An epic world book for the Rifts® series.
Compatible with the entire Palladium Books® Megaverse®!

Dedicated to John Zeleznik who continues to work his artistic magic on one great cover after another — not to mention dynamic black and white on Skraypers™ and more books to come.

— Kevin Siembieda, 1998

Coming for Rifts in 1999
Rifts® Canada
Rifts® Free Quebec
Rifts® Scotland
Rifts® Splynn Dimensional Market (Atlantis)
Rifts® Australia Two
The Rifter™ Sourcebook series continues
and much, much more ...
Check out all the latest news at *www.palladiumbooks.com*

The cover is by John Zeleznik, and depicts a Gypsy Sorcerer summoning spirits from a fire. Behind her is one of the few rebuilt cities of Western Russia — probably Kiev.

First Printing — December, 1998

Palladium On-Line: www.palladiumbooks.com

Rifts® World Book 18: Mystic Russia™ is published by Palladium Books Inc., 12455 Universal Drive, Taylor, MI 48180. Printed in the USA.

PALLADIUM BOOKS® PRESENTS:
RIFTS® WORLD BOOK 18:
MYSTIC RUSSIA™

Written by: **Kevin Siembieda**

Additional Text & Concepts for Spells:

> **Mark Sumimoto**
>
> **Randi Cartier**

Editors: **Alex Marciniszyn**

> **Jim Osten**
>
> **Wayne Smith**

Proofreader: **Julius Rosenstein**

Cover Painting: **John Zeleznik**

Interior Artists: **Wayne Breaux Jr.**

> **Ramon Perez Jr.**
>
> **Scott Johnson**
>
> **Michael Dubisch**
>
> **Michael Wilson**
>
> **Mark Dudley (DSS)**
>
> **Brandon C. Clark (DSS)**
>
> **Ka Xiong (DSS)**
>
> **Drunken Style Studio**

Art Direction, Maps & Keylining: **Kevin Siembieda**

Cover Logo: **Niklas Brandt**

Typography: **Maryann Siembieda**

Base on the RPG rules, characters,

concepts and Megaverse® created by Kevin Siembieda.

Palladium Books On-Line: www.palladiumbooks.com

Special Thanks to Mark and Randi for their contributions to the Necromancy spells, to all my artists, and to Maryann, Alex, Jim, Jules, Wayne and the rest of the Palladium demon-stompers.

— *Kevin Siembieda, 1998*

Contents

Quick Find Tables

Russian Player O.C.C.s

Optional Player O.C.C.s

Russian Magic

Bone Magic

Note: Double P.P.E. cost if not a Necromancer.

A few words from the Author

Before I began my research for **Mystic Russia**, I was initially given the impression that Russian myths and legends were not very plentiful or unique. In fact, I had a few people suggest that Russian lore was very similar to Norse mythology. Nothing could be further from the truth. I found a rich tapestry of legends and folk tales about gods, demons, woodland spirits, witches and sorcery. While Russian myths did present gods of thunder and lightning and other figures reminiscent of Thor, Odin and other Norse gods, their deities have distinctly unique characteristics and different qualities than Norse or Teutonic gods. Furthermore, one of the most unique things about Russian mythology is that it is a combination of folk superstitions, shamanism, spiritualism, and Christianity with touches and influences from a dozen different cultures, peoples and places. It seems to me that every people to neighbor or invade Russia has left some indelible aspect of their culture and beliefs upon the region. Yet despite all the outside influences, the Russian belief in evil spirits, demonic creatures, witches, sorcerers, magic and the supernatural remained strong and largely unchanging well into the 19th and even 20th Centuries.

The appearance and influence of Christianity started in some regions in the 9th Century but didn't eradicate the old beliefs, legends and practices as much as alter them, giving the old a new spin — a facelift, if you will. In fact, the so-called "pagan" traditions were so strong and smoothly integrated into the new Christianity that many historians, scholars and religious leaders considered the Russian people to maintain a dual faith, keeping in their hearts the old and new ways. For example, evil woodland spirits, witches and supernatural beings were no longer just malignant forces of darkness and magic that inhabited the deep forest, swamps and frightening places, but became the servants or aspects of the "devil."

Like many rural and agricultural societies, much of the "magic" and "monsters" involved the everyday fears and troubles of the farmer and peasant. These included storms, crop failure, successful harvesting of crops, ailments, disease, blights, the forces of nature, good fortune, romance, success, telling the future, birth, death, and strange occurrences. Many of their "magical" spells, rituals, and cleansing were, from our modern perspective, silly, unscientific, and clearly wrapped in centuries of superstition. Many magical rituals involved fire, water, wood and protection from evil forces. Most were simple: bury this, bless that, and hang it from a tree at midnight, etc.

It is interesting to observe that the belief in magic and the supernatural permeated all strata of society, from peasant and clergyman to noble and king. Sorcery was both respected and feared. Many leaders outlawed magic and systematically killed, tortured and burned sorcerers and witches. Yet, the belief in magic and its practice lived on into the modern age.

The premise of **Rifts® Mystic Russia** is that the Russian people's steadfast beliefs in magic and the supernatural was well founded, and that their belief and ancient knowledge helped prepare them for the return of magic to Earth. Their ancient superstitions and myths allowed them to understand and deal effectively with the many supernatural beings that have invaded Mother Russia. They are not taken aback by the monsters, but accept them as part of their world, and respond accordingly. For some, this means a return to magic themselves — to fight magic with magic. For others, like the Warlords of Russia, Bogatyr and other heroes, they are prepared to address the invaders with firm resolve and weapon in hand. For them, it doesn't matter that these "invaders" are demonic, magic wielding, mega-damage beings. An invader is an invader, and must be driven from Mother Russia. Thankfully, the old myths, legends and superstitions have given these patriots and heroes the insight and information they need to combat the monsters. Among the heroes, some are determined to destroy the demonic invaders, while others are intent on driving the hellish creatures away, or simply protecting and helping their fellow humans from the clutches of evil. Meanwhile, the Gypsies and other practitioners of magic see the return of mystic energy and many of the old ways as a means to garner power and/or wealth. Thus, they use magic and sometimes supernatural beings for their own advancement, as well as offering their magical services to protect and battle evil forces; usually for some sort of payment or favor. The worst of the sorcerers are the Witch, Shifter, and Necromancers, villains who call upon dark forces and supernatural evil to get what they want.

This is the backdrop of Rifts Russia, a vast range of wilderness overridden by demonic beings, all manner of supernatural forces and ancient magic. It is not engulfed by any one Demon Empire like the New German Republic. Nor has it the battlefield for several warring supernatural forces like China. However, it is a battleground nonetheless. An expansive territory that is as dangerous as it is beautiful. A realm of opportunity and mystery. A place where heroes, mercenaries and adventurers dare to take a stand and fight true monsters so that their fellow man may crawl from the lingering Dark Age and reclaim their homeland and identity. A place where survival on the simplest level is fraught with danger. A place of magical wonderment and unspeakable evil. A world unto itself that will challenge the boldest of champions.

— Kevin Siembieda, 1998

Rifts Russia & The Supernatural

Disclaimer

Mystic Russia is *inspired* by the ancient myths, legends, folk tales and superstitions of the ancient Russian people. The monsters, demons, magic, and Occupational Character Classes (O.C.C.s) that appear in this book are *not* real. They are fictional conglomerations inspired by myth, heavily changed and extrapolated upon, and spun into fictional magic and imaginary characters by the fertile imagination of the author. None of the magic or monsters are real.

Likewise, no real-life people, gypsies, cultures or religious faith have been portrayed. Although Christianity played a large role in Russian history, it is only occasionally and vaguely presented as a bit of color and background. This is a work of fiction about a future and alien Earth where magic and technology collide and ancient legends and mythical gods and monsters walk the planet.

With a few exceptions, like the Aborigines of Australia, few people on Rifts Earth possessed as keen an understanding and innate acceptance of the supernatural as the Russian people. Even with the advent of Christianity in the 9th Century, many Russians, especially the poor peasants who lived under Medieval conditions and lifestyle until the 20th Century, practiced old "pagan" beliefs, superstitions and magic concerning nature spirits, ancient gods, demons, witches and the arcane. Even into the golden age of technology and science, a good number, especially rural people, held on to the old beliefs and continued to tell ancient folk tales.

Even the people of Rifts Russia cannot explain why these ancient beliefs were so fervently embraced and kept for thousands of years. Some scholars and sorcerers have suggested that, somehow, the Russian people held in their psyche the knowledge that magic and supernatural beings were real; perhaps some unique form of racial memory or inherent instinct. Others attribute it to divine intervention or inspiration. Whatever the reason, this unique understanding and acceptance of the supernatural has given the people of Rifts Russia an edge. They remembered and embraced old folk tales and superstitions which provided warnings, advice and information about countering dark magic and defending against supernatural evil. They quickly recognized the demons, gods and monsters from ancient myths. The old folk tales, legends, and beliefs were given a new validity and provided the Russian people with an understanding about what was happening around them that helped them to accept and adapt to the supernatural world in order to survive.

Old practices and nearly forgotten forms of magic were revived to do battle against the encroaching evil returned to the world. Many of the old stories, sayings, superstitions, and myths provided clues and warnings for dealing with, fighting and avoiding demonic creatures. They also provided similar information about certain types of magic. Ironically, most Russians are not practitioners of magic and avoid its study and use in any form. Only select types of Russian heroes, warriors, wisemen, gypsies and clergy dare to draw upon the ancient mystic arts. Such individuals are both revered and feared by the common man. Even most of the Warlords utilize magic in a minimal way, with less than 4% of their troops (often less than 1%) skilled in the mystic arts.

Ironically, it is the same historical myths and knowledge that helps them to accept and combat demons and monsters that keeps most Russians from embracing magic and welcoming the supernatural. According to the old tales (validated by the return of magic and monsters), the practice of magic, all magic, draws upon a mysterious force of nature not meant for mortal man to wield. The legends and superstitions warn that only true heroes and the greatest of warriors blessed with strong spirits and pure hearts may dare to use magic. Yet even many of these heroes are not masters of magic and few summon and command supernatural forces. Instead, most possess either a limited range of magic abilities, or a handful of special powers and/or resistance to magic or monsters. Any magical weapons, armor or charms that they possess are usually gifts given to them by the gods, priests, and good practitioners of magic, or won in battle against supernatural demons and evil practitioners of magic. Consequently, except for a few magical occupations, like the *Mystic Kuznya, Russian Sorcerer* and *Old Believer*, magic and those who use it are feared and shunned. Even such characters as the *Demon Slayer, Gypsies*, and benevolent *Ley Line Walker/Sorcerers* are often avoided. However, the people always try to show masters of magic some measure of respect and reverence, and frequently consult with them or turn to them for relief from demons, monsters, evil sorcerers and foul enchantments. Likewise, a mage is often invited to hold a place of honor at ceremonies and sometimes given special posts within a community in the hope that this "honor" will placate the mage and get him to intercede on the people's behalf against incursions by rival or evil practitioners of magic and hostile demons. Common folk will even try to show a Witch or Necromancer some degree of courtesy and respect, out of fear if nothing else (afraid that to do otherwise will result in vengeful repercussions; spoilings, curses, and trouble from demons).

How Russians view the various magic O.C.C.s

Since the old beliefs dissuade the acceptance and use of magic, and since many of these old beliefs and legends have been proven true, the average Russian will never embrace magic like those in the Americas and other parts of Rifts Earth. Never. This is true of the lowliest peasant and clergy, to the most intelligent and worldly warrior, warlord or scholar. Many (98%) are convinced it has been their remembrance and practice of the old ways that has helped them to survive against overwhelming demonic forces that plague Mother Russia. Consequently, since those same teachings admonish the use of magic, they follow that practice as well. Nothing will change their minds, and nothing will get them to accept magic. The bottom-line is that *all* practitioners of magic possess knowledge, insight and power denied to the ordinary person, thus removing them, at least one step, from ordinary men and placing them closer to the very demonic beings they oppose.

- **Biomancy and the Anti-Monster** are not known beyond South America (see **Rifts® World Book Six: South America One** for more details).

- **Bio-Wizardry, Rune Magic**, and the use of symbiotes are unknown to the people of Russia. These secrets are held and guarded by the Splugorth. The demonic Lords of Atlantis have little influence or presence in Russia (see **Rifts® Atlantis** for details about this magic).

- **Conjurers** are not found in Russia (see **Rifts® Federation of Magic** for details about this O.C.C.), although adventurers from other lands occasionally visit.

- **Ley Line Walkers of Russia:** The Ley Line Walkers of Russia are fundamentally the same as those found elsewhere in the world except they can choose from two different types of spell magic, either those found in the **Rift® RPG** or the *Living Fire Magic* presented elsewhere in this book.

- **Gypsy Magic** is hated, feared and avoided. Generally speaking, Rifts Russians regard Gypsies, as a whole, as deceitful, self-serving thieves and cutthroats who will dare anything and associate with dangerous magic and demonic forces if they think they can profit from it. **Note:** See the section on Russian Gypsies elsewhere in this book for more information.

- **Mystics** are among the most common practitioners of magic in Russia. Such characters are generally regarded as "mystic wisemen" or "born sorcerers" (naturals who inherit a power over magic rather than study it. Consequently, a "born sorcerer" may be considered an unwilling participant in magic, or as having been "chosen" by a god or other power of goodness (or evil). They are generally recognized as being less powerful than those who willingly elect to study magic, but a power to be reckoned with nonetheless. The Born Sorcerer is viewed with some degree of suspicion and fear, and may be politely avoided by ordinary folk. **Note:** The innate psychic potential that creates a Mystic can also be channelled and reshaped to create a Major or Master Psychic like those found in the pages of **Rifts® World Book 12: Psyscape™**. Evil characters with such an innate magical aptitude can become an evil Mystic or a Mystic Knight (see **Rifts® Federation of Magic™** for details).

- **Mystic Knights (NPC Villains)** *are* found in Rifts Russia (see **Rifts® Federation of Magic** for details about this O.C.C.).

- **Magic of the Three (Magi):** This specialized magic, involving automatons and other specialized areas, is limited to the *Federation of Magic* in North America (see **Rifts® Federation of Magic** for details about this O.C.C.).

- **Necromancy** is the most hated and feared type of magic. Its practice is absolutely forbidden and the Warlords of Russia actively hunt down and kill Necromancers (and Witches) as part of their efforts to protect Mother Russia.

  The practice of Necromancy is believed to have originated in Africa (or possibly China), but has been adopted by evil practitioners of magic in Russia. This is probably due to the presence of demonic creatures and violent wars over territory by supernatural beings and mages where a legion of animated dead and the horrible skills of a Necromancer are welcomed. **Note:** See the Russian Necromancer O.C.C. described elsewhere for more details.

- **Old Believers** are sorcerers or mystics who understand and practice the "old ways." They know about demons, monsters, magic and healing. They are reasonably respected by common folk and most are practitioners of nature or fire magic.

- **Shifters/Summoning Magic** is considered one of the most feared and forbidden mystic arts because it calls upon and attempts to enslave supernatural beings and forces. Russians believe that the most well intentioned of those who use Summoning magic are misguided fools destined to suffer and die, but most are regarded as wicked people and demon worshippers. Such a character will get no help or kindness from the common man, and may find himself run out of town or slain. The latter is especially true when a Shifter/Summoner is discovered doing things that work against the village or somebody in the community.

  This having been said, Shifters are one of the few practitioners found in Russia. This is due, in part, to the vast number of demonic and supernatural beings available for such a character to control. The majority are evil (55%) or self-serving (30% are anarchist).

- **Techno-Wizardry** is unknown to Russians and most people and places in the World, particularly in Europe and Asia. It is a relatively *new* area of mystical study that originates and prospers in North America. Furthermore, because of their superstitions and outlook, Techno-Wizards and the devices created by their magic will never be welcomed or accepted. The mages themselves would be feared and shunned, while their mechanical creations would be smashed and/or buried.

- **Temporal Magic** practiced by humans is very rare in this part of the world, although the inhuman Temporal Raider is counted among the rarer monsters that plague Russia and China. Most Temporal Raiders are self-serving transdimensional adventurers who have little interest in conquering Mother Russia or her people. Instead they seek knowledge, magic and excitement. They may associate with demon lords, gods, and practitioners of magic.

- **Stone Magic** is unknown to the people and monsters of Russia (see **Rifts® Atlantis** for details about this magic).

- **Tattoo Magic** is unknown to the people and monsters of Russia (see **Rifts® Atlantis** for details about this secret magic of True Atlanteans).

- **Witchcraft and Witches:** The Russian "witch" is a figure of legendary evil. These vile individuals are typically women who wield dark magic for their own wicked or selfish desires and who consorts with demons. No form of witchcraft or demon worship is accepted by the Russian people. Thus, witches are among the most hated and feared users of magic. See the Russian Witch O.C.C. described elsewhere for details about this unique and monstrous figure. **Note:** The ancient practices of Wicca and Druidism are not considered witchcraft or demon worship, although Russian people will have nothing to do with either of them.

Who is acceptable?

Only the *Mystic Kuznya* (Smith) and *Superhuman Hero* are welcomed with open arms and enjoy an honored place in Russian society. However, depending on the actions and attitudes of the individual *Old Believer, Znakhari (Wiseman), Demon Slayer,* or *Line Walker/Sorcerer*, these practitioners of magic can often earn some measure of respect, acceptance and even lasting friendship, as well as achieve hero status.

Dragons, werebeasts, and similar creatures of magic are generally regarded as inhuman monsters and seldom earn the trust or friendship of an entire community no matter how kind, generous and helpful they may be. For the people of Russia, magic is a dangerous force and the supernatural is evil. They must be rooted out, not accepted. In fact, the magical and demonic are such overwhelmingly prevalent forces that the peasants tend to blame almost every ill on one or the other (sometimes both). This can include a mysterious illness, blight, drought, crop failure, a missing child or resident, strange or sudden storm, and so on. They may turn to heroes and the few trusted practitioners of magic to help them battle the supernatural, but they seldom engage in the study and cultivation of magic themselves. Good sorcerers are the lesser of two evils, and magic wielding heroes are a godsend.

Russian Ley Lines

Despite the return of ancient gods, spirits and hordes of demons, for its size, Russia is comparatively devoid of ley line energy. What few ley lines and nexus points exist are located in clusters and usually hundreds, sometimes thousands of miles apart.

Consequently, these places of magic are coveted by the demons, dragons and evil sorcerers who dominate the land. Skirmishes between the Warlords and demonic enemies are frequent at these locations, and they are the sites of the bloodiest battles. For the Warlords and most Russians, ley lines and nexus junctions are a curse upon the land, for no sooner do the defenders of Mother Russia bleed to rid the region of one supernatural menace, than another takes its place.

The Demon Plague

Only China has a greater number and variety of supernatural beings — demons, ghosts and spirits — than Russia. People trying to colonize Mother Russia for humans regard the multitude of supernatural beings as a plague. A pestilence that strikes out at, hurts and kills humans, often in a chaotic, random manner.

In addition to supernatural beings not of this Earth, there are wicked humans as evil and powerful as any demon. These include Witches, Necromancers, and evil practitioners of magic of all kinds (Gypsies are frequently included among them). Indeed, the average peasant feels surrounded by persons and creatures possessing supernatural powers, able to cast dangerous magic upon him or his crops, and/or send demonic minions against him. Truth be told, those living in Russia know that there is no place guaranteed to be safe from the supernatural, although some places are safer than others. As noted in **Warlords of Russia™**, the deep woods, as well as swamps, caves and subterranean catacombs, are among the most dangerous of places, for they serve as the abodes of demons and evil spirits. See the section on *The New Frontier* starting on page 15, with particular attention to Dangers on the Road, Deep Forests, and The Danger of Ley Lines.

Most Russians regard demons, witches and, to a lesser degree, woodland spirits, to be a pestilence. A plague or blight as commonplace as the ones that afflict their crops. These monstrous beings are hated and feared, but accepted as a part of life in Russia.

The Peasant Homestead

The poorest and most common communities are gatherings of impoverished peasants who pool their numbers and resources to work the land. In addition to the shared communal farmland where they work together to grow crops and raise livestock, each family in the community typically has its own small farm or garden (roughly the size of a large backyard or field) and a small pen for hogs, sheep, goats, or fowl (mostly ducks, geese and chickens). The inhabitants of such communities typically build houses nestled relatively close together, with as few as a dozen to as many as one hundred homes and farmland claiming a 1-4 mile (1.6 to 6.4 km) region.

There are also independent homesteads (a house and a small, independent farm or ranch worked by one family), hunting lodges and cabins where lone individuals, families or clans live off the land. They are not members of any particular community but independent settlers and woodsmen trying to make a living.

The simplest and most common peasant house ("izba") has one main room where the entire family lives and sleeps. Most have one large fireplace and a woodburning iron stove. The part of the house closest to the stove is typically surrounded by heavy shelves or cupboards, and a short, stout table that functions as the kitchen area. On the shelves are bowls, drinking mugs, pots, pans, empty jars and containers, along with containers of preserved fruits, vegetables, and dried or pickled meats, as well as spices and other food ingredients. The largest pots and pans hang from pegs on the wall along with a meat cleaver, ladle, large two-pronged fork (for stabbing meat), large wooden stirring spoon, and a few other large cooking utensils. One or two barrels of flour and/or other grains, a barrel of drinking water, a small sack of sugar, and a couple of large sacks of potatoes are usually nearby. The best china and dinnerware is often kept in a trunk or cedar chest. At night, this area also becomes the sleeping area because it is closest to the warmth of the stove and/or fireplace.

Across from the kitchen area is what might be considered the dining and living room. Here there is typically a long, sturdy table big enough to accommodate the family and at least four guests. Benches rather than chairs are used at the table, and can also be pulled over to the fireplace or easily moved to any part of the house. A bench or two also usually rests near one of the other walls as well. There are only two chairs at the table, one at its head and foot. Shelves, clothes closets and dressers typically line one wall. Furs may be hung from the wall to serve as both a decoration and additional rugs to sleep on, or blankets for visitors.

A cellar is often built under one part of the house, or in a small attached room that resembles a closet. The cellar is accessible from inside the house because a separate one outside would be impossible to get to during the winter, covered by many feet of snow and ice. The cellar contains additional sacks and barrels of grain, flour, potatoes, cheese, lard, canned foods, jams, jelly, honey, syrups, preserved meats, alcohol (typically Vodka and home brewed wines) and other food supplies that are preserved in a dark, cool (freezing in winter) storage bin. Sometimes paint, varnish, lamp oil, coal (or other fuels), seeds for planting and other supplies are also kept in the cellar.

Outside, a giant pile of chopped wood typically lines one entire wall of the house, plus another pile is likely to be stacked nearby or against a tool shed or storage hut.

The most prosperous of the farmers or peasants will have a water pump outdoors near the house (the richest may have one indoors), plus a storage shed or barn, and an outhouse. Some may also have a coop or pen for chickens, ducks and geese, and/or a small barn or stable 30-80 yards/meters from the main house. However, livestock are difficult to keep during winter, especially by homesteads in the northern half of Russia, so a dog or two, goat and/or a few egg-laying chickens or ducks may also be found living inside the house. Villages and communal farms have the best chance of keeping livestock in the winter months and are likely to have generators to power heaters and provide electricity. Only in the largest towns and small cities will there be a mill and/or modern means of power to provide electricity, power, heat, and other modern amenities to 40-70% of the homes and 85-96% of the businesses. Remember, Rifts Russia is a comparatively poor and low-tech place, even among the "civilized" communities under the watchful eyes of the Warlords. And while within each of the Warlords' Spheres of Influence there are 1-4 small cities and 4-12 sizeable towns, most of the many small villages and farms are poor and low-tech, and most communities are scattered miles apart.

The Heart of Winter

The heart of winter is so cold and dangerous that family members may not leave the grounds of their homestead for a month or two, holing up like bears in hibernation. During the long winter months, deep snow covers the fields and makes work outside, except for the occasional hunting or fishing trip, impossible. Likewise, travel in the deep snow is a difficult and arduous task taking 10 times the usual time and effort to travel the same distance when it is free of snow. Consequently, visitors in the winter are a rarity, even by the Warlords' Camps, and the appearance of visitors is reason for concern. In many cases, travelers, especially lone travelers at night, are sent away at gunpoint for fear that they are a disguised demon, woodland spirit, witch, evil mage, or bandit. However, most people will offer some measure of hospitality to avoid getting a witch, mage or monster angry with them and placing a curse on the home or causing other trouble. This hospitality usually extends to offering directions, basic information, fresh water, a drink or two of booze (typically Vodka) and a bowl of hot porridge, soup or stew. **Note:** Soups and stews are a common winter foodstuff because they stretch available food stocks (water can be had by melting snow), warm the body, are healthy, tasty, and can last for days, especially when stored in freezing to near freezing cold cellar.

If the visitor(s) seems to be convincingly human, the home owner *may* allow him or her to come inside to be warmed by the fire and sometimes to spend the night. However, this is a rarity unless a neighbor or somebody else known to the family vouches for the individual(s). When a trusted individual vouches for strangers, the door is opened and all the reasonable hospitality of the home is offered, including warm clothes, hot food, drink and roof over their heads for a few days (longer if the visitors bring food and other valuable goods offered in trade for the homeowner's generosity and a place to stay; otherwise strangers who stay without contributing to the home drain it of the necessary food stores and resources they need to survive).

Travel outdoors is usually limited to getting firewood, the occasional *daytime* visit to a neighbor (often to make certain they are well) or trading lodge. The occasional trip to go ice fishing, hunting, skating or crosscountry skiing (the latter done to visit neighbors or to gather wood or collect other resources rather than for fun or sport) may also be entertained. On comparatively sunny and warm days, children may be allowed to go outside to play in the snow. Travel at night is avoided at all costs, because that's when the demons and woodland spirits roam. The most cautious even avoid venturing out on gloomy days.

When stuck indoors, storytelling, songs, playing musical instruments, and dance are favorite pastimes. Games of darts, checkers, chess, and carving wood, whittling, weaving, knitting, and the making of clothes, crafts, tools and toys are also done in the winter. Children play with toys, draw, and help with chores, while the few who are literate may read or write.

Villages and towns are more active during the winter, and are likely to have a snow removal system to clear local roads and bridges. However, even here, the snow is deep and the cold frightful, thus keeping most people indoors and travel limited to neighbors, and local stores, taverns, and places within the community. Villages are also more likely to keep comparatively large numbers of livestock through the winter, provided they have proper shelter and saved enough feed for them. Here too, strangers are viewed with suspicion and concern, although there is usually an inn or boarding house that can take them in. After all, one never knows who or *what* a stranger may really be.

Most homesteads, farms and villages scattered throughout Russia are positively medieval. Most are low-tech, with a smattering of technology in the way of M.D.C. armor, the occasional modern vehicle, and M.D. weapons or magic. Most are simplistic, rural, agrarian communities, many of whom struggle to survive from season to season. They are also places beset by trouble at the hands of supernatural thieves, vandals, tormentors and monsters.

The Inhuman Menace

Evil supernatural beings, mischievous and thieving woodland spirits, witches, D-bees and bandits see human settlements (from the smallest to the largest) as places of opportunity where they can plunder, play and hunt. At any given time, the typical communal farm or village is (often secretly) plagued by one or more supernatural menaces, from woodland spirits to dragons, demons or evil sorcerers.

Supernatural predators see humanoid communities as an excellent place to hunt and feed. Depending on the creature, their prey may be either or both animal livestock and people. Others see homesteads, farms and villages simply as targets for plunder or entertainment: stealing or damaging crops and/or stored food and grains, stealing horses and livestock, slaughtering animals for fun, robbing houses, mugging villagers and visitors, spreading disease, spoiling food, sabotaging bridges and creating mishaps, and worse, kidnaping, torturing, raping, and murdering for sport and pleasure. All common acts of *play* among demons and similar wicked beings, including evil woodland spirits, and human witches and necromancers.

Cunning and cruel, many supernatural beings use hit and run tactics or cloak their real identities to create greater confusion and fear, or to draw attention away from them and their real hiding place or scheme. They love to create mystery, fear and panic — it's part of their games. Thus, a single demon or small group may be responsible for many (if not all) the current trouble experienced by a community. When the monster(s) gets bored, it will either leave, to return for more fun and games at a later date, or turn to some new "game."

One must remember that most of the so-called "demons" and many other supernatural beings prey on humanoids for food, but more importantly, one must never lose sight that most demonic

creatures are malicious and vile savages who find beauty and goodness abhorrent, and torment, destroy, maim, and kill for the sheer enjoyment of it. These sadistic monsters love to harass and torment humans, D-Bees and any beings weaker than they. Frequently, they kill only those who represent the greatest threat to them, or who dare to oppose them, leaving the rest alive so they have living playthings to continue to torment and play with. Their motivation and pleasure comes from causing fear, sorrow, turmoil, and pain more than a desire to kill — not that they don't engage in wanton destruction from time to time. For Russian demons, to create an air of terror, confusion and chaos is like a magnificent symphony or epic game to revel in. The sorrow and suffering of the mortals around them is to be enjoyed and drunk deeply like a sweet nectar. Such cruelty and depravity lays at the very essence of their being, and the root of their sardonic pleasures. And these are just the run-of-the-mill demons — the everyday sort of troubles with which the Russian people must contend.

The most powerful and intelligent hell-spawned demons and other malignant forces (including dragons, woodland spirits and human witches, necromancers, evil sorcerers, bandits and tyrants), may try to dominate or enslave an entire village, town or people, or establish a small nightmarish kingdom, or gather a horde of misanthropes and monsters who roam the land as demonic bandits, killers, or ravaging gangs that strike terror into the hearts of men. These power-mongers and madmen usually have larger, more sweeping plans, and crave power and/or wealth. They are often the dark forces behind the most insidious plots, treachery and evil.

Adventurers & Demons

Adventurers known or suspected of being (or have the potential to be) heroes are often invited by individuals and villagers to investigate mysteries, disappearances, murders, etc., in the hope that they can find the supernatural cause and put an end to it. For their trouble, all these appreciative homesteaders, farmers and villagers can usually offer is a warm place to stay, food and basic supplies. Some can offer a small payment and/or valuable information, on top of their undying gratitude (the heroes will have made friends for life). Unfortunately, truly desperate villages and individuals may send adventurers to their doom, like sheep to slaughter. This can accidently result if the menace outguns the adventurers, but can also arise from a deliberate ruse on the part of the villagers. Some send "strangers" to their death to appease the monster(s) that plague them, rather than lose more villagers, friends and loved ones. If by some miracle the heroes win and kill the creature(s) tormenting them, it's a win, win situation. While such action is deplorable, and can be the practice of evil people in league with evil forces, it is more often an act done out of insane desperation or absolute terror.

Demonic overlords, tyrants and tormentors don't usually care where their "entertainment" comes from, and (often literally) welcome "new blood" from strangers led to slaughter or tricked into conflict with them. Most demons derive pleasure from the challenge of such confrontations and amusement from the satisfaction of winning. This brings up an interesting point which demon-slayers and heroes can use to their advantage: Russian demons, ancient gods, and many supernatural beings tend to regard humans and most mortals as their inferiors and usually underestimate them. Consequently, the monsters never *expect* to

lose. This is a good thing, because it allows capable and savvy heroes to get the upper hand and destroy these horrific creatures. And destroy them utterly they must, for demons are notoriously vindictive and vengeful. Mercy is not a virtue when dealing with demons who usually have no sense of honor and are the living embodiment of evil. If even one demon should survive, it will eventually seek retribution against the champions who embarrassed and defeated it and destroyed its brothers. Furthermore, a demon's sense of revenge is likely to spill over to the villagers who dispatched the adventurers to it, even if they were only obeying its orders. Demonic beings possess all the worst and most vile qualities of humankind and rarely any of the good. Thus, they never feel responsible for their own failures, so they blame others and strike out in anger and frustration to save face and prove how powerful or better they really are. They also crave revenge against those who bested them, often seeing anybody who reminds them of those people as an extension of them to be punished or destroyed (i.e. all Bogatyrs, Line Walkers, and Demon Slayers may induce intense emotions and hate that drives the demon to attack or torment them). Many greater demons, demon lords, Witches and Necromancers become obsessed with revenge to the point that they may dedicate their lives to achieve it, and are willing to take any risk and lose everything to get it. Ah, but then to a demon, Witch or Necromancer, there is nothing sweeter than complete and utter revenge.

Thankfully, the supernatural beings Russians consider "woodland spirits" — lesser demons, werebeasts, and Faerie-like creatures — are typically less deranged, depraved, murderous and vengeful. While such beings may hold a grudge, play pranks on, and relish seeing an old foe or antagonist get into serious trouble, few become obsessed with revenge. In fact, even the most malicious woodland spirits eventually let such feelings go and seldom engage in schemes or acts that threaten their lives or will cause them to lose everything they hold dear. In that regard, they are much more practical and pragmatic — "Hey, sometimes you lose. Those squishy flesh bags beat me. I hate 'em, but what can I do?" And that's pretty much the end of it. Many woodland spirits also appreciate that retreat or surrender can be the better part of valor, and that it allows them to fight another day. Don't confuse this common sense with honor or a sense of fair play, because most foul spirits lie, cheat, back-stab and kill without hesitation or regret to get what they want. Many are nearly as malicious and cruel as demons.

As noted in **Warlords of Russia** and elsewhere, from the human perspective, one of the saving graces regarding demons and woodland spirits is that they dislike each other almost as much as mortals. This means they seldom gather into large groups and are typically encountered as lone villains, pairs or in small groups of 3-8. That doesn't mean a dozen to scores of these horrid creatures may not be operating in the same region, or plaguing a particular village(s), it just means they are not a cohesive group, but several independent individuals and tiny private interest groups with their own (often conflicting) agendas and rivalries. As a result, humans rarely have to deal with more than a dozen supernatural menaces at a time (typically 1-8). There are, of course, exceptions. The most common of which is demons marshalled under the leadership of a greater demon, dragon, witch, evil practitioner of magic, or other powerful being (humans included). Under the thrall of powerful and conniving leaders, one to several dozen demons, probably combined with mortal henchmen and other creatures, may be molded into a large gang, tribe or small army. However, kill the leader and most of the others are likely to scatter.

Supernatural Horrors

Russia is a wilderness. Even the comparatively populated region of western Russia, the Warlords' domain, is mostly untamed wilderness. One can travel a hundred miles without coming upon anything larger than a farm or outpost, sometimes not even that. The communities that do exist are generally small towns, villages and farmsteads. Cities, real cities, are a rarity. Yet to call Russia an unpopulated wilderness is not entirely true, for while one may be at a loss to find technologically advanced humans or D-Bees, the land is swarming with demons, monsters, spirits and superhuman creatures. The people of North America, where the Coalition States and other human and D-Bee powers exist, have no concept of a savage, demon-haunted wilderness when compared to Europe, Russia, and China. With the exception of the American West and large portions of Canada, even the so-called American wilderness is dotted with low and high-tech towns, cities and fledgling kingdoms. By contrast, Germany, the old Slavic countries, Russia and much of Asia is largely a wilderness devoid of civilization and dominated by the inhuman and demonic.

The monstrosities described in the following section are generally regarded as "Russian Demons" — foul creatures of Pre-Rifts myths and legends come to life. Demonic spirits and vile monsters that seem to have some historical (and magical?) ties to the Russia of the past and present. The "Russian" or "Archaic Demons" are known to the Megaverse-spanning Dimensional Raiders, True Atlanteans, Splugorth, Demons of Hades, and the other powerful demons presented in **Rifts® Conversion Book One**. However, Russian "demons" are not from the same demonic lineage as the Demons of Hades. Still, demons are demons and the Archaic Demons often associate and work with other evil supernatural beings. The Archaic Russian demons are an older, more primordial and elemental race of foul supernatural beings from another dimension. They are frequently regarded as inferior savages by most other demons and alien intelligences (talk about the pot calling the kettle black) and treated like second-class members of the tribe. The Russian Demons established dimensional links to Russia at least fifteen thousand years before the Great Cataclysm and are ancient enemies of True Atlanteans. When magic energy faded from Earth, their presence also faded, but with the return of mystic energy and seething ley lines, they have returned in droves.

While the Archaic Demons are less numerous and have little influence throughout the *Megaverse*, they have a tremendous presence in the Russia and Asia of Rifts Earth. Hundreds of thousands, perhaps millions, can be found throughout these parts of the world. Here, the Archaic demons are a constant source of consternation and trouble to mortal men. They regard Russia as their own (the truly demon-infested lands of China/Asia must be shared with many powerful demonic forces), and the mortals who inhabit these lands their playthings.

Archaic demons have no sense of culture or civilization so their outlook is more like that of predatory animals who prowl the land and regard mortals as both their prey and possessions. For them, humans and D-Bees are little more than herds of animals or slaves to be hunted, slaughtered, and toyed with for their twisted amusement.

Unlike the Gargoyle and Brodkil Empires to the west, the demons, ghosts and woodland spirits of Russia do not gather in organized kingdoms, nations or armies. They have no organized society or civilization, nor much of a culture. Although demon lords and dark gods lay claim to millions of demonic subjects in other dimensions, and sometimes command armies of thousands of Archaic demons, most so-called "Russian Demons" are only loosely allied to these higher powers. This means they often do as they please, operating as lone, rogue individuals and small groups. Archaic Demons fear and respect power and brutality, so evil sorcerers, witches, necromancers, dragons, greater demons, and supernatural beings of immense power and/or vicious ruthlessness are the only ones who can organize and control a band of more than a few dozen.

Tiny groups of 3D4 demons or malignant spirits are typical among Russian demons, with small to medium groups of 16-30 being the next most common size for a demon gathering. Large groups of Archaic demons numbering 40-160 (4D4x10) are extremely unusual, but do occur from time to time. That having been said, a region may be infested with scores of small to medium groups and dangerous individuals numbering in the thousands. Most of these groups are not particularly friendly or cooperative toward one another, yet few are warring rivals. Some rivalry and competition exists between all the groups, but most act like wild animals who share the same territory and treat others of their kind with relative ambivalence. They may squabble, threaten, abuse and play pranks on one another, but there is no organized effort to band together into any sort of large community, kingdom, or army, nor to destroy rival demon bands unless they represent a constant source of trouble. This is due largely to the fact that, like animals, Archaic demons don't make an effort to conquer any specific place, resource, or people. Thus, while a particular individual, group or groups of Archaic demons may live in the same region and torment the same villages, they are like roving predators who simply like living and hunting in the same area. What animals, humans and resources that may exist are taken for granted and used by all parties. Should their prey and resources dry up, they simply move on to find a new hunting ground. Likewise, unless they are bothered by them, Archaic demons just don't concern themselves with woodland spirits or other supernatural beings who may also share their domain.

What few rules exist between Archaic demons are fairly simple and straightforward: Avoid conflict with other demons, stay out of their affairs, and don't steal from, pester, challenge, or openly malign other groups and individuals (although it's okay to do these things among friends). And, of course, respect, revere and fear power (i.e. those more powerful than you). Follow these simple rules and all will be right in the world.

Since might makes right, those who break these basic covenants face violent retribution from those they have angered, typically a beating, humiliation, servitude/slavery, and sometimes torture, but rarely death. Demons tend not to destroy their own kind unless commanded to do so by a demon lord or god, or when extracting a terrible retribution. Sub-demons, like Gargoyles and Brodkil, don't count, as they are seen as lesser beings subservient to all of demonkind. This being the case, the Gargoyle and Brodkil Empires are something of an anomaly, annoyance and embarrassment to most "true" demons.

Physical and emotional torture are second nature to most Archaic demons. An instinct that serves them well. Thus, a demon knows he can inflict greater pain and suffering by killing a single child or beloved figure than slaying a dozen people. They also like to inflict prolonged torment and visit pain upon a select target (be it an individual, group or entire village) in a pattern of evil spread over a period of months or years. Such tactics breed delicious fear, dread, and sorrow in their victims that can crush the human spirit and breed chaos and insanity. Although some Russian demons are small and even humorous looking, all are despicable, evil creatures.

When not actively engaged in hurting or molesting humans and D-Bees, demonkind can be found torturing animals, plucking the wings (and other body parts) off of Faeries, gorging themselves on food, drinking themselves into a stupor (many

build stills and brew homemade alcohol of potent quality), swapping stories, searching for lost treasure, sleeping (most are lazy), and gambling. Their favorite game of chance is throwing "bones" (rolling dice), often made from real human bone! The also play cards and smoke tobacco like chimneys.

Russian demons frequently associate with other evil creatures, including forest spirits, ghosts, entities, dragons, monsters and humans. They are attracted to evil and find wicked humans, be they sorcerer or witch, thief or killer, amusing and delightfully fun to associate with. Likewise, one or more demons can often be found as members of groups with a mixture of races and occupations, but all will be evil or anarchist. They are especially fond of murderers, depraved madmen, Witches, Necromancers and Shifters, and often serve them as minions, partners and advisors.

Among other demons, the Archaic Ones are generally considered to be barbarians compared to their infamous cousins from Hades and the conniving undead. Most Demons of Hades and other powerful demonic creatures such as the Goqua, Mindolar, Sowki, Death Weaver Spider Demon, and others (all found in **Rifts® Conversion Book One**), tend to look at Russian demons as inferior, less dangerous, less cunning and unsophisticated. This sentiment has created some feelings of resentment among the more powerful members of the Russian Demons, but most accept their place and grudgingly serve as lesser demons. Many Russian demons are also found in Mongolia and China, just as so-called Chinese and Indian demons are frequently encountered in Russia. At least one third to half of the demons and monsters that roam the Russian Frontier have migrated from the demon-plagued lands of China and Asia. An-

other 12% come from India, Afghanistan and Iran. The remaining 40-50% originate from Russian Rifts linked to their otherworldly home dimension.

Note: See **The Palladium Fantasy Role-Playing Game®, 2nd Edition** for additional details about the Demons of Hades, and Deevals, and **Dragons & Gods™** (complete with M.D. stats) for more information about demon lords, dark gods and dragons.

Supernatural Creatures of Russia

Lesser Russian Demons
The Unclean
Demon Claw
Hell Horse
Il'ya Demons
Kaluga Hag
Kladovik Guardian Demon
Nalet
Serpent Hound
Stone Demon
Water Demon
Wood Demon

Note: Also see the Night Witch and/or Shifter for details about *Demon Helpers.*

Greater Russian Demons
Khitaka Abductors
Koshchei the Deathless Ones
Midnight Demon (Polunochnitsa)
Morozko Frost Demons
Nightfeeder
Whirlwind
Wolf-Serpent

Woodland or Forest Spirits
Domovoi
Polevoi
Leshii
Vodianoi
Rusalka
Firebird
Spirit Wolf
Werewolves
Vampires

Lesser Russian Demons

The Unclean

Unclean Spirits are known as "nechistaia sila" (Unclean Force), or simply "The Unclean." They are creatures of darkness and usually shun the light of day and even the light of a campfire, bonfire, fireplace or artificial light. The only light they do not fear is the blue radiance of ley lines. The comforting darkness of night and the deep shadows of the forest or subterranean

hiding places gives them courage and increased physical strength — physical M.D.C. and P.S. are increased by 50% at night or in darkness. Consequently, most Unclean Spirits hide or sleep during the light of day and come out at night. They are among the demons who prey upon night travelers and people who get lost or linger in the woods at night.

To be deceitful and tricky, they often disguise themselves through metamorphosis. The Unclean can turn into a black cat, black or dark mottled pig, a mangy-looking dark grey or black wolf, or a black rat. They use this disguise to spy on potential victims, to cause mischief, engage in vandalism, slaughter cattle, spoil food and strike without warning. The light of day (including a Globe of Daylight) and the flash of lightning reveals their true demonic nature, forcibly making them assume their natural demon form.

Unclean Spirits often travel, hunt and cause trouble in pairs or small packs of 3-8. They rarely go out into the world alone, so when one is found, 1D6 others are certain to be nearby. Such packs may also associate with, or serve, other more powerful demons, witches or other creatures of darkness, including human sorcerers, thieves and murderers.

The Unclean come in a variety of shapes and sizes, but all share a basic body shape and features. They are somewhat satyr-like with the lower body of a goat, pig or deer (all animals with cloven hooves) and stand only 4-5 feet (1.2 to 1.5 m) tall. Each has a corresponding tail per its animal type. The upper body is human in general appearance and usually very muscular. The skin is usually dark grey or black and cold to the touch. The hair is dark brown or grey, and often long and shaggy. The head tends to be pointed at the top, and is crowned with a pair of horns — those of the antelope (tall and tapered), stag (deer antlers; large or small), or ram (curled). The ears are also pointed, and the teeth sharp, with canine-like fangs. The eyes are a sickly pale green or dull grey, but glow in the dark. About one third have huge, muscular, oversized arms and hands, and tend to be more aggressive and warlike.

Unclean Spirits are malevolent demons who spoil food, damage crops, slaughter livestock, lure travelers into danger, waylay people at night, abduct children, steal, bully and generally delight in causing hardship, suffering and death among humans and D-Bees. The Unclean are sadistic, murderous creatures who enjoy hurting, torturing and killing mortals. They also instigate trouble among mortals foolish enough to listen to them. One of their favorite activities is to mislead, corrupt or encourage acts of evil by fanning the flames of envy, greed, revenge, hatred and fear. Other favorite pastimes include getting drunk, gluttonous eating, smoking (pipes and cigars in particular), rape and torture.

The Unclean Demon NPC Villain

Also Known as Unclean Spirits or Unclean Force (nechistaia sila).
Race: Lesser Archaic Demon
Alignment: Always miscreant or diabolic.
Attributes: I.Q. average human intelligence but cunning and sadistic: 1D4+6, M.E. 1D6+6, M.A. 1D6+6, P.S. 2D6+12 (half in daylight), P.P. 2D6+10, P.E. 2D6+10, P.B. 1D6, Spd 2D6+18; a minimum speed of 22 (15 mph/24 km); supernatural P.S.
M.D.C.: P.E. number +2D4x10+8, but increase by 50% at night or in darkness (on S.D.C. worlds the Unclean has 1D6x10

+P.E. number for Hit Points and 1D4x10 S.D.C.; increase both by 50% at night. A.R. 11, increase to 13 at night).
Horror Factor: 9 for an individual, H.F. 12 for a pack of four or more.
Size: 4-5 feet (1.2 to 1.5 m) tall.
Weight: 100-150 pounds (45 to 67.5 kg)
Average Life Span: Uncertain, 1000+ years; may be immortal.
P.P.E.: 3D4x10 +P.E. attribute number
Natural Abilities: Fair speed and can run without pause or exhaustion for 1D4 hours. They can also leap up to 15 feet (4.6 m) high and lengthwise, climb 80%/70%, swim 90%, can hold its breath for 2+1D6 minutes, survive depths of up to 500 feet (152 m), prowl 50% (+15% in animal form), track humanoids using sense of smell and vision 60% (+10% in animal form), and 40% to track animals. Nightvision is one mile (1.6 km). Unclean Spirits can dimensional teleport 55% and bio-regenerate 1D6 M.D. per minute.

Knows all Languages: Magically understands and speaks all languages 90%, but cannot read.

Limited Flight (special): Can ride the wind of a storm, including tornados and hurricanes, without injury. In fact, they think it's a hoot! During a storm the Unclean effectively fly, and are able to dive, swoop, and hover, but only so long as they are moving in the same direction as the storm winds, and stay just ahead of the heart of the storm. Under these conditions, they can attain a speed of 40 to 90 mph (64 to 144 km; exact speed is up to the demon) during a normal storm, but as fast at 180 mph (288 km) during a *ley line storm*. In the latter case, the creatures must stay ahead of the storm and stay on the ley line.

Limited Metamorphosis (special): The Unclean can turn into a black cat, black or dark mottled pig, mangy dark grey or black wolf, or a black rat three times per night for as long as the entire night. Metamorphosis is impossible during the light of day, and a Globe of Daylight or the flash of lightning (natural or magical) will force an instant transformation back into its true demonic form.

Limited Invulnerability (special): The Unclean are impervious to normal S.D.C. weapons unless they are made of silver or the wood of a juniper or birch tree, in which case the weapon inflicts the equivalent S.D.C. damage as M.D. (i.e. a wooden staff that inflicts 2D6 S.D.C. would inflict 2D6 M.D. to the Unclean if made of juniper or birch). They are also impervious to disease, cold, and heat. Man-made Mega-Damage weapons inflict half their normal damage, M.D. fire does full damage, and magic weapons, spells and psionics do full damage. Millennium Tree weapons do full damage. Lightning does double damage. The light of day (including the magical Globe of Daylight) reduces the demon's P.S. and M.D.C., inhibits their ability to metamorph, and makes them feel exposed and insecure.

Also see magic.

O.C.C.: Not applicable.

R.C.C. Skills: Horsemanship (exotic animals), land navigation 80% and wilderness survival 90%, plus select three skills from each of the following skill categories: W.P. Ancient Weapons, Rogue, and Espionage; all get a +15% skill bonus and one skill gets an additional +10%. Proficiency in these skills do not advance. Also see Natural Abilities, above.

R.C.C. Combat: Attacks Per Melee: Four

Damage: Bite 1D4 M.D., head-butt with horns, punch or kick M.D. varies with supernatural P.S., or by weapon or magic.

R.C.C. Bonuses: +3 on initiative, +3 to strike, +2 to parry, +1 to dodge, +4 to pull punch, +3 to roll with impact or fall, +2 to save vs Horror Factor. R.C.C. bonuses are all in addition to any possible attribute bonuses.

Magic: All Unclean can cast the following spells, provided the demon has sufficient P.P.E.: Fool's Gold, Multiple Image, Levitate, Mask of Deceit, Repel Animals, Compulsion, Spoil (Food/Water), Sickness, Shadow Meld, and Cloak of Darkness (*Federation of Magic*). Spell potency is equal to a 3rd level sorcerer.

Psionics: None

Enemies: All mortals, particularly humans. Greatly dislike Gargoyles and Brodkil and consider all "sub-demons" to be inferior and subservient to them.

Allies: Others of its kind, greater demons, powerful practitioners of magic, and other powerful beings with agendas that involve murder, torture and mayhem.

Value: None

Habitat: Woodlands (especially deep forests and swamps), ruins, abandoned buildings, slums, waste dump sites, caves, and subterranean networks (sewers, catacombs, etc.) throughout Rifts Rifts Russia, China and much of Asia. Although one or more bands of Unclean Spirits may plague a farm, village or city on a nightly basis, few, if any, will actually live in a human community. Most will invade the community at night from lairs in the surrounding wilderness or underground. However, most will have one or more hiding places in the community, typically alleys, garbage dumps, graveyards, abandoned buildings, sewers and basements or catacombs where they can find momentary refuge.

The Demon Claw

"And the hand of evil shall reach out to try to snare the human spirit, and failing that, go forth and crush the body of men of all faiths." — Or so it is said of the abomination known as the Demon Claw.

This particular demon has a gnarled, bone encrusted body that resembles a crab, or that of a giant, demonic four-fingered claw. Each finger-like leg ends in a sharp, cutting and stabbing claw, as if the beast were walking on spear tips or the blade of a sword. The finger-like legs can face forward, sideways or completely backwards, that's how flexible the demon is. The creature can strike opponents with one pair of its legs and the arms of the upper torso, effectively giving it two pairs of arms to fight with. The Demon Claw can also rear up on its hind legs and stab or parry with both the clawed hands of its upper torso and front legs. On top of the giant claw-like body is a humanoid torso encrusted in the same bony armor and spines. The two oversized hands are themselves massive claws, each with three blade-like fingers and a bladed thumb. The entire body is encased in a rock hard exoskeleton studded with lumps and spines and the color of wind dried bone. The humanoid head is also encased in a natural helmet of stone, with a pair of small horns protruding from the side of the head and pointed teeth jutting from the large snapping mouth.

The Demon Claw is the embodiment of hate and fury, thus it strikes out at all things gentle and beautiful, as well as the enemies of its master. Humans (and D-Bees) are hated for their propensity toward good and their love of life. However, the Demon Claw finds humans who have given themselves to hatred and wickedness to be admirable beings and worthy allies. Thus, this demon may ally itself to Necromancers, Witches and other foul humans. Thankfully, when not allied to or summoned by greater forces, the Demon Claw tends to be a loner, seldom gathering in groups larger than three of its own kind, and is usually found in swamps, polluted waters, deep lakes and near ley line nexus points. However, they can be found in or near any body of water including oceans and seas throughout the world, and any environment from tropical or desert to the snow swept tundra and glacial wastelands. They also serve as the minions, typically guardians, enforcers, and soldiers, of evil Shifters/Summoners, Witches, Necromancers, Nalets and greater demons. As minions, they can be found anywhere and in larger groups of their own kind and other demons.

The Demon Claw loves to kill and feast on the bones and flesh of its victims. The monster is a merciless and relentless fighter devoid of any sense of fair play, justice, or mercy. They are also said to be absolutely fearless and willing to fight to the death, taking as many enemies to the grave with them as they can. When left to their own devices, Demon Claws are savage brutes and bullies who use straightforward tactics, brute force and intimidation to bully, cow and defeat "lesser" beings. Comparatively dull-witted, Demon Claws are easily provoked into pursuit, combat or reckless behavior. They never use man-made weapons, preferring their raw strength, slashing sword-like finger claws, and large stabbing and slicing legs. They possess little in the way of innate magical ability, but the powers they do have, they wield expertly.

KA XIONG '98

The Demon Claw NPC Villain

Also Known as the Hand of Evil and Claw of Death.

Race: Lesser Archaic Demon

Alignment: Always miscreant or diabolic.

Attributes: I.Q. low to average human intelligence but a fierce hunter and fighter: 1D4+5, M.E. 1D6+2, M.A. 1D6+2, P.S. 5D6+23, P.P. 2D6+12, P.E. 2D6+12, P.B. 1D4, Spd 2D6+28 (running or swimming); a minimum speed of 30 (20 mph/32 km); supernatural P.S. and P.E.

M.D.C. by Location: Main Body: P.E. number x3 plus an an additional 160 points, increase by 50% when on a ley line (on S.D.C. worlds the Demon Claw has 1D6x10 Hit Points +P.E. number and 2D6x10 S.D.C.; increase both by 50% at ley lines and places of magic. A.R. 16).; each of the four legs has 100 M.D.C. (or 90 S.D.C.), the large claw hands 70 M.D.C. (or 60 S.D.C.).

Horror Factor: 14.

Size: 7-8 feet (2.1 to 2.4 m) tall, 7 feet (2.1 m) long and 12 feet (3.6 m) wide.

Weight: 1200 pounds (540 kg)

Average Life Span: Uncertain, 1000+ years; probably immortal.

P.P.E.: 2D4x10 +P.E. attribute number.

Natural Abilities: Fair to excellent speed and can run, fight or swim without pause or exhaustion for 24 hours! They can also leap up to 15 feet (4.6 m) high or across, climb 70%/60%, swim 98%, run on the top of water, float (by filling up an internal air bladder), breathe underwater (indefi- nitely), survive depths of up to 3,000 feet (914 m), prowl 45%, track humanoids using sense of smell and vision 75%, and 30% to track animals. Nightvision is 2000 feet (610 m) and Demon Claws can dimensional teleport 25% bio-regenerates 2D6 M.D. per melee round and regenerates lost limbs within 24 hours.

<u>Knows</u> <u>all</u> <u>Languages</u>: Magically understands and speaks all languages 90%, but cannot read.

<u>Ride</u> <u>the</u> <u>Waves</u> (special): The demon can ride the waves of a river, lake, sea or ocean, including tidal waves without injury. This power also gives them the ability to walk and run on the surface of water at their normal speed.

<u>Limited</u> <u>Invulnerability</u> (special): Demon Claws are impervi- ous to cold, drowning, disease, and normal S.D.C. weapons un- less they are made of silver or the wood of a juniper, ash or birch, in which case, the weapon inflicts the equivalent S.D.C. damage as M.D. (i.e. a wooden staff that inflicts 2D6 S.D.C. would inflict 2D6 M.D. to the demon if made of juniper, ash or birch). Also impervious to disease and cold. Millennium Tree weapons do full damage.

Man-made Mega-Damage weapons inflict their normal dam- age, as do most types of magic weapons, spells and psionics. Magical fire does 50% greater damage, while lightning and electrical attacks do half damage. Although they prefer murky or polluted waters, overcast skies and darkness, they are not negatively affected by the light of day. Also see magic.

O.C.C.: Not applicable.

R.C.C. Skills: Land navigation 80% and wilderness survival 90%, plus select three skills from the Wilderness skill category; all skills get a +5% skill bonus. Also see Natural Abilities, above.

R.C.C. Combat: Attacks Per Melee: Six

Damage: Bite 1D6 M.D., head-butt, (closed-fist) punch, leg-strike/kick (without using the point or inner blade side) does M.D. equal to the monster's supernatural P.S.; or by weapon or magic. Stabbing and slicing attacks with the lower legs or large, sword-like hand-claws inflict M.D. equal to the creature's supernatural P.S. +3D6 additional M.D.

R.C.C. Bonuses: +3 on initiative, +3 to strike, +5 to parry, +2 to dodge, +2 to pull punch, +2 to roll with impact or fall, +10 to save vs Horror Factor. R.C.C. bonuses are all in addition to any possible attribute bonuses.

Magic: All Demon Claws can cast the following spells, provided they have sufficient P.P.E.: Float in Air, Levitate, Chameleon, Fear, Fire Bolt, Fire Ball, Agony and Spoil (Water only). Spell potency is equal to a 2nd level sorcerer.

Psionics: None

Enemies: All mortals, particularly humans. Greatly dislike Gargoyles, Brodkil and Aquatics (demons) and consider all "sub-demons," as well as mortals, to be inferior.

Allies: Others of its kind, greater demons, powerful practitioners of magic, and other powerful beings with agendas that involve war, murder, torture and mayhem.

Value: None

Habitat: Typically encountered in or near swamps and other bodies of water, especially if polluted. Found throughout Rifts Russia, China and much of Asia.

Hell Horse

The Hell Horse, or "Chertu Baran" (meaing the Devil's Mount), is a stark white or pale grey, and skeletal thin demonic horse. The head looks like the skull of a dead animal with flesh pulled tight to reveal the nasal cavity, teeth and sunken eyes and cheeks. From the deeply shadowed eye sockets radiates a green light, and the mane and tail are composed of ethereal white or pale green wisps of mist or smoke. Monsters empowered by wickedness and magic, the Chertu Baran can run across the ground and through the air at tremendous speed. In ancient times, the Chertu Baran were believed to be the cursed spirits of those who committed suicide, and who now hated the living, condemned to live all eternity as the work animals of demons. However, they are demonic creatures in their own right, lesser demons who enjoy bringing chaos and participating in carnage. Thus, they gladly carry other demons through the sky and across the land to spread evil. In fact, they are frequently seen running and soaring through the clouds, along ley lines or galloping through graveyards carrying 2-4 small demons like the Unclean or Il'ya or a single hellspawned warrior. Sometimes wagons and chariots are hooked to the creatures, as they possess tremendous strength and can pull heavy weights. When large groups of demons gather into small armies, it is the "Devil's Mount" who carries many of them into battle.

Although far more than a dumb animal, these lesser demons possess a low intelligence and usually serve as the riding animals and servants of other demons. They don't care to make decisions and are poor at developing and implementing strategies or subterfuge. Consequently, they are content to follow the orders of those more cunning than they.

The Hell Horse Demon NPC Villain

Also Known as "Chertu Baran"/Devil's Mount and Demon Horse.

Race: A lesser demon.

Alignment: Always miscreant or diabolic.

Attributes: I.Q. 1D4+3, M.E. 1D6+4, M.A. 1D6, P.S. 3D6+22, P.P. 2D6+16, P.E. 2D6+12, P.B. 1D6, Spd 2D6x10+100 running (80 mph/128.7 km minimum speed, and 220 flying (150 mph/241 km maximum); double along ley lines! Supernatural P.S. and can pull or carry 600 times its P.S. in pounds (well over 6 tons).

M.D.C.: P.E. number +2D6x10 +30; double during ley line storms (on S.D.C. worlds the demon has 1D6x10 +P.E. number for Hit Points, and 1D6x10 S.D.C. with an A.R. 12).

Horror Factor: 10 for an individual, 12 for a pack of four or more. **Size:** About the size of normal horse, 6 feet (1.8 m) tall at the shoulders.

Weight: 1500 pounds (675 kg)

Average Life Span: Uncertain, 1000+ years; probably immortal.

P.P.E.: 2D6x10 +M.E. attribute number

Natural Abilities: Superhuman speed on the ground or running in the air! It can also stand and hover in the air, and run without pause or fatigue for 24 hours; maximum altitude is 10,000 feet (3048 m). The demonic beast can leap up to 25 feet (7.6 m) high and 40 feet (12.2 m) lengthwise without actually flying, swim 70% (at one third normal speed), prowl 45%, track humanoids using sense of smell and vision 65%, 50% to track animals. Nightvision is one mile (1.6 km). Hell Horses can dimensional teleport at 61% accuracy and bio-regenerate 2D6 M.D. per minute.

<u>Knows</u> <u>all</u> <u>Languages</u>: Magically understands and speaks all languages 75%, but cannot read.

<u>Lightning</u> <u>Ride</u> (special): The Hell Horse can turn itself and its riders into a bolt of lightning twice per night (never during the day) to travel a distance of up to 100 miles (160 km) in two seconds (counts as one melee action).

<u>Limited</u> <u>Metamorphosis</u> (special): The Hell Horse can turn into a normal looking black or dark colored horse three times per night for as long as all night. Metamorphosis is impossible during the light of day, and a Globe of Daylight or the flash of lightning (natural or magical) will force an instant transformation back into its true demonic form.

<u>Limited</u> <u>Invulnerability</u> (special): The Hell Horse is impervious to normal S.D.C. weapons unless made of silver or the wood of juniper or birch trees, in which case the weapon inflicts its normal S.D.C. damage as M.D. (i.e. a wooden staff that inflicts 2D6 S.D.C. would inflict 2D6 M.D. if made of juniper or birch). Also impervious to disease, cold, and heat.

Mega-Damage weapons and those made from the wood of a Millennium Tree inflict their normal damage. Magical M.D. fire, magic weapons, spells and psionics also do full damage. Impervious to lightning and electricity.

The light of day (including the magical Globe of Daylight) reveals the true nature of a Hell Horse disguised by metamorphosis, and reduces its running speed and maximum attainable altitude by half while caught in its light.

O.C.C.: Not applicable.

R.C.C. Skills: Land navigation 90%, wilderness survival 90%, herd cattle 85%, plus select two skills from each of the following skill categories (keeping in mind the limitations of the horse form): Espionage and Wilderness; all get a +10% skill bonus.

R.C.C. Combat: Attacks/Actions Per Melee: Four

Damage: Bite 2D4 M.D., head-butt 1D6 M.D., punch or kick M.D. depends on the supernatural P.S., however, a kick with both rear legs simultaneously inflicts 2D6 M.D. in addition to supernatural P.S. damage. Hell Horses are known to eat the flesh of fallen enemies, corpses and rotted food and garbage.

R.C.C. Bonuses: +4 on initiative, +2 to strike, +5 to auto-dodge (this dodge does not use up a melee attack/action, but must be rolled on 1D20), +1 to pull punch/kick, +3 to roll with impact or fall, +1 to save vs magic, +4 to save vs Horror Factor. These are all in addition to any possible attribute bonuses.

Magic: Although a supernatural and mystical creature, it is incapable of casting spells; see natural abilities.

Psionics: None

Enemies: All mortals, particularly humans. Hates Gargoyles and Brodkil and considers all "sub-demons" to be inferior and potential enemies. They also hate all Deevils but are sometimes forced to serve them as mounts (they serve most of demonkind willingly).

Allies: Other Archaic demons, others of its own kind, greater demons, dark gods, high level Necromancers and Witches, as well as other powerful and diabolical practitioners of magic, and evil beings involved in murder, war, destruction and mayhem.

Value: None

Habitat: Woodlands (especially deep forests and swamps), the Steppe, grasslands, and mountain regions throughout Rifts Russia, China and much of Asia. They are seldom encountered without a "master" or one or more riders, but when they are, they are usually found in pairs or groups of 1D4+2 (hundreds may be part of a demon army).

Il'ya Demons

Il'ya demons are small to medium-sized demons who are malicious and murderous in nature. They are strange in that Il'ya demons appear in the sky during ferocious thunder and/or lightning storms, as well as during ley line storms. During the worst storms, the ancient god Perun appears in a chariot of fire in hot pursuit of the vile creatures. They try to escape Perun, Demon Slayers and others who hunt their kind (psychics, sorcerers, the Warlords, Bogatyrs, etc.) by turning into animal or human form. This shapechanging ability is why Russian peasants and farmers are wary of strangers and stray animals who appear during storms. Unfortunately, this often means ordinary, mortal travelers will be ignored and left to soak in downpours.

The natural appearance of Il'ya demons is hunchbacked men and women who stand 3-5 feet (0.9 to 1.5 m) tall, but who have the heads of a demonic animal (typically cow, bull, ox, boar, deer, wolf or hound) and a pair of small, feathered wings. Their skin is either dirty grey or black, and their eyes (in demon form) glow with red or yellow energy. Those with the head of a wolf or hound can transform into both canine or human form (male or female), but all other Il'ya demons can only assume the shape of the animal-type represented in their demonic form. For example,

an Il'ya demon with the head of an ox can transform into most types of bovine; cow, bull, ox, musk ox, etc.

Most Il'ya demons are somehow "Rifted" to Russia during supernatural thunder or lightning storms along ley lines. During such storms, small flocks of 3D6 demons will appear a moment after a flash of lightning, and thousands can appear during a single storm. Thankfully, only 1D6 Il'ya demons appear during the worst natural storms and in both cases, three quarters disappear with the storm, sucked back into their hellish dimension at the end of the violent weather. However, that leaves twenty-five percent on Earth. These miscreant beings typically assume the shape of an animal or a human vagabond and engage in violent and malicious activities. The demon animals will attack travelers, maidens, elders and lone warriors, drag children into the wilderness where they frighten, abuse and threaten them, but often leave them hanging from tree branches or pinned under logs and rocks rather than kill them. The monsters enjoy the panic and ensuing manhunt for the lost/stolen child/children or maiden and often use this as an opportunity to "pick-off" and maim or kill members of the search party. The kidnap victim is little more than bait in their traps and mad games.

For reasons unknown, the Il'ya demons cannot enter a home or camp unless invited to do so. This is where their shapechanging abilities become important, and why peasants and those familiar with demon lore are wary of strangers and stray animals. If invited or brought into a home, barn or campsite even once, that particular demon can come and go as he pleases from that day forward. Many Il'ya demons are so skillful at their animal disguises that the victims never realize the "animals" are really transformed demons. Demons disguised as animals may maim or slaughter livestock, spoil or eat food reserves, frighten other animals, and fight or kill guard animals, especially dogs, cats and horses who are all very sensitive to the supernatural and who can usually sense the creature's true demonic nature. They will also frighten, bully and hurt children, the elderly and impaired.

The Il'ya Demon NPC Villain

Also Known as Storm Demons.
Race: Lesser Archaic Demon
Alignment: Anarchist (20%), miscreant (50%) or diabolic (30%).
Attributes: I.Q.: 1D6+8, M.E. 1D6+8, M.A. 1D6+8, P.S. 2D6+14, P.P. 2D6+8, P.E. 2D6+8, P.B. 1D6 as demon, 2D6+6 in metamorphed animal or human form, Spd. Running: 3D6+30 (+30 in animal form); Flying is possible only when in demon form at speeds of 1D6x10+40. Supernatural P.S.
M.D.C.: P.E. number +1D6x10+14, but increase by 50% at night (on S.D.C. worlds the Il'ya has 1D4x10 +P.E. number for Hit Points and 1D4x10 S.D.C.; increase both by 50% at night. A.R. 10, increase to 12 at night).
Horror Factor: 9
Size: 3-5 feet (0.9 to 1.5 m) tall; average around 4 ft (1.2 m).
Weight: 100-150 pounds (45 to 67.5 kg)
Average Life Span: Uncertain, 1000+ years; probably immortal.
P.P.E.: 3D4x10 +P.E. attribute number.
Natural Abilities: Excellent running and flying speed and can run or fly without pause or exhaustion for 1D4+2 hours. They can also leap up to 10 feet (3 m) high and lengthwise, climb 85%/80%, swim 80%, can hold breath for 2+1D6 minutes, survive depths of up to 500 feet (152 m), prowl 50% (+15% in animal form), track humanoids using sense of smell and vision 60% (+15% in animal form), and 45% to track animals (+15% in animal form). Nightvision is 1000 feet (305 m). Il'Ya can dimensional teleport 55% and bio-regenerate 2D6 M.D. per minute.

Knows all Languages: Magically understands and speaks all languages 90%, but cannot read.

Storm Flight (special): Il'ya can also ride the wind of a storm, including tornados and hurricanes, without injury. During a storm the Il'ya effectively fly, and are able to dive, swoop, and hover, but only so long as they are moving in the same direction as the storm winds and stay just ahead of the heart of the storm. Under these conditions, they can attain a speed of 40 to 90 mph (64 to 144 km; exact speed is up to the demon) during a normal storm, but as fast at 180 mph (288 km) during a *ley line storm*. In the latter case, the creatures must stay ahead of the storm and stay on the ley line.

Limited Metamorphosis (special): The Il'ya can turn into the type or family of animals represented by its physical appearance. All Il'ya have the head or facial features and tail of a cow, bull, ox, boar, deer, wolf or hound (and a pair of small, feathered wings that disappear when the metamorphosis is used). This means demons who have a boar-like head can turn into a boar, wild pig or any type of domesticated pig; those with the head of a deer can change into any variety of deer or elk; a bull or ox into various large types of bovine (typically male), cow into any variety of cow (female animal), hound into any type of dog, etc. Those with the head of a *wolf* or *hound* can transform into both canine or human form (male or female).

In all cases, the Il'ya demon can maintain their "false" appearance as an animal (or human) indefinitely — hours, days, weeks, or months. However, they are only likely to maintain such a charade only as long it is fun for them, i.e. they can continue to cause trouble without being discovered. Neither the light of day nor lightning have any adverse affect on the disguise of the Il'ya. However, a negate magic spell will force an instant transformation back into its true demonic form.

Limited Invulnerability (special): The little demons are impervious to normal S.D.C. weapons unless made of silver or the wood of juniper or birch trees, in which case the weapon inflicts its normal S.D.C. damage as M.D. (i.e. a wooden staff that inflicts 2D6 S.D.C. would inflict 2D6 M.D. if made of juniper or birch).

Mega-Damage weapons and those made from the wood of a Millennium Tree inflict their normal damage. Magical M.D. fire, magic weapons, spells and psionics also do full damage.

Impervious to lightning, electricity, disease, cold, and heat. Also see magic.

O.C.C.: Not applicable.
R.C.C. Skills: Horsemanship (exotic animals), land navigation 75%, wilderness survival 75%, plus select three skills from each of the following skill categories: W.P. Ancient Weapons, Rogue (ideally thief skills), and Domestic; all get a +15% skill bonus on all skills, and one particular skill gets an additional +10%. Also see Natural Abilities, above.
R.C.C. Combat: Attacks Per Melee: Four
Damage: Bite 1D6 M.D., head-butt with horns, punch or kick M.D. varies with supernatural P.S.; or by weapon or magic.
R.C.C. Bonuses: +3 on initiative, +3 to strike, +2 to parry, +2 to dodge, +2 to pull punch, +3 to roll with impact or fall, +4 to save vs Horror Factor. R.C.C. bonuses are all in addition to any possible attribute bonuses.
Magic: All Il'ya can cast the following spells, provided the demon has sufficient P.P.E.: Thunderclap, Heavy Breathing, Fingers of Wind, Float in Air, Wind Rush, Compulsion, Spoil (Food/Water), Sickness, Minor Curse, Call Lightning, Electric Arc, and Influence the Beast (the last three spells are found in *Federation of Magic*). Spell potency is equal to a 2nd level sorcerer.
Psionics: None
Enemies: All mortals, particularly humans. Greatly dislike Gargoyles and Brodkil, and consider all "sub-demons" to be inferior and subservient to them.
Allies: Others of its kind, other demons, greater demons, powerful practitioners of magic, and other powerful beings with agendas that involves murder, torture and mayhem.
Value: None

Habitat: Woodlands (especially deep forests and swamps), ruins, abandoned buildings, slums, waste dump sites, caves, and subterranean networks (sewers, catacombs, etc.) throughout Rifts Rifts Russia, China and much of Asia. Not only is it likely that one or more bands of Il'ya demons plague a farm, village or city on a regular basis, but many will actually live among humans disguised as an ordinary animal or fellow human. Il'ya take great pride in their ability to disguise themselves and walk among mortals unnoticed. This also makes them the natural spies and thieves of the Archaic demons.

Kaluga Hag

The Kaluga Hag is one of the ugliest and most feared of the Russian demons. It appears as a leprous old hag covered in poisonous pimples. She has an unusually long tongue (three times longer than a normal human) that is as flexible as that of a snake. The eyes are red with a purple iris, the teeth yellow and crooked, and her scraggly hair is grey or white. Despite her withered, aged and diseased appearance, the Kaluga Hag is quick and strong, and her long, broken nails cut like M.D. blades.

The demon hag is renowned for her acts of cruelty and manipulation. Unlike many of the other Russian demons, the Kaluga Hag often acts alone and avoids the company of others, especially other hags. When it does work with other demons, it is usually because the scheme involves mass suffering or death. They love to make large groups of people suffer and, eventually, die. The Demon Hag also likes to enforce her depraved will over others while slowly driving them to despair, insanity or depravity. Bringing an entire village or town to its knees is one of the Hag's greatest pleasures and triumphs. When the people are completely lost or the community destroyed, the venomous creature moves on to find her next set of victims. This imposition of her will and the subjugation of people through terror, intimidation and murder is not born from a desire for power as much as it is an unfathomable desire to devastate others for the sheer pleasure of it. The Kaluga Hag does what she does because she can. To punish those who will not submit to her will, and when angry or just feeling mean, the Hag will unleash a blight, disease or pestilence upon one or more targets, sometimes entire villages. Most peasants regard the Hag as a harbinger of death and destruction.

When the Kaluga Hag does associate with other evil forces, they are often humans and other mortals dedicated to inflicting pain, suffering and/or destruction upon the weak and helpless. This demon is especially fond of reaping mass suffering, death and destruction. The Hag may also claim a village as "hers," forcing the people into her service and depravity lest they watch their loved ones suffer from disease and foul magic. Villages who try to resist are either themselves stricken by a debilitating curse, blight, wasting disease, or demonic minions, or (more likely) see their loved ones maimed, become ill, die or worse in their place — Kaluga Hags are masters of manipulation and their favorite ploy is to capture, threaten or hurt loved ones to get the real target of their evil to submit or break. Thus, victims of Kaluga Hags are left with only three choices: 1) Submit, 2) flee before the Kaluga Hag can get to them or those they hold dear (knowing that innocent villagers will pay for their crimes

of insurrection), or 3) somehow manage to kill the Hag. Note that driving the Demon Hag away is only a temporary solution, because few other demons can match the obsessive need for revenge that will take hold of a Kaluga Hag. This venomous creature has no concept of mercy and will return to extract a terrible vengeance upon those who have defied or defeated her. And such revenge always involves long suffering before an excruciating death.

The Kaluga Hag Demonic NPC Villain

Also Known as Demon Hag or Witch Demon.

Race: Lesser Demon, but some rank her among the greater demons because she is so powerful and uses her abilities so cleverly that it makes the Hag a terrible foe.

Alignment: Always miscreant or diabolic.

Attributes: I.Q. 2D6+6, M.E. 1D6+10, M.A. 2D6+10, P.S. 2D6+22, P.P. 2D6+10, P.E. 2D6+10, P.B. 1D6, Spd 2D6+18; a minimum speed of 22 (15 mph/24 km); supernatural P.S.

M.D.C.: P.E. number +3D6x10, but increases by 30% at night (on S.D.C. worlds the demon has 2D6x10 H.P. +P.E. number and 1D6x10 S.D.C. with an A.R. 10).

Horror Factor: 12

Size: 5-6 feet (1.5 to 1.8 m) tall.

Weight: 100-180 pounds (45 to 55 kg)

Average Life Span: Uncertain, 1000+ years; probably immortal.

P.P.E.: 3D6x10+60

Natural Abilities: Fair speed, can run without pause or exhaustion for six hours, leap up to 15 feet (4.6 m) high and lengthwise, does not breathe air, can eat spoiled or poisoned food and drink, climb 70%/65%, prowl 65%, and recognize poisonous chemicals, drugs, toxins and plants at 90%. Nightvision is one mile (1.6 km), the Hag can dimensionally teleport 50% (+25% at a ley line nexus) and bio-regenerates 2D6 M.D. per melee round.

<u>Knows</u> <u>all</u> <u>Languages</u>: Magically understands and speaks all languages 90%, but cannot read.

<u>Poisonous Tongue</u> (special): The Hag's tongue is poisonous and she can contaminate water, wine and other drinks simply by taking a sip from the container — the drink becomes a deadly poison that does 1D4x10 points of damage direct to hit points for every sip taken (3D6 M.D. if the drinker is an M.D.C. creature). This damage is also inflicted by the Hag's kiss or the lick of her tongue on bare flesh!

<u>Poison</u> <u>Pimples</u> (special): Breaking a pimple by touch (including punch and kick) releases pus that burns like acid. It inflicts 6D6 points of damage directly to Hit Points on mortal beings and 1D6 M.D. to the skin of Mega-Damage creatures or body armor. Worse than the initial damage is that any wound inflicted by the acid pus will not heal through normal means; S.D.C./Hit Points cannot be restored. For dragons, other creatures of magic and supernatural beings, this means their bio-regenerative powers are ineffective on these wounds. Healing potions, magic and psionics will restore half the lost damage they would heal normally, but remains an open, ulcerated sore. The only way to heal the wound completely is to have the Hag remove it with her magic (a simple wave of her hand or touch of the finger and her expending 10 P.P.E. points does the trick), the healing touch of a god or demigod, or by one of the following magical means: *Greater Healing* or *Super Healing* (in

both cases, the spell heals the hideous ulcer and restores 1D4 H.P.; subsequent magical healing repairs injury as per normal — see Federation of Magic, page 143 and 152 respectively, for details), *Purge Self* (see Federation of Magic, page 148, for details), *Purge Others* (see Federation of Magic, page 151, for details), *Negate Magic* (roll 1D20, a 16 or higher saves and the sore disappears), *Remove Curse,* and *Restoration.*

Limited Metamorphosis (special): Twice per night, the Hag can transform into a beautiful woman with a P.B. of 1D6+18 (poisonous tongue/kiss and contamination of drinks by touch all still apply). However, this metamorphosis can only be performed at night and lasts for one brief hour at a time.

Limited Invulnerability (special): The Kaluga Hag is impervious to poison, acid, disease, pollution and even magic potions, magical illness and curses, as well as normal cold and heat (magic cold and heat-based attacks do full damage). Normal S.D.C. weapons do no damage unless made of silver or the wood of juniper or birch trees, in which case the weapon inflicts the equivalent S.D.C. damage as M.D. (i.e. a wooden staff made of juniper or birch that inflicts 2D6 S.D.C. inflicts 2D6 M.D. against the Hag).

Mega-Damage weapons, M.D. fire, magic weapons, spells and psionics inflict their normal damage. Lightning and electrical blasts do double damage. The light of day (including the magical Globe of Daylight) reduces the demon's P.S., Speed and available P.P.E. by half.

Also see magic.

O.C.C.: Not applicable.

R.C.C. Skills: Horsemanship (exotic animals), land navigation 80%, wilderness survival 70%, identify plants, recognize poisons, and brewing all at 90%, plus select *two* skills from each of the following skill categories: W.P. Ancient Weapons, Domestic or Technical, and Rogue or Medical; all get a +20% skill bonus and two skills get another +10% bonus on top of the first.

R.C.C. Combat: Attacks Per Melee: Five

Damage: Bite 1D4 M.D., punch or kick M.D. is equal to the supernatural P.S., a claw strike adds +2D6 M.D. to supernatural P.S. damage; or by weapon or magic.

R.C.C. Bonuses: +3 on initiative, +4 to strike, +2 to parry, +1 to dodge, +3 to pull punch, +2 to roll with impact or fall, +6 to save vs Horror Factor. These are all in addition to any possible attribute bonuses.

Magic: All Kaluga Demon Hags are effectively Necromancers and possess a large range of spell casting abilities. They possess all Necromancy spells levels 1-12, plus the following spells from the *Rifts® RPG*: Fly, Repel Animals, Fear, Trance, Calling, Domination, Compulsion, Agony, Life Drain, Negate Magic, Minor Curse, Luck Curse, Sickness, Spoil (food and water), Commune with Spirits, Negate Poisons/Toxins, Cure Minor Disorders, and Cure Illness.

The Kaluga Hag can also cast the following spells as described in *Federation of Magic™*: Cleanse, Watchguard, Forcebonds, Distant Voice, Instill Knowledge, Horror, Aura of Death, Aura of Doom, Aura of Power, Death Curse, Fortify Against Disease, and Plane Skip. Spell potency is equal to a 5th level Necromancer.

Psionics: None

Enemies: All mortals, particularly humans. Dislikes Gargoyles, Brodkil and considers all "sub-demons" to be inferior and subservient to her.

Allies: Tends to be a loner, although Hags do occasionally associate with Necromancers, other demons, greater demons, and dark gods. They are particularly fond of human Witches and Necromancers, and may associate with other powerful beings who have an agenda that involves mass murder, mass destruction, mass suffering and anarchy.

Value: None

Habitat: Woodlands (especially deep forests and swamps), ruins, abandoned buildings, slums, and strange or ugly places throughout Rifts Russia, China and much of Asia. They can be encountered day or night, although they prefer the night. They typically live in a dilapidated hut or house, and may live in or near a human or D-Bee community. Many grow a garden of poisonous plants, mushrooms and dangerous herbs. At least one Kaluga Hag will be found living at or near most ley lines.

Kladovik Guardian

The Kladovik demon thrives on combat and brutality. Unlike the Nalet and Kaluga Hags, they rarely bother with strategies or tactics, and simply look for an opportunity to fight, slaughter and kill. They enjoy intimidating and torturing others, but lack the patience to stretch such sweet agony out for more than a few hours before killing their victims. Consequently, these psychopathic killers are used as demon shock troops and savage guardians by the more intelligent and powerful Archaic demons. In fact, they are often placed on a leash and literally reined in like mad dogs. gs.

As demon guardsmen they are used to protect "unclean" places, like caves, strange rock formations, swamps and sinkholes that serve as lairs, hideouts or gathering places for other demons. They are also used to guard dimensional portals, treasure troves, prisoners, and sacred or magical artifacts, as well as being used like attack dogs. These are all wise uses of the Kladovik because they understand simple, straightforward assignments like, "kill anybody who enters this room," or "let none pass," or "let no one touch the altar," or "kill all who try to escape," or "find him and kill him," and so on. Although anxious and fidgety, a Kladovik demon will hold his post indefinitely, each passing day making him or her more bloodthirsty than the previous. When the prey or enemy appears, the Kladovik strikes with unbridled fury and demonic savagery. There is no room for discussion, deal-making, fast-talking, cat and mouse games, or pleas for mercy. The monster strikes to kill and does not stop fighting until its quarry lies dead. The harder the fight, the better the demon likes it. If the monster has any fear of death, he never shows it, smiling and laughing or giggling during the entire battle, and engaging opponents who clearly outmatch or outnumber him without any sign of hesitation. The demon follows orders into battle with absolute glee. Fighting, even to the death, is ecstacy.

When not under the thrall of greater beings (including evil Shifters, Necromancers and black-hearted sorcerers), the Kladovik will terrorize the countryside with insane killing sprees or wholesale slaughter of people and livestock. It is under

this circumstance that the Kladovik demon may engage in cat and mouse games, luring Demon Hunters and angry townspeople after it so that the murderous fiend can engage in ambushes and skirmishes where it can pick and choose its battles and ultimately take on all challengers; or go to terrorize and kill those holed up in town or in what they consider a sanctuary while their heroes and defenders are off on a wild goose chase. Kladovik are as despicable as any demon, but none are more bloodthirsty.

These crazed demon fighters have one serious flaw that is rooted in their very soul; they cannot resist a challenge or ignore an insult. Even the most insignificant of slights or challenges will send most Kladovik at the throat of the person responsible. Only a powerful master can stem this trigger response, but even such influential beings can contain the fury for only so long before the demon(s) breaks rank to attack his accusers. Left on their own, Kladovik stalk and hunt as lone predators or in pairs, but dozens can serve under a powerful master, and when a demon army is raised, the front-line will be composed of hundreds of them.

Fortunately, Kladovik have little use for magic or weaponry, preferring to tear their opponents apart with their bare hands, and rip out their throats with their teeth. This makes the demon susceptible to long-range attacks and magical countermeasures. Unfortunately, they are smart enough to lie in ambush and strike without warning. So when a Kladovik attacks, he is probably already within close combat range and pouncing on his opponent.

Kladovik are tall, lithe humanoids with a tall, conical head, pointed ears, crazed eyes, and wide mouth filled with sharp teeth. Four pairs of long arms end in snapping, crescent shaped claws that slash and stab, as well as snap closed like scissors — they love to literally chop their opponents to pieces and dismember or flay victims under torture. The sickening white skin feels like rubber and a network of thin, blue and violet veins snake through the forearms, lower legs and membranes between the arms, sometimes giving them a scaly appearance. Their huge feet end with two taloned toes used to claw and slash opponents, as well as pin those who have fallen. The large feet also give the demon better balance and traction.

Kladovik Guardian Demon, NPC Villain

Also Known as The Bloodletters and Demon Guardians.
Race: Lesser Demon.
Alignment: Always diabolic.
Attributes: I.Q. 1D6+4, but even the most dull-witted is a natural and cunning predator; M.E. 1D6, M.A. 1D6, P.S. 3D6+24, P.P. 2D6+12, P.E. 2D6+12, P.B. 1D4, Spd 3D6+30; a minimum speed of 33 (22.5 mph/36 km); supernatural P.S.
M.D.C.: P.E. number +2D4x10+50 (on S.D.C. worlds the demon has 2D4x10 +P.E. number for Hit Points and 1D6x10 S.D.C., with an A.R. 11).
Horror Factor: 13
Size: 8-9 feet (2.4 to 2.7 m) tall.
Weight: 300-400 pounds (135 to 180 kg)
Average Life Span: Uncertain, 1000+ years; probably immortal.

P.P.E.: 2D4x10

Natural Abilities: Fair to good speed, can run or fight without pause or exhaustion for 12 hours, leap up to 20 feet (6 m) high and lengthwise, does not breathe air, can eat spoiled or poisoned food and drink, climb 95%/90%, prowl 60%, swim 90% and track by blood scent up to two miles (3.2 km) away at 72% proficiency. Nightvision is 1000 feet (305 m), plus the demon can see the invisible, dimensionally teleport 30% (+15% at a ley line nexus) and bio-regenerate 3D6 M.D. per melee round.

<u>Knows</u> <u>all</u> <u>Languages</u>: Magically understands and speaks all languages at 90%, but cannot read.

<u>Limited</u> <u>Metamorphosis</u> (special): The Kladovik can transform into a pale grey, long-legged spider the size of a man's fist. However, this metamorphosis can only be performed at night and only twice during that period.

<u>Limited</u> <u>Invulnerability</u> (special): The Kladovik demon is impervious to poison and disease (eats spoiled meat and rotting corpses), as well as normal cold and heat (magic cold and heat based attacks do full damage). Normal S.D.C. weapons do no damage unless made of silver or wood (any type), in which case the weapon inflicts the equivalent S.D.C. damage as M.D. (i.e. a wooden staff that inflicts 2D6 S.D.C. inflicts 2D6 M.D. against the Guardian Demon). Weapons made from the wood of a Millennium Tree inflict double damage.

Mega-Damage weapons, M.D. fire, electricity, magic weapons, spells and psionics inflict their normal damage. The demon finds the light of day glaring and harsh, but it has no adverse effect.

Also see magic.

O.C.C.: Not applicable.

R.C.C. Skills: Horsemanship (exotic animals), land navigation 70%, wilderness survival 90%, plus select *two* skills from each of the following skill categories: Military, Espionage, and Wilderness; all get a +10% skill bonus.

R.C.C. Combat: Attacks Per Melee: Seven, and knows all types of kick attacks.

Damage: Bite 3D6 M.D., blunt elbow, punch/jab or kick inflicts M.D. equal to the supernatural P.S., slashing, stabbing or scissor-like cutting strikes do supernatural P.S. damage +2D6 M.D; or by magic.

R.C.C. Bonuses: +4 on initiative, +5 to strike, +6 to parry, +3 to dodge, +3 to pull punch, +5 to disarm, +1 to roll with impact or fall, and is impervious to Horror Factor. These are all in addition to any possible attribute bonuses.

Magic: All Kladovik can cast the following spells, provided the demon has sufficient P.P.E.: Death Trance and Fear, plus Shatter, Magic Shield, and Fists of Fury, the latter three described in *Rifts® Federation of Magic*™. Spell potency is equal to a 3rd level sorcerer.

Psionics: None

Enemies: All mortals, particularly humans. Hates Gargoyles and considers most "sub-demons" to be inferior misanthropes, but likes Brodkil. Many Kladovik consider the Warlords of Russia and their Camps to be their number one enemy, with Bogatyrs, Demon Slayers, Mystic Kuznya, good practitioners of magic and psychics next on the list, pretty much in that order.

Allies: Guardian Demons can be found just about anywhere in Rifts Russia, the Slavic Countries (including Poland), China

and much of Asia. They frequently associate with other bloodthirsty creatures and serve greater demons and deities.

Value: None

Habitat: Woodlands (especially deep forests and swamps), ruins, abandoned buildings, slums, and strange or ugly places throughout Rifts Russia, China and much of Asia are preferred, but can be found almost anywhere. They can be encountered day or night, although they prefer the dark.

The Midnight Demon

The "Polunochnitsa," the Midnight Demon, is an evil spirit that can only appear between the hours of midnight and three a.m. It is responsible for nightmares and extreme behavior associated with the full moon and the Witching Hour. This particular demon is a consummate liar who specializes in "mind games." The Midnight Demon likes to draw upon its victims' own fears, insecurities, desires and anger. It knows how to fan the flames of discontent better than most, and is expert at getting individuals to act on emotion without stopping to think about what they are doing. To this end, the Midnight Demon can, at least for the moment, justify anything. It can agitate trouble out of a simple disagreement and grow betrayal, reprisal and murder from the seeds of envy, jealousy, sorrow, hate and similar emotions.

The Midnight Demon is also known to torment people with thoughts and feelings of despair, anguish, sorrow and doom — all things more easily contemplated in the quiet, lonely hours after midnight, when the mind often wanders before it goes to sleep. This can be done by softly whispering in a person's ear or through the use of magic. Midnight Demons may also torture parents by kidnapping and hiding children as well as luring children and unsuspecting travelers into the woods where they get lost and are left to fend for themselves and battle the elements, predators and other demons. Insidious manipulators, Midnight Demons are seldom directly responsible for murder, i.e. kill with their own two hands, but rather manipulate emotions, people and situations so that they lead to tragedy.

The natural form of this foul creature is that of a black mist or vapor twice the size of a man. It has the face or head of a black demon, with spindly arms and clawed hands emerging from the inky blackness. The Midnight Demon shuns the light of day and is said to seek shelter in the shadows of swamps, underground sewers, deep forests and caves.

The Midnight Demon NPC Villain

Also Known as the Black Mist and Dream Ghost.

Race: Lesser Archaic Demon

Alignment: Always miscreant or diabolic.

Attributes: I.Q. 1D6+13, M.E. 1D6+13, M.A. 1D6+13, P.S. 1D6+13 (half in daylight), P.P. 1D6+13, P.E. 1D6+13, P.B. 1D6, Spd 2D6+18 floating and moving as a mist or mist-like phantom; a minimum speed of 22 (15 mph/24 km); supernatural P.S.

M.D.C.: P.E. number +2D4x10, but increases by 50% between the hours of Midnight and 3 a.m. (on S.D.C. worlds the Midnight Demon has 1D6x10 +P.E. number for Hit Points and 1D4x10 S.D.C.; increase both by 50% between Midnight and 3 a.m. A.R. 8 when in the form of an imp, not applicable as a mist).

Horror Factor: 13

slight swish, like a gentle breeze. It is also virtually invisible in total darkness or dimly lit areas, and can hover, float and move as high as 10 feet (3 m) above the ground (it must effectively go up stairs or scale a wall to reach a window or floor several stories high). The demon can also glide across water, slip under closed doors through the crack under the door, or through openings as small as a keyhole.

In mist form the Midnight Demon impervious to all physical attacks, gas, poison, disease, and normal weapons, including those made of silver and wood. It is also impervious to Magic Net, Carpet of Adhesion, Forcebonds and most magic barriers and other *spells* of restraint, however it is affected by magic circles and the sanctum spell.

All energy blasts, explosions, M.D. weapons, cold and heat based magic, and magical weapons inflict half the usual damage to the ghostly black mist. Lightning (magical or natural) doesn't hurt the creature, but will temporarily transform it into the demon's weak and vulnerable imp form. Psionic attacks will have full effect, but the demon is resistant to psionics.

Limited Flight (special): As a mist, the demon can hover and float at the rate indicated under the speed attribute. The demon can also ride the winds of a storm, including tornados and hurricanes, without injury the same as The Unclean.

Limited Metamorphosis (special): The demon can turn into a black magpie/raven once per night for as long as the entire night, but most prefer their mist form. Metamorphosis is impossible during the light of day, and a Globe of Daylight or the flash of lightning (natural or magical) will force an instant transformation into its frail form as a tiny imp. However, at night, the demon will recover and return to its deadly mist form within 1D4 melee rounds after being transformed or escaping the harsh light of day from the magical Globe.

Limited Invulnerability (special): See the Mist Form, above, for superior invulnerability. However, during the day, while in its tiny imp form, or at night in the form of a magpie, the Midnight Demon is vulnerable to all manner of M.D. attacks as well as weapons made of silver or wood (any type), which inflict the equivalent S.D.C. damage as M.D. (i.e. a wooden staff that inflicts 2D6 S.D.C. would inflict 2D6 M.D. to the Midnight Demon) They are also impervious to disease, gases, poison, cold, and heat in all forms.

The Midnight Demon has only a fraction of its power during the light of day (including when exposed to the magical light from a Globe of Daylight), and is so weakened and insignificant that it appears as a tiny, two foot (0.6 m) tall, skeletal, black imp, with a small, squeaky voice. During this time of day, the demon's physical attributes, available P.P.E. and attacks per round are all reduced by half! Worse, the potency of its magic is reduced to the equivalent of a 2nd level mage. The light of day shows just how small and petty this phantom really is when not supplemented by the darkness of the night, self-pity and dark emotions.

Also see magic.

O.C.C.: Not applicable.

R.C.C. Skills: Land navigation 80%, wilderness survival 80%, streetwise 80%, and seduction 50%. Also see Natural Abilities, above.

R.C.C. Combat: Attacks Per Melee: Four; typically the casting of a spell counts as two melee actions.

Size: A mist that is about twice as a man.

Weight: Insubstantial and ghost-like although physical attacks by the demon inflict damage; effectively weightless.

Average Life Span: Uncertain, 2000+ years; probably immortal.

P.P.E.: 3D6x10 +100

Natural Abilities: Fair speed as a mist and can float around and cause trouble all night long without fatigue. Prowl 80% (+10% in total darkness), climb 65%/60%, nightvision is one mile (1.6 km), can see the invisible, can perform dimensional teleport 45% (+20% at a ley line nexus) and bio-regenerate 2D6 M.D. per minute.

Knows all Languages: Magically understands and speaks all languages 90%, but cannot read.

Natural Form is that of a Black Mist: As a black mist, the Midnight Demon moves without making a sound other than a

Damage: M.D. from a punch varies with supernatural P.S., add 1D6 M.D. for claw strikes; or by weapon or magic.

R.C.C. Bonuses: +2 on initiative, +2 to strike, +1 to parry, +1 to dodge, +3 to pull punch, +4 to roll with impact or fall, +1 to save vs magic, +2 to save vs psionic attack, +4 to save vs illusions, +10 to save vs possession, +6 to save vs Horror Factor. R.C.C. bonuses are all in addition to any possible attribute bonuses.

Magic: All Midnight Demons can cast the following spells, provided the demon has sufficient P.P.E.: *Rifts® RPG:* See Aura, Sense Magic, Sense Evil, Death Trance, Fear, Fingers of the Wind, Levitation, Astral Projection, Ley Line Transmission, Calling, Sleep, Apparition, Compulsion, Spoil (Food/Water), Sickness, and Shadow Meld.

Plus these spells found in *Federation of Magic*: Weight of Duty, Aura of Death, Aura of Doom, Mental Shock, Enemy Mind, Disharmonize, Id Alter Ego, Mindshatter, Soul Twist, Beat Insurmountable Odds, Distant Voice, Instill Knowledge, Superhuman Endurance, and Swap Places. **Note:** For *Nightbane®* aficionados, the Midnight Demons can travel through the Dreamstream™ and are effectively 4th level Dream-Makers.

Spell potency during the day is equal to a 2nd level sorcerer, at night 4th, and between the hours of Midnight and 3 a.m., 6th level.

Psionics: None

Enemies: Humans, other mortals and sub-demons aren't seen as enemies but as playthings. They despise Vampires because they see them as rivals.

Allies: Others of its kind, greater demons, dark gods, evil practitioners of magic, and other powerful beings with agendas that involve subjection, manipulation and mental or emotional torment. They find evil Mind Melters, Mind Bleeders and others who can manipulate the mind and emotions particularly alluring. Although the Splugorth and their minions are seen as dangerous rivals, most Midnight Demons hold them in high regard as masters of manipulation.

Value: None

Habitat: The Midnight Demon shuns humanity and civilization during the day and most of the night, but between Midnight and three a.m. they seek out mortal victims to agitate and torment. This demon is most common in Rifts Russia, Mongolia and China, but can be found throughout Western Europe, India and Asia, and occasionally elsewhere.

Nalet

Nalet means "to come flying" or to "swoop down upon." It is one of the most powerful and feared of the Archaic demons, but one of the less common ones. Strong, aggressive and forceful, the Nalet are often the leaders of demon bands. They are natural born fighters with an innate skill for strategy and tactics, setting traps and laying in ambush. All Nalet see the mortal troops of the Sovietski and Warlords as their sworn enemies and a threat to their dominance over humankind. As a result, the flying demons lead small to medium-sized bands of demons (with 1D4+4 fellow Nalet) in raids against the human warriors, as well as attack small squads and reconnaissance teams, sabotage camps, ambush leaders, and encourage other evil beings and enemies of humanity to rise up against them.

To incite trouble and insurrection, the Nalet often promises to aid disenchanted people in actions against their mutual enemies. This can mean alliances with traitorous or power hungry forces within a War Camp, would-be conquerors, rebellious villagers, vengeful warriors or victims of these military powers, and evil sorcerers, witches and monsters. Slick and convincing liars, the Nalet may promise an army of demons, magical weapons, or a tactical strike guaranteed to weaken, divide and conquer the enemy. However, such promises are rarely fulfilled and the fools who trust a Nalet are destined to failure if not death. From the Nalet's point of view, these alliances are amusing and fun. When such a hapless ally rushes into battle inspired by the Nalet, the winged demon feels proud, content and happy that his deception came to a satisfying climax. Whether the duped ally wins or loses (most are crushed and die a horrible death), the demon doesn't care. His goal was to cause havoc, bloodshed, and human death, all things he's accomplished whether his stupid, human ally survives or not. More importantly, the demon has struck a blow against his hated Warlord or Sovietski enemy.

The Nalet appears as a tall, thin, but muscular humanoid with large, tattered wings and prehensile tail. The demon is the color of a red hot coal and actually seems to glow as if a fire or burns beneath his tough hide. The head is bald, as the Nalet have no body hair whatsoever, with a pair of small, bright white horns jutting from the forehead. The hands have long, slender fingers that end in wicked, curved nails used for slashing and cutting, as well as for precise torture. The tail functions as a third limb that slashes and strikes like a whip or to entangle a limb or weapon of an opponent.

Nalet are bloodthirsty and cruel in the extreme, so any act of mercy is likely to have an ulterior motive. They love to cast suspicion on innocent people and turn allies against one another, so an apparent act of kindness or mercy is likely to be used to cause just that.

The Nalet Demonic NPC Villain

Also Known as the Crimson Flyer and Blood Demon.

Race: Lesser Archaic Demon

Alignment: Always miscreant or diabolic.

Attributes: I.Q. 1D6+8, M.E. 1D6+8, M.A. 2D6+8, P.S. 4D6+16, P.P. 2D6+16, P.E. 2D6+8, P.B. 1D6+8, Spd. running: 2D6+8; flying: 6D6+40, minimum speed of 46 (32 mph/51 km); supernatural P.S.

M.D.C.: P.E. number +2D6x10 +36 (on S.D.C. worlds the Nalet has 2D4x10 Hit Points +P.E. number and 1D6x10+20 S.D.C.; A.R. 14).

Horror Factor: 11

Size: 10 feet (3 m) tall, plus horns and wings.

Weight: 400 pounds (180 kg)

Average Life Span: Uncertain, 2000+ years, but is probably immortal.

P.P.E.: 2D6x10 +60 and M.E. attribute number.

Natural Abilities: Good to excellent speed and can run or fight without pause or exhaustion for 1D4+3 hours. They can also leap up to 20 feet (4.6 m) high and lengthwise without taking flight, fly (maximum altitude of 30,000 feet/9144 m), hover, climb 60%/55%, swim 50%, prowl 55% (+20% at reduced size), track humanoids using vision 70%, engage in "tailing"/following a target 60% (+20% at reduced size; can not use surveillance equipment), breathes without air and

33

nightvision is one mile (1.6 km). Nalet demons can dimensionally teleport 65% and bio-regenerate 2D6 M.D. per melee round (15 seconds).

Knows all Languages: Magically understands and speaks all languages 90%, but cannot read.

Reduce Size (special): The demon can reduce its size by two thirds, shrinking down to about three and a half feet (one meter) tall. This shrinking power is used to prowl, follow and spy on people, as well as to spring surprise attacks. The act of shrinking or growing back to full size takes about six seconds and counts as two melee attacks/actions. While small, the Nalet's P.S. and Spd. are reduced by 20%, but all other attributes are unchanged.

Limited Invulnerability (special): The demon is impervious to disease, normal cold, heat and fire, including M.D. and magical fire. Impervious to normal S.D.C. weapons unless they are made of silver or the wood of a juniper or birch tree, in which case the weapon inflicts the equivalent S.D.C. damage as M.D. (i.e. a wooden staff that inflicts 2D6 S.D.C. would inflict 2D6 M.D. to the demon if made of juniper or birch). Millennium Tree weapons do full damage.

Man-made Mega-Damage weapons inflict *half* their normal damage, but M.D. electrical attacks and electrical magic weapons, and most spells and psionics do full damage, including the Fire of Perun and Celestial Fire of Perun. The light of day has no negative impact on the Nalet and they are frequently encountered during the daytime.

Also see magic.

O.C.C.: Not applicable.

R.C.C. Skills: Horsemanship (exotic animals), land navigation 98%, navigation (flying/air) 80%, basic math 90%, seduction 70%, and wilderness survival 80%, plus select four skills from each of the following skill categories: W.P. Ancient Weapons and Espionage; all get a +20% skill bonus and one skill gets an additional +10%. Also see Natural Abilities, above.

R.C.C. Combat: Attacks Per Melee: Six, including the use of the prehensile tail.

Note: Nalets are among the few supernatural creatures who will consider using modern energy weapons, as well as magic items. However, they prefer melee weapons above all others.

Damage: Bite 1D4 M.D., claw strike adds 1D6 M.D. plus the usual damage as per supernatural P.S.; head butt with horns, punch or kick M.D. varies with supernatural P.S.; or by weapon or magic.

R.C.C. Bonuses: +4 on initiative, +4 to strike, +3 to parry, +2 to dodge, +4 to dodge while in flight, +6 to pull punch, +2 to roll with impact or fall, and +5 to save vs Horror Factor. R.C.C. bonuses are all in addition to any possible attribute bonuses.

Magic: All Nalet can cast the following spells, provided the demon has sufficient P.P.E.: See Aura, See the Invisible, Sense Magic, Blinding Flash, Ignite Fire, Fuel Flame, Fire Bolt, Fire Ball, Circle of Flame, Wind Rush, Aura of Power, Fireblast, Fire Blossom, Fire Gout and Lightblade (the last five are found in the *Federation of Magic* sourcebook). Magic is used carefully and judiciously. Spell potency is equal to a 4th level sorcerer.

Psionics: None

Enemies: All mortals, particularly humans and True Atlanteans (the latter being old enemies). The Nalet frequently lead small to medium-sized groups of other Nalet and/or demon, sub-demons, monsters and misanthropes against the War Camps (occasionally large groups and small armies numbering up to a thousand), making the Nalet among the most hated of the Russian Demons by the Warlords' warriors; the Whirlwind and Wolf-Serpent are a close second and third.

Nalet see Gargoyles, Brodkil, and all "sub-demons" as inferiors who are meant to serve them and all "true" demons. They often force a dozen to a several score of them into service as troops to strike against the human War Camps. Sub-demons who dare to defy or challenge the will of a Nalet is beaten into submission or slain. Actually, many sub-demons, particularly Gurgoyles and Brodkil, fear and respect these powerful demon warriors and willingly serve them.

Nalet regard vampires as deadly competition and destroy them whenever they are encountered. They dislike the arrogant Demons of Hades and Deevals of Hell, but respect their power and dominance in the Megaverse. They also respect the Splugorth and many of their minions, including the Kitanni.

Allies: Its own kind, other demons, greater demons, powerful practitioners of magic, and other powerful beings with agendas that involve combat, war, murder, torment and mayhem.

The Unclean, Il'ya, Kladovik, Demon Claw, Serpent Hound and Hell Horse respect Nalet to be their superiors and usually follow them without resistance. Other lesser demons *may* also accept the Nalet as a military leader, but are likely to question or defy their leadership in other matters, preferring the roles of either independent operative or leader for themselves. Nightfeeders can sometimes be pressed into service by the Nalet if given enough respect and freedom, however, most Nightfeeders regard the Nalet as inferior and weak; the two are constantly at odds.

Value: None

Habitat: Although especially common in Rifts Russia, they can be found anywhere throughout the Slavic countries (including Poland and Germany), China and much of Asia, but seem to favor the Steppe and other grasslands, and mountain regions. They are encountered during the day more than at night, and are considered by most to be the warriors of the Archaic demons. They enjoy combat, tests of fighting skills and brute strength, and battles to the death.

Note: The Nalet are also occasionally found in North America, particularly around the Calgary and St. Louis Rifts.

Stone Demon

The Stone Demon is a demonic spirit that inhabits a particular mountain peak, cave, hill, rock formation, boulder, or even the foundation of a building or part of an ancient (pre-Rifts) ruin. Such demons are more likely to be encountered near or on a ley line, but can be found anywhere. Stone Demons tend to be very territorial and consider everything within a ten mile (16 km) radius of the actual stone they inhabit to be their domain, including the people and animals who live on the land. Those who disturb that region (war, mining, development, etc.) will

face the wrath of the Stone Demon. It can magically form a body out of stone to walk among men, to cause trouble, or to strike at invaders, despoilers and enemies. Like most demonkind, the Archaic Stone Demon likes to torment humans and bring them grief and disaster.

The wrath of a Stone Demon is not reserved for intruders. Like all demons, this malignant spirit is cruel and mischievous, so it likes to confront, torment and destroy things of beauty, humans and other life forms. Thus, it may attack a group of adventurers or raid a village simply because they were there and it has the power to do so.

Stone Demon NPC Villain

Also Known as The Cursed Earth.
Race: Lesser Archaic Demon.
Alignment: Always miscreant or diabolic.
Attributes: I.Q. average human intelligence, but cold and vindictive: 1D6+5, M.E. 1D6+5, M.A. 1D6+5, P.S. 2D6+40 (half in water or in the air), P.P. 2D6+10, P.E. 2D6+18, P.B. 1D6, Spd 2D6+5; supernatural P.S.
M.D.C.: 2D4x10 +200 (on S.D.C. worlds the demon has 2D6x10 Hit Points and 140 S.D.C.; A.R. 15 day and night).
Horror Factor: 11
Size: 6-16 feet (1.8 to 4.9 m) tall.
Weight: 1-10 tons
Average Life Span: Uncertain, 1000+ years; probably immortal.
P.P.E.: 3D4x10 +60
Natural Abilities: Slow speed, but can run or fight without pause or exhaustion indefinitely. Swim 30%, does not breathe air, can survive depths of up to two miles (3.2 km), nightvision is one mile (1.6 km), dimensional teleport 30% (+20% at a ley line nexus), and bio-regenerate 4D6 M.D. per melee round as long as it is touching the Earth (cannot regenerate if suspended in the air, space or water). If reduced to

20% or less of its M.D.C., the demon is weakened and needs to hibernate to regenerate; all M.D.C. and lost body parts are regenerated within 12 hours.

Note: Draws its power from the Earth, so if removed from contact with the Earth/ground (i.e. suspending in air, space, water, etc.) reduce the P.S. and potency of magic spells by half.

<u>Knows</u> <u>all</u> <u>Languages</u>: Magically understands and speaks all languages 90%, but cannot read.

<u>Earth</u> <u>Link</u> <u>&</u> <u>Powers</u> (special):

- Recognize/identify any mineral on sight at 88%.
- Sense and identify seismic disturbances, including earthquakes, explosions, mining, or movement of heavy equipment (like troops or giant robots) in a radius of 50 miles (80.4 km) at 75%.
- Sense dangers in the earth or rock, such as loose dirt/rocks, mud slides, quicksand, land mines, and creatures in burrows at 88%.
- Sense and predict (within 1D6x10 minutes) the coming of an earthquake, volcanic eruption or other natural disturbance in the earth's crust at 66%.

<u>Limited</u> <u>Metamorphosis</u> (special): Other than the power to make a physical body of earth and stone, this demon has no ability to change its shape. This demonic spirit is effectively powerless unless it takes physical form — a creature of earth and stone. If the physical body is destroyed, there is a 01-65% chance that the Stone Demon will be automatically cast back to the otherworldly dimension from which it originates. A percentile roll of 66-00 means it remains on Rifts Earth, but is so weakened that it cannot take physical form again for 3D6 months. To avoid being sent back to another dimension, the demon can shed its animated physical body (counts as two melee attacks/actions and looks like the thing is being absorbed into the ground) and seek refuge in the particular piece of earth (boulder, mountain peak, hill, etc.) that it normally inhabits. This is the demon's true link to the Earth. The one thing that bonds it to this dimension. Destroy or exorcise that particular part of the earth and the Stone Demons is sent back to his native dimension; cannot return to Rifts Earth for 2D6x10 years. However, any such attempt to rid the "Cursed Earth" of the evil force that lives within it will result in the physical manifestation and a battle to the death!

<u>Limited</u> <u>Invulnerability</u> (special): The Stone Demon is impervious to normal S.D.C. attacks and weapons, even those made of silver or wood. Suffers half damage from falls and all kinetic attacks such as M.D. punches, kicks, sword strikes, bullets, rail guns, explosions, rock slides and falls. Lightning also does half damage. Impervious to disease, poison, toxins, gases and normal cold and heat.

Other man-made Mega-Damage weapons, magic weapons, spells and psionics inflict their normal damage. The light of day has no negative impact on this demon.

Also see magic.

O.C.C.: Not applicable.
R.C.C. Skills: Land navigation 95%, identify plants and fruits, prospecting, recognize weapon quality, military fortification, trap construction, trap/mine detection, whittling/sculpting (many of these skills can be found in **Rifts® New West**) and basic math, all at 75%. Also see Natural Abilities, above.

R.C.C. Combat: Attacks Per Melee: Five

Damage: Bite 1D6 M.D., head-butt, punch or kick M.D. varies with supernatural P.S., or by weapon or magic.

R.C.C. Bonuses: +2 on initiative, +3 to strike, +2 to parry, +1 to dodge, +4 to pull punch, +3 to roll with impact or fall, +4 to save vs Horror Factor. R.C.C. bonuses are all in addition to any possible attribute bonuses.

Magic: Chameleon, Fool's Gold, Repel Animals, Spoil (Food/Water), Sickness, Negate Poison, Stone to Flesh, plus the following Earth Warlock spells (described in *Rifts® Conversion Book One*, starting on page 68): All level one and two spells plus Mend Stone, Crumble Stone, Earth Rumble, Wall of Stone, Wall of Thorns, Quicksand, Sand Storm, River of Lava, Earthquake, Travel through Walls, Travel Through Stone, and Petrification.

Plus the following spells found in *Rifts® Federation of Magic™*: Manipulate Objects, Shatter, Throwing Stones, Create Wood, Ironwood, Mend the Broken, Fortify Against Disease, Mystic Fulcrum, Influence the Beast, Tame the Beast, Lifeblast, and Bottomless Pit.

Spell potency is equal to a 4th level sorcerer.

Psionics: None

Enemies: All mortals, humans in general and the Warlords and their War Camps in particular (they see these warriors as a people driven to tame the land and destroy demonkind). They consider all "sub-demons" to be inferior and subservient to them, thus the Gargoyle Empire is an abomination.

Allies: Others of its kind, other demons, greater demons, powerful practitioners of magic, evil warlocks, and other powerful beings with agendas that involve murder, torture and mayhem. Stone Demons sometimes manipulate Elementals.

Value: None

Habitat: Wilderness throughout western Europe, India, Russia, Mongolia, China and Asia. Occasionally found in a village.

Water Demon

A demon or spirit made of water. Traditionally, it appears as a pale skinned woman (human-looking and human-sized) with long, flowing black hair, black eyes, and simple robes that are actually made of water. Although strangely attractive, there is also something ominous about the creature. For superior speed and aquatic abilities, the demoness can metamorph into a monster with the head and upper torso of a woman but the lower body of a water serpent.

These she-demons or "chertovka" (demoness) usually inhabit swamps, and deep or dangerous areas of lakes and rivers. Where the Water Demon lives the water turns black. Water demons can rise out of the water, walk on its surface (as well as land) and ride the waves. They are cold, heartless creatures who enjoy bringing trouble and sorrow to humans and other lesser beings. Their usual victims are fishermen, millers, swimmers, boaters and travelers, but they can molest and trouble anybody who comes close to their watery domain. Like the Stone Demon, the Water Demons or "Bereginia" (Bank Spirit) tend to be very territorial and consider everything within a ten mile (16 km) radius of their actual watery lair to be their domain, including the people and animals who live in the water and neighboring land. Those who disturb that region (war, fishing, building a dam or

mill, pollution, development, etc.) will face the wrath of the water demon. Like most demonkind, the Bereginia likes to toy with, trick, frustrate, and torment humans. When denied or angered, the Water Demon strikes out with deadly force and kills without hesitation or regret.

Although born of water, the Bereginia can walk on and function on dry land for up to 72 hours. At the end of this period she must either willingly return to her watery lair, or is magically transformed into a mist and is forcibly returned to her underwater domain (the mist turning into rain once she has returned home). The cruel games and vindictive escapades of a Water Demon are not limited to those who defile or disturb her domain. Like all demons, this pernicious beast is cruel and mischievous, so it likes to confront, torture and destroy things of beauty, humans, and other life forms, particularly noble heroes. Thus, it may attack a group of adventurers or raid a village simply because it feels like it. Water Demons are also notoriously jealous of others and will often try to maim, disfigure or kill those who are incredibly attractive, or enjoy adoration and fame. Likewise, these demons will steal or kill and take objects of great value and magic and keep them on the floor of their underwater lair.

Water Demon NPC Villain

Also Known as The Black Water and Bereginia.

Race: Lesser Archaic Demon.

Alignment: Always miscreant or diabolic.

Attributes: I.Q. average to high human intelligence, but cold and treacherous: 1D6+8, M.E. 1D6+2, M.A. 1D6+8, P.S. 2D6+20 (half in dry, hot environments), P.P. 2D6+8, P.E. 2D6+8, P.B. 1D6+14, Spd 2D6+8 on dry land, but 2D6+60 in water (double when in serpent form); supernatural P.S.

M.D.C.: 2D6x10 +70 (on S.D.C. worlds the demon has 2D6x10 Hit Points and 1D4x10+40 S.D.C.; A.R. 12 day and night).

Horror Factor: 9

Size: 6-7 feet (1.8 to 2.1 m) tall.

Weight: 200 pounds (90 kg)

Average Life Span: Uncertain, 1000+ years; probably immortal.

P.P.E.: 3D4x10 +60

Natural Abilities: Good speed and can swim or fight without pause or exhaustion for 12 hours. Swim 98%, does not breathe air, can survive water pressure at any depth, nightvision is one mile (1.6 km), see the invisible, dimensional teleport 40% (+20% at a ley line nexus), and bio-regenerate 2D6 M.D. per melee round as long as it is within ten miles (16 km) of its watery lair or is touching water (rain, fog, snow, pond, marsh, bathtub, pool, etc.; cannot regenerate if farther away). If reduced to 20% or less of its M.D.C., the demon is weakened and needs to hibernate to regenerate; all M.D.C. and lost body parts are regenerated within 12 hours.

Note: Draws its power from water, so if taken out of range of its domain and placed in a dry environment reduce the P.S. and potency of magic spells by half.

Knows all Languages: Magically understands and speaks all languages 90%, but cannot read.

Water Link & Powers (special):

- Recognize/identify any mineral on sight at 50%.
- Recognize/identify all aquatic life forms at 80%.

- Knows the time and direction by scanning the heavens and tides at 88%.
- Sense the direction and speed of winds, water currents and tides, changes in the currents and tides, and underwater disturbances at 88%.
- Sense the approach of tidal waves, rainstorms, hurricanes and atmospheric disturbances involving water at 80%.
- Sense impurities, chemicals, poisons, and particles in the water at 75%.
- Nightvision to 1 mile (1.6 km) and see through fog and mist without any impairment of vision.
- Dowsing; same as the spell, only triple the range.

Limited Metamorphosis (special): As noted previously, the Water Demon can take the form of an attractive human-like maiden as her physical body. In the alternative, the demon can transform into a hideous part human, part serpent (snake) for superior speed swimming (double normal swim speed) and bonuses (+1 on initiative, +1 to strike and dodge); has no other ability to change its shape. If the physical body is destroyed, there is a 01-65% chance that the Water Demon will be automatically cast back to the otherworldly dimension from which it originates. A percentile roll of 66-00 means it remains on Rifts Earth, but is so weakened that it cannot take physical form again for 3D6 months. To avoid being sent back to another dimension, the demon can hide in deep water that is its lair where it is invisible to all means of detection until it desires to make a physical body. This is the demon's true link to the Earth and the one

thing that bonds it to this dimension. Destroy or exorcise that particular part area of water and the Water Demon is sent back to her native dimension and cannot return to Rifts Earth for 2D6x10 years. However, any such attempt to rid the "Black Water" of the evil force that lives within it will result in the physical manifestation and a battle to the death!

Limited Invulnerability (special): The Water Demon is impervious to ocean depths, drowning, tidal waves, lightning, cold, disease, hurricane and tornado winds, rain, storms, and toxins, as well as ordinary S.D.C. attacks and weapons, even those made of silver or wood. However, an S.D.C. weapon coated in ice or weapons made of ice (i.e. using a large icicle as a knife or bludgeon, a snowball or chunk of ice as a thrown object, etc.) inflict half the S.D.C. damage as M.D. (so a thrown ball of ice that might normally do 1D6 S.D.C. damage will inflict half that damage as M.D. on the demon).

Suffers half damage from falls and all kinetic attacks such as M.D. punches, kicks, sword strikes, bullets, rail guns, explosions, rock slides and falls. Other man-made Mega-Damage weapons, magic weapons, spells and psionics inflict their normal damage. The light of day has no negative impact on this demon. M.D. fire, plasma, and magic fire do double damage!

Also see magic.

O.C.C.: Not applicable.

R.C.C. Skills: Astronomy, navigation, land navigation, basic mathematics, boat building, pilot sail and row boats (including canoes), brewing, chemistry, and lore: demons and monsters, all at 86%. Also select two rogue skills of choice

(+20% bonus). Also see Natural Abilities, above.

R.C.C. Combat: Attacks Per Melee: Five

Damage: Head-butt, punch or kick does M.D. equal to the creature's supernatural P.S., or by weapon or magic.

R.C.C. Bonuses: +4 on initiative, +3 to strike, +2 to parry, +3 to dodge (+6 underwater), +4 to pull punch, +2 to roll with impact or fall, +1 to save vs magic, +5 to save vs Horror Factor, and impervious to possession. R.C.C. bonuses are all in addition to any possible attribute bonuses.

Magic: Globe of Daylight, Globe of Silence, Turn Dead, Energy Bolt, Float in Air, Seal, Escape, Water to Wine, Summon Fog, Summon Storm, Spoil (Food/Water), and Negate Poison, plus the following Water Warlock spells (described in *Rifts® Conversion Book One*, starting on page 79): All level one and two spells plus Command Fish, Calm Waters, Circle of Rain, Create Water, Earth to Mud, Whirlpool, Part Waters, Rain Dance, Summon Storm, and Drought.

Plus the following spells found in *Rifts® Federation of Magic™*: Cleanse, Lantern Light, Electric Arc, Sustain and Lifeblast.

Spell potency is equal to a 5th level sorcerer.

Psionics: None

Enemies: All mortals, humans in general and the Warlords and their War Camps in particular (they see these warriors as a people driven to tame the land and destroy demonkind). They consider all "sub-demons" to be inferior and subservient to them, thus the Gargoyle Empire is an abomination to be destroyed (the demon is jealous of their impressive accomplishments); Brodkil are regarded as bumbling fools, Demon Claws and Guardians as mindless brutes, and Kaluga Hags are despised as dangerous rivals.

Allies: Others of its kind, other demons, greater demons, powerful practitioners of magic, and other powerful beings with agendas that involve murder, torture and mayhem. Water Demons sometimes manipulate Elementals and are attracted to evil Water Warlocks, Woodland Spirits, Witches and evil practitioners of magic who have mastered the rare arts of Ocean Magic (see *Rifts® Underseas*). Tends to be a loner and rarely gets involved with plots or groups with other demons.

Value: None

Habitat: Wilderness throughout western Europe, India, Russia, Mongolia, China and Asia. Occasionally found in Rifts North America where it is considered a most foul and evil spirit.

Wood Demon

A Wood or Tree Demon is a demonic spirit that inhabits a particular large, ancient or strangely shaped tree or cluster of trees. Such demons are more likely to be encountered near or on a ley line, but can be found anywhere. Wood Demons are territorial and consider everything within a ten mile (16 km) radius of the actual tree they inhabit, to be their domain, including the people, plants, crops/farms and animals on that land. Those who disturb or despoil that region will face the wrath of the Wood demon. To take any type of action, physical or magical, the demon must magically create a body out of wood. This body resembles that of a gnarled tree with a vaguely humanoid shape. It has tree bark for skin and a long, very thin body, arms, and legs. The fingers are also long and spindly, like tree branches. The demon is typically 8-12 feet (2.4 to 3.6 m) tall.

Like most demonkind, the Archaic Wood Demon likes to harass, frighten, torment and kill humans. Their favorite targets are human and D-Bee woodsmen, hunters, loggers, farmers and travelers, as well as Faerie Folk and the gentler members of Russian Woodland Spirits. The Warlords and their War Camps are counted among the demon's most dangerous enemies, for they are managing to conquer and settle wood lands, and destroy demonkind in the process.

Unlike most of the other Archaic demons who take a very active and openly aggressive stance against humanoids, the Wood Demon is much more subtle and secretive, prefer to strike in small ways when nobody is looking. Consequently, unexplained disappearances, deaths and freak accidents in the wilderness, especially in deep forests, are blamed on the Wood Demon. Indeed, these malicious fiends quietly watch and wait until the right opportunity avails itself, then they strike! Although they can be murderous, most are not as bloodthirsty as some demons and do things that cause confusion, panic, and terror to drive settlers away, terrify travelers into avoiding that part of the forest, or ultimately lead intruders to more serious trouble and danger, like into the arms of bandits, rival War Camps or other hostile forces, witches, monsters or other demons, as well as swamps, bogs, mud slides, pits, traps, etc. They are famous for misleading travelers and trading secrets to both humans and their fellow demons. Tree Demons are extremely patient, silent and observant, and make excellent spies and cunning stalkers and assassins.

Wood Demons are tolerant of other elemental demons and may share a region or part of an overlapping area with a Water or Stone Demon. These demons don't usually see each other as rivals unless one or the other constantly brings danger or destruction to the area. In fact, those who share overlapping territory frequently come to each other's aid in times of need. Wood

and Water Demons are especially compatible. **Note:** Although the Wood Demon considers a specific 10 mile (16 km) radius "its" domain, the demon can travel beyond this territory, but rarely more than a hundred miles.

Wood Demon NPC Villain

Also Known as the Tree Demon and Woodland Demon.
Race: Lesser Archaic Demon.
Alignment: Always miscreant or diabolic.
Attributes: I.Q. 1D6+6, M.E. 1D6+9, M.A. 1D6+6, P.S. 2D6+24, P.P. 2D6+9, P.E. 2D6+9, P.B. 2D6, Spd 2D6+9; supernatural P.S.
M.D.C.: 2D6x10 +45; increase 30% during the "day" (on S.D.C. worlds the demon has 2D6x10 Hit Points and 100 S.D.C.; increase 30% during the day. A.R. 12 day and night).
Horror Factor: 10
Size: 8-12 feet (2.4 to 3.6 m) tall.
Weight: 1-2 tons.
Average Life Span: Uncertain, 2000+ years; probably immortal.
P.P.E.: 3D4x10 +40
Natural Abilities: Slow speed, but can run or fight without pause or exhaustion for 12 hours. Swim/float 90%, does not breathe air, nightvision is 2000 feet (610 m), dimensionally teleport 30% (+20% at a ley line nexus), and bio-regenerates 3D6 M.D. per melee round as long as it is touching the Earth (cannot regenerate if suspended in the air, space or water). If reduced to 20% or less of its M.D.C., the demon is weakened and needs to hibernate to regenerate. To do this, the demonic spirit abandons its animated tree form, which either falls to the ground as an old, rotting log, or turns into a withered looking sapling, and return to the tree or grove of trees it possesses — this is its true link to the physical plane. All M.D.C. and lost limbs on the mobile body are regenerated within 12 hours of hibernation/inactivity, after which a new body can be formed out of thin air.

Note: The Wood Demon draws its power from the Earth, so if removed from contact with the Earth/ground (i.e. suspending in air, space, water, etc.) reduce the P.S. and potency of magic spells by half.

Knows all Languages: Magically understands and speaks all languages 90%, but cannot read.

Earth Link & Powers (special):

- Recognize/identify any tree, plant, fruit, nut/seed, root, vegetable or type of wood on sight at 90%.

- Sense and identify seismic disturbances, including earthquakes, explosions, mining, or movement of heavy equipment (like troops or giant robots) in a radius of 50 miles (80.4 km) at 50%.

- Knows the time and direction at 90% by scanning the heavens.

- Sense wind direction, changes in wind direction, the approach of storms and atmospheric disturbances at 80%.

Limited Metamorphosis (special): This demon can assume two shapes, one is the mobile, physical body of wood, the other is a real tree sapling of any type, usually to disguise its demonic nature and hide. In tree form the Wood Demon cannot move or cast spells, but can see and hear everything around it — the perfect measure for spying. To attack or take action, the demon

must negate the metamorphosis and return to its animated, monstrous tree form. This metamorphosis can be done at will and maintained indefinitely. Magically, only a Detect Evil, Detect Magic or See Aura directed at that particular sapling will reveal its true supernatural nature. Of course, Dog Boys, Psi-Stalkers and psychics with the ability to sense supernatural evil may be able to pinpoint the fiend as well. However, in all cases, the character must know about demons or spirits that can possess or turn into trees, otherwise he must assume that an evil being, concealed in some way, is hiding in the tree.

If either of the physical bodies is destroyed, there is a 01-65% chance that the Wood Demon will be automatically cast back to the otherworldly dimension from which it originates. A percentile roll of 66-00 means it remains on Rifts Earth, but is so weakened that it cannot take physical form again for 3D6 months. To avoid being sent back to its home dimension, the demon can shed its animated physical body (counts as two melee attacks/actions) and seek refuge in the particular real tree that it normally inhabits. This is the demon's true link to the Earth, the one thing that bonds it to this dimension. Destroy or exorcise that particular tree and the Wood Demon is sent back to its native dimension; cannot return to Rifts Earth for 2D6x10 years. However, any such attempt to rid the "Cursed Earth" or "Demon Tree" of the evil force that lives within it will result in the physical manifestation and a battle to the death!

Limited Invulnerability (special): The Wood Demon is impervious to normal S.D.C. attacks and weapons, even those made of silver or wood. All other types of M.D. weapons, magic and psionics do full damage. Impervious to drowning, disease, poison, toxins, gases and normal cold and heat, but M.D. fire does double damage.

The light of day actually energizes this demon, increasing its M.D.C. by 50% and providing one extra attack per melee round.

Also see magic.

O.C.C.: Not applicable.
R.C.C. Skills: Basic Math, botany, carpentry, whittling/sculpting, holistic medicine, camouflage, detect traps, intelligence, farm lore, and cattle/animals lore (see *Rifts® New West*) all at +80%.

Land navigation 65%, military fortification 50%, trap construction 45%, trap/mine detection 60%,(many of these skills can all be found in *Rifts® New West*). Also see Natural Abilities, above.
R.C.C. Combat: Attacks Per Melee: Four (+1 during the day).
Damage: Punch or kick M.D. varies with supernatural P.S., or by weapon or magic.
R.C.C. Bonuses: +2 on initiative, +3 to strike, +4 to parry, +1 to dodge, +4 to pull punch, +3 to roll with impact or fall, +2 to save vs magic, +6 to save vs Horror Factor. R.C.C. bonuses are all in addition to any possible attribute bonuses.
Magic: The following Earth and Air Warlock spells (described in *Rifts® Conversion Book One*, starting on page 62): All level one Earth and Air spells plus Chameleon, Crumble Stone, Earth Rumble, Wall of Thorns, Wither Plants, Grow Plants, Repel Animals, Heavy Breathing, Howling Wind, Mesmerism, Whisper of the Wind, Leaf Rustler, Call Lightning, and Suspended Animation.

Plus the following spells found in *Rifts® Federation of Magic™*: Create Wood, Ironwood, Mend the Broken, Mystic Fulcrum, Life Source, and Lifeblast.

Spell potency is equal to a 4th level sorcerer.

Psionics: None

Enemies: All mortals, humans in general and the Warlords and their War Camps in particular (they see these warriors as a people driven to tame the land and destroy demonkind). They consider all "sub-demons" to be inferior and subservient to them, thus the Gargoyle Empire is an abomination. They also despise vampires and delight in their torture and destruction.

Allies: Others of its kind, other demons, greater demons, powerful practitioners of magic, evil warlocks, and other powerful beings with agendas that involve murder, torture and mayhem. Wood Demons often befriend and work with other evil woodland spirits, Faerie Folk, druids, and gypsies, as well as sometimes manipulate lesser Elementals.

Value: None

Habitat: Wilderness throughout western Europe, India, Russia, Mongolia, China and Asia. Occasionally found in a village.

Serpent Hound

Reminiscent of a small, winged dragon, the Serpent Hound is a willing minion of other demons, particularly the Nalet, Unclean, and greater demons, as well as evil practitioners of magic, especially Witches and Shifters/Summoners. The Serpent Hound is a creature of anarchy and the harbinger of trouble, namely because they usually serve a greater evil, so if a Hound is seen, others cannot be far behind. Although cunning and treacherous, these demons prefer to follow others rather than take charge. Most will obey the commands of masters they fear and/or respect without question or pause, even if that master is human.

They are massive, muscular, red or bronze skinned beasts with large bat wings, and taloned claws. The head resembles a demonic hound with huge teeth. The tiny eyes burn like a pair of hot coals and smoke rises from the nose and corners of the mouth when the Serpent Hound is angry or excited. The body of the demon is a long, thick serpent and entirely smooth and free of hair.

Also Known as the Fire Hound and Demon Hound.

Race: Lesser Archaic Demon

Alignment: Always miscreant or diabolic.

Attributes: I.Q. average human intelligence but cunning and sadistic: 1D4+6, M.E. 1D6+6, M.A. 1D6+6, P.S. 3D6+24 (half in daylight), P.P. 2D6+10, P.E. 1D6+18, P.B. 1D6, Spd 2D6+20 running; 1D6x10+80 flying; supernatural P.S.

M.D.C.: P.E. number +3D4x10, but increase by 50% at night or in darkness (on S.D.C. worlds the Hound has 1D4x10 +P.E. number for Hit Points and 2D4x10 S.D.C.; increase both by 50% at night. A.R. 13 day or night).

Horror Factor: 12

Size: 5-6 feet (1.5 to 1.8 m) tall at the shoulders, 3-4 feet (0.9 to 1.2 m) wide at the shoulders, 15 feet (4.6 m) long, and has a wingspan of 15 feet (4.6 m) when wings are fully extended.

Weight: 1000 pounds (450 kg)

Average Life Span: Uncertain, 1000+ years; probably immortal.

P.P.E.: 3D4x10 +66

Natural Abilities: Excellent speed and can fly or fight without pause or exhaustion for 48 hours. They can also leap up to 15

feet (4.6 m) high and lengthwise, climb 70%/60%, swim 95%, doesn't breathe air, can survive depths of up to one mile (1.6 km), prowl 60%, track humanoids using sense of smell and vision 90%, track animals 60%, nightvision is one mile (1.6 km), dimensionally teleport 25% (+25% at ley line nexus) and bio-regenerate 2D6 M.D. per melee round.

Knows all Languages: Magically understands and speaks all languages 90%, but cannot read.

Prehensile Tail (special): The tail can be used like a tentacle to grab, entangle or punch, use a hand-held melee weapons, etc.

Infrared and Thermo-Imaging Vision: Can see perfectly in smoke. Range: 3000 feet (914 m). Track via heat signatures at 70% (-40% in temperatures of 90+ degrees Fahrenheit).

Breathe Fire (special): Each blast of fire breath counts as one melee attack and inflicts 4D6 M.D.; range is 200 feet (61 m).

Limited Metamorphosis (special): The Demon Hound can turn into a large snake or elkhound day or night, twice per 24 hours. This disguise can last indefinitely, but most Serpent Hounds don't like to hide and keep the disguise for only short periods, usually to spy upon the enemy.

Limited Invulnerability (special): The demon is impervious to normal S.D.C. weapons unless they are made of silver or the wood of a juniper or birch tree, in which case the weapon inflicts the equivalent S.D.C. damage as M.D. (i.e. a wooden staff that inflicts 2D6 S.D.C. would inflict 2D6 M.D. to the demon if made of juniper or birch). They are also impervious to fire (even magic and M.D. fire), disease, cold, and heat.

Man-made Mega-Damage weapons and lightning inflict full damage, as do magic weapons, spells and psionics. Cold based magic and magic weapons do double damage. The light of day (including the magical Globe of Daylight) reduces the demon's P.S. and M.D.C., but does not inhibit its ability to metamorph.

Also see magic.

O.C.C.: Not applicable.

R.C.C. Skills: Land navigation 95%, navigation 90%, and wilderness survival 90%, plus select three skills from each of the following skill categories: W.P. Ancient Weapons and Espionage; all get a +15% skill bonus and one skill gets an additional +15%. Proficiency in these skills does not advance. Also see Natural Abilities, above.

R.C.C. Combat: Attacks Per Melee: Five

Damage: Bite 6D6 M.D., head-butt, punch or kick M.D. varies with supernatural P.S., or by weapon or magic.

R.C.C. Bonuses: +4 on initiative, +4 to strike, +2 to parry, +4 to dodge (+6 when flying), +3 to pull punch, +3 to roll with impact or fall, +5 to save vs Horror Factor, +2 to save vs mind control, possession and illusions. R.C.C. bonuses are all in addition to any possible attribute bonuses.

Magic: All Serpent Hounds can cast the following spells, provided the demon has sufficient P.P.E.: Blinding Flash, Cloud of Smoke, Fuel Flame, Ignite Fires, Fire Bolt, Circle of Flame, Energy Disruption, Fire Ball, Call Lightning, Negate Magic, Dispel Magic Barrier and Reduce Self, plus these spells found in *Rifts® Federation of Magic*: Lantern Light, Light Blade, Fireblast, Fire Blossom, Fire Gout, and Fire Globe.

Spell potency is equal to a 4th level sorcerer.

Psionics: None

Enemies: All mortals, particularly the Warlords of Russia, their War Camps, Demon Slayers, and heroes — they constantly engage these guys in combat. They also dislike Gargoyles, Brodkil and vampires, and frequently attack them without provocation.

Allies: Often gather in small packs of 3-6, and frequently associate with other Russian demons, as well as greater demons, powerful practitioners of magic, and other powerful beings with agendas that involve combat, murder, and mayhem.

Value: None

Habitat: Can be found almost anywhere throughout western Europe, India, Russia, Mongolia, China and Asia, but tend to prefer forested and mountainous regions. As winged creatures, they can be found as lone individuals or small packs almost anywhere. In fact, approximately one thousand have rifted to North America and roam the northern Rockies and western Canada.

They are especially numerous in Eastern Russia, the domain of the Warlords, where they constantly lock horns with squads, platoons and small companies of human troops. The Serpent Hound is cunning and fairly good at tactics, so they use guerilla warfare and rarely fight to the death — hit and run. Their favorite attacks are night raids when they and any demon allies will be at their strongest. The Hounds often join forces with Nalet, Unclean, Il'ya, and Kladovik demons. As fighters, they are usually on the move from one place to another and seldom establish anything more than a base camp for current operations. They are most likely to be found in ruins, caves, deep forests, mountain peaks or underground during the day. **Note:** Serpent Hounds can be encountered day or night, but tend to be nocturnal predators.

Greater Russian Demons

Khitaka Abductors

The Khitaka demon is a frightening, hulking mass of muscles, horns and claws. It towers 9 feet tall, even though it is hunched over and the neck and head hang over the chest. The arms, chest and legs are hairy, but the rest of the body, including the head, hands and feet, is completely free of hair. Rising from the demon's back, just below the shoulder blades, is a pair of large, hooked horns pointed downward. Smaller demon allies like The Unclean and Il'ya, or evil woodland spirits, are often seen riding on the Abductor's back by holding onto or leaning against the two horns. The skeletal face, third eye, horns and menacing fangs of the large mouth all add to the demon's frightful visage. Two horns slope downward from the forehead and a third juts from the chin. The hands are large, with three thick fingers and a thumb, each ending in a wicked talon. The feet are also oversized and sport four clawed, prehensile toes, but have no "thumb" toes, making the feet less articulated than those of a monkey or ape. However, their prehensile toes and claws help in balance, climbing and making sudden moves.

The demon earns the name "Khitaka," or Abductor, because the monster is amazingly stealthy, sneaky and skilled at breaking and entering, assassination and abduction. The Khitaka is known to kidnap children, maidens, important villagers and enemies. The kidnap victim may be used for extortion (to force someone to do something, or not do something, through threats and intimidation) or black-mail (as a means to acquire wealth/valuables, magic items, prisoners, or information), as bait for a trap (to lure out heroes, enemies, etc.), revenge or punishment for failing to pay tribute or for defying the demon, or just for fun. Those abducted for a specific purpose *may* be unharmed and returned if friends and loved ones comply with the Abductor's demands. However, those taken for fun ("fun" including causing panic, fear and chaos), punishment or retribution are seldom found alive, but are slain only after being brutalized and tortured, sometimes over a period of hours, other times, days. Victims who amuse the Abductor, for whatever reason, may be kept alive for days or weeks, not that most wouldn't welcome death. Khitaka demons love to intimidate and manipulate lesser beings like humans, and are one of the few Russian demons who will lord over a village or town as its tyrant ruler. Khitaka demons are also likely to try to take leadership of demon and bandit gangs or will be found among the gang's higher-up members. Yet, although the Khitakas are frequently involved with groups, they are powermongers who shy away from large groups where they must serve as underlings, instead preferring positions of power and leadership. They are equally happy as lone predators and stalkers doing as they please. As a lone wanderer, the Khitaka may pause to cause trouble for cities, villages, farms, mercenary camps, Warlord Camps, heroes and travelers. They are just as likely to decide, for at least a little while, to join forces with a group of mercenaries, bandits, and even adventurers, provided the demon feels they represent opportunity and amusement. However, Khitaka are evil through and through and will at some point, either abandon the group without warning (a best case scenario) or turn against them.

The Khitaka Demon NPC Villain

Also Known as the Abductor and Nighthunter.

Race: Greater Archaic Demon of considerable raw power and magic.

Alignment: Always miscreant or diabolic.

Attributes: I.Q. 1D6+9, M.E. 1D6+10, M.A. 1D6+11, P.S. 3D6+30, P.P. 2D6+12, P.E. 2D6+12, P.B. 1D6, Spd 2D6+28; a minimum speed of 30 (roughly 20 mph/32 km); supernatural P.S.

M.D.C.: P.E. number +5D6x10, but increase by 50% at night or in darkness (on S.D.C. worlds the Khitaka has 2D6x10 Hit Points and 2D6x10+20 S.D.C.; increase both 50% at night. A.R. 12, increase to 15 at night).

Horror Factor: 13

Size: 9-10 feet (2.7 to 3 m) tall.

Weight: 700-900 pounds (315 to 405 kg)

Average Life Span: Uncertain, 2000+ years; probably immortal.

P.P.E.: 6D6x6 +140

Natural Abilities: Fair speed and can run or fight without pause or exhaustion for 24 hours. The demon can also leap up to 20 feet (6 m) high and 30 feet (9 m) lengthwise (increase by 50% with a running start), climb 98%/95%, swim 90%, does not breathe air, can survive depths of up to 1500 feet (457 m), prowl 80%, track humanoids using sense of smell and vision 80%, track animals 60%, see the invisible, nightvision is one mile (1.6 km), dimensionally teleport 55% (+20% at a ley line nexus) and bio-regenerates 3D6 M.D. per melee round.

Knows all Languages: Magically understands and speaks all languages 90%, but cannot read.

Invisibility (special): The Khitaka can turn invisible at will for up to an hour at a time during the night or when in darkness; equal to Superior Invisibility where the demon is invisible to the naked eye and mechanical optic systems (cannot be seen via infra-red or starlight nightscope). The act of turning invisible counts as one melee action.

Limited Flight (special): Can ride the wind of a storm, including tornados and hurricanes, without injury, just like The Unclean. During a storm the demon can effectively fly, and is able to dive, swoop, and hover, but only so long as he is moving in the same direction as the storm winds, and stays just ahead of the heart of the storm. Under these conditions, the demon can attain a speed of 40 to 90 mph (64 to 144 km; exact speed is up to the demon) during a normal storm, but as fast at 180 mph (288 km) during a *ley line storm*. In the latter case, the creature must stay ahead of the storm and stay on the ley line.

Limited Invulnerability (special): The Khitaka are impervious to normal S.D.C. weapons unless they are made of silver or juniper or birch trees, in which case the weapon inflicts the equivalent S.D.C. damage as M.D. (i.e. a wooden staff that inflicts 2D6 S.D.C. would inflict 2D6 M.D. to the Khitaka if made of juniper or birch). They are also impervious to disease, cold, and heat.

Most man-made Mega-Damage weapons inflict their normal damage, however M.D. fire, including magic fire, does half

damage. Most other magic weapons, spells, psionics and lightning do full damage. Millennium Tree weapons and Lightning do double damage.

The light of day (including the magical Globe of Daylight) dispels any magical disguises or metamorphosis, turns an invisible demon visible, and attacks per melee round are reduced to four.

Also see magic.

O.C.C.: Not applicable.

R.C.C. Skills: Land navigation 80%, wilderness survival 75%, horsemanship (general & exotic animals) 80%, surveillance systems (tailing only 86%), detect ambush 82%, detect concealment 80%, escape artist 70%, intelligence 75%, camouflage 75%, plus select three skills from the Rogue category, each +20% and two Ancient and two Modern W.P.s — the Khitaka is one of the few demons who will use energy weapons. Also see Natural Abilities, above.

R.C.C. Combat: Attacks Per Melee: Six

Damage: Bite 1D6 M.D., head-butt with horns, punch or kick M.D. varies with supernatural P.S. of the individual, a slashing claw strike adds 3D6 M.D. to usual punch damage; or by weapon or magic.

R.C.C. Bonuses: +5 on initiative, +5 to strike, +4 to parry, +3 to dodge, +8 to pull punch, +3 to disarm, +2 to roll with impact or fall, and +6 to save vs Horror Factor. R.C.C. bonuses are all in addition to any possible attribute bonuses.

Magic: All Abductors can cast the following spells, provided the demon has sufficient P.P.E.: Blinding Flash, Fire Bolt, See Aura, Sense Magic, Levitation, Magic Net, Carpet of Adhesion, Escape, Magic Pigeon, Calling, Purification, Spoil (Food/Water), Sickness, Chameleon, Shadow Meld, Mystic Portal, Teleport: Lesser, Teleport: Superior, and, from *Rifts® Federation of Magic*: Cloak of Darkness, Mystic Fulcrum, Armor Bizarre, Distant Voice, Crushing Fist, Sheltering Force, Phantom Mount, Power Weapon, Power Bolt, and Forcebonds. All spells are equal to a 5th level sorcerer.

Psionics: None

Enemies: All mortals, particularly humans, and sees them as potential slaves, pawns and playthings. Hates Gargoyles and Brodkil, and considers all "sub-demons" to be inferior and subservient to them. Anybody they can lord over and torment, they will. The Abductors are old enemies and rivals of True Atlanteans and Temporal Raiders.

Allies: Others of its kind, other demons, greater demons, Splugorth and their minions, powerful practitioners of magic, and other powerful beings with agendas that involve intimidation, extortion, murder, torture and mayhem.

Value: None

Habitat: Can be found anywhere throughout Rifts Russia, western Europe, China and Asia, from woodland hideaways to a mansion or tower in the heart of a city or village.

The Nightfeeder

The dreaded Nightfeeder is one of the most horrible of Russian Demons. The head looks like the skull of some monstrous alien with two nose openings, horn-like cheek bones, a gaping maw filled with jagged teeth, and a pair of tiny black pincers implanted in the jaw bone. The eyes are two large, black orbs more reminiscent of an insect than an animal. Above the bony eye ridges are a pair of large, curved horns. Jagged spines that look like rough, wooden stakes hammered from the inside out through the skull, appear in the center of the forehead and run down the middle of the skull and the back of the neck. The humanoid shaped body looks as if it has no skin, but a network of sinew and muscles stretched like taffy or rubber bands pulled over thick bone — observers can actually see through some of the spaces in the body. The hands also appear as bare muscle ending in long, narrow black nails (the feet have a similar appearance). All this makes for a terrifying effigy, but there is more.

Emerging from the mass of sinew that composes the chest and abdomen are four retractable, scrawny, but powerful insect-like appendages, two on each side. At the end of each of these arms is a jagged pincer used to stab, cut, and tear out hunks of the Nightfeeder's prey. These pincers can ravage the physical body or protective armor of an opponent in under a minute, literally tearing the person apart. One particularly horrible tactic is to plunge one or more of the pincer arms through a hole in an opponent's armor and into his body, enabling the demon to tear and chop internal organs. The pincer arms and

long, razor-sharp nails on the hands are also used to torture, flay skin, extract organs (without initially killing their victim), and tear out chunks of meat.

As the name suggests, Nightfeeders eat mortal humanoids and find the flesh of humans and True Atlanteans (old enemies) to be the most delicious. When a Nightfeeder slaughters and butchers livestock and other animals, the monster does so out of spite, anger or vengeance, or to create an aura of fear and foreboding, not for food. Nightfeeders love to create an atmosphere of terror and play cat and mouse games with humans and D-Bees, a penchant that sometimes overlaps into their dealings with other demons as well. Nightfeeders are much too selfish and cruel to be effective leaders, but love to dominate lesser beings, rule over (or terrorize) entire communities, and lead small bands of bloodthirsty demons, woodland spirits or other misanthropes (including humans and D-Bees). They so delight in the subjugation, abuse and torture of other beings that they have no desire for wealth or genuine power, and little concern for what their henchmen or colleagues are doing, so long as it doesn't interfere with their fun and games. To this end, cunning and careful "colleagues" can amass sizeable treasure hoards, use the Nightfeeder for their own gain, or build small pockets of power for themselves. However, anybody involved with Nightfeeders must always be the model of discretion and constantly on their guard, and always act genuinely subservient. The alternative is to invoke the murderous ire and wrath of their demon "leader." Nightfeeders are notoriously unpredictable and hot-tempered killers who lash out at the slightest provocation. They see the solution to all their problems as torture and/or murder. If an underling is suspected of stealing, lying, conspiring or speaking out against the Nightfeeder, innocently questions the beast, or just makes the demon angry for a moment, the fiend is likely to (but not always) either subdue and torture the poor soul (for fun and information), or kill him on the spot.

Whenever a Nightfeeder is part of a group where it is not the leader, one can be assured that it is either plotting ways to usurp control, or the being in charge is powerful or cunning enough to keep the demon happy in its lesser role. In the latter case, this typically means the Nightfeeder holds a high position within the group (in name, if not actual power), and is given a tremendous amount of latitude and freedom. Such latitude includes letting the beast come and go as it pleases, engage in frequent acts of torture, punishment and murder, and indulge in schemes and activities of its own, as long as they don't interfere with the true leader's plans or the group's effectiveness. As one might guess, the more the Nightfeeder's attention can be directed toward murder, torture, and the abuse and domination of lesser creatures, the happier and more fulfilled it will be and thus the less likely to consider seizing leadership for itself — they are narrowly focused and rather obsessive creatures.

Nightfeeder Demon NPC Villain

Also Known as Nightkillers.

Race: Greater Archaic Demon.

Alignment: Always diabolic; aggressive and cruel.

Attributes: I.Q. average human intelligence but cunning and sadistic: 1D4+7, M.E. 1D6, M.A. 1D6, P.S. 2D6+30 (half in daylight), P.P. 2D6+12, P.E. 2D6+12, P.B. 1D4, Spd 2D6+12; supernatural P.S.

M.D.C.: P.E. number +3D4x10+42, but increase by 50% at night or in darkness (on S.D.C. worlds the Nightfeeder has 2D4x10 +P.E. number for Hit Points and 100 S.D.C.; increase both by 50% at night. A.R. 14 day or night).

Horror Factor: 16

Size: 6-7 feet (1.8 to 2.1 m) tall.

Weight: 200-250 pounds (90 to 112.5 kg)

Average Life Span: Uncertain, 2000+ years; probably immortal.

P.P.E.: 5D6x10 +P.E. attribute number.

Natural Abilities: Fair speed and can run or fight without pause or exhaustion indefinitely. They can also leap up to 8 feet (2.4 m) high and 12 feet (3.6 m) lengthwise, climb 80%/70%, swim 90%, do not breathe air, can survive depths of up to 2000 feet (610 m), prowl 60%, track humans using sense of smell and vision 75% (-25% when tracking any other life forms). Nightvision is one mile (1.6 km), see the invisible, dimensional teleport 55% (+25% at a ley line nexus) and bio-regenerates 4D6 M.D. per melee round!

Knows all Languages: Magically understands and speaks all languages at 90%, but cannot read.

Limited Flight (special): Can ride the wind of a storm, including tornados and hurricanes, without injury. During a storm the demon can effectively fly and is able to dive, swoop, and hover, but only so long as it is moving in the same direction as the storm winds, and stays just ahead of the heart of the storm. Under these conditions, they can attain a speed of 40 to 90 mph (64 to 144 km; exact speed is up to the demon) during a normal storm, but as fast at 180 mph (288 km) during a *ley line storm*. In the latter case, the creatures must stay ahead of the storm and stay on the ley line.

Limited Metamorphosis (special): The Nightfeeder can turn into a leprous old man or hag once per night for as long as the entire night. Metamorphosis is impossible during the light of day, and a Globe of Daylight or the flash of lightning (natural or magical) will force an instant transformation back into its true demonic form.

Limited Invulnerability (special): The Nightfeeder is impervious to normal S.D.C. weapons unless they are made of silver or the wood of a juniper or birch tree, in which case the weapon inflicts the equivalent S.D.C. damage as M.D. (i.e. a wooden staff that inflicts 2D6 S.D.C. would inflict 2D6 M.D. to the Nightfeeder if made of juniper or birch). They are also impervious to disease, cold, and heat.

Man-made Mega-Damage weapons inflict half their normal damage, M.D. fire does full damage, and magic weapons, spells and psionics do full damage. Millennium Tree weapons do full damage. Lightning does double damage.

The light of day (including the magical Globe of Daylight) reduces the demon's P.S. and M.D.C. by half, and inhibits their ability to metamorph, however, nothing makes them feel insecure or any less aggressive.

Also see magic.

O.C.C.: Not applicable.

R.C.C. Skills: Horsemanship (general & exotic animals), land navigation 70%, wilderness survival 80%, plus select three skills from each of the following skill categories: W.P. Ancient Weapons and Rogue. All elective skills get a +25% skill bonus and one skill gets an additional +10%. Proficiency in these skills does not advance. Also see Natural Abilities, above.

R.C.C. Combat: Attacks Per Melee: Eight! Casting a spell typically uses up two attacks.

Damage: Bite 3D6 M.D., head-butt with horns does the usual supernatural P.S. damage +2D6, punch or kick M.D. varies with supernatural P.S., pincer attacks do 4D6 M.D. (disregard supernatural P.S.), slashing or stabbing claw strike inflicts the usual supernatural P.S. damage +3D6,; or by weapon or magic.

R.C.C. Bonuses: +4 on initiative, +4 to strike, +5 to parry, +2 to dodge, +7 to pull punch, +3 to disarm, +1 to roll with impact or fall, +8 to save vs Horror Factor. R.C.C. bonuses are all in addition to any possible attribute bonuses.

Magic: Available spells from the *Rifts® RPG* include: Fool's Gold, Multiple Image, Levitate, Mask of Deceit, Repel Animals, Compulsion, Spoil (Food/Water), Sickness, Shadow Meld, and Cloak of Darkness.

From *Federation of Magic:* Aura of Power, Magic Shield, Fire Blast, Ballistic Fire, Desiccate the Supernatural, Crushing Fist, Frequency Jamming, Negate Mechanics, Distant Voice, Influence the Beast, Tame the Beast, and D-Step.

Spell potency is equal to a 4th level sorcerer.

Psionics: None

Enemies: Humans aren't seen so much as an enemy as they are playthings and prey. Of course, foolish heroes, mages and Demon Slayers are regarded as impudent upstarts to be made an example of through prolonged torture and death. Nightfeeders take a similar view of Gargoyles, Brodkil and all "sub-demons," expecting all to accept Nightfeeders as their lords and masters (and the sub-demon better bow and scrape), and killing any who dare to stand against, defy or annoy them. Despises Vampires because they see them as rivals.

Allies: Others of its kind, greater demons, powerful, evil practitioners of magic, and other powerful beings with agendas that involve subjecting, tormenting and killing other life forms. They find Necromancers and evil Shifters/Summoners especially attractive.

Value: None

Habitat: Anywhere throughout Rifts Russia, China and much of Asia. Occasionally encountered in Poland, Germany and even Africa and North America.

Koshchei the Deathless Ones

The Koshchei are the elite vanguard of the Russian Demons, warriors with skeletal faces and black armor and garments. Each wears a crown to show their high place among demons and wields a crooked magical sword. Exactly how many exist is unknown, but it is believed that there are fewer than one thousand scattered throughout the Megaverse (and at least 100 on Rifts Earth in Russia and Asia). According to legend, there is a set number of these warrior demons, and when one actually dies, a new one is recruited from their legion of mortal assassins and cutthroats.

The Deathless Ones serve both the gods and their demon brothers (i.e. the Archaic Demons). Each is wise, cunning in the ways of war and combat, a master swordsman and maker of enchanted weapons. They distribute these weapons to champions of evil among the Archaic demons and humankind which the Koshchei deem worthy of such a great gift. These honored damned must be anarchist or evil and show a great penchant for evil. This doesn't mean a willingness and ability to slaughter the helpless, but the ability to see the larger picture and the rare qualities of leadership, guile and treachery that can motivate an army, demoralize a nation, and lead to great chaos, war and disaster. These are the rare and chosen champions of evil honored by the Koshchei.

The War Camps of the Warlords hate and fear the Deathless Ones more than any other demon, for not only are these vicious demon warriors incredibly powerful — virtually indestructible — but they are also the only demon that can raise an army of thousands to fight against them. Such armies are typically 6D6x100 with at least half being composed of other Archaic demons (most lesser ones) and sub-demons (usually gargoyles, gurgoyles and Brodkil), and the remaining 35-50% other foul creatures, including monsters, D-Bees and traitorous humans. In addition to these formidable armies, the Koshchei also establish and help support a network of villains from human brigands, spies, assassins and cutthroats to Witches, Necromancers, evil sorcerers, dragons and small bands of demons (6D6x2) to pillage the countryside and make small strikes and incursions against the Warlords, their War Camps and the communities who embrace them. How such a powerful demonic patron gives courage to low-life humanoid villains and lesser demons alike, even if that patron may be gone for months at a time is unclear. In addition to helping organize these factions, the Deathless

Ones settle disputes, pass out judgements, and, most importantly, help to give these brigands goals, plans for various continuing operations, and basic strategies and tactics. When the Koshchei return, they expect to be treated like a warrior-king (or god). When the Koshchei call their networks together to form a unified army or engage in coordinated attacks or special missions, the demons demand complete obedience.

While it is true the Koshchei are excellent generals and military strategists, they are also known to act alone. There are many reports of a lone Deathless One attacking heavily armed squads, platoons (40 troops) and even companies (160 troops), hurling devastating magic and engaging troops hand to hand in a frenzy of martial combat. According to several War Camps, a single Koshchei is capable of killing 10-40 men single-handedly, in less than 15 minutes or before the demon is destroyed or vanishes. Whispered rumors tell of a Deathless One accompanied by a fellow Koshchei and a dozen or two other demons wiping out entire companies of soldiers. The Warlords and their Camps adamantly deny this, and their success against the demon hordes, Koshchei included, would seem to support the notion that such rumors are baseless, but the rumors (perhaps started by the Koshchei) linger. The reputation of the Deathless Ones is such that their mere presence is enough to send cowards, inexperienced troops and low level Reavers fleeing in terror — a reaction the Koshchei enjoy immensely. In fact, the Deathless Ones rarely have their minions pursue and slaughter any man who runs without firing a single shot; a mocking act of mercy. Even veteran Soldati and War-Knights have been known to flee when face to face with the superhuman onslaught of a Deathless One. Only the insane Cyborg Shocktroopers and bold Wingriders and Cossacks are said to have never fled before such demons, even if it meant every last warrior perished in the battle against it — according to modern day myths, the *Wingriders* and *Cossacks* are the only human warriors the Deathless Ones truly respect, and regret killing. They cannot respect cyborgs who are more machine than man.

Surprisingly, Deathless Ones rarely hold a grudge. Instead, they are cold-blooded, calculating and merciless fighting machines who try not to let emotion blind them to the military task at hand.

Koshchei Demon General & NPC Villain

More Commonly Known as the Deathless Ones.
Race: Greater Archaic Demon of immense power.
Alignment: Aberrant (55%), Miscreant (25%), Diabolic (15%), Anarchist (5%).
Attributes: I.Q. 1D6+16, M.E. 1D6+16, M.A. 1D6+20, P.S. 3D6+32, P.P. 1D6+16, P.E. 1D6+16, P.B. 1D6, Spd 2D6+16 running; supernatural P.S.
M.D.C.: P.E. +6D6x10+16 (on S.D.C. worlds Koshchei have 3D6x10 Hit Points +P.E. number and 3D6x10 S.D.C.; natural A.R. of 12).
M.D.C. Armor: The demon warrior also wears a suit of magical armor that gives it an additional 160 M.D.C. (on S.D.C. worlds the armor has 160 S.D.C. and an A.R. of 15).
Horror Factor: 15
Size: 7 feet (1.8 m) tall.
Weight: 200 pounds (90 kg)
Average Life Span: Probably immortal.
P.P.E.: 1D4x100 +216

Natural Abilities: Fair speed and can fight without pause or exhaustion for 12 hours. The demon can also leap up to 20 feet (6 m) high and 40 feet (9 m) across, climb 90%/85%, prowl 60%, swim 90%, does not breathe air, can survive depths of up to 1000 feet (305 m), see the invisible, nightvision is one mile (1.6 km), dimensional teleport 50% (+32% at a ley line nexus) and bio-regenerates 1D4x10 M.D. per melee round!

Knows all Languages: Magically understands and speaks all languages 95%, but cannot read.

Conditional Immortality (special): The Koshchei are called "The Deathless Ones," because it is almost impossible to kill them. Their life essence, or souls, does not reside inside their bodies. Consequently, although their bodies *can* be destroyed, that same Koshchei will be reborn, with all the same memories, experience, power, and weapons, within 72 hours unless the place where its cursed soul resides can be found and its essence freed.

The life essence of each Deathless One is contained in a separate, ordinary looking duck's *egg*. This egg is hidden by each individual Koshchei, usually in some remote and desolate place, and often guarded by loyal beasts or (1D6) trusted minions (typically demon or nonhuman). The life essence is released, and the Koshchei slain, simply by cracking the egg open (it has two S.D.C). This is the only way to permanently kill a Deathless One! The moment the egg is broken, the Koshchei, wherever it may be, will instant fall to the ground as a pile of old, dry bones. The armor and weapons once in its possession vanish into thin air, as do all weapons the fiend may have created and given to its mortal allies, a sign to them that their demon patron is gone forever.

Note: If just the physical body of the Deathless One is destroyed, its armor, weapons and possessions vanish, only to re-appear 72 hours later when the Deathless One reappears, totally healed. Also note that the egg containing the creature's life essence can be no more than 300 miles (482 km) away at any given time. As a result, if an enemy retreats or makes a stand beyond the maximum range, the Koshchei cannot give chase and must stop short, although the demon can send his troops ahead without him. To go beyond this point, the Koshchei must retrieve the egg and find a new hiding place for it. Of course, the demon warrior can travel without restrictions if the egg is on his person, but this foolishness is rarely done.

Limited Invulnerability (special): The Koshchei is impervious to normal S.D.C. weapons unless they are made of silver, in which case the weapon inflicts the equivalent S.D.C. damage as M.D. (i.e. a silver plated sword that inflicts 2D6 S.D.C. would inflict 2D6 M.D. to the demon). The demon is also impervious to natural heat, cold, disease, and poison.

Man-made Mega-Damage weapons, magic weapons, spells, and psionics inflict their normal damage, however M.D. lightning and electricity does double damage. The light of day has no negative effect on the Deathless Ones.

Also see magic and combat abilities.

O.C.C.: Effectively a Demon Knight.
R.C.C. Skills: Horsemanship: knight and exotic animals, land navigation 70%, wilderness survival 75%, plus *all* Military and Espionage skills at 75%. Also has W.P. Sword (equal to 8th level skill) and five of choice (any including modern

weapons), all equal to 5th level skill experience. Also see Natural Abilities, above.

R.C.C. Combat: Attacks Per Melee: Seven physical, or two physical and two by spell magic.

Damage: Punch or kick M.D. varies with supernatural P.S. of the individual, or by weapon or magic.

R.C.C. Bonuses: +6 on initiative, +5 to strike, +4 to parry, +4 to dodge, +6 to pull punch, +4 to disarm, +2 to roll with impact or fall, +2 to save vs magic, +8 to save vs mind control and illusions, +10 to save vs possession and +10 to save vs Horror Factor. R.C.C. bonuses are all in addition to any possible attribute bonuses.

Magic: All Koshchei are the equivalent of 8th level *Mystic Kuznya*, with all their metal-working and weapon-making abilities.

In addition, the demon warrior has the following spell knowledge: See Aura, Sense Evil, Sense Magic, Detect Concealment, Turn Dead, Energy Disruption, Fly, Fly as the Eagle, Call Lightning, Fire Ball, Time Slip, Dispel Magic Barrier, Negate Magic, Spoil, Time Hole, and Close Rift.

Plus the following from *Rifts® Federation of Magic™*: Light Target, Deflect, Reflection, Ricochet Strike, Barrage, Ballistic Fire, Spinning Blades, Dragon Fire, Power Bolt, Power Weapon, Speed Weapon, Frost Blade, Frequency Jamming, Energize Spell, Implosion Neutralizer, Sorcerous Fury, Summon Ally and Enchant Weapon.

All spells are equal to a 6th level sorcerer.

Psionics: None

Enemies: All mortals, particularly humans. They see all humans as slaves, pawns and playthings. Thus, the Warlords and their War Camps are impudent fools who need to be crushed. Consequently, Deathless Ones frequently engage warriors and soldiers in battle, cause trouble and try to undermine the Warlords' efforts whenever possible. They also engage Bogatyrs, Demon Slayers and other "heroes." They tend to instigate the least trouble among the Cossacks out of respect for their courage and fighting expertise.

The Deathless Ones regard vampires as their mortal enemy above all others and destroy them whenever encountered. They think little of Gargoyles, Brodkil, and other "sub-demons," and are surprised that such inferior beings could build and hold an Empire. They don't give them too much credit, however, because they recognize the fact that the Gargoyle Empire survives through strength of numbers and superior supernatural ability over the lesser humans. As for the Brodkil Empire, it is already a shambles and won't last more than another decade.

Allies: Others of its kind, other Archaic demons (lesser and greater), dragons (they hold adult and ancient dragons in high regard and often welcome them as allies), and dark gods. Evil mortal practitioners of magic and wicked humans, D-Bees, creatures of magic and other evil beings are welcome to *serve* the Koshchei and its demon brethren, but are never considered equals on any level.

Value: None

Habitat: Can be found anywhere throughout Europe and Asia, but are mainly found in Rifts Russia and Mongolia. Twenty-four are known to be actively engaged in action against the Warlords of Russia, their War Camps and the people who swear allegiance to them. Another 76 are said to be scattered throughout the rest of Rifts Russia and Asia.

Morozko Frost Demons

Old Man Morozko is a demon lord and King of the Frost Demons (12th level, 2000 M.D.C., anarchist, possesses all the magic known to the greater Frost Demons, plus all level 1-3, and 15th level wizard spells). He rarely interferes in the affairs of mortals, but there are legions of comparatively less powerful Frost Demons that do. These are greater demons often confused with the demon lord himself, or sometimes said to be his multitude of children. Whether they are actually Old Man Morozko's offspring is unlikely, but they consider him their ultimate master, share many similar powers and are elemental in nature. Consequently, they are generally referred to as "The Morozko," or "Frost Demons." They never gather in large numbers unless summoned by Lord Morozko and are typically encountered as lone, solitary figures or commanding a group of lesser demons or evil woodland spirits. The Frost Demons may also associate with evil humans, particularly black-hearted men of magic.

Frost Demons are cruel and cold-hearted. They enjoy causing hardship and suffering for lesser creatures and frequently battle the human War Camps. This includes stirring up other demons and instigating trouble. They prefer to use their own natural abilities and innate magical powers, but are willing to use man-made weapons. Furthermore, they recognize the power of human science and high-technology, and rarely underestimate the power of high-tech weaponry, machines, science or magic.

All Frost Demons are tall, thin, and menacing looking humanoid beings with pale (whitish) or light blue colored skin and piercing, ice blue eyes. Their bodies feel firm and their skin cold to the touch. Most are ill-tempered, mean-spirited, spiteful and vindictive. Many wear fur trimmed boots, a tall, fur trimmed hat, and pants for show, and light armor that seems to be made of crystallized ice. Others wear little more than a loin cloth and a few bits of crystal armor. All can magically create a Frostblade that inflicts 4D6 M.D. (does 6D6 M.D. to creatures of fire/fire elementals).

Morozko Demon NPC Villain

More Commonly Known as the Frost Demon. Also known as the Children of Morozko.

Race: Greater Archaic Demon of considerable power.

Alignment: Anarchist (30%), Miscreant (30%) or any evil alignments (Old Man Morozko, Lord of the Frost Demons, is himself anarchist).

Attributes: I.Q. 1D6+10, M.E. 1D6+10, M.A. 1D6+10, P.S. 2D6+20, P.P. 2D4+10, P.E. 2D6+10, P.B. 2D6, Spd 2D6+12 running (triple when sliding on snow or ice, and does so without leaving a trail); supernatural P.S.

M.D.C.: P.E. +6D6x10 (on S.D.C. worlds Frost Demons have 2D6x10 Hit Points +P.E. number and 3D6x10 S.D.C.; A.R. 12).

Horror Factor: 13

Size: 6-7 feet (1.8 to 2.1 m) tall.

Weight: 300 pounds (135 kg)

Average Life Span: Uncertain, 2000+ years; probably immortal.

P.P.E.: 1D4x100 +50.

Natural Abilities: Fair speed and can fight without pause or exhaustion for 12 hours. The demon can also leap up to 20 feet (6 m) high and 30 feet (9 m) across (increase by 30% with a

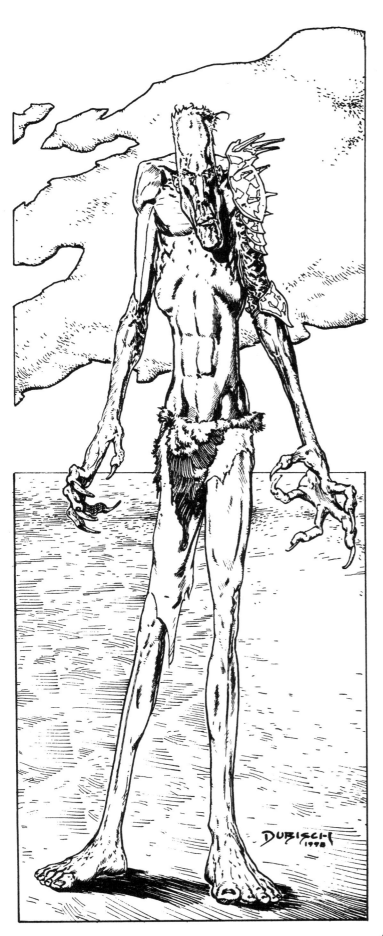

running start), swim 90%, skate 98%, does not breathe air, can survive depths of up to 1000 feet (305 m), prowl on snow or ice 90% (-40% on dry ground), track humanoids in snow 75% (-40% on dry ground), see the invisible, nightvision is one mile (1.6 km), dimensionally teleport 40% (+25% at a ley line nexus) and bio-regenerate 3D6 M.D. per melee round.

Frost Powers (special):

- Can walk on top of snow and the thinnest ice without making noise, falling through or leaving track (impossible to track).
- Can climb pillars of ice, glaciers, fir and pine trees equal to a skill of 95%/90%.
- Skate across ice and ski across snow with grace and at triple the demon's normal running speed, and +1 on initiative, +1 to strike and +3 to dodge.
- Knows the precise time and direction by scanning the heavens (day or night) at 80%.
- Sense the direction and speed of the wind, as well as the air temperature 90%.
- Sense the approach of snow, snow storms, and ice storms involving air and freezing water at 90%, up to 100 miles (160 km) away.

Knows all Languages: Magically understands and speaks all languages 95%, but cannot read.

Frost Touch (Special): Same as the spell Wave of Frost but does not cost P.P.E. to perform. Each frost touch counts as two melee actions.

Frost Breath (Special): The Frost Demon can blow an ice cold burst of wind that will send chills through the body of everybody who feels its touch (-1 on initiative, -5% on skill performance), does 2D6 S.D.C./H.P. damage and covers glass, goggles, face plates, and other surfaces with a sheet of white frost (must be scraped away to see). Range: 200 feet (61 m), cutting a six foot (1.8 m) wide swath. Does not cost P.P.E. to perform, but each breath counts as two melee attacks.

Limited Invisibility (special): Completely invisible and undetectable by modern machines while in a snowstorm unless within 6 feet (1.8 m) or closer. The same is true if the demon dives into snow and covers himself completely.

Limited Flight (special): Can ride the wind of a *snowstorm* to effectively fly, and is able to dive, swoop, and hover, but only so long as he is moving in the same direction as the storm winds, and stays just ahead of the heart of the storm. Under these conditions, the demon can attain a speed up to 40 mph (64 km; exact speed is up to the demon). Cannot fly during a *ley line storm*.

Limited Invulnerability (special): The Frost Demon is impervious to normal S.D.C. weapons unless they are made of silver, or juniper or birch trees, in which case the weapon inflicts the equivalent S.D.C. damage as M.D. (i.e. a wooden staff that inflicts 2D6 S.D.C. would inflict 2D6 M.D. to the demon if made of juniper or birch). The demon is also impervious to the most frigid cold, and cold-based magic has no affect and does no damage. Furthermore, because cold and ice is the demons' natural environment, Frost Demons don't need any source of warmth, clothing or protection even in sub-zero temperatures. Impervious to disease, and electricity does half damage.

Man-made Mega-Damage weapons, magic weapons, spells, and psionics inflict their normal damage, however M.D. fire, including magic fire, does double damage. The light of day has no negative effect on the Frost demon.

Also see magic.

Vulnerabilities: Heat: Frost Demons dislike summer or any time or place where the temperature rises above 60 degrees Fahrenheit. In such "hot" environments the Morozko feel weak and uncomfortable, spell potency is reduced to 3rd level, while physical M.D.C., Speed and Attacks per Melee Round are reduced by half. According to legend they flee to the bottom of cool lakes, or the tops of mountains and glaciers to avoid the summer warmth, but thrive in the cool and cold months, which in most of Rifts Russia typically spans from October through April, giving the Morozko 9 months of activity at full strength.

Normal fire does Mega-Damage! An ordinary flaming club, torch or arrow will inflict 2D6 M.D., being knocked into a bonfire does 4D6 M.D., while Mega-Damage fire, plasma and magic fire (including flaming swords) inflict double damage. However, heroes and mages who wield fire are the first ones attacked and incapacitated by these intelligent and clever menaces.

O.C.C.: Not applicable.

R.C.C. Skills: Land navigation 60% (+30% in the winter and snow), wilderness survival 85%, horsemanship: general and exotic (includes the Hell Horse), plus whittle/sculpt (ice only), art, dance, and intelligence, all at 75%. Also select three skills from W.P. (any including modern weapons), Wilderness and Technical, all get a +20% bonus. Also see Natural Abilities, above.

R.C.C. Combat: Attacks Per Melee: Six

Damage: Bite 1D6 M.D., head butt with horns, punch or kick M.D. varies with supernatural P.S. of the individual, a slashing claw strike adds 3D6 M.D. to usual punch damage; or by weapon or magic.

R.C.C. Bonuses: +3 on initiative, +4 to strike, +4 to parry, +3 to dodge, +2 to pull punch, +2 to disarm, +1 to roll with impact or fall, +2 to save vs magic, +6 to save vs possession and +8 to save vs Horror Factor. R.C.C. bonuses are all in addition to any possible attribute bonuses.

Magic: All Frost Demons can cast the following spells, provided the creature has sufficient P.P.E.: Air & Water elemental spells found in *Rifts® Conversion Book One*, starting on page 62: Create Light, Create Mild Wind, Stop Wind, Create Air, Levitate, Northwind, Northern Lights, Freeze Water, Snow Storm, Hail, Shards of Ice, Sheet of Ice, Wall of Ice, Ten Foot Ball of Ice, Encase in Ice, Dowsing, Float on Water, Water Seal, and Calm Storm (snow, hail and ice storms only), plus the following from *Rifts® Federation of Magic*: Cleanse, Light Target, Chromatic Protection, Orb of Cold, Wave of Cold, Frost Blade, Ice, House of Glass, Sheltering Force, and Phantom Mount.

All spells are equal to a 6th level sorcerer.

Psionics: None

Enemies: All mortals, particularly humans. They see all humans as potential slaves, pawns and playthings and the Warlords and their War Camps as dangerous upstarts trying to tame the land and destroy demonkind. Consequently, Morozko fre-

quently engage warriors and soldiers in battle, cause trouble and try to undermine their efforts whenever possible. The Frost Demons also plague villages who have sworn allegiance to the Warlords until they promise to break their bonds with these insane wild men.

Morozko hate vampires and destroy them whenever encountered. They also dislike Gargoyles and Brodkil, and considers all "sub-demons" to be inferior and subservient to them. Anybody they can lord over, frighten and abuse, they will. However, only a handful put themselves in place as lords over communities of mere mortals. Frost Demons tend to be free spirits who expect to come and go as they please.

Allies: Others of its kind, other demons (especially Water Demons and Woodland spirits), greater demons, dragons (they hold dragons in very high regard and often welcome them as allies and partners), and other powerful beings. The Morozko tend to be suspicious of and avoid practitioners of magic, dislike Witches and Necromancers and hate the Kaluga Hags.

Value: None

Habitat: Can be found anywhere throughout Europe, but are mainly found in Rifts Russia, Scandinavia, Mongolia, China and Asia, from woodlands hideaways to a mansion or tower in the heart of a city or village.

Whirlwind Air Demons

Whirlwind demons appear as wicked-looking angel-like beings, that is to say, they are human in appearance with curly golden or black hair, sparkling eyes, and graced with red, grey and black wings. The face usually has a wicked or cruel expression, the nose is often beakish, and their ears large, pointed and hairy. The feet are like the talons of a bird of prey, reflecting their insatiable hunger for inflicting suffering and predatory nature. Many, especially the males, are gluttonous and obese. Most enjoy dressing in fine Chinese silk and may use magic weapons.

Whirlwind are cunning and mean. They delight in tormenting all lesser beings from humans and young dragons to fellow supernatural beings (good and evil). They are bullies who find self-worth in tricking, belittling, enslaving and tormenting others. If a an individual — ally or enemy — shows a sudden weakness or vulnerability, the Whirlwind seizes the opportunity to get the upper hand, extract revenge or eliminate competition. Creatures of air and wind, their temperaments are ethereal and change in a heartbeat. One minute the Whirlwind may be cold and indifferent, the next, a raging maniac. When mad, one can see the anger roll over the demon like storm clouds, and in a matter of seconds (one melee round), see lightning, hate and aggression crackling from the monster's smoldering eyes. They are quick to anger and violent reaction. Abusive and cruel, the Whirlwind's knee-jerk reaction is to lash out and smash the cause of its anger, sorrow, embarrassment or frustration. They are incredibly petty, vindictive and vengeful, and hold grudges that can span centuries.

Untrustworthy, fickle and selfish creatures, they find other demons, even their fellow Archaic demons, to be inferior to them. Whirlwinds respect no man or god, although they appreciate and fear great power, so they can be pressed into service by powerful sorcerers, demon lords and deities. However, they are

completely untrustworthy and will do all manner of little things to strike back at their so-called "masters." When the being who commands them is hurt or loses his power (i.e. faces defeat), the Whirlwind are the first to abandon or turn on him, and may torture or even kill him, although they are more likely to loot his treasure trove, vandalize the lair, and leave, believing it is better to leave the poor creature alive to suffer the agony of his defeat.

For reasons unknown, they are frequently encountered in groups of three, although pairs and lone Whirlwind predators are also common. Some force humans, D-Bees and sub-demons to serve them as slaves and underlings; the biggest kiss-ups and boot lickers earning the Whirlwinds' greatest confidence and kindness. Lone air demons seem to be attracted to establishing "kingdoms on Earth," where they rule as tyrant kings. However,

most such "kingdoms" are rarely larger than a village or town with a few hundred to a thousand subjects. Such "kingdoms" are most commonly found south and east of the Warlords' Spheres of Influence.

The Whirlwinds see the Warlords and other mortal leaders and heroes as insolent, arrogant and defiant upstarts, and delight in bringing them trouble and war. As a result, these demons frequently attack squads and platoons, raid camps or simply plow through them as ... well ... whirlwinds, to create panic, cause destruction and then fly away. They also entice lesser demons and humanoid brigands to take action against the War Camps, often joining forces to, quote, "insure their success". However, Whirlwinds find it funny to pump-up people, lead them into battle and then, halfway through the conflict, leave them to fend for themselves (which almost always ends in crushing defeat and high casualties). They also send storms, freak winds and bad weather against the humans allied to the Warlords, both warriors and civilians. The monsters raid and harass villages and cities, scatter (sometimes slaughter) cattle, damage crops, topple church steeples, frighten visitors, send bad weather and generally torment communities who have sworn allegiance to the Warlords. The only people they hate more are self-proclaimed "demon slayers" and heroes who have built a reputation for battling demons.

Whirlwind Demon NPC Villain

Also Known as the Evil Wind and Demon Angel.
Race: Greater Archaic Demon.
Alignment: Anarchist, miscreant or diabolic; usually evil.
Attributes: I.Q. average to high human intelligence, but violent and treacherous: 1D6+7, M.E. 2D6, M.A. 2D6, P.S. 3D6+20, P.P. 1D6+17, P.E. 1D6+17, P.B. 1D6+7 (males), 1D6+14 (females), Spd 2D6+7 on the ground, but 2D6+88 flying (approx. 65 mph/104 km); supernatural P.S.
M.D.C.: 5D6x10 +70 (on S.D.C. worlds the demon has 4D4x10 Hit Points and 2D6x10 S.D.C.; A.R. 11 day and night).
Horror Factor: 10
Size: 7-8 feet (2.1 to 2.4 m) tall.
Weight: 200-400 pounds (90 to 180 kg).
Average Life Span: Uncertain, 2000+ years; probably immortal.
P.P.E.: 7D6x10+35
Natural Abilities: Good speed and can fly or fight without pause or exhaustion for 24 hours. Nightvision is two miles (3.2 km), see the invisible, track with hawk-like vision 90% and can see an Imp sitting on a log up to three miles (4.8 km) away! Dimensionally teleport 37% (+40% at a ley line nexus), and bio-regenerates 2D6 M.D. per melee round.

Knows all Languages: Magically understands and speaks all languages 90%, but cannot read.

Air Elemental Powers (special):

- Recognize and speak to true elementals at 84%.

- Knows the precise time and direction by scanning the heavens (day or night) at 91%.

- Sense the direction and speed of the wind, as well as the air temperature at 91%.

- Sense the approach of rain, snow, storms, tidal waves, hurricanes and atmospheric disturbances involving air or water at 91%, up to 100 miles (160 km) away.

- Sense and pinpoint odors, smoke, impurities, chemicals, poisons, pollution and particles in the air at 84%, up to 100 miles (160 km) away.

- See through fog and mist without any impairment of vision.

Limited Metamorphosis (special): The Whirlwind can transform into either an attractive looking human (P.B. 1D6+14) or a real, tornado-like Whirlwind at will. This can be done as often as once per hour. In human form, the demon retains all of its powers, except flight, but appears perfectly normal. This appearance is used to walk among humans and is ideal for efforts in seduction, corruption, spying, infiltration, sabotage and theft. This appearance can be maintained for up to 14 hours.

In Whirlwind form, the creature becomes a swirling force of destructive wind, roughly equal to the Whirlwind Air Warlock spell in power and size (see page 66 of *Rifts® Conversion Book One*). In this elemental form, only attacks utilizing psionics, magic, elemental forces and explosives have any effect on the raging funnel of living wind. Physical attacks do no damage to the "wind," and most M.D. weapons only inflict 10% of their normal damage. However, M.D. explosives and particle beam weapons do half damage. The Vacuum spell will dispel the Whirlwind, returning the demon to its normal physical form. Other spells ideal for stopping a Whirlwind windstorm are Negate Magic, Anti-Magic Cloud (both forcing the demon to resume its physical form), Sanctum (keeps it out), Id Barrier, Tornado, Hurricane (both are strong storms that won't hurt the Whirlwind demon but will temporarily get it caught in their stronger swirling winds), Sonic Blast, Shockwave, Wall of Wind (cannot pass through it) and Immobilize, to name just a few. This wind form can be maintained for 14 minutes at a time.

Limited Invulnerability (special): The Air Demon is impervious to storm winds while in physical form (gets sucked into them and temporarily becomes part of them when in whirlwind form), as well as lightning, electricity, cold, and disease. It is also impervious to ordinary S.D.C. attacks and weapons, even those made of silver or wood.

Magic, magic weapons, psionics and M.D. weapons inflict full damage. The light of day has no negative impact on this demon. Also see magic.

O.C.C.: Not applicable.
R.C.C. Skills: Astronomy, navigation, land navigation, basic mathematics, and lore: demons and monsters, all at 91%. Also select two W.P. (any, equal to 4th level proficiency), two Rogue and two Technical skills of choice (each gets a +28% bonus). Also see Natural Abilities, above.
R.C.C. Combat: Attacks Per Melee: Six
Damage: Head-butt, punch or kick attacks inflict M.D. equal to the creature's supernatural P.S., or by weapon or magic.
R.C.C. Bonuses: +5 on initiative, +4 to strike, +2 to parry, +2 to dodge (+6 when flying), +2 to pull punch, +3 to roll with impact or fall, +1 to save vs magic, +5 to save vs Horror Factor, and +3 to save vs possession. R.C.C. bonuses are all in addition to any possible attribute bonuses.
Magic: All air elemental magic levels 1-8 (described in *Rifts® Conversion Book One*, starting on page 62), plus the following spells found in *Rifts® Federation of Magic™*: Cleanse, Lantern Light, Electric Arc, Wall of Wind, and Heavy Air.

Spell potency is equal to a 5th level warlock.

Psionics: None
Enemies: All mortals, humans in general and the Warlords and their War Camps in particular, because they see these warriors as a people driven to tame the land and destroy demonkind. They consider all "sub-demons" to be inferior and subservient to them, thus the Gargoyle Empire is an abomination to be destroyed (the demons are jealous of their impressive accomplishments); Brodkil are regarded as bumbling fools, Demon Claws and Guardians as mindless brutes, and Kaluga Hags are despised as dangerous rivals. They also frequently clash with Hindu and Chinese demons. Actually, they don't get on well with most creatures, including other demons.

Allies: Others of its kind, other demons (particularly Nalet, Il'ya, Midnight Demons and Wolf-Serpents), other greater demons, powerful practitioners of magic, and other powerful beings with agendas that involve murder, war, torture and mayhem. Whirlwinds sometimes manipulate lesser Air Elementals and are attracted to evil Water Warlocks, Druids, evil priests, Witches and evil practitioners of magic. They are friendly rivals with Wolf-Serpents and like to think they can manipulate these craven and cunning demons, but 99 out of 100 times it is the Wolf-Serpent who manipulates the Whirlwind, often without the Air demon realizing it.

Value: None

Habitat: Anywhere throughout the world, but are most common in Rifts Russia, Mongolia, China and Asia. Occasionally encountered in Poland, Germany, Africa and North America. In North America, Whirlwinds are considered most foul and evil spirits, but are comparatively rare; perhaps less than six hundred are scattered throughout Canada, the US, and Mexico.

Wolf-Serpent

The Wolf-Serpent is a hideous predatory demon with the body of a giant rattlesnake and the head of a Man-Wolf. The head has both the features of a human and a wolf. It is completely black, with a large mouth, large dark red eyes, and the ears and fur of a black or grey wolf. Behind the head and running down the length of the spine are protective plates reminiscent of some ancient dinosaurs. A hideous pair of lizard-like legs, stubby arms and claws, and two pair of spine-like appendages (slightly reminiscent of an insect) are located in the top third of the snake body, and give the Wolf-Serpent a truly strange appearance. The multitude of different limbs give the demon hands for using tools and operating machines, and natural defensive weapons (claws and stabbing spines) for protection, combat and climbing. The tail ends with a rattle that is used when angry and ready to attack, to frighten would-be combatants, and when content.

The Wolf-Serpent enjoys terrorizing and frustrating humans and other lesser beings, but its true pleasure is sowing the seeds of corruption and evil. It is both a tempter and corruptor, frequently offering humans healing, knowledge, insight to the future, and its assistance in extracting revenge — it may even offer to maim or murder on behalf of the troubled individual. Of course, the Wolf-Serpent always encourages the most extreme and hurtful course of action, and the knowledge it offers is usually hurtful or damning or suggestive information. For instance, a jealous man, suspicious that his wife is having an affair, may enlist the aid of the Wolf-Serpent. The next day the demon has information like, "Yesss, I followed your wife as you asked of me, and yesss, I sssaw her at your neighbor's home. He was most familiar with her and they laughed about you." In many cases, this is all the Wolf-Serpent may need to do, because the husband may now return home to beat his wife and/or kill her or her apparent lover. The monster just happens to leave out the reason she is seeing the man is because he is arranging the delivery of a special gift for the husband's birthday. In other cases, the corruptor will fuel the flames of foul emotions, suggesting that the individual is being made a fool, a laughingstock, etc., and even suggest murder or other foul acts of revenge. It may even offer "free" advice on how to do the deed.

The "price" of knowledge, advice and help from the Wolf-Serpent rarely involves money or trade goods, but a favor. Exactly what that favor may be can vary dramatically. Sometimes it will involve something as simple as telling a particular person something, telling a lie, spreading a rumor, bearing false witness against another, playing a (seemingly innocent) prank, and similar little things. Of course these actions are rarely innocent and are usually designed to trigger a strong reaction and ignite or escalate trouble with other people. More obvious and dangerous prices involve spying, public and obviously damaging lies or perjury to ruin a person's reputation, stealing (sometimes something as minor as a lock of hair or recently worn article of dirty clothing), meeting a particular person, passing on messages (often to demons, witches, or brigands), making a delivery, tampering with evidence, placing false evidence, threatening or beating up another person, to kidnapping, extortion and murder.

As a rule, the Wolf-Serpent is willing to live up to his end of the deal first, by providing information or help (threats, torture, murder or any of the things it might ask of another as noted above), and *trusts* the individual to fulfill the "favor" asked of him afterwards. Those who fail to fulfill the favor, whatever it may be, will be plagued by an escalating series of misfortune orchestrated by the Wolf-Serpent, or killed by it or one of its many evil henchmen or people who owe it a favor.

A clever person will ask what the favor is *before* receiving any information, advice or help from the demon, because the price is often more than many people are willing to pay. Leaving it open for later is asking for serious trouble. Likewise, the cruel and evil Wolf-Serpent always takes the most vicious, mean, destructive and extreme approach to accomplishing whatever is asked of it. This means saying something like, "I hate him, I want him out of my life," is likely to result in that person's murder, when all the character may have wanted was for that person to leave him alone, or leave town. Furthermore, it will hurt or kill anybody who gets in the way, which means innocent people are likely to be hurt.

Some rules of thumb for dealing with Wolf-Serpents:

Rule number one, *NEVER* go to a Wolf-Serpent for help in the first place! It's not worth it! Don't do it! It will only lead to moral decay, tragedy, sorrow, and death or ruin. Player characters of good alignment may drop to selfish then evil alignment if they willingly or regularly turn to a Wolf-Serpent for aid and advice, especially if the demon and his advice leads them to inadvertently hurt innocent people and/or murder and other acts of treachery and evil. Even the most simple and innocent "favor" is usually much more than it seems and will result in the hurting of others.

Rule number two, *NEVER* think that one can outsmart, outmaneuver or deceive a Wolf-Serpent. NEVER! The damned creature will twist and warp whatever good one may think they will accomplish into something evil or hurtful. If not, it is because the Wolf-Serpent is setting that person up for future trouble or the deed is setting some other, yet unseen, set of events into motion.

Rule number three, those who cheat, trick or renege on a Wolf-Serpent *will* pay. And the price will be a horrible one.

Rule number four, the only way to escape the wrath of a Wolf-Serpent is to destroy it. Slaying a Wolf-Serpent will not be easy.

Rule number five, forget rules 2-4 and don't ever turn to a Wolf-Serpent to begin with. They are evil incarnate!

The Wolf-Serpent NPC Villain
Also Known as The Poisonous Liar.
Race: Greater Archaic Demon
Alignment: Always miscreant or diabolic.
Attributes: I.Q. high intelligence, guile and cunning: 1D6+13, M.E. 1D6+13, M.A. 1D6+20, P.S. 1D6+20, P.P. 1D6+13, P.E. 1D6+13, P.B. 1D6, Spd 2D6+20 (double in wolf form); supernatural P.S.
M.D.C.: +3D6x10+88, but increase by 30% at night or in darkness (on S.D.C. worlds the demon has 2D6x10+16 Hit Points and 100 S.D.C.; increase both by 30% at night. A.R. 12 day or night).
Horror Factor: 14
Size: Typically sits coiled, raising the head to eye level with whomever the Wolf-Serpent is dealing with; 25-30 feet (7.6 to 9.1 m) long.
Weight: 600 pounds (315 kg)
Average Life Span: Uncertain, 3000+ years; probably immortal.
P.P.E.: 1D4x100 +130 plus P.E attribute number.
Natural Abilities: Fair speed and can hunt or fight without pause or exhaustion for 12 hours, climb 85%/80%, swim 98%, does not breathe air, can survive depths of up to 1500 feet (457 m), prowl 66% (+10% in animal form), track humanoids using sense of smell and vision 80% (+10% in animal form), nightvision is one mile (1.6 km), dimensionally teleport 45% (+25% at ley line nexus) and bio-regenerates 1D6 M.D. per melee round.

Knows all Languages: Magically understands and speaks all languages 98%, and can read Russian and Dragonese/Elven.

Poisonious Bite (special): The creature can elect to inject poisonous venom from its bite in any of its forms, snake, wolf, or demon. A nonvenomous bite does 2D6 M.D., a poisonous bite does 4D6 M.D. plus an additional 2D6 M.D. for 1D4 melee rounds from the poison. Damage and the continuing damage from the injected poison is cumulative from multiple bites. A successful save vs poison means the victim suffers 2D6 M.D. from the bite and 1D4 additional from the poison, but no additional poison damage over the next 1D4 melees. The Wolf-Serpent can use its poisonous bite as part of its attack *twice* per melee round.

Limited Metamorphosis (special): The Wolf-Serpent can turn into a large, dark colored rattlesnake or a large black wolf three times per 24 hours and it can be maintained for up to 12 hours at a time. Metamorphosis is possible during the day and night. The Wolf-Serpent prefers its natural appearance and uses metamorphosis only to spy, hunt and kill unsuspecting prey.

Limited Invulnerability (special): The Wolf-Serpent is impervious to normal S.D.C. weapons unless they are made of silver or the wood of a juniper or birch tree, in which case the weapon inflicts the equivalent S.D.C. damage as M.D. (i.e. a wooden staff that inflicts 2D6 S.D.C. would inflict 2D6 M.D. to the demon). The demon is also impervious to disease, poison, toxins, cold, and heat.

Man-made Mega-Damage weapons, M.D. fire, lightning and magic weapons, most spells and psionics do full damage. Millennium Tree weapons do double damage. The demon is not adversely affected by the light of day except that its spell potency is less.

Also see magic.

O.C.C.: Not applicable.

R.C.C. Skills: Land navigation 80%, wilderness survival 70%, basic math 98%, intelligence 90%, escape artist 80%, streetwise 85%, seduction 75%, and all lore 75% each, plus select three skills from each of the following skill categories: W.P. (any, including modern ones; equal to 4th level proficiency), Rogue, Science, and Communications or Technical; all get a +30% skill bonus, but proficiency in these skills does not advance. Also see Natural Abilities, above.

R.C.C. Combat: Attacks Per Melee: Six in demon form, four in wolf or snake form.

Damage: Bite (nonpoisonous) 2D6 M.D., poisonous bite 4D6 M.D. +2D6 M.D. from the poison for 1D4 melee rounds after the initial bite per each poison bite, tail or head strike/butt does M.D. equal to punch damage appropriate for the supernatural P.S., or by weapon or magic.

R.C.C. Bonuses: +3 on initiative, +3 to strike, +2 to parry, +2 to dodge, +6 to pull punch, +3 to roll with impact or fall, +3 to save vs magic, +4 to save vs illusions, +2 to save vs Horror Factor, and impervious to possession. R.C.C. bonuses are all in addition to any possible attribute bonuses.

Magic: All Wolf-Serpents possess the following spells as found in the *Rifts® RPG*: All level one spells plus Second Sight, Oracle, Create Magic Scroll, Amulet, Sanctum, Charismatic Aura, Invisibility: Simple, Invisibility: Superior, Eyes of Thoth, Ley Line Transmission, Commune with Spirits, Negate Magic, Dispel Magic Barrier, Mystic Portal, Constrain Being, Banishment, Control/Enslave Entity, Befuddle, Agony, Life Drain, Sickness, Spoil, Blind, Mute, Luck Curse, Minor Curse, Phobia Curse, Remove Curse, Healing Touch, and Restoration.

Plus the following from *Federation of Magic™*: Reflection, Armorbane, Enemy Mind, House of Glass, Wall of Defense, Wall of Not, Create Wood, Create Steel, Mend the Broken, Instill Knowledge, Sustain, Distant Voice, Power Weapon, Speed Weapon, Energize Spell, Implosion Neutralizer, Fireblast, Summon & Control Serpents, and Re-Open Gateway.

Spell potency is equal to a 6th level sorcerer at night, 4th level during the day.

Psionics: None

Enemies: All mortals, particularly humans and True Atlanteans (the latter being old enemies). They consider Gargoyles, Brodkil and "sub-demons" (as well as most lesser demons) to be inferior and subservient to them. They also love to trick, taunt, bug and get the best of the arrogant Whirlwind demons, a relatively easy task for the smarter, sneaky and cunning masters of lies and treachery. Wolf-Serpents have a field day with the War Camps of the Warlords, and are a constant source of insurrections, treachery, murder and sabotage. They even sometimes organize raids and attacks with Nalet against the Camps. Vampires are seen as a pestilence to be destroyed whenever discovered.

Allies: Many Wolf-Serpents prefer to work alone, although most have 2D4 lesser demons (typically Unclean, Il'ya or sub-demons, and/or humanoids) as henchmen and servants (they love to trick Whirlwinds into doing things for them). They also usually have connections with human and D-Bee criminals and low-lifes, as well as mortal "agents" — henchmen who directly serve the fiends as solicitors, thieves, assassins and servants. Such agents are always willing servants of evil. Then, of course, there are those lost souls who owe the Wolf-Serpent favors.

Wolf-Serpents involved with larger groups will often hold high positions within that organization, particularly when it involves espionage, undermining the enemy or assassination. They may also lead or ally themselves with other demons (lesser or greater), creatures of magic, powerful practitioners of magic, and other powerful beings with agendas that involve corruption, treachery and tormenting or playing with lesser beings.

Value: None

Habitat: Anywhere throughout Rifts Russia, China and much of Asia. Occasionally encountered in Poland, Germany and even Africa and North America. Although most maintain a secret lair, they like to be available for people who seek them out, so they usually have a second, known abode typically in the woods but near one or more communities.

Woodland Spirits

Although referred to by Russians as "spirits," these strange creatures are physical, flesh and blood beings more closely related to *Faerie Folk* than ghosts, entities or supernatural beings. All are *creatures of magic* and the majority are forest and nature creatures found only in the wilderness or near villages rather than in them, and rarely in or near modern cities. Of course, since most of Rifts Russia and Asia is wilderness, they are found everywhere.

Most of these "spirits" avoid demons because they dislike and/or fear them, or consider them to be dangerous rivals and chaotic destroyers (most Woodland Spirits appreciate beauty and nature and try to cultivate and preserve it most demons are destroyers who hate beauty and don't give a damn about nature). However, some of the more mischievous and evil Woodland Spirits consort or trade with demons, and some will join gangs and packs of evil D-Bees, bandits or demons.

As one might expect, most get along with Faerie Folk, who are probably cousins or distant relatives of some kind. However, Woodland Spirits are shy, elusive and mischievous beings who watch humanoids from afar and make contact or attack only when the desire strikes them or they feel like causing trouble. Most serious clashes result when the creature feels its life, friend or home is threatened. Unfortunately, "home" is often unrecognizable to humans (an old tree, moss covered log, meadow, pond, boulder, etc.), and a "friend" might include an animal, tree or favorite field of flowers.

Like Faerie Folk, Russian Woodland Spirits usually seem to be lost in their own business. By civilized standards, these bizarre *creatures of magic* seem quite insane, content on a vagabond life of mischief and wandering. Volatile in temperament, Woodland Spirits can exhibit extraordinary degrees of emotion and malice over the most trivial of matters (trivial to humans, that is). Like spoiled children, they do, say, and act as they damn well please and woe to the person that dares to interfere in their play or defile what they consider to be their home (house, farm, or stable to an old tree, pile of rocks, pond, field, meadow, etc.). It is during the vengeful temper tantrum of a perturbed Woodland Spirit where malice comes to the fore.

Their mischief stems from their selfish, carefree, wild, scatterbrained antics and lack of understanding about big people (or any non-Faerie Folk). They will pick fruits and vegetables and engage in food fights with one another, scatter and chase livestock, ride animals wildly throughout the night, tease dogs or twirl cats by their tails, and create a ruckus that could wake the dead all in the name of fun, not thinking or caring about the trouble such antics might cause for big people. Other favorite antics include moving or hiding objects (often into the pockets of unwitting bystanders and then tattling on them with accusations of thievery), picking pockets, tying shoelaces together, physically tampering with weapons, spoiling food or milk, howling, hooting, stomping or banging around, whispering lies, telling wild stories (all or mostly all untrue), tattling on others, frightening big people, misleading them so they get lost, pinching, pulling hair, stealing freshly baked bread, fruit pies, milk, jam, honey, candy and wine (the latter four they love with a passion), and other similar mischief.

They are far from harmless pranksters and can be positively deadly. Even under the most innocent of circumstances with the friendliest Woodland Spirit, a wise person will mind his tongue, avoid insults and beware of acts of seemingly selfless kindness. Furthermore, unlike Western Faerie Folk, many of the Russian Woodland Spirits are large, strong and cantankerous, if not downright mean. Even their harmless pranks can become deadly since they have little understanding of the human condition, laws, or morals. And many are intolerant of humans and humanoids who show no understanding or respect for nature.

On the other hand, the nicer and gentler Woodland Spirits will often attempt to cheer a sad person with gifts of fruit and flowers, mending their clothes, or by performing songs, dances and/or acrobatics. They have also been known to appear before travelers, adventurers and heroes to warn them of nearby danger (particularly about witches, necromancers and demons), to offer helpful news and information, to point lost travelers in the right direction, or even lead them back to the road, leading or chase them (gotta have their fun too) to food or water or herb, frightening away dangerous animals, and so on. Sometimes such acts of kindness are given as gifts other times there is a price. The price is usually one of three things: 1) Trade of food (ideally candy, honey or wine) or some trinket, 2) some silly action, like making the person sing, dance, stand on his head, or imitate an animal, or 3) do the Spirit a favor. Favors can involve just about anything from healing a hurt animal "friend," to building something, finding somebody, getting a particular article for trade (from food or drink, to clothing or building materials) to getting rid of a menace (settlers infringing on their homeland, D-Bee gang, dragon, witch, demon, etc.).

Although rumors of secret woodland treasure troves abound — these can be a trunk of gold, to a powerful magic item or items, to natural wonders — most Woodland Spirits have no need or desire for gold, jewels, weapons, magic items or any other valuables, and never keep them. They are more likely to keep a bag of candy, jar of honey, bottle of wine or vodka, a feathered hat and the occasional weapon or trinket that strikes their fancy. The latter item(s) might be magical or rare, but there will only be one to a handful of such items, which does not represent a treasure trove by any stretch of the imagination. As for natural wonders, many Woodland Spirits know about plants and nature and may know where to find certain medicinal herbs valuable or important to humans. If one is nice and lucky, he may be able to convince a woodland spirit to trade him a selection of herbs for something he can provide.

Note: Unlike Faerie Folk, there are no tell-tale mounds or circles of flowers or mushrooms to identify the home or range occupied by Woodland Spirits. On the other hand, Russian Spirits rarely gather in large groups, although a cluster of different spirits may inhabit the same part of the woods. Also note that traditional Faerie Folk are uncommon in Rifts Russia and virtually unheard of in Asia. Most Woodland Spirits are M.D. creatures, but *are* vulnerable to poison and disease. The damage inflicted by these things do the equivalent of half damage in M.D.C. while symptoms and penalties are unchanged.

Weapon Note: Woodland Spirits are minor Mega-Damage Creatures of Magic, so unless stated otherwise, most ordinary weapons and S.D.C. attacks do no damage to them. M.D. weapons, magic and psionic attacks inflict full damage.

Woodland Spirits of Rifts Russia

Domovoi
Polevoi
Leshii
Rusalka
Vodianoi
Russian Firebird
Spirit Wolf
Man-Wolf (a sort of Russian Werewolf)
Werebeasts
Vampires

Domovoi — House Spirit

According to Russian lore, the Domovoi is a "house goblin." Unlike goblins in other parts of the world, the Domovoi might be considered a miniature, dwarf-like Sasquatch or Big Foot and seems likely to be the Russian cousin to the more renowned and recognized Faerie Folk of the British Isles and other parts of the world. The creature stands two feet (0.6 m) tall and, except for his hands, feet and face, is covered in dark brown or black fur from head to toe. The face looks extremely human with beard, moustache and bushy eyebrows. The hair on the head and face is the same as the fur covered body, except that it grows longer, creating a bushy beard and moustache and an unruly mane of hair. Their hands are small and delicate, while their feet are furry on top and the bottoms hard like dry leather. Males and females look nearly identical, except that the female is minus the facial hair.

Although a Domovoi can be mean and spiteful toward those they don't like, and even downright murderous, most are gentle beings who come to like and care for the humanoids whose house they invade. Most consider themselves to be (an unofficial) part of the family, with the house being as much theirs as the humans or D-Bees who built it.

A benevolent protector of the home/farm and family ,it often performs simple tasks and chores to help around the house or farm; i.e. milk the cow, spin wool, chop wood, pitch hay, gather fruit and vegetables, sweep the floor, wash dishes, feed and watch over pets and livestock, extinguish small but potentially dangerous fires, and attempt to frighten away animal predators, as well as warn the family of danger by making loud noises. Such warnings typically involve stirring up the animals and making them squeal and howl, banging on or slamming a door, beating on or knocking down pots or pans, ringing bells (most farms have a bell or ringer to alert workers in the field and to announce visitors), and so on. They may also catch mice and get rid of other pests, as well as gather small piles of food, such as berries, nuts, herbs, or honey for the enjoyment and head of "their" family. The "big" inhabitants should reciprocate by leaving a bowl of porridge, soup, stew and sweets for their "House Guardian Spirit."

Although they avoid contact with adults, Domovoi often appear to babies and children. The furry little spirits are usually very maternal and protective of youngsters, especially females, and will play with and defend children. Domovoi are infamous for keeping watch over children and helping to keep them out of harm's way. Thus, they will pull them away from wells or the edge of a river (or other danger), help them find their way home, protect them from wild animals, and even from witches, demons, vile Faerie Folk, and wicked beings, both human and supernatural. This helpful, protective nature can also manifest itself in dangerous ways. A parent, relative or friend who is neglectful or openly abusive (acts of cruelty and brutality above and beyond a spanking or harsh words), is usually disliked, if not hated by the Domovoi. This means that individual will be targeted by the Domovoi for pranks and acts of aggression such as a thorn or barb slipped into a shoe, tripping or pushing the individual down the stairs, breaking or hiding his or her personal possessions, a glass or bottle of booze being tipped over and spilled, secretly tear holes in pockets, socks or sacks, as well as the theft of small things like a knife, shoelaces, compass, etc. If the hated individual is responsible for serious injury to, or the death of, the child, the house spirit may try to kill him. This can be done by causing him to trip or pushed down a well, stairs, out of a hay loft, etc, or be lead into a pack of animals or demons, and so on. The cause of death often looks like an accident, and Domovoi *never* kill in obvious ways, such as slice the throat while the hated one sleeps.

It is said one or two Domovoi inhabit every wilderness home and a third of the houses in Russian cities. However, truth be told, one or two of these woodland creatures can be found in only about 30-40% of the wilderness homes and about one tenth of those in and around cities or large towns. Still, these are fairly large numbers suggesting that there could be a million or more scattered throughout Russia and Asia. At least 75% of the Russian peasants regard the little creature as good or a shy but likeable and welcome house pets. By contrast, about half the city dwellers consider them pests.

Most Domovoi are rarely seen, and when they are, they're glimpsed only for a second or two, or their presence is known only from their small acts of kindness (cleaning, etc.) and/or by of candy, nuts and fruit left as gifts — the more at home, welcomed, and happy the Domovoi, the more the creature will do for the big people who share its home. They easily avoid direct contact with big people because they are masters of stealth, can turn invisible at will, and are small in stature. Most sleep under the stove, or bed, or other large, heavy piece of furniture where it's relatively warm and cozy (some prefer the attic, cellar, or barn, chicken coop, or shed). Most will have 1D4 hiding places, often under floor boards, where they hide treasured possessions such as nuts, candy, feathers, cap or hat, toys, and the occasional dagger, Vibro-Blade and other stolen or found odds and ends.

Domovoi Non-Player Character or Villain

Also known as the House Guardian.

Player Note: If desirable, the Game Master can allow a Domovoi as an optional player character, however, the character will be extremely limited in its range of skills and abilities and the vast majority (95%) of Domovoi dislike and abstain from adventure. They are by nature, "house" spirits and prefer to live work and play at and around one particular, inhabited (usually by a family or group of people) home or farmstead — most stay in one place for generations. The Domovoi (pronounced Dom o voy) has little need or interest in money/credits/gold or other valuables, nor magic items or modern technology. They are simple free spirits who care about people (especially other Domovoi and children) and finding peace and happiness.

Race: Woodland Spirit/creature of magic.

Alignment: Any, but the majority are unprincipled (40%) or anarchist (30%).

Attributes: I.Q. low to average human intelligence but alert, clever and compassionate: 1D4+6, M.E. 1D6+10, M.A. 1D6+10, P.S. 1D6+8, P.P. 1D6+10, P.E. 2D6+10, P.B. 1D6+6, Spd 2D6+10; supernatural P.S.

M.D.C.: P.E. number +1D4x10 (on S.D.C. worlds the Domovoi has 3D6 +P.E. number for Hit Points and 4D6 S.D.C.; A.R. 10).

Horror Factor: 9

Size: Two feet (0.6 m) tall.

Weight: 20-40 pounds (11.3 to 18 kg)

Average Life Span: Uncertain, 1000+ years; may be immortal.

P.P.E.: 6D6x2 +P.E. attribute number.

Natural Abilities: Fair speed and can run or work without pause or exhaustion for four hours. They can also leap up to 6 feet (1.8 m) high and lengthwise, prowl 70%, climb 90%/80%, swim 80%, can hold its breath for 4+1D4 minutes, survive depths of up to 300 feet (91.5 m), track humanoids 50%, track animals 60%, nightvision 300 feet (91.5 m, but is not nocturnal), bio-regenerate 1D4 M.D. per hour, see the invisible, and turn invisible at will as often and for as long as it likes, but typically only uses invisibility to avoid detection, sneak away and hide.

Knows all Languages: Magically understands and speaks all languages 75%, but cannot read.

Limited Metamorphosis (special): The Domovoi can turn into a brown or grey house cat or small dog two times per 24 period for as long as two hours at a time. Metamorphosis is possible day or night and the animal usually looks like the family pet.

Also see magic.

O.C.C.: Not applicable.

R.C.C. Skills: Horsemanship (general), land navigation 80%, wilderness survival 80%, plus select two skills from each of the following skill categories: W.P. Ancient Weapons, Domestic, Technical (lore only), and Wilderness; all get a +15% skill bonus, but these skills do not advance. Also see Natural Abilities, above.

R.C.C. Combat: Attacks Per Melee: Four

Damage: Bite 1D6 S.D.C., head-butt, punch or kick M.D. varies with supernatural P.S., or by weapon or magic.

R.C.C. Bonuses: +3 on initiative, +1 to strike, +2 to parry, +3 to dodge, +3 to pull punch, +3 to roll with impact or fall, +6 to save vs poison and disease, +2 to save vs Horror Factor. R.C.C. bonuses are all in addition to any possible attribute bonuses.

Magic: All Domovoi can cast the following spells, provided they have sufficient P.P.E.: Chameleon, Sense Evil, Sense Magic, Repel Animals, and Escape, plus the following as described in *Federation of Magic™:* Lantern Light, Cleanse, Throwing Stones, Mystic Fulcrum, Mend the Broken, Influence the Beast and Life Source. Spell potency is equal to a 3rd level sorcerer.

Psionics: None

Enemies: None per se, other than those who threaten it, its house or its family and friends. Dislikes all demons and evil people, from humans to fellow Woodland Spirits.

Allies: Others of its kind, most other Woodland Spirits and other members of the household.

Value: None, per se, although a Necromancer may have some use for it.

Habitat: Occasionally grasslands and woodlands out in the wild, but prefers rural areas where it can live on a farm, house or in a small village. As House Guardians, most Domovoi adopt a house and its family as their own and live there for generations.

Leshii — Forest Spirit

The Leshii are giant, belligerent, Sasquatch-like creatures known to whistle, grunt, bellow, shout and threaten. Most humans, especially city-folk and members of the Warlords' Camps, fear them and insist they represent a dangerous force that has no love for humans. Old Believers, Bogatyrs, druids, huntsmen and others who understand the woods well, know better. Most Leshii are good natured and have a wonderful sense of humor — not that most humans, humanoids or demons appreciate it. Leshii see themselves as the protectors of the forest, and have a profound love for nature, animals and life. Consequently, they frown upon humans and other life forms that recklessly or wantonly destroy wildlife or abuse the land. It is such defilers

and miscreants who suffer the wrath of these big, walking mounds of fur and muscle, and who return to civilization with stories about scary encounters with the insane and savage Leshii (and/or other Woodland Spirits). Warriors who lay waste to the land, polluters, lumbermen who cut down the forests without any effort for conservation, sportsmen who think slaughter is fun (and do not eat and use all that they kill), and black-hearted fiends who bring evil and unnatural forces to the land are all targeted by the Leshii.

If the villain(s) is an evil destroyer, the Leshii, armed with its sense of justice, has no qualms about slaying him and all who follow in his path. However, the lumbering nature spirit is not a bloodthirsty monster and is usually content with chasing such people out of its forest, or frustrating them to such a degree that they leave of their own accord. To this end, the Leshii engage is vandalism, theft, and sabotage, as well as scare tactics and mischief. They love to pull pranks that confuse and confound. One favorite tactic is to lead an enemy or pursuers around and around on a merry chase for hours (sometimes days), only to have them arrive back where they started with no sign of the Leshii at the end of trail. They also love to taunt and lead antagonists deep into the forest where they get lost and spend many worrisome days trying to find their way out (typically made all the more frightening by strange sounds and animal cries secretly made by the Leshii). Other tricks and tactics involve chasing away animal prey, smashing traps, freeing trapped animals, causing mischief and chases disguised as an animal, rendering vehicles inoperable, stealing equipment or supplies and hiding them high up in trees, leading people into mud pits, bogs, and swamps, setting traps where one steps into animal feces or it is dropped on his head, and so on. Like the Domovoi, the Leshii are especially compassionate toward children, and will often guide lost little ones to safety and protect them from the dangers of the deep forest, including demons.

Leshii are roughly humanoid in appearance, although their heavy legs and hindquarters are those of a goat, complete with cloven hooves and short tail. The spirit stands over ten feet (3 m) tall, is covered head to toe in shaggy, light brown to black fur, has a human face with moustache and long pointed beard, glowing red eyes, and short thick horns. Only one out of every eight is a female, minus beard and moustache.

The forest giant, despite its mass and size, is said to move through the forest as quiet as a mouse and wields powerful earth magic that gives it complete reign over forest animals. They are often seen in the distance as cheerful giants whistling or singing loudly, but can vanish in the blink of an eye. In addition to music, the Leshii likes to startle human intruders with loud handclaps, laughter, barking, howling, and other sounds. Many are the reports of the creatures wailing and screaming after finding a favorite tree chopped down, or favorite stream dammed up, or a woodland creature slain or tortured for sport, or a friend or child injured or slain. Their favorite weapon is a huge tree branch, sizable sapling or small tree used as a club or cudgel (inflicts 2D6 M.D. plus the usual punch damage from the Leshii's supernatural P.S.).

Leshii Non-Player Character or Villain

Also known as the Master of the Forest and Guardian of the Beasts.

Player Note: If desirable, the Game Master can allow a Leshii as an optional player character, however, the character will be extremely limited in its range of skills and abilities and the vast majority (95%) cannot tolerate prolonged war or stays away from their beloved forests. Grasslands like the Steppe are too open to feel completely comfortable, and cities are horrid to these are forest creatures. However, unlike the Domovoi, the Leshii (pronounced les she) enjoy wandering, combat and pitting their cunning in games against others. Furthermore, most have no love for demons, witches, necromancers or other evil and destructive creatures, and will consider joining forces with others to rid the forest of such pestilence. Unfortunately, the Leshii will never accept or use modern weapons or technology, nor can they understand or appreciate the laws, rules and (too often conflicting) morals of human beings. They feel trapped and alone in towns and even dislike the confines of small villages. Likewise, most humans cannot accept these giants as anything but dangerous monsters, and regard even the most heroic Leshii as a dangerous and savage animal that could pounce and kill at any moment. The nature spirit has little need or interest in money/credits/gold or other valuables, nor magic items or modern technology. They are simple free spirits who care about nature, forests, animals and personal freedom.

Race: Woodland Spirit and creature of magic.

Alignment: Any, but the majority are unprincipled (40%) or anarchist (30%).

Attributes: I.Q. low to average human intelligence but alert, clever and compassionate: 1D4+8, M.E. 1D6+8, M.A. 1D6+8, P.S. 2D6+30, P.P. 1D6+14, P.E. 2D6+14, P.B. 1D6+6, Spd 2D6+30; supernatural P.S.

M.D.C.: P.E. number +4D4x10 (on S.D.C. worlds the Leshii has 2D4x10 +P.E. number for Hit Points and 2D4x10 S.D.C.; A.R. 10).

Horror Factor: 12

Size: 10-12 feet (3-3.6 m) tall (according to legend, the Leshii could be as small as a blade of grass or as tall as the biggest tree).

Weight: 600-1000 pounds (270-450 kg)

Average Life Span: Uncertain, 1000+ years; may be immortal.

P.P.E.: 1D4x100 +P.E. attribute number.

Natural Abilities: Good speed and can run or work without pause or exhaustion for eight hours. The giant can also leap up to 15 feet (2.6 m) high and 20 feet (6 m) lengthwise (increase by 50% with a running start). Other abilities include prowl 65%, climb 90%/85%, swim 80%, can hold its breath for 6+1D6 minutes, survive depths of up to 300 feet (91.5 m), track humanoids 50% (+15% in animal form), track animals 90% (+5% in animal form), nightvision 600 feet (181 m), see the invisible, impervious to normal cold, takes half damage from cold based magic, and bio-regenerate 3D6 M.D. per hour.

Knows all Languages: Magically understands and speaks all languages 70%, but cannot read.

Limited Metamorphosis (special): The Leshii can turn into a number of different animals, including the fox, wolf, hare, horse, pig (domestic) or wild boar, and most medium to large birds, from pheasant, goose or duck to falcon, magpie, or rooster. The animal metamorphosis can be performed four times per 24 hours and maintained for as long as the spirit desires. Once per day, the giant can assume the form of an ordinary looking, elderly human. This guise is the least frequently used transformation and done to walk among men. It is said those who gaze deeply into the eyes the old man will see the Leshii for its true identity.

Also see magic.

O.C.C.: Not applicable.

R.C.C. Skills: Horsemanship (knight and exotic animal), land navigation 98%, wilderness survival 98%, W.P. Blunt (equal to 5th level), all animal, farm and plant lore, plus select three skills from each of the following skill categories: Domestic and Wilderness; all selected skills get a +35% bonus, but these skills do not advance. Also see Natural Abilities, above.

R.C.C. Combat: Attacks Per Melee: Six

Damage: Bite 4D6 S.D.C., head-butt and punch M.D. varies with supernatural P.S., 2D6 M.D. plus supernatural P.S. punch damage from kick or giant cudgel, or by weapon or magic.

R.C.C. Bonuses: +3 on initiative, +4 to strike, +2 to parry, +3 to dodge, +5 to pull punch, +2 to roll with impact or fall, +2 to save vs poison, +8 to save vs disease, +4 to save vs Horror Factor. R.C.C. bonuses are all in addition to any possible attribute bonuses.

Magic: All Leshii can cast the following spells, provided they have sufficient P.P.E.: Blinding Flash, Thunderclap, Heavy Breathing, Fingers of the Wind, Chameleon, Shadow Meld, Reduce Self (down to six inches), and all summoning spells involving animals, plus the following as described in *Federation of Magic*: Cleanse, Influence the Beast and Tame Beast. Spell potency is equal to a 5th level sorcerer.

Psionics: M.E. x3 for I.S.P. Psi-powers include: Mind Block, Dowsing, Resist Fatigue, Resist Hunger, Resist Thirst and Healing Touch.

Enemies: Anybody who threatens them or the forest. The War-lords and their War Camps are seen as warring savages and destroyers, as are most demons, other than those of Wood, Earth and Water. Dislikes humans in general and sees them as reckless, careless, selfish and destructive.

Allies: Others of its kind, most other Woodland Spirits, Mega-Steeds, animals in general. In addition to protecting animals and the forest, the Leshii often come to the aid and defense of other Woodland Spirits and small children.

Value: Varies, approx. 800-2000 credits as component parts. The horns are used in magic potions that impart control over animals and healing potions, plus Necromancers can always find various uses for the bones of these formidable giants.

Habitat: Occasionally found in or near the Steppe, other grass-lands, farmlands or villages, but typically found only in the expansive northern and northwestern forests that cover most of the northern half of Rifts Russia. Rarely found in China or Asia, but is sometimes reported in the forests of Scandinavia and northern Poland and Germany.

Polevoi — Field Spirit

The Polevoi are anarchist and spiteful spirits of the field who have little tolerance for humans or stupidity, and are known for playing mean and often deadly jokes. They are bold, arrogant and self-absorbed. They are easily provoked and quick to lash out in some mean or violent way.

The Polevoi appear as small humanoids the color of the Earth (black or dark brown), with long stringy grass on the top of their heads or long leafy green hair, brown eyes and clothes woven from vines. They stand only four feet (1.2 m) tall and sometimes carry a walking stick, sickle or scythe as a weapon — some-times such items are enchanted. They may also use the bone weapons of the Necromancer. Known as the Midday Spirits, they are strongest during the hours of noon to 3 P.M.

Polevoi Player Character or Villain

Also known as the Master of the Field and the Midday Spirit; females are known as "Poludnitsa."

Player Note: If acceptable to the Game Master, he or she can allow a Polevoi as an optional player character. This character will tend to be fickle, bombastic and independent to the point of causing trouble for his companions. Polevoi (pronounced pole-voy) act like spoiled children who frequently say and do as they please, wander off on their own, insult and annoy, and pro-voke brawls and conflict with their condescending and haughty words and attitude. Although limited in their range of skills and abilities, most make good scouts, spies and thieves. They prefer grasslands like the Steppe and wide open spaces. The longer they stay in a village, town or city, the more irritable and mis-chievous these troublemakers become. They have no under-standing of human laws and etiquette, and consider themselves above "human law." Consequently, short visits to a village and civilization are recommended; 1-4 days would not be too pain-ful. Moreover, the Polevoi's free-spirited, selfish and anarchist nature just doesn't mix well in groups — the Polevoi like to do as they please and cause mischief no matter what.

On the other hand, they are resourceful and adventurous be-ings who are not afraid of anybody (even when they should be). They are also reasonably good fighters and users of magic. Fur-thermore, most have no love for demons, witches, necromancers or other evil and destructive creatures. The nature spirit has little need or interest in money/credits/gold or other valuables, or modern technology, but is attracted to valuable gems and magic items. They are chaotic and troublemaking free spirits who care more about themselves, playing jokes and causing trouble for others, than anything else. Having a Polevoi in the group is probably more trouble than it is worth.

Race: Woodland Spirit and creature of magic.

Alignment: Any, but the majority are anarchist (55%), miscre-ant (20%), or unprincipled (10%).

Attributes: I.Q. average human intelligence but alert, clever and tricky: 1D4+9, M.E. 1D6+7, M.A. 1D6+7, P.S. 2D6+20, P.P. 1D6+16, P.E. 2D6+16, P.B. 1D6+9, Spd 2D6+50 (double during midday); supernatural P.S.

M.D.C.: P.E. number +2D4x10, double during midday (on S.D.C. worlds the Polevoi has 1D4x10 +P.E. number for Hit Points and 1D4x10 S.D.C.; double during midday. A.R. 12).

Horror Factor: 9

Size: Males are four feet (1.2 m) tall, females are four to four feet, six inches (1.2 to 1.3 m) tall.

Weight: 70-100 pounds (32-45 kg).

Average Life Span: Uncertain, 1000+ years; may be immortal.

P.P.E.: 2D4x10 +50

Natural Abilities: Fast and can run or play without pause or exhaustion for eight hours. The impish spirit can also leap up to 12 feet (3.6 m) high and 18 feet (5.4 m) lengthwise (increase by 30% with a running start). Other natural abilities include prowl 55%, climb 70%/65%, swim 70%, can hold its breath for 2+1D6 minutes, survive depths of up to 300 feet (61.5 m), track humanoids 50% (+15% in animal form), track animals 70% (+15% in animal form), nightvision 100 feet (30.5 m), see the invisible, impervious to normal cold, takes half damage from cold based magic, and bio-regenerates 3D6 M.D. per hour.

Knows all Languages: Magically understands and speaks all languages 70%, but cannot read.

Limited Metamorphosis (special): The Polevoi can turn into a hare/rabbit or squirrel, and during noon to 3 p.m. he can turn into a magpie/raven. The animal metamorphosis can be performed four times per 24 hours and maintained for as long as the spirit desires.

Also see magic.

O.C.C.: Not applicable.

R.C.C. Skills: Horsemanship (knight and exotic animal), land navigation 90%, wilderness survival 95%, all animal, farm and plant lore, plus select three skills from each of the following skill categories: W.P. (4th level equivalent), Rogue and Wilderness; all selected skills get a +25% bonus, but these skills do not advance. Also see Natural Abilities, above.

R.C.C. Combat: Attacks Per Melee: Five

Damage: Bite 2D4 S.D.C., head-butt, punch and kick M.D. varies with supernatural P.S., or by weapon or magic.

R.C.C. Bonuses: +4 on initiative, +3 to strike, +2 to parry, +4 to dodge, +3 to pull punch, +2 to roll with impact or fall, +3 to save vs poison, +6 to save vs disease, +5 to save vs Horror Factor. R.C.C. bonuses are all in addition to any possible attribute bonuses.

Magic: All Polevoi can cast the following spells, provided they have sufficient P.P.E.: Globe of Daylight, Befuddle, Concealment, Detect Concealment, Fingers of the Wind, Chameleon, Reduce Self (down to six inches), Repel Animals, and all level one Earth Warlock spells, Wither Plants, Grow Plants, Mend Stone, and Travel Through Walls, starting on page 68 of *Rifts® Conversion Book One*. Spell potency is equal to a 3rd level sorcerer most of the day, but 6th level potency between the hours of noon and 3 p.m.

Psionics: M.E. x2 for I.S.P. Psi-powers include: Mind Block, Presence Sense, Impervious to Fire, Impervious to Poison, and Telekinetic Push.

Enemies: Anybody who threatens them or the area they consider their home. Actually, anybody who annoys them. The Warlords and their War Camps are seen as troublesome, disruptive, noisy brutes who are fun to torment and tease, as are demons, other than those of Wood, Earth and Water. Finds humans, in general, annoying and equally fun to scare, annoy and play with.

Allies: Others of its kind and most other Woodland Spirits. It frequently comes to the defense of other Woodland Spirits. The Polevoi can be nice and helpful, sometimes coming to the aid of farmers, huntsmen, heroes, maidens and children.

Value: None per se.

Habitat: Occasionally found in woodlands and cities, but typically encountered in the Steppe, other grasslands, farmlands and fields of Rifts Russia, Poland and, to a lesser degree, the plains of Mongolia and China. Polevoi are rare compared to Domovoi or even Leshii.

Rusalka — Air Spirit

Rusalka appear as beautiful young maidens with pale skin and long, flowing, light brown or green hair down to their feet. The hair is usually decorated with wildflowers and/or a garland of flowers. They are dark green skinned and their beauty is alluring and seductive. These spirits seem playful and cheerful, often giggling and laughing as they play in a field of flowers, swing from the branches of trees or swim in a pond. However, they are cruel and malicious spirits that like to tease, trick, torment and kill humans and other intelligent creatures. Fools who treat them harshly or cruelly will be hurt or killed. Those who make them angry will suffer cruel tricks and meanspirited retribution.

They are nocturnal creatures and especially cranky and vile when woken prematurely from their sleep. However, the Rusalka can come out during the day or evening and are especially fond of spring rainshowers and thunderstorms where they can be seen dancing in the rain. All Rusalka are seductresses who like to toy with the emotions, love and lust of mortal males. Unfortunately, they often rob and kill those they seduce (see allies & enemies for more details).

Although they have little use for money, gems or valuables, these petty and envious spirits often covet the things others hold dear, and may try to steal them. Jewelry, expensive knick-knacks (small sculptures, crosses, toys, etc.) scarves and even photographs are the main targets of the Rusalka, along with small magic items, particularly charms, rings and other types of pretty jewelry.

Rusalka Player Character & Villain

Also known as the Forest Seductress.

Player Note: If acceptable to the Game Master, he or she can allow a Rusalka as an optional player character, but such cruel and petty creatures are not recommended as player characters. The Rusalka is best suited as a villain — not quite a demon, but close. This character tends to be fickle, petty, spiteful, jealous and cruel. They do as they please, belittle others, and laugh at those who try to curb their amorous nature. They lie, steal, cheat, seduce and torture. Rusalka have little regard for humanoid life or the feelings of any intelligent creature. They have a passing respect for nature, their fellow Woodland Spirits, Old Believers and Witches, but that's about all. Most are evil and nothing but trouble.

Race: Woodland Spirit and creature of magic.

Alignment: Any, but the majority are miscreant (50%), anarchist (35%) or diabolic (10%).

Attributes: I.Q. low to average human intelligence but alert, cunning and treacherous: 1D4+7, M.E. 1D6+7, M.A. 1D6+14, P.S. 2D6+21, P.P. 1D6+14, P.E. 2D6+14, P.B. 1D6+14, Spd 2D6+30 (double at night); supernatural P.S.

M.D.C.: P.E. number +2D4x10, double between midnight and dawn (on S.D.C. worlds the Rusalka has 1D4x10 +P.E. number for Hit Points and 1D4x10 S.D.C.; double late at night. A.R. 11).

Horror Factor: 10

Size: Six feet (1.8 m) tall; always appears as a beautiful woman.

Weight: 100-150 pounds (45 to 67.5 kg).

Average Life Span: Uncertain, 1000+ years; may be immortal.

P.P.E.: 2D4x10 +42

Natural Abilities: Fair to good speed and can run or play without pause or exhaustion for eight hours. The spirit can also leap up to 12 feet (3.6 m) high and 20 feet (6 m) lengthwise (increase by 30% with a running start), swim like a fish 98, can breathe underwater, survive any depth, track humanoids 50%, climb 95%/95%, nightvision one mile (1.6 km), see the invisible, impervious to normal cold, takes half damage from cold based magic, and bio-regenerates 1D6 M.D. per minute.

Knows all Languages: Magically understands and speaks all languages 80%, but cannot read.

Limited Metamorphosis (special): The Rusalka can turn into a seemingly normal, long haired, beautiful human maiden with sparkling eyes. The metamorphosis can be performed four times per 24 hours and maintained for as long as the spirit desires. However, her true, inhuman nature is revealed in the light of the full moon.

Also see magic.

O.C.C.: Not applicable.

R.C.C. Skills: Horsemanship (general and exotic animal), land navigation 95%, wilderness survival 95%, acrobatics and gymnastics 95%, seduction 80%, and dance 98%, plus select two skills from each of the following skills categories: W.P. (4th level equivalent) and Rogue; all selected skill get a +30% bonus, but these skills do not advance. Also see Natural Abilities, above.

R.C.C. Combat: Attacks Per Melee: Five

Damage: Bite 1D6 S.D.C., head-butt, punch and kick M.D. varies with supernatural P.S., or by weapon or magic.

R.C.C. Bonuses: +3 on initiative, +4 to strike, +3 to parry, +4 to dodge, +4 to pull punch, +1 to roll with impact or fall, +7 to save vs poison and disease, +7 to save vs Horror Factor. R.C.C. bonuses are all in addition to any possible attribute bonuses.

Magic: All Rusalka can cast the following spells, provided they have sufficient P.P.E.: Befuddle, Concealment, Detect Concealment, Chameleon, Fingers of the Wind, Float in Air, Levitate, Ignite Fire, Fuel Flame, Fire Bolt, Invisibility: Simple, Energy Disruption, Impervious to Energy, Escape, Fly as the Eagle, Spoil, Water to Wine, and Mask of Deceit. Spell potency is equal to a 3rd level sorcerer most of the day, but from midnight to dawn, is equal to a 6th level sorcerer.

Psionics: M.E. x2 for I.S.P. Psi-powers include: Mind Block, Empathy, Sense Time and Empathic Transmission.

Enemies: Anybody who threatens them or tries to stop them from doing as they desire. They also like teasing and tor-

menting humans and D-Bees in general, particularly heroes, adventurers and travelers. These seductive and murderous female spirits love to target the Warlords' soldiers, seduce them, have their way with them and then, the lucky ones are left naked (their armor and clothing tossed in a river or pond, or placed up in a tree), and the unlucky ones (at least half) slain — treachery and backstabbing are these spirits' trademark. Rusalka hate Water demons (jealous rivalry) and dislike most others, but frequently befriend and associate with Kaluga Hags, Nalet, Frost demons and Morozko. **Note:** The Rusalka's two favorite ways to kill is to strike without warning, usually while her victim is seduced (stabbing and throat-cutting are common), and drowning her victims.

Allies: Others of its kind, some demons, and mean and wicked Woodland Spirits and people, but especially Kaluga Hags, Nalets (who are sometimes their lovers), Morozko Frost Demons, Koshchei the Deathless Ones, Wolf-Serpents, witches and evil practitioners of magic.

The evil spirit enjoys watching people struggle and suffer in traps and trouble, but may come to the aid or defense of cute and attractive animals. Petty and envious, this foul spirit hates beautiful women above all others. Consequently, attractive females are often the target of their most vicious attacks. Rusalka will try to ruin a woman's life (often by trying to seduce her lover), damage her reputation, steal from her and try to hurt, torture, disfigure or even kill her. Virile and powerful males, on the other hand, are the target of the Rusalka's mercurial affections. Ironically, while the demonic spirit will be frustrated and angry from rejection, it rarely lashes out with murderous rage, instead seeing that individual as a challenge and prize to be won. However, those who have slept with a Rusalka and then reject, anger or displease her, may be slain or tormented. On the other hand, they are just as likely to be ignored, as if they never existed — although if the spurned lover tries to win the spirit back or pester her in any way, she is likely to make his life a living hell, or slay him.

Value: None per se.

Habitat: Found mainly in woodlands and near the banks of rivers, lakes, streams, ponds and mills throughout what was once the Ukraine and southern Russia. They are much less common in the tundra, Mongolia and China. A Rusalka may live near and visit a village or city (usually to tease, rob and torment its residents), but rarely lives among mortals.

Vodianoi — Water Spirit

The Vodianoi is a treacherous and murderous water spirit similar in temperament to the Leshii, only more murderous and cruel. Most Vodianoi appear as an ugly, old man clad in a loincloth or rags. The creature has a human head and form, but the skin is pale white, the stomach bloated, and the body usually covered in slime. The hands are the paws of a wolf, the eyes are pale blue, and the beard and hair are a shaggy, tangled mass of green. They are water spirits and usually encountered in and around swamps, deep lakes and other bodies of water. In fact, the Vodianoi are said to live in swamps and on the floor of lakes and rivers at their deepest point (but never oceans). By contrast, female Vodianoi (only one in ten are female) are usually thin, gaunt and pale, also with a long green tangle of hair.

The Warlords and the soldiers of their War Camps are seen as despoilers and haughty invaders unwilling to submit or show respect to the spirits of nature. Consequently, the Vodianoi target them regularly, tricking and attacking small squads and encampments, capsizing boats and drowning the unsuspecting.

A small percentage of Vodianoi are selfish and even good. Good and aberrant evil spirits tend to be more disciplined, caring and have a pleasant appearance. These males are still fat, but have a jolly appearance and disposition. Most have long green or white hair and tangled beards that run down to their waists. Females are thin and beautiful, with long, wet hair that hangs below their waists. Most wear nice clothes or decorative armor. Unlike their evil kin, these free spirits help fishermen, save drowning people and help protect children and maidens. Unfortunately, only one in 500 is a good or civilized Vodianoi. For their own protection, they often gather in small underwater communities of 2D4x10 members.

Vodianoi Non-Player Character & Villain

Also known as the Swamp Demon, Evil Water Spirit and Vodianoi.

Player Note: This character is a malevolent, murderous being as evil and vile as any demon, and not suitable as a player character, unless it is one of the rare good or anarchist ones (and acceptable to the Game Master). Even a good or selfish water spirit tends to be easily provoked, cocky and quick to fight. Like most Faerie Folk and Woodland Spirits, all Vodianoi tend to be self-absorbed free spirits with little concern or understanding about mere mortals or the laws of men. They tend to do as they please and abuse those they dislike. Anarchist spirits will cheat, lie, steal, batter, torture and kill with little thought about the consequences its actions may have on the group. However, they have a respect for raw power, magical power and cunning, so they can be impressed and held in line to some degree by mages, heroes and warriors who win their respect. They also respect most of their fellow Woodland Spirits, Old Believers, Mystic Kuznya, and greater demons. Most are evil and nothing but trouble.

Race: Woodland Spirit and a creature of magic.

Alignment: Any, but the majority are miscreant (40%), diabolic (30%) or anarchist (20%); and most are ruthless and cruel.

Attributes: I.Q. low to average human intelligence but alert, cunning and treacherous: 1D6+6, M.E. 1D6+6, M.A. 1D6+6, P.S. 2D6+18, P.P. 1D6+12, P.E. 2D6+12, P.B. 1D6+6, Spd on dry ground: 2D6+6 (increase by 50% at night), speed swimming: 2D6+40 (increase by 50% at night), a minimum of 30 mph (48 km/26 knots); supernatural P.S.

M.D.C.: P.E. number +2D4x10, double at night (on S.D.C. worlds the spirit has 1D4x10 +P.E. number for Hit Points and 1D6x10 S.D.C.; double both at night. A.R. 12 day and night).

Horror/Awe Factor: 7 for good ones, 12 for evil ones.

Size: Males stand 4-5 feet (1.2 to 1.5 m) tall and potbellied. Females are 5-6 feet (1.5 to 1.8 m) tall and thin.

Weight: 150-250 pounds (67.5 to 76 kg).

Average Life Span: Uncertain, 1000+ years; may be immortal.

P.P.E.: 2D4x10 +60

Natural Abilities: Fair speed on dry land, especially at night, but amazing speed when swimming. The Vodianoi can swim or fight without pause or exhaustion for eight hours. They swim flawlessly and faster than most fish 98%, can dive up to 1000 feet (305 m), can breathe underwater, survive any

depth, and can also climb 60%/50%, see in muddy and murky water, see in the infrared spectrum of light, nightvision one mile (1.6 km), see the invisible, impervious to normal cold, take half damage from water or cold based magic, and bio-regenerate 2D6 M.D. per minute. **Note:** Fire based attacks do double damage.

Knows all Languages: Magically understands and speaks all languages 80%, but cannot read.

Limited Metamorphosis (special): These demonic spirits of nature can transform into a human of average appearance twice per night, but the palms of their hands, skin and clothes are always moist, and the creature always leaves a trail of wet footprints wherever it goes regardless of the form it takes. Furthermore, this transformation cannot be maintained in the light of day (yes, a Globe of Daylight will reveal a metamorphed Water Demon for what it really is). The creature can also turn into a merman/mermaid with the upper body being a potbellied human and the lower half that of a giant fish. This one can be done twice per 24 hour period, day or night. Double swimming speed when transformed into this man-fish form.

Also see magic.

O.C.C.: Not applicable.

R.C.C. Skills: Underwater and sea navigation 95%, wilderness survival 95%, plus select two skills from each of the following skill categories: W.P. (4th level equivalent), Rogue and Wilderness; all selected skills get a +30% bonus, but these skills do not advance. Also see Natural Abilities, above.

R.C.C. Combat: Attacks Per Melee: Five

Damage: Bite 2D4 S.D.C., head-butt, punch and kick M.D. varies with supernatural P.S., or by weapon or magic.

R.C.C. Bonuses: +3 on initiative, +3 to strike, +3 to parry, +2 to dodge (double when in water), +2 to pull punch, +1 to roll with impact or fall, +4 to save vs poison and disease, +5 to save vs Horror Factor. R.C.C. bonuses are all in addition to any possible attribute bonuses.

Magic: All Vodianoi can cast the following spells, provided they have sufficient P.P.E.: All level one and two Water Elemental spells as described in *Rifts® Conversion Book One*, starting on page 78, plus Create Water, Command Fish, Summon Sharks & Whales, Summon Storm and Drought.

Spell potency is equal to a 3rd level sorcerer during the day but increases to 5th level at night.

Psionics: M.E. x2 for I.S.P. Psi-powers include: Mind Block, Exorcism, Telepathy, and Hydrokinesis.

Enemies: Anybody who threatens them or tries to stop them from doing as they desire. They also like teasing and tormenting humans and D-Bees in general, particularly heroes, adventurers, travelers, fishermen and sailors. They find the Warlords' troops to be easy targets and attack them regularly, especially those foolish enough to wander away from the rest of the group.

Allies: Others of its kind, some demons, and mean and wicked Woodland Spirits and people, but especially Leshii, Nalets, Morozko Frost Demons, Serpent Hounds, Demon Claws, and Stone, Wood, and Water Demons. Dislikes the temperamental and attractive Rusalka Woodland Spirits but will associate with them from time to time. The evil spirit enjoys watching people (including children) agonize in fear and suffer almost as much as they enjoy killing. The Vodianoi engage in cat and mouse games, stalking, terrorism, torture and murder.

Value: None per se.

Habitat: Found in swamps, ponds, mill ponds, lakes, rivers and seas throughout Rifts Russia, Mongolia, and parts of Asia. One or more Vodianoi or Water Spirits and other vile creatures may regularly stake out a particular road, bridge, beach/bank, area of a river or lake, or even a particular area of a farm, village, or city to hunt and play its deadly games. The Vodianoi frequently rob their victims and build small to medium treasure troves of (water damaged) weapons, magic items, gems, precious metals and other valuables. Such treasures (worth 4D6x10,000 credits) are usually kept hidden away at the bottom of the deepest part of a river, lake or sea. Civilization does not scare these monsters, although they rarely live in the city proper, preferring a neighboring body of water.

Russian Firebird

The Russian Firebird is a strange and mystical creature of magic. It has a low intelligence and lives, for the most part, as a bird, feeding on apples, fruits and seeds. Fewer than four hundred are said to exist in the entire world. The magical bird is the size and shape of a sleek pheasant, and its golden feathers radiate with the light of the sun. A single feather glows with more light than a multitude of candles or ten fireplaces, but does not radiate any heat, only the light of day. Vampires and creatures of darkness cannot come within 1000 feet (305 m) of the wondrous bird and even humans must cover their eyes within 500 feet (152 m) or be blinded by its brilliance. The magical Firebird is greatly coveted for its feathers — a single small feather is equal to three lanterns, a medium one to six lanterns and a large/long feathers equal to twenty lanterns — and all are practically weightless, can be covered by a small dark pouch, and glow with a brilliance of the which can reveal night-demons and hold vampires at bay for a distance of 100 feet (30.5 m). Best of all, the feather will radiate sunlight for 4D6x10 years after having been plucked, and as long as no more than one third of the feathers are plucked from a live Firebird, the magical creature will regrow the lost feathers in 4D4 years. However, plucking more than 33% will kill the bird.

The bird avoids contact with humanoids, dragons, and supernatural creatures, preferring to keep to itself and avoiding the trouble and conflict associated with intelligent beings. If it has a human intelligence it is comparatively low. However, the Firebird is intuitive and known to display some level of compassion toward humans and other creatures. Folktales include stories that tell how a lone Firebird has sat in a tree above a lost child, sweetly singing the entire night (and keeping demons and vampires at bay) to comfort the child and/or bring searchers to the location, for the bird shines with a brilliance that cannot be mistaken or missed in the deep woods. One story tells how a particular Firebird followed a group of Vampire Hunters and would appear at the most opportune time to blind and hurt vampires with its light.

A similar story tells of a tiny village so far northeast that even heroes and trappers never visited it. One day a band of vampires took sway over the town and the people began to suffer greatly at their hands. Then, as if in answer to their prayers, a mated pair of Firebirds roosted in the church steeple. Their combined brilliance was such that the entire village and surrounding

farms were illuminated with the light of day. After eight nights the pair flew away and the vampires emerged from their hiding places. The undead immediately began to search for human prey, for they were hungry. Suddenly, a great light grew in the distance as the pair of Firebirds returned. The vampires fled from the village, never to return. The Firebirds, knowing they were safe among the appreciative villagers, stayed for eight years before leaving the village, every year giving birth to two young Firebirds who flew away with each passing season. When the magical birds finally left, they knocked their nest off the steeple. Inside the nest, the villagers found a bedding of "Firefeathers," enough to light every room of the church and one for each and every home in the village. And the village prospered.

Other stories tell how, on occasion, the Firebird will pluck one of its own small or medium feathers and drop it into the lap of an Old Believer, Druid, or Bogatyr as an act of kindness or reward for their compassion and kindness to others. It is also known to sometimes leave behind one of its feathers to those who save it from traps or hunters, and is said to have the power to heal those it touches. Of course, such encounters and apparent acts of sentience are extremely rare (except for Old Believers who consider the Firebird to be a sacred symbol of hope and the light of knowledge. And whom, it is said, meet the magical bird at least once in their lives to receive a Firefeather).

Firebird Non-Player Character/Animal

Also known as the Sunbird and Bird of Hope.

Player Note: Not applicable as a player character.

Race: Woodland Spirit & Creature of Magic.

Alignment: Any selfish or good alignment.

Attributes: I.Q. low human intelligence but alert and compassionate: 1D4+2, M.E. 1D6+10, M.A. 1D6+20, P.S. 1D6+6, P.P. 1D6+10, P.E. 1D6+10, P.B. 1D6+20, Spd running: 2D6+6, Spd flying: 1D6x10+100; low supernatural P.S.

M.D.C.: P.E. number +1D4x10 (on S.D.C. worlds the Firebird has 3D6 +P.E. number for Hit Points and 4D6 S.D.C.; A.R. 10).

Horror Factor: 9

Size: Approximately 2 feet (0.6 m) long and one foot (0.3 m) tall.

Weight: 12-20 pounds (5.4 to 9 kg); and tastes fabulous.

Average Life Span: Uncertain, at least 500 years; maybe 1000+.

P.P.E.: 1D4x100, making them coveted by Necromancers and evil sorcerers for their vast P.P.E. which is doubled during a blood sacrifice.

Natural Abilities: Excellent flying speed and can fly or sing without pause or exhaustion for 12 hours straight. They can also prowl 60%, climb 70%/50%, swim 50%, have keen vision and hearing, see the invisible, and bio-regenerate 1D6 M.D. per hour.

Knows all Languages: Perhaps. They seem to (60%).

Limited Metamorphosis (special): The Firebird can hide its light for up to six hours per 24 hour period by metamorphing into a pheasant or hummingbird!

Also see magic.

O.C.C.: Not applicable.

R.C.C. Skills: Land and air navigation 98%, wilderness survival 88%. Also see Natural Abilities, above.

R.C.C. Combat: Attacks Per Melee: Three

Damage: Bite/Peck 1D4, M.D. or claw strike with its feet 2D6 M.D., or by psionics or magic.

R.C.C. Bonuses: +5 on initiative, +4 to dodge, +7 to dodge when flying, +1 to roll with impact or fall, +7 to save vs poison and disease, +3 to save vs Horror Factor. R.C.C. bonuses are all in addition to any possible attribute bonuses.

Magic: All Russian Firebirds can cast the following spells: Sense Evil, Sense Magic, Blinding Flash, Repel Animals, Resist Fire, Negate Poison, and Turn Dead. Spell potency is equal to a 3rd level sorcerer.

Psionics: M.E. x10 to determine I.S.P. Psi-powers include Healing Touch, Increased Healing, Suppress Fear, Empathy, and Mind Block.

Enemies: Demons, Necromancers and unscrupulous, greedy and evil people of all kinds.

Allies: Others of its kind, Old Believers, and most champions of good. Most other Woodland Spirits will help to protect the Firebird and come to its aid in times of need, and vice versa.

Value: A phenomenal 1-2 million credits! A single feather can typically command 10,000 to 15,000 credits, plus there is the bird's value as a sacrificial animal, and it tastes wonderful.

Habitat: Approximately 100-200 are believed to live scattered throughout Rifts Russia, as well as another 100-200 scattered throughout India and Asia.

Spirit Wolf

The Spirit Wolf is a creature of magic that looks like an ordinary large Grey wolf. It has a low human intelligence but incredible cunning and guile. A spirit of nature, it usually lives life as a normal wolf, but finds humans, D-Bees and other intelligent creatures to be irresistibly alluring and interesting. Consequently, it often watches the affairs of men and demons from afar and, from time to time, joins adventurers, heroes or brigands for fun and adventure. If the Spirit Wolf takes a liking to a particular village, it may elect to become its unofficial protector. Likewise, the Wolf sometimes becomes the companion of heroes, knights and adventurers, at least for a while. Unfortunately, the creature hates being confined, and often finds responsibility, even to simple villagers and friends, to be too restricting and uncomfortable. Thus, the Spirit Wolf may suddenly announce one day that it is leaving a group or area to find adventure elsewhere, or just disappear. However, the Great Wolf never forgets a friend (or enemy) and will always be glad to meet old friends, staying with them for a while or lending a helping hand.

Not all Spirit Wolves are benevolent and helpful creatures. In fact, most are selfish, not entirely reliable and irrepressibly independent. This independent mind means they often ignore the laws of men (unless obeying it serves their purpose), generally do as they please (although not to the detriment or endangerment of friends) and like to play tricks and games on people, especially antagonists. They are also very spur-of-the-moment types who tend to wander off wherever their current interest takes them. Worst, when angered, a Spirit Wolf can be savage and merciless.

Spirit Wolf Non-Player Character & Villain
Also known as the Great Wolf.

Player Note: If acceptable to the Game Master, he or she may allow a Spirit Wolf as an optional player character. This character will tend to be sarcastic, funny, fickle, clever and independent to the point of causing regular trouble for his companions.

They have a good understanding of human laws, morality and etiquette, but don't think any of it applies to them. While most are not thieves, many are natural and cunning con-artists who can talk candy out of the mouth of babes. The Spirit Wolf is at its most dangerous when provoked or bored, so short visits to a village and civilization are recommended; 2-12 days should not be too bad. Moreover, when bored, the Spirit Wolf's natural free spirit and anarchist nature just doesn't mix well in groups and the creature can become alarmingly obstinate, sarcastic and persnickety.

On the other hand, they are observant, cunning, resourceful and adventurous to the extreme, willing to take wild chances and great personal risk for the sake of adventure or a great challenge. They are also reasonably good spies, con-artists and fighters. Furthermore, most have no love for demons, witches, necromancers or other evil and destructive creatures. The nature spirit has little need or interest in money/credits/gold or other valuables, or modern technology, but is sometimes attracted to valuable items that others have a great interest in as a prize to win. They respect cunning and resourcefulness over brute strength and magic, and tend to be attracted to risk-takers and beloved heroes and warriors. They also like and respect most of their fellow Woodland Spirits, Gypsies (because of their cunning and free spirit), Old Believers, Mystic Kuznya, and psychics. They recognize demons as a genuine threat to them and to the world, but don't actively engage in their extermination.

Race: Woodland Spirit and a Creature of Magic.

Alignment: Any, but the vast majority are anarchist (40%), unprincipled (30%), aberrant (10%) or miscreant (10%).

Attributes: I.Q. low to average human intelligence but cunning and bold: 1D6+6, M.E. 1D6+18, M.A. 1D6+8, P.S. 2D6+18, P.P. 1D6+18, P.E. 1D6+18, P.B. 1D6+18, Spd: 3D6+118, a minimum of 82 mph (131 km; swimming speed is half); supernatural P.S.

M.D.C.: 6D6x3 (on S.D.C. worlds the Spirit Wolf has 3D4x3 +P.E. number for Hit Points and 1D6x10 S.D.C.; A.R. 12 day and night).

Horror/Awe Factor: 10.

Size: Stands 4 feet (1.2 m) tall at the shoulders.

Weight: 150-250 pounds (67.5 to 76 kg).

Average Life Span: Uncertain, 1000+ years; may be immortal.

P.P.E.: 3D4x10 +P.E. attribute number.

Natural Abilities: Great speed and can run without pause or exhaustion for 72 hours! The Spirit Wolf can leap 20 feet (6 m) high and 30 feet (9 m) across (increase by 50% with a running start) and is excellent and speedy swimmer (85%), can dive up to 300 feet (91.5 m), and can hold its breath for 3D4+6 minutes underwater, but maximum depth is only 500 feet (152 m). Other natural abilities include climb 60%/50%, track by scent alone 75%, nightvision one mile (1.6 km), see the invisible, impervious to normal cold, and bio-regenerates 2D6 M.D. per minute. **Note:** Electrical based attacks do double damage, silver S.D.C. weapons inflict M.D., and all other types of M.D. attacks do full damage.

Knows all Languages: Magically understands and speaks all languages 85%, but cannot read.

Limited Metamorphosis (special): These demonic spirits of nature can transform into a handsome human once per 24 hours. However, the body is unusually hairy, and the hair on the head is long and grey. The light of the full moon and the flash of lightning will negate the metamorphosis to reveal the Spirit Wolf for what it is.

Also see magic.

O.C.C.: Not applicable.

R.C.C. Skills: Land navigation 90%, wilderness survival 95%, intelligence 80%, surveillance (tailing only) 80%, prowl 70%, and streetwise 65%, plus select two skills from each of the following skill categories: W.P. (4th level equivalent), Rogue and Wilderness; all selected skills get a +20% bonus, but these skills do not advance. Also see Natural Abilities, above.

R.C.C. Combat: Attacks Per Melee: Five

Damage: Wolf-bite 3D6 M.D., head-butt, punch and kick M.D. varies with supernatural P.S., or by weapon or magic.

R.C.C. Bonuses: +3 on initiative, +3 to strike, +1 to parry, +4 to dodge (double when running faster than 60 mph/96 km), +3 to pull punch, +1 to roll with impact or fall, +6 to save vs poison and disease, +5 to save vs Horror Factor. R.C.C. bonuses are all in addition to any possible attribute bonuses.

Magic: All Spirit Wolves can cast the following spells, provided they have sufficient P.P.E.: See the invisible, Sense Magic, Sense Evil, Globe of Daylight, Chameleon, Shadow Meld, Locate, Repell Animals, and Escape. Spell potency is equal to a 3rd level sorcerer.

Psionics: M.E. x2 for I.S.P. Psi-powers include: Mind Block, Exorcism, Telepathy, and Hydrokinesis.

Enemies: Anybody who threatens them or tries to stop them from doing as they desire. They also like teasing, tricking and besting people, from humans to demons, which can get the Wolf and its companions into trouble. They find the Warlords' troops very interesting, and might join them on an adventure if not for the fact that these "crazy humans" attack all supernatural beings. Those who attack it first, frequently suffer the anger and wrath of the Great Wolf.

Allies: Other people of all kinds, especially humans, and other Woodland Spirits, but seldom fellow Spirit Wolves. Sometimes demons, bandits and other unsavory or monstrous forces. Depends largely on the temperament, goals and alignment of the Wolf.

Value: To Necromancers, the feet of a Spirit Wolf can give him the animal's amazing speed. The paws the clawing power to inflict 1D6 M.D. and the skull the power to see the invisible and nightvision for one mile.

Habitat: Forests and grasslands of Rifts Russia and Asia, both of which are plentiful in this part of the world. The Spirit Wolf is not intimidated by people or civilization, but tends to find large towns and cities too confining, and villages and farms too boring to stay for any length of time — but may visit regularly.

Man-Wolf

The Man-Wolf is often confused with the more famous *were-wolf*, but they are different. The Man-Wolf always starts life as a mortal human or D-Bee. However, for whatever reason, the individual sees himself as a misfit, somebody who doesn't fit in the world of men. Somehow the suffering and longings of these misanthropes draws the magic energy of the ley lines to them. Unhappy in the world of men, the magic energies fuse with the pathetic and lost individual and transform him into a creature of magic that is neither human nor animal, but both. Exactly how or why this strange phenomenon occurs in Russia is not entirely known. Certainly part of the answer lies in the prevailing atmosphere of superstition that has kept the old Russian myths, folk tales and beliefs alive. This belief combines with the subconscious mind and intense emotions helps to direct the mystic energy to create the Man-Wolf. It is also likely that the handful of individuals who become such animal-men (and despite the name, a Man-Wolf can be male or female) are latent psychics or have the potential for becoming Wisemen, Old Believers or Mystics. Unfortunately, the self-loathing and feeling of being completely out of place takes the misdirected energy, funneling it inward and, fueled by the legend of the Man-Wolf, turns them into said creature. Or so most practitioners of magic believe.

Unfortunately, because the Man-Wolf originates from such a sense of loneliness, loss, and low self-esteem, most are pitiful creatures who find they don't fit into the world of animals any better than in the world of humans. The Man-Wolf typically tries to forget he was ever human by living like an animal. However, he cannot stomach the taste of carrion, blood or raw meat, and when he looks into a mirror, pool of water or any reflective material, he sees the sad face of a human staring back at him, even when in wolf form. Neither man nor animal, the pitiful soul is tortured all the more. They often become loners who live in the wilderness as huntsmen by day and wolves by night. Many struggle to find some measure of peace and happiness, and are usually accepted by the other Woodland Spirits, although mocked and tormented by most demons and the Rusalka and Vodianoi. The majority are unsure of themselves and frightened, and avoid their once fellow humans. However, some join bands of adventurers, heroes, explorers, druids, huntsmen or warriors (a few War Camps include one to a half dozen Man-Wolves). It is these lost souls who try to do something pro-

down are toyed with before being lured to their doom. Occasionally, a Devil-Wolf will seize control of a town where it serves as a demonic, tyrant lord delivering misery and injustice to all who live under its rule.

By day, the Man-Wolf appears as a human, usually with a long, unruly tangle of hair, and a wild look in the eyes (the Devil-Wolf is often excessively hairy and has slightly longer canines than normal). At night, the Man-Wolf becomes a hulking beast of a wolf, standing five feet (1.5 m) at the shoulders and tall enough to look most men in the eye. The teeth are yellow, the breath fetid, and the eyes an eerie crimson. When slain, the Man-Wolf reverts to his original human appearance and is said to die with a peaceful expression on his face, because his hell on Earth is finally over.

The nightly transformation is beyond the character's control and happens whether he or she wants it to or not. Hence, the Man-Wolf is often seen as a cursed individual. During the day, the Man-Wolf looks (mostly) normal, but can turn into his wolf persona for a brief period lasting not longer than 2D6+2 minutes. Such a transformation can be brought on through intense willpower and at moments where the Man-Wolf truly believes his life is in jeopardy. In the latter case, the creature fights only enough to make good his escape.

Man-Wolf Non-Player Character & Villain

Also known as the Devil-Wolf and King-Wolf. In Romania they are called "ruvmanush" or wolf-man (*ruv* meaning wolf and *manush*, man).

Player Note: If the Game Master allows it, the Man-Wolf can be used as a player character. Presumably, such a character is a misguided misanthrope of a selfish or good alignment. As a Man-Wolf, he or she will tend to be a quiet, private, and shy (even fearful) individual. In human form in particular, the character will exhibit a lack of confidence and decisiveness. However, when angry and at night, when he becomes the Wolf, the character is much bolder, aggressive and confident. This can be a fun and challenging character to play. Remember that most people, from peasants, warriors, and wizards to Warlords and demons, will regard Man-Wolves (and the people who associate with them) with suspicion and concern. Those given to violent rage and acts of terror will bring tragedy and destruction to everybody they associate with.

Race: Woodland Spirit and Creature of Magic.

Alignment: Any, but the majority are unprincipled (25%), anarchist (35%), or miscreant (25%).

Attributes: I.Q. human: 3D6, M.E. 3D6, M.A. 3D6, P.S. 3D6+28, P.P. 3D6+13, P.E. 3D6+13, P.B. 3D6, Spd 3D6+50; supernatural P.S.

M.D.C.: P.E.x2 +1D6x10, increase by 50% at night when in wolf form (on S.D.C. worlds the Man-Wolf has 2D4x10 for Hit Points and 1D6x10 S.D.C.; increase by 50% at night. A.R. 12 at night in wolf form, A.R. 6 as a human). The Devil-Wolf gets an additional 3D6 M.D.C (or S.D.C.).

Horror/Awe Factor: 12

Size: 5 feet (1.5 m) tall at the shoulders with eye level being around 6 feet (1.8 m).

Weight: 250 pounds (76 kg) of muscle and sinew as a wolf; an average weight when in human form.

Average Life Span: Adds 3D6x10 years to the life of a human.

P.P.E.: 2D4x10

ductive and meaningful with their lives, who, ironically, come to find their humanity and some level of peace if not their place in the world.

The worst give in to their animal side and become savage predators. Cruel and ruthless beastmen who hunt, torture and kill for pleasure and who wallow in self-pity, self-hatred and delude themselves with thoughts of revenge against those who fear, hate or reject them. Such a lost soul becomes known as a Devil-Wolf, a beast ruled by his hatred and anger. A monster who believes the only way it can prove its own self-worth is by belittling, terrifying, hurting and slaying those weaker than it. Such beings frequently consort with all manner of evil, from thieves and assassins to witches, demons and practitioners of the black arts. Whether alone or with a marauding gang, the Devil-Wolf roams the countryside slaughtering cattle and sheep (for fun or out of cruelty), plundering travelers, heroes, villages, and War Camps, and terrorizing any who cross their path. The Devil-Wolf is known to smash down the doors of woodland abodes to terrorize or slaughter those inside, as well as rape, kidnap, extort, rob, maim, kill and engage in wholesale murder. Those monsters who adopt a village or part of a city as their domain, terrorize the inhabitants and ravage whomever they please. Any authorities or would be heroes who try to hunt them

Natural Abilities: Good to excellent speed and can run without pause or exhaustion for 12 hours! The Man-Wolf can leap 12 feet (3.6 m) high and 18 feet (5.5 m) across (increase by 50% with a running start). They hate water and are only fair swimmers (45% swim skill). Other natural abilities include climb 60%/50%, track humanoids or animals by scent alone 85% (-50% as a human), nightvision one mile (1.6 km, reduce by 80% when in human form), see the invisible (in wolf and human form), impervious to normal cold, and bio-regenerates 2D6 M.D. per hour.

Vulnerability: Silver S.D.C. weapons inflict double damage as M.D., and all other types of M.D. attacks do full damage. Magic and psionics have full affect. Weapons made of the Millennium Tree also do double damage.

Knows all Languages: Magically understands and speaks all languages 85%, but cannot read unless taught as a human.

Limited Metamorphosis (special): These frail creatures of magic automatically turn into a huge Grey wolf every night as soon as the sun goes down. In wolf form, they are powerful and more animalistic, but retain their memories, knowledge/skills, and can speak in the human tongue. The Man-Wolf can also will himself to turn into a wolf during the day but only for 2D6+2 minutes.

O.C.C.: Not applicable.

R.C.C. Skills: Land navigation 95%, wilderness survival 90%, plus select three skills from each of the following skill categories: W.P., Domestic, Technical, and Wilderness or Rogue; all selected skills get a +15% bonus, but are -30% when in wolf form. Selected skills increase by level. Also see Natural Abilities, above.

Level of Experience: NPCs are typically 1D4+2 levels in experience, player characters (if allowed) start at first level and use the same experience table as the Dragon Hatchling.

R.C.C. Combat: Attacks Per Melee: Three in human form, but five as a wolf (six if the more savage and evil Devil-Wolf).

Damage: Bite 4D6 M.D.C., claw strike, punch and kick (in either form) does M.D. as per supernatural P.S., or by weapon.

R.C.C. Bonuses: +3 on initiative, +3 to strike, +2 to parry, +3 to dodge (double when running in wolf form), +1 to pull punch, +1 to roll with impact or fall, +7 to save vs poison and disease, +8 to save vs possession, +2 to save vs mind control, +4 to save vs Horror Factor (+6 if a Devil-Wolf N.P.C.). R.C.C. bonuses are all in addition to any possible attribute bonuses.

Magic: None.

Psionics: M.E. x2 for I.S.P. Psi-powers include: Intuitive Combat, Empathy, Commune with Spirits, Object Read, Sense Time, Sense Evil, Sixth Sense and Mind Block.

Enemies: Anybody who threatens them. Devil-Wolves hate humans and beauty. Many Man-Wolves and Devil-Wolves deeply hate the Warlords and their Camps. This is because they often try to exterminate them (at least troublesome and murderous ones), and because they represent the civilization and humanity whose world the tortured creature could never fit into. Some even blame them for what they have become. On the other hand Man-Wolves, and even Devil-Wolves who can control their baser instincts and follow orders, have been recruited by some of the War Camps. Both Warlords Sokolov

and Orloff have at least two dozen Man-Wolf warriors among their Reavers.

Allies: Others of its kind, werebeasts, demons, and Woodland Spirits. Devil-Wolves typically associate only with evil Woodland Spirits, demons, witches and other evil beings. However, most demons, even lesser ones, consider them to be no better than sub-demons and meant to serve or be submissive to them. Brodkil and Gargoyles welcome them as equals.

Value: None per se.

Habitat: Man-Wolves can be found anywhere in Rifts Russia, Mongolia, Hungary, Romania, Bulgaria and Poland, especially in forest and mountain regions.

Werebeasts

Werebeasts are a race of intelligent shapechanging creatures found throughout the world, but particularly in Rifts Russia, Hungary and Poland. They are especially common in Russia along the Ural and Caucasus Mountains. The most common of the werebeasts are the Werewolf and Werebear. The rare Weretiger can be found in the northern forests of the tundra and India.

Note: See *Rifts® Conversion Book One*, starting on page 191, for complete stats and details. Sorry, space limitations prevent us from reprinting them here.

Vampires

The undead are a constant and reoccurring problem throughout Europe and Asia. They seem to have the strongest link and chronic manifestation in the Caucasus Mountains, Hungary and Romania.

Note: See *Rifts® Vampire Kingdoms™* for comprehensive information about the classic vampire.

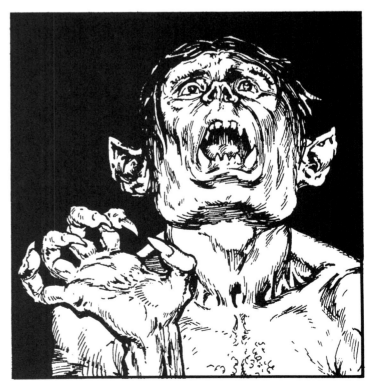

Russian Magic

Men of Magic O.C.C.s

Born Mystic or Mystic Wiseman
Mystic Kuznya/Smith
Old Believer
Russian Demon & Serpent Slayer
Russian Fire Sorcerer
Russian Necromancer
Russian Sorcerer/Line Walker
Russian Shifter/Summoner
Pact Witch
Night Witch
Hidden Witch
Note: Also see Gypsies

Russian Witches

Please note, that none of the so-called, stereotypical evil "witches" presented in this book are meant to represent any real religious belief, faith or practice, and should not be confused with Wicca.

An historical glimpse of the Russian Witch

The "Witch" (and to a lesser degree, the sorcerers) plays a large role in Russian myth as they appear time and time again throughout the ages. The Russian "Witch" of folk tales often appears as the traditional Fairy-Tale Character — a decrepit looking, wicked, old hag. Other legends suggest a Witch looked like an ordinary human, except she had a short tail (easily concealed) that marked her as more than human. Historically, a witch was female, with her male counterpart being an evil sorcerer. This foul-hearted woman possessed dangerous magical powers that gave her the ability to hurt and heal. She was typically mean-spirited and motivated by base human emotions such as jealousy, lust, greed, anger, hate and revenge. Most were just plain cruel and vindictive, causing pain and suffering whenever they felt like it. The old crones were capable of making magical potions and powders, casting spells and curses (the "evil eye"), and riding broomsticks or fireplace pokers and other objects (Baba Yaga flew in a mortar, propelling herself with a pestle, while steering and erasing her tracks with a broom).

The mythical Russian Witch kept black cats and poisonous snakes, could summon or dispel vermin (mice, rats, spiders, flies, etc.) and often associated with or commanded demons and evil spirits. Many were cannibals who kidnapped and ate children or babies. Some lived like hermits in the woods while others lived in or near villages — historically, most every village believed it harbored one or two witches and/or sorcerer or magic healer.

Witches were blamed for times of ill fortune, crop failure, disease, sudden or inexplicable deaths, freak accidents, strange occurrences, or any bad luck that befell a community or could not be easily explained. If misfortune fell upon somebody who had a falling out with a Witch, the villagers saw this as no coincidence, and the Witch would be deemed responsible for an act of cruel revenge. One of their greatest powers, especially in the low-tech agrarian society that dominated Russia into the 20th Century, was the power to "spoil." The Russian Witch could cause cows and other milking animals to go dry and be unable to give fresh milk, she could also spoil milk, make eggs go rotten, and spoil meat and food with her magic. She could also bring ruin to crops by tying a shaft of wheat in a knot and make animals miscarry, go lame or become ill by tying a knot in their tail. They could also bring vermin and disease to a community.

Ironically, although feared, and generally considered evil and dangerous in the extreme, Witches (and many sorcerers) could heal as well as destroy. Witches knew much about illness and thus knew how to combat disease, help a mother (woman or animal) give birth, and dispel magical sickness and spoilage as well as make healing potions, salves, and balms. Consequently, they were frequently called upon to heal sickness, defend against disease, remove curses, and protect a village or family from other (worse and rival) witches and sorcerers. However, all Witches were ultimately evil and *tolerated* out of fear rather than acceptance or respect by villagers. During periods of rampant plague and famine, the Witch was often held responsible (even when not), and usually slain by an angry mob; often beaten or tortured and then burned at the stake (in the Ukraine, witches were drowned, elsewhere they were hung). Throughout history, many regional lords, Tsars and church leaders outlawed the practice of magic and engaged in active campaigns to drive out or destroy anybody believed to be practicing magic, particularly witches — the persecution of witches in Russia and the Ukraine were particularly intense and dramatic in the 16th and 17th Centuries. However, most villages still had one or two people believed to be a witch or sorcerer quietly plying their mystical trade well into the early 20th Century.

The Pact Witch

The classic "Pact" Witch, presented in **Rifts® Conversion Book One** (as well as *The Palladium Fantasy RPG®, 2nd Edition* and *Beyond the Supernatural*™), is in league with a powerful supernatural force, typically a demon lord, dark god or alien intelligence. His (yes, males can be a classic witch too) or her powers are "gifts" granted by the evil supernatural being as the result of a pact. The greater the sacrifice and level of allegiance offered by the Witch through the pact, the greater the gift. This type of Witch is usually considered a demon worshipper and/or willing servant of supernatural evil. Such Witches are relatively common throughout Rifts Russia, Europe and Asia. See **Rifts® Conversion Book One**, pages 55-58, for details.

Night Witch O.C.C.

Note: The Night Witch O.C.C. presented in this book keeps with the Russian view of the evil, haggish Witch of myth and superstition. A foul, depraved and cruel creature who associates with supernatural evil and uses foul magic. The character is presented as an evil, Non-Player Character *villain*. No slight is intended to well intentioned modern witches or traditional practitioners of wicca, druidism or shamanism. The Night Witch is a fictional presentation and not meant to portray any real-life people or religious belief.

The Night Witch

One of the things that makes the Night Witch so reviled is that as a creature of darkness who enjoys corrupting and "spoiling" the human spirit and tarnishing all that is good, healthy and beautiful. Consequently, the Night Witch will gladly help other people who are evil or on the path of losing their innocence, morality, compassion and/or goodness. The Night Witch will even help old rivals and enemies provided such aid will ultimately make them indebted to her and ultimately worse off. It is common knowledge that anyone who willingly seeks a Night Witch's help consorts with evil and opens himself to danger and treachery, if not the corruption of his very soul — for the Night Witch is a wicked creature who knows nothing of compassion and uses her dark magic to inflict suffering and destroy good. She is the friend of the envious, ambitious, greedy, hate-filled, and vengeful, eager to convince and help lost souls to follow her path, and hurt, betray and destroy others. What makes her alluring at all, is that she appeals to the dark side in each human, and makes acts of revenge, selfishness and greed sound delicious and just, as opposed to bitter and cruel.

Those in denial might argue that their hands are clean of blood and treachery, for it was the Witch who actually did the deed. However, they are deluded or liars, for the conscious act of commissioning a Night Witch to perform one's dirty work for them is a deliberate act of evil, initiated by that individual, and he bears the guilt of what happens next. Such cowardly villains might as well have done the evil themselves, for the Night Witch is nothing more than their instrument. A fact they take great joy in. Cruel and vindictive, the Night Witch usually takes the most brutal and destructive path, destroying hope and beauty, and hurting everything she touches. This means she will take the most extreme and devastating path to accomplish her "client's" request, which is often much more terrible, expansive and personal than he had ever imagined or intended. Ah, but such is the risk one takes when associating with this creature of darkness. **Note:** Characters of good alignment who turn to a Night Witch, Necromancer or Demon for help in extracting revenge, justice or to harm others, automatically drop to anarchist alignment. If the deed involves the character's willful participation in acts of torture or murder, that individual's alignment will change to an evil one, probably miscreant. Likewise, further acts of deception, treachery and evil will warp the alignment into evil. Worse, once started down the path of selfishness and evil, it is difficult to change course.

The fabled, evil witch Baba Yaga — said to be the grandmother of all (ancient) witches — was a Night Witch. These are vile, wicked humans (or any mortal being) who practice a form of necromantic sorcery. Half of all Night Witches engage in cannibalism and often threaten to eat people unless they get their way. They also kidnap children to use as slaves or to eat or use in blood sacrifices. Many associate with and favor Necromancers, demons, evil Woodland Spirits, thieves, murderers, and brigands of all kinds.

The Warlords see Witchery and dark magic as both a genuine danger to the people and future of Mother Russia, and a threat to their rule. As a result, they have made its practice a crime punishable by death. As a rule, all witches, but especially those who consort with demons, are actively hunted down and destroyed. This has made these two rival factions hated enemies. Pact Witches and Night Witches actively engage in actions that undermine, cripple and destroy members of the War Camps. In addition to act of open aggression and combat, they also encourage, support and protect the Warlords' enemies, criminals, evil sorcerers, monsters, and demons. This can involve magical assistance, sanctuary, supplies and information; sometimes directly, but often without these brigands ever knowing who their secret benefactor really is — being men of little moral character, they don't care from whom or how they get this assistance.

The Special Powers & Abilities of the Night Witch

1. Becomes a minor Mega-Damage creature. The Night Witch has P.E. x2 for physical M.D.C., plus 2D6 M.D. per each level of experience. P.S. is supernatural.

2. Strongest at night. Increase physical M.D.C., P.S. and Spd by 30% at night.

3. Long Life. The old adage that the good die young, but evil is hard to kill, is true of the Night Witch. Unless slain, this foul wretch will live 3D4x10 years over the age of 80!

4. Bio-Regeneration. The Night Witch can bio-regenerate 2D6 M.D. per hour, but only at night — no healing occurs during the hours of daylight. She can also regrow severed limbs, but such an impressive feat takes 1D6+6 months to accomplish.

5. Deceptively alluring and attractive. In their youth, most Night Witches (men and women, although 90% are females) are attractive, even beautiful; +1D6+1 to P.B. attribute. However, as they get older, their evil takes on a physical manifestation that makes them ugly, old hags. At age 40, reduce the character's P.B. by two points. Continue to reduce P.B. by two points for every additional five years of age. Stop when P.B. is down to 4 or 5.

6. The shapechanging powers of the Night Witch: Traditionally, the Night Witch could change into the following animals: Cat, pig, mare, toad, dark colored dog (not a wolf), magpie/raven, as well as into the identity of somebody she met or knows (i.e. a fellow villager, an acquaintance, adventurer who may have bumped into her, etc.).

In the latter case, the Witch needs a bit of that person's hair or fingernails, or blood (dried blood on a rag or bandage is acceptable), or an unwashed article of clothing worn by the person she hopes to impersonate. That individual can be female, male or D-Bee, provided he is a mortal (no creatures of magic, supernatural beings, or mega-damage creatures). The magic turns the Night Witch into an exact copy of that individual and the metamorphosis lasts as long as the witch desires, provided she wears whatever the personal article of clothing, or has the hair or fin-

gernails worn on her body. Hair, nail clippings, bloody bits of clothes, or a vial of blood is typically worn in a locket or as a charm on a string or chain hung around the neck or wrist. If the item is clothing, that piece (scarf, hat, shirt, gloves, skirt, dress, wrap, shoes, etc.) must be worn as such. Many Night Witches keep several articles of clothing and samples of hair, nails, and blood in vials, jars, and lockets as part of their magical treasure hoard to be drawn upon as needed.

When the item that links the disguise to the genuine individual is removed, the spell is instantly broken. If it is completely destroyed by fire, the shape and image the item once represented can *never* be used by the Night Witch again. Otherwise, the witch can maintain her magically created appearance as long as she desires, or use that appearance again and again, whenever she pleases. Most Night Witches have 2-4 favorite fake appearances they assume regularly. However, if the individual she is imitating is dead, the magical transformation can only be maintained during the hours of night.

Note: The body of the transformed witch is completely physical and will withstand any physical examination. Likewise, the sound of the voice and any verbal inflections of the person being imitated are given to the witch while in that body. However, all physical and mental attributes, skills, knowledge, memories and abilities are those of the witch regardless of the form her physical body may take.

7. Demon Helpers! Lesser demons, typically The Unclean, Il'ya, Gargoylites, Grave Ghouls, Lasae or Imps (the Imp is actually a Deevil), are inevitably drawn to the Night Witch as her willing minions and servants. One will come to her at levels 2, 4, 6, 8, 10, 12 and 14. Whenever one is slain, it is permanently gone and there is no replacement. If the Witch is slain, her minions will run to her lair, fight over her treasure, steal what they can and vanish into the wilderness.

At times of need, the Night Witch can summon 1D4+1 additional demons of the same type already in her service. These extra minions will consider serving her for up to 24 hours per level of her experience. However, they are not bound to the Witch who summoned them and must negotiate a "deal" to serve her. These deals will require room and board, some kind of fair payment in valuables or magic items, plus the opportunity to torment and spill the blood of innocent people or causing harm, inflicting terror, and other acts of wickedness that will hurt others (emotionally, morally or physically). If the opportunity to kill and do evil is excellent, the price the demons demand will be low, even downright paltry (a token payment). If the work is something that is unappealing or potentially deadly, they have the freedom to reject the offer or to charge a ridiculously high payment. If no deal can be reached in a matter of a few minutes, the free willed demons vanish back from whence they came.

P.P.E. Cost: 120 points. The P.P.E. is expended prior to determining the number summoned, so whatever the character gets is the luck of the draw.

Limitations: Can only include the types of supernatural creatures already in the Night Witch's service, and they will only serve the *Witch* (this same power is available to the *Rifts Shifter* and Palladium Fantasy RPG Summoner when used in a Rifts® setting). Furthermore, this spell can only be performed twice in an individual's entire life, so it is used carefully.

Note: The Night Witch can keep the extra demons by permanently sacrificing 6D6 of her own P.P.E. and 1D6 points from her M.D.C.

The Curse of Demon Helpers: Demon Helpers who are bound to the Witch (or Shifter) indefinitely (including those who come from every other level or experience), remain with that individual until the day she dies. The creatures cannot be "freed" or "dismissed" by the Night Witch, nor can they be sent on faraway journeys, sold like slaves to another person, or locked away. The summoning power and spell is such that they become linked to serve the one who summoned them. Escape is impossible because the Demon Helpers will never go more than 200 miles (320 km) away from their master, won't stay gone for more than three days at a time, and magically sense their master's exact location.

The horrid creatures won't do anything to harm their master and faithfully serve and obey. However, they get easily bored and constantly pester their master for things to do — from the most mundane and unpleasant work to delightful tasks like spying, stealing, and killing. Some Night Witches and Shifters will keep their Demon Helpers busy during quiet times by giving them difficult to impossible tasks, like counting all the needles in a pine tree, or the number of stones leading from the walkway at the gate to the front door, or picking fleas off the back of a hound, and so on. Otherwise, the Night Witch or Shifter is constantly pestered and shadowed by the bored Helpers, or they get into arguments and brawls among each other which makes noise, breaks things, etc.

The demons serve their master in good faith and will do anything that is asked of them except that which would be suicidal or deadly to their fellow Helpers. They will even spy on, fight and steal from other demons and sorcerers. Of course, if caught, the Demon Helpers, under minimal torture, will name their master, or may accidentally lead an enemy or victim to her. Remember, they are lesser demons and not overly intelligent.

8. The power to Spoil. All Night Witches possess the knowledge of Magic Spoiling. All spells are known to the Witch; described elsewhere in this section.

9. P.P.E.: Like all practitioners of magic, the Night Witch is a living battery of mystic energy that she can draw upon at will. *Permanent Base P.P.E.:* 2D4x10 +P.E. attribute number. Add 2D6 P.P.E. per level of experience. Additional P.P.E. can be drawn from ley lines and blood sacrifices (see **Rifts® RPG**, page 162, *Taking P.P.E. from the living*). Most Night Witches and evil Necromancers have no qualms about animal and human sacrifices to acquire the doubled P.P.E. released by the victim at the moment of their death.

10. Mystic Knowledge: Starts with *all* Spoiling Magic and 2D4 additional wizard/Line Walker spells (*Rifts® RPG* and *Federation of Magic*) selected from levels 1-4 or 1D4 Necromancer Bone magic spells (any). Additional common spells can be learned by the usual means. N.P.C. villains are likely to know 2-4 times more wizard spells; seldom more.

11. O.C.C. bonuses: +5 to save vs Horror Factor, +8 to save vs possession, +4 to save vs poison and disease. All are in addition to possible attribute or other bonuses. +1 to spell strength at levels 3, 6, 9, and 13.

Notable Vulnerabilities of the Night Witch

- The light of day is unwelcomed and unpleasant (prefers the night, shadows and cloudy days).
- Magical fire and M.D. plasma do double damage.
- Rainwater collected during the first thunderclap of a storm burns like acid, inflicting 4D6 M.D. per level of experience. Holy Water is bitter and stings the flesh, but does no damage.
- The Night Witch has no special saves vs magic of any kind, not even charms and talismans work for them, they are vulnerable to magic.
- Insanity. Roll for one phobia at level two, roll for one obsession at level four and roll for one random insanity at level six.
- Lastly, they are vulnerable to their own greed, lust and vengeful nature. This means the Night Witch finds it difficult to resist extracting revenge or trying to get something or somebody they want, and causes them to overplay their hand, stand and fight when they should retreat, and to take foolish chances. Their lust for wealth, valuables, and power, as well as lust for revenge, can also be used to lure them out in the open and into ambushes and traps. However, the cunning and ruthless Night Witch is no stranger to deception and guile, and will anticipate treachery and unleash her full power against those fools who dare to challenge her. In addition, should the witch triumph or escape, she will not forget or forgive their attack and plot her retribution (makes for a great recurring villain).

Night Witch Optional O.C.C. & N.P.C. Villain
Alignment: Any selfish or evil, but most are miscreant (50%).
Racial Restrictions: None, although the vast majority (75%) are human.
Roll The Eight Attributes as normal for that race, although the witch is a minor M.D.C. being and has supernatural P.S.
Average Level of Experience (N.P.C.): 1D6+2
Psionics: Psionic abilities are not a requirement, but approximately 15% possess minor or major psionics.
Attribute Requirements: I.Q. 8, and an evil heart.
O.C.C. Skills:
  Basic Math (+20%)
  Speaks Russian at 98%
  Speaks Euro and two other languages of choice (+20%).
  Literacy: Russian (+10%)
  Lore: Demons & Monsters (+20%)
  Lore: Two of choice (+10%)
  Herbology (+20%)
  Land Navigation (+10%)
  Wilderness Survival (+5%)
  W.P. Ancient, one of choice (any).
  W.P. Energy Weapon, one of choice (any).
  Hand to Hand: Basic to start, but can be changed to Expert for the cost of one O.C.C. Related Skill or two skills for Martial Arts or Assassin.
O.C.C. Related Skills: Choose eight other skills at level one and two additional at levels 3, 6, 9 and 12.
  Communications: Any
  Domestic: Any (+5%)
  Electrical: None
  Espionage: None

Mechanical: None
Medical: Any (+20%)
Military: None
Physical: Any, except Gymnastics and Acrobatics.
Pilot Skills: Any, except robots, power armor, military vehicles, ships and aircraft.
Pilot Related Skills: Any
Rogue Skills: Any
Science: Any (+10%)
Technical: Any (+10%; +15% to language and lore skills).
W.P.: Any
Wilderness: Any

Secondary Skills: The character also gets to select three Secondary Skills from the previous list at level one and one additional at levels 3, 5, 7, 9 and 13. These are additional areas of knowledge that do not get the advantage of the bonus listed in parentheses. All secondary skills start at the base skill level. Also, skills are limited as previously indicated.

Standard Equipment to Start: Light suit of M.D.C. body armor, a Vibro-Knife (1D6 M.D.), one M.D. weapon of choice, one silver knife, one sacrificial sword, wooden cross, mallet and six wooden stakes, two medium sacks, one large, backpack or satchel, bedroll, canteen or water skin, belt, boots, flashlight, language translator, note pad, 2D4 pencils, basic clothing, and a handful of personal items. Additional weapons, special items and magic items may be acquired over time.

N.P.C.s are likely to have 2-4 Demon Helpers, 2D4 henchmen, a lair (their own house, a place they took or rent, a hideout, etc.), 1D4 magic items, and 2D6x10,000 in gold, credits and valuables, plus a collection of herbs, poisons and components necessary for their magic and sinister plots. The villain may also have one or more guard dogs, a cat and other pets, friends and safeguards as the G.M. sees fit.

Vehicle: Starts with none. Whether an N.P.C. has a vehicle is up to the G.M. A witch who can not drive may have a servant to drive her.

Secret Resources: Varies dramatically with each specific character. Some have few friends, allies or resources, while others will have an expansive network of henchmen and allies, as well as underworld connections and associates in all walks of life.

Money: Player characters start with 1D6x1000 credits, and 1D6x100 in tradeable goods. N.P.C.s start with 2D6x10,000. Many build strong reputations and some amass sizable fortunes. Some are even rulers and leaders of towns, clans and gangs.

Cybernetics: None; avoids them as unnatural and unnecessary.

Spoiling Magic ———————

One of the most impressive and terrible powers of the Night Witch is the ability to "spoil." It is always a harmful magic transmitted through touch, pinch, kiss or spell, as well as through enchanted food, drink and objects such as goblets, glasses, spoons and forks (i.e. utensils used to convey food or drink). Magic that can be done through staring and concentration are considered part of the Night Witch's "Evil Eye" power.

Note: Spoiling magic is exclusive to the various Witch O.C.C.s

and no other. The Night Witch possesses all these spells and rituals, the Pact Witch may only select them as part of a *Gift of Magic* (any spoil magic can be substituted for the more traditional magic spells).

Level One

Sense Poison
Range: Touch or within 12 feet (3.6 m); line of sight. Can be performed on oneself or two others by touch.
Duration: The sensing ability lasts for five minutes per level of the spell caster.
Saving Throw: Not applicable.
P.P.E. Cost: 3

The character can sense if the food has been poisoned, even if it appears to be perfectly fine. Moreover, he or she knows exactly what the poison is and the level of danger it represents.

Sense Bad Food & Drink
Range: Touch or within 12 feet (3.6 m); line of sight. Can be performed on oneself or two others by touch.
Duration: The sensing ability lasts for five minutes per level of the spell caster.
Saving Throw: Not applicable.
P.P.E. Cost: 4

The character can sense if food or drink is spoiled or magically tainted even if it appears to be perfectly fine. The sense is so acute that those enchanted can pinpoint the specific tainted food or drink out of a banquet table full of food.

Spoil Water
Range: Touch or within 40 feet (12.2 m).
Duration: Permanent
Saving Throw: -4 to save because the target is not a living creature. As much as ten gallons per level of the witch can be affected. A successful save means the magic fails and has no effect.
P.P.E. Cost: 3

The witch spoils the water or any type of drink by spitting into it. The water is discolored, has a slight odor, and tastes so bitter or acidic that it is impossible to drink. Water blessed by a priest or Old Believer, as well as holy water and alcohol, are impervious to this magic.

Curdle Milk
Range: Touch or within 40 feet (12.2 m).
Duration: Permanent
Saving Throw: -4 to save because the target is not a living creature. A successful save means the magic fails and has no effect.
P.P.E. Cost: 3

The Night Witch can spoil and cause milk (any kind) to curdle by either dipping her finger into the milk, or by staring at it for one full melee round (15 seconds). As much as five gallons per level of the witch can be affected. The milk is sour and foul smelling, and impossible to drink. This power can also be used to ruin fruit juices, cottage cheese, cream, ice cream and butter

Level Two

Spoil Wine
Range: Touch or within 40 feet (12.2 m).
Duration: Permanent
Saving Throw: -4 to save because the target is not a living creature. A successful save means the magic fails and has no effect.
P.P.E. Cost: 6

In much the same way that the Night Witch can spoil milk (any kind) by dipping her finger into the liquid, or by staring at it for one full melee round (15 seconds), she can turn wine to vinegar. As much as two gallons per level of the witch can be affected.

Spoil Eggs
Range: Touch or within 40 feet (12.2 m).
Duration: Permanent
Saving Throw: -4 to save because the target is not a living creature. A successful save means the magic fails and has no effect.
P.P.E. Cost: 6

The Night Witch can rot fresh eggs (any kind) still in their shell or eggs prepared for eating by touching them (affecting as many as she can hold in her arms) or by staring at them for one full melee round (15 seconds). As much as two dozen per level of the witch can be affected. The moment the egg is cracked open there is a foul smell, indicating the egg is no good, and the yoke is grey with specks of blood.

Level Three

Spoil Sleep
Range: Touch or up to 60 feet (18.3 m) away; line of sight.
Duration: Eight hours per level of the spell caster.
Damage: Superficial, but those deprived of sleep will be tired, irritable and function in a reduced capacity; reduce initiative by half, Spd by 30% and skill performance by 30%.
Saving Throw: Standard
P.P.E. Cost: 8

Causes the bed to become infested with bedbugs, fleas, spiders, cockroaches, mice and similar small but disgusting biting and squirming creatures. No matter what is done, the bed remains infested with the creatures, making sleep even in the same room impossible. The witch can cancel the magic at any time, or the bed can be "cleansed" through Dispel Magic, Remove Curse, and Circle of Protection: Superior.

Use Poison Flawlessly
Range: Self or as many as two others by touch.
Duration: Five minutes per level of the spell caster.
Saving Throw: Not applicable.
P.P.E. Cost: 6

When this spell is cast, the witch can use poisonous, toxic, and acidic substances without fear of infecting herself, spilling a pinch, or misuse. All brews, concoctions and applications are mixed or applied perfectly.

Level Four

Cursed Bread
Range: The cursed bread affects all who eat it.
Duration: Symptoms and penalties last two hours per level of the witch.
Saving Throw: For those eating the bread the save is standard. A successful save means the magic has no ill effect.
P.P.E. Cost: 10

Note: Can curse two loaves of bread per level of experience.

Those who eat the cursed bread suffer from bloating, stomach pain and 1D6 points of damage direct to Hit Points. Penalties last for two hours per level of the witch: -2 on initiative, -1 to on all combat maneuvers, and reduce speed and skill performance by 10%.

The magic Negate Poisons spell will negate the symptoms and penalties, but not the damage inflicted. Those who are impervious to poison are not affected. Mega-Damage creatures only suffer one point of damage and -1 on initiative as they feel a little light-headed.

Dry Mother's Milk
Range: Touch or within 60 feet (18.3 m).
Duration: 24 hours per level of the spell caster.
Saving Throw: -1 to save because the target is typically an animal. A successful save means the magic fails and has no effect.
P.P.E. Cost: 13

By tying a knot in a milking animal's tail, that animal can no longer give milk until the knot is undone or cut out, and a successful Remove Curse is performed, or the spell duration lapses. It causes the afflicted cow, goat or similar milk giving animal to go dry; incapable of giving milk.

The Night Witch can stop the curse at any time. It also stops when the witch is slain. This magic can also afflict human mothers trying to breast feed; same basic process but with the witch pinching a breast. The milk from animals such as cows and goats is usually very important to farmers and peasants. The purpose of this cruel magic is to prevent proper nourishment and confound farmers and herdsmen. In some cases, depriving an entire village or farmstead.

Level Five

Impervious to Disease
Range: Self or as many as two others by touch.
Duration: 30 minutes per level of the spell caster.
Saving Throw: Not applicable.
P.P.E. Cost: 13

The individual(s) protected by this magic is immune to all normal and magical diseases, no matter how potent, deadly or debilitating.

Spoil & Taint Food
Range: Touch and sprinkle of component.
Duration: Permanent
Saving Throw: -4 to save because the target is not a living creature. The base save is 12, but a successful save means the magic fails and has no effect. People who eat spoiled food must make a

save vs non-lethal poison (16 or higher), although the damage inflicted may be deadly to children, the sick and elderly.

P.P.E. Cost: 15

A spell that requires the symbolic sprinkling of a pinch of living or powdered insects (typically fly larvae/maggots) or other poisonous or repulsive substance. Affects up to 20 pounds (9 kg) of food per level of the witch. She can affect any food from grains to processed meats and canned foods. Every item touched even by a single grain of the sprinkled substance is spoiled. In each case, 1D6x10% of the food +2% per level of experience is obviously spoiled, but the rest can be salvaged. However, the salvaging of edible food may be too time intensive to make it practical to save much if any of it.

The Cause of the spoiling is one of the following:
Spoiled by insect infestation;
Mold and mildew;
Rot and bacteria;
Vermin and/or their waste (mice, rats, etc.).

Note: Eating spoiled food results in food poisoning that inflicts 3D6 points of damage direct to Hit Points, unless the victim makes a successful save vs poison. A successful save means no damage and all penalties are reduced to half.

A failed roll to save means the character suffers the 3D6 damage to Hit Points, plus feels feverish, dizzy and nauseous (no initiative, -2 on all combat maneuvers, and reduce speed and skill performance by 25%). Symptoms and penalties linger for 1D4 days.

The magic Negate Poisons spell will negate the symptoms and penalties, but not the damage inflicted. Those who are impervious to poison are not affected. Mega-Damage creatures only suffer one point of damage and -1 on initiative as they feel a little light-headed.

Level Six

Spoil Concentration
Range: Touch or within 60 feet (18.3 m); line of vision.
Duration: One hour per level of the spell caster.
Saving Throw: Standard
P.P.E. Cost: 15

The victim is easily distracted and not very alert or focused, missing even many obvious things. Reduce skill performance by 10%, initiative by half, and -1 melee attacks/actions.

Remove Curse and Restoration spells will restore the concentration and negate any skill penalties. Psionic probes will reveal a magical mental block but only the psionic powers of *Hypnotic Suggestion* (used in this case, to remove the magical block) and *Mind Bond*, or the Mind Bleeder's power of *Mental Block Removal* can destroy the magic and restore spoiled concentration.

Track Thy Enemy
Range: Self or other by touch; line of sight up to 40 feet (12 m) away.
Duration: One hour per level of the spell caster, or until the soil is spilled or put down.
Saving Throw: 16, standard for rituals. A failed roll means the victim can be easily followed wherever he goes. A successful save means the magic fails. New components must be gathered to attempt the magic again.

P.P.E. Cost: 15

The Witch gathers the soil around the footprint of the character she intends to track. The soil is put in a small bag or pouch and either hung around the neck or held in hand. The tracking ability can be transferred to one of her demon minions or human henchmen by touch while the spell is being cast. Whomever the tracker may be, it is that individual who must hold onto the soil. As long as that character wears or holds the soil, he can track that one person (or animal) flawlessly (98%). The moment the small bag of soil is put down or spilled, the magic is broken. Those magically pursued in this fashion can not successfully cover or hide their trail from this enchanted tracker, not even by climbing a tree or walking through water. Flying disrupts the tracking enchantment, but even then, the tracker will have a genuine idea of what direction the character has travelled, and can pick up the trail at a later time where the pursued sets his feet back to Earth.

Level Seven

Spoil Memory
Range: Touch or within 60 feet (18.3 m); line of vision.
Duration: One hour per level of the spell caster.
Saving Throw: -2 to save.
P.P.E. Cost: 20

The victim can either be made to have trouble remembering things in general (the performance of all skills are -20% and they take 25% longer to perform), or to forget one small, specific thing, such as having seen the witch or one of her associates, the date and/or time of an appointment, the name of a particular person, the location of a particular item, and so on. In the alternative, one entire skill, fighting ability, spell, or memory of a specific person or event can be temporarily spoiled and forgotten, but it will return as soon as the spell duration lapses or the witch is slain. Of course, the witch can remove the spell at any time.

Remove Curse and Restoration spells will restore the memory and negate any skill penalties. Psionic probes will reveal a magical mental block but only the psionic powers of *Hypnotic Suggestion* (used in this case, to remove the magical block) and *Mind Bond*, or the Mind Bleeder's power of *Mental Block Removal*, can destroy the magic and restore spoiled memory.

Level Eight

Spoil the Mind with Numbing Madness
Range: Touch or within 60 feet (18.3 m); line of vision.
Duration: Three minutes per level of the spell caster.
Saving Throw: Standard
P.P.E. Cost: 25

The afflicted individual stares out blindly, reacting only to attacks specifically directed at him. During this period, the victim froths at the mouth and is incapable of performing skills, taking action (other than self-defense), speaking or thinking. While under the enchantment, he or she can be led by the hand, pushed or dragged, and similarly manipulated, provided the manipulator has no ill intent on the individual. However, the afflicted character will instantly recognize the evil mage who has ruined his mind. All other people are barely noticed. If he should slay the Night Witch, the magic is instantly broken and all others cursed by the witch are restored to normal.

Wither Thy Enemies

Range: 10 miles (16 km) per level of the spell caster. This is a ritual requiring the enchantment of components. The victim must be within the range of the spell to be affected.
Duration: Until the victim dies or the magic spell is broken.
Saving Throw: Special; see below.
Damage: See penalties and wasting below. Can result in death.
Saving Throw: -2
P.P.E. Cost: 30 against mortals, 60 against Mega-Damage beings who are not supernatural or creatures of magic (they are immune).

This spoiling magic makes its victim sick and waste away. It requires bits of the intended victim's hair or that person's footprint to cast harmful magic upon him. In the latter case, the Witch gathers the soil around the footprint and puts it in a bag or pouch and attaches it to a tree or chimney.

As the hair or earth dries, so too does the victim of the enchantment wither away. The victim suffers from an unquenchable thirst, feels feverish and hot. With each passing day the victim looks more worn out and gaunt, regardless of how much rest, food or water he might get. Suffers the following penalties and deterioration with each passing day: -1 point from S.D.C. and Hit Points, -1 from Spd attribute, -5% to skill performance, and healing potions and magic have no effect. After the tenth day, the victim also sees his attacks/actions per melee round reduced by half and any combat bonuses reduced to zero. He continues to wither and waste away until down to six hit points. At this point the character gets to try to save vs magic. If that roll fails, the character will lapse into a coma and die in six days!

The witch can break the spell at any time. The spell can also be instantly broken by finding the bag with the soil or hair, removing it from its perch in a tree or on a chimney and spilling the contents on the ground, or by killing the witch responsible. A successful Remove Curse can also break the spell.

Moving out of range of the magic only offers conditional relief; the disease stops progressing, but the victim does not recover any Hit Points or S.D.C. by any means. Furthermore, the ailment continues the moment he reenters the enchanted area around the sack.

Level Ten

Demon Charms

Range: Touch or within 60 feet (18.3 m); line of vision.
Duration: The toxic magic on the enchanted object lasts for 15 minutes per level of the spell caster, and poisons every bit of food or drink it touches. The venomous curse on the object can be made permanent as well.
Saving Throw: Standard
P.P.E. Cost: 75 for a temporary cursed item, 200 to make the item permanently cursed. Permanently enchanted items have 50 M.D.C. but can be destroyed. Furthermore, all such cursed items become inert and return to the ordinary the instant the evil witch dies.

These cursed "charms" are not pieces of jewelry but utensils used in the preparation, serving or eating of food and drinks. The Night Witch has the power to enchant one particular object such as a fork, spoon, ladle, pot, pan, pitcher, goblet, glass, etc., cursed with spoilage. Any food it touches (or in the case of pots, pans and other containers, any food or drink placed inside it) becomes magically, but imperceptibly spoiled/poisoned. In this particular case, the food or drink is not obviously tainted and tastes good. However, all who eat the bad food get seriously ill.

Eating the bad food inflicts 6D6 points of damage directly to Hit Points, unless the victim makes a successful save vs lethal poison. A successful save means no damage and all penalties from illness are reduced to half. Duration is also halved.

A failed roll to save means the character takes 6D6 points of damage directly to Hit Points, plus suffers from high fever, dizziness, headache and nausea. Penalties: No initiative, reduce combat bonuses, attacks per melee round, speed and skill performance by 50%! Symptoms and penalties linger for 1D4+2 days. Victims also continue to suffer 1D6 points of damage, directly to Hit Points, every day that they are ill! Vile witches can make entire communities sick, and kill scores of people (children and the elderly being the most susceptible) by using one such item. Just imagine the harm that could be done by serving stew or soup with a cursed Demon Charmed ladle at a church or social function — each scoop of food is sickness and potential death.

The magic Negate Poison spell will prevent further physical damage but the symptoms and penalties persist unabated. Only the witch who made the cursed item(s) or a successful Remove Curse spell can negate the penalties and illness. **Note:** Those who are impervious to poison are not affected. Mega-Damage creatures only suffer 2D6 M.D. and 1D4 M.D. per each subsequent day, and all penalties are half of those previously noted.

The Hidden Witch O.C.C.

Also Known as the Gypsy Witch

The Hidden Witch is a practitioner of dark magic who appears to be a completely ordinary person, male or female, but possesses supernatural and magical powers. Most (90%) Hidden Witches are females and possess the powers to heal and hurt. However, the Hidden Witch does not derive her powers from some demonic supernatural being like the Pact Witch, nor does she start life as a vile, black soul, like the Night Witch. Most start their career in witchcraft as strong-willed and self-serving individuals who see this dark magic as a way to acquire wealth, power and prestige. Most convince themselves that they are strong enough to control the magic and escape its corrupting influences. Most are wrong.

The majority of Hidden Witches are of anarchist, miscreant and aberrant alignments. Many actually try to do some good with their magic, but are ultimately self-serving and use their craft as a means to their ends. In this regard, the Hidden Witch is similar to a thief — a fundamentally self-serving individual

who uses and abuses others, ignores the law, and lies, cheats, steals and even kills, to get what they want. Like the thief, they are usually secretive, often have an innocent-looking public persona, and are cunning, careful and subtle about their underworld dealings.

This particular witch is arguably the least powerful and least vile of the Russian witches. She does not command Demon Helpers or a Demon Familiar, and often avoids consorting with demons, Night Witches, Pact Witches and Necromancers. That having been said, the Hidden Witch is a master of deceit and treachery. Most are reasonably good thieves, associated with criminals and cutthroats, as well as other Hidden Witches and sorcerers, and may also build a relationship with Woodland Spirits.

The Hidden Witch is said to originate among the Gypsies, and is frequently found among their clans. Consequently, she is also known as the "Gypsy Witch," and because the Hidden Witch usually commands the powers of both life and death, pain and pleasure, she is often known as the "Mistress of Life and Death."

The Special Powers & Abilities
of the Hidden Witch

1. Becomes a minor Mega-Damage creature. The Hidden Witch has P.E. x2 for physical M.D.C., plus 1D6 M.D. per each level of experience. P.S. is *not* supernatural nor is her life extended. The Hidden Witch ages naturally.

2. Bio-Regeneration. The Hidden Witch can bio-regenerate 1D6 M.D. per hour, day or night, but can not regrow severed limbs.

3. The shapechanging powers of the Hidden Witch: The witch can shapechange into a black cat, black magpie/raven, or grey fox once per 24 hours. She can speak in her animal disguise, but can not cast spells and skills are performed at -80% due to the inappropriate animal form. Otherwise, she looks, acts and has all the natural abilities of that particular animal. The animal metamorphosis can be maintained for up to one hour per level of the Hidden Witch.

4. P.P.E.: Like all practitioners of magic, the Hidden Witch is a living battery of mystic energy that she can draw upon at will. *Permanent Base P.P.E.:* 2D4x10 +P.E. attribute number. Add 1D6+2 P.P.E. per level of experience. Additional P.P.E. can be drawn from ley lines and blood sacrifices (see **Rifts® RPG**, page 162, *Taking P.P.E. from the living*). However, most Hidden Witches tend to avoid human sacrifices to acquire the doubled P.P.E. released by the victim at the moment of their death. Of course, the most evil don't have any qualms about killing.

5. Limited & Specialized Mystic Knowledge: The Hidden Witch is not the trained adept that the Night Witch and other practitioners of magic are. She has the following magic knowledge and powers and rarely learns more than one additional common wizard spell every other level of experience, if that much. The Hidden Witch is more like a Mystic who instinctively knows a new set of spells at various junctions in her life.

- At level one the character possesses 1D4+2 Spoil Magic spells of choice (excluding 8th level or higher), plus Sense Evil, Fear, Domination, Agony, Life Drain, Minor Curse, Sickness, Spoil and Blind.

- At level two she gets an animal familiar (typically a cat, dog, fox, ferret, ermine or rat), via the Familiar Link spell (see *Rifts® RPG*, page 182). **Note:** Does not have Demon Helpers or a Demon Familiar.
- At level three she possesses many healing spells, including: Negate Poison/Toxin, Cure Minor Disorder, Cure illness, Heal Wounds, Cure Illness, Purification (of food and water), and Remove Curse.
- At level five the character knows the following spells from *Rifts® Federation of Magic:* Cleanse, Mend the Broken, Life Source, Fortify Against Disease, Heal Self, and Greater Healing.
- At level seven, the Hidden Witch knows, Second Sight, Charismatic Aura, Mask of Deceit, Multiple Image, and Fool's Gold.
- At level nine, the character knows Metamorphosis: Animal and Negate Magic.
- At level eleven, she knows Oracle, Exorcism and Commune with Spirits.
- At level thirteen, she learns Constrain Being and Curse Phobia.
- At level fifteen, she knows the following spells from *Rifts® Federation of Magic:* Death Curse, Deathword and Restore Life.

6. O.C.C. bonuses: +1D4 to P.B., +1 one melee attack, +4 to save vs Horror Factor, +1 on initiative, +4 to save vs possession, +1 to save vs magic, and +2 to save vs poison and disease. All are in addition to possible attribute or other bonuses. +1 to spell strength at levels 3, 7, and 11.

The Inner Demon of the Hidden Witch

Whether good, selfish or evil, the powers commanded by the Hidden Witch are more than she can completely control. As a result, her inner demon may be unleashed while she slumbers, even when she doesn't want to! This is not a conscious decision or attack, but a reflection of her inner thoughts, fears, desires and hatred. This inner demon is most typically activated by feelings and desires of hate, revenge and envy. The Inner Demon rises out of the witch and becomes a magical manifestation of her subconscious mind and powers. This "manifestation" takes physical form as a flying creature. Among good and selfish characters, it typically takes the form of a large grey moth with flecks of color, or a small bird, while the Inner Demon of evil Hidden Witches appears as a bat, small owl or raven.

The Inner Demon takes flight with the sole purpose to find the source of its foul emotions and punish, hurt or kill those responsible. Occasionally, if a Hidden Witch of good or selfish alignment is terribly concerned about somebody, her Inner Demon will serve as a secret protector, going forth while she sleeps to watch over him or her. The secret protector makes its presence known only when the person she is worried about is directly attacked. The wrath of the Inner Demon, even when protecting somebody, is terrible and usually murderous.

Fortunately, the Inner Demon is only a dim reflection of the Gypsy Witch and as such, has only a fraction of the witch's power. Available P.P.E. is only 33% of the amount currently available to the slumbering witch.

All spells are cast at 33% the witch's current level of experience.

Physical attacks by the Inner Demon are also possible (typically bite or claw strike with its feet), but only inflict 2D6 S.D.C./Hit Point damage or one M.D. point to Mega-Damage creatures and structures.

And, lastly, the Inner Demon is primarily a primordial extension of the Hidden Witch, so it is incapable of elaborate schemes, treachery, clever traps or long-range plans. Instead all its actions tend to be aggressive and direct. They are focused only upon the specific cause of their emotional turmoil and those who get in its way.

The Inner Demon:

The manifestation can only occur once a night and seldom happens more frequently than once a week, unless the witch is burning with hate or other strong emotions (then it could appear every 36 hours, but only when she sleeps). More typically, such a demon plagues the same individual once every month or so.

Maximum Range: 500 miles (800 km). If its quarry is out of range, it returns back to the witch or turns its aggression toward others who provoke or vex the witch in her waking hours.

Flying Speed: Hover to 60 mph (96 km).

Attacks per Melee Round: Equal to half those of the witch.

Hit Points/M.D.C.: Considered a Mega-Damage creature fueled by powerful emotions, the thing has 1D4+2 M.D. per level of the witch.

Symbiotic Link: Every point of damage the Inner Demon suffers, the Hidden Witch loses an equal number. When 40% of her M.D.C. has been drained, there is a 01-80% likelihood that the slumbering witch will awaken, causing the Inner Demon to immediately vanish. If the witch fails to awaken, each additional attack that does damage to the Inner Demon (even if as little as one point) has a 01-95% chance of waking the character. The Hidden Witch will remember the battle only as a nightmare that jarred her awake. Like most dreams, the details are vague, although she will remember seeing the target of her hate/rage/subconscious emotions fighting some terrible monster who was trying to kill him. She won't recognize the monster as being her own Inner Demon/desires, although sometimes (01-33% chance) she will see herself in the dream, fighting her enemy.

Hidden Witch Optional O.C.C. & N.P.C. Villain

Also known as the Gypsy Witch and Mistress of Life and Death.

Alignment: Any, but most are anarchist (40%), unprincipled (20%), aberrant (15%) and miscreant (15%).

Racial Restrictions: None, although the vast majority (80%) are human.

Roll The Eight Attributes as normal for that race, although the Hidden Witch is a minor M.D.C. being.

Average Level of Experience (N.P.C.): 1D4+3

Psionics: Psionic abilities are not a requirement, but approximately 20% possess minor or major psionics.

Attribute Requirements: I.Q. 9, M.E. 9, or higher.

O.C.C. Skills:
Basic Math (+20%)
Speaks Russian at 95%
Speaks Euro and one other language of choice (+20%)
Lore: Demons & Monsters (+15%)
Lore: One of choice (+10%)
Animal Husbandry (+10%)
Paramedic (+10%)
Cook (+20%)
Brewing (+15%)
Seduction (+13%)
Land Navigation (+10%)
W.P. Ancient, one of choice (any).
W.P. Energy Weapon, one of choice (any).
Hand to Hand: Basic to start, but can be changed to Expert for the cost of one O.C.C. Related Skill or two skills for Martial Arts (or Assassin, if evil).

O.C.C. Related Skills: Choose three Rogue skills, plus six other skills at level one and one additional at levels 3, 5, 7, 10 and 13.
Communications: Any (+5%)
Domestic: Any (+10%)
Electrical: None
Espionage: Any
Mechanical: None
Medical: Any (+10%)
Military: None
Physical: Any, except Boxing, Gymnastics and Acrobatics.
Pilot Skills: Any, except robots, power armor, military vehicles, ships and aircraft.
Pilot Related Skills: Any
Rogue Skills: Any (+5%)
Science: Any (+10%)
Technical: Any (+10%).
W.P.: Any
Wilderness: Any (+5%)

Secondary Skills: The character also gets to select four Secondary Skills from the previous list at level one and one additional at levels 4, 6, 8 and 12. These are additional areas of knowledge that do not get the advantage of the bonus listed in parentheses. All secondary skills start at the base skill level. Also, skills are limited as previously indicated.

Standard Equipment to Start: Light suit of M.D.C. body armor, an S.D.C. dagger (1D6), Vibro-Knife (1D6 M.D.), one M.D. weapon of choice, one silver knife, silver cross, mallet and six wooden stakes, two medium sacks, one large, backpack or satchel, bedroll, canteen or water skin, belt, boots, flashlight, language translator, note pad, 2D4 pencils, a nice wardrobe of clothing, and a handful of personal items. Additional weapons, special items and magic items may be acquired over time.

N.P.C.s are likely to have an animal familiar, their own residence or business (the latter is often a house of healing, fortune-telling or gambling, tavern or Gypsy's wagon), 1D4 magic items, and 1D6x10,000 in gold, credits and valuables, plus 2D4x1000 worth of favorite jewelry, a collection of herbs, poisons and components necessary for their magic and scheming. The Hidden Witch may also have one or more guard animals, a lover or other protector(s), loyal assistants, and dangerous or influential friends and safeguards as the G.M. sees fit.

Vehicle: Starts with none. Whether an N.P.C. has a vehicle is up to the G.M. Those who can not drive may have a servant to drive them.

Secret Resources: Varies dramatically with each specific character. Approximately 48% are Gypsies and are loyal to their clan and family. Those who are not actually Gypsies themselves know and associate with them. Furthermore, most Hidden Witches establish friendships, deals and connections with underworld figures, mercenaries, cults, and other influential people in all walks of life; from thieves and spies to ruling powers and members of the Warlords' Camps. Just how expansive that network may be, depends on the character, circumstance and the G.M.

Money: Player characters start with 1D6x1000 credits, and 1D6x100 in tradeable goods. N.P.C.s start with 1D6x10,000. Many build notorious reputations and some amass sizable fortunes. Some are even rulers and leaders of towns, clans and gangs.

Cybernetics: None; avoids them as unnatural and unnecessary.

The Necromancer

NPC Villain & Optional Player Character

Necromancy is an obscure area of magic said to have originated either in Africa or China, although some credit the ancient Atlanteans. It is a black art that draws power from the dead and dying, and involves blood sacrifices, torture and murder. In addition to the acquisition of knowledge and magical power through ritual killings and evil ways, many Necromancers consort with ghosts, entities, spirits and demons, as well as with witches and other evil practitioners of magic. Thus, it is generally a mystic art shunned by people who value life. However, necromancy is appealing to wicked, depraved, ruthless and rather extreme individuals. It is especially popular among some of the monster races like ogres, trolls and orcs.

Indeed, except for cults within the infamous and fearsome *Federation of Magic*, its practice is virtually unheard of in North America, even among the vampire kingdoms of Mexico. Nor is it practiced in Canada, Central or South America, Australia, Japan, or most of Europe. Even the Splugorth and monsters of Atlantis stay clear of this particular death magic. And while necromancy *may* have originated in China, its practice has been abandoned for centuries, although recent rumors suggest a number of Death Cults may be making a resurgence in Asia.

By far and away, necromancy is most common in *Africa* and parts of southern Europe, most notably *Southern France*. It is also practiced to varying degrees in *Yugoslavia, Albania, Bulgaria, Turkey, Syria, Arabia, Egypt, Libya, Sudan, Ethiopia, Iraq* and *Iran*. The reason necromancy is so popular among these countries is the influence of forces in Rifts Africa, including the insane Pharaoh Rama-Set, the Four Horsemen of the Apocalypse, and the popularity of the so-called Egyptian Gods of Darkness where "death gods" play an important roll. Except in Africa, the parts of the world where necromancy is comparatively common, it is generally regarded as one of the black arts to be avoided by god-fearing creatures and men of noble and good hearts. In many places, Death Magic is often relegated to small cults or practitioners among the monster races and evil supernatural beings.

Unknown to the western world, Necromancy has blossomed in Russia. This practice is likely to have grown from Demon worship. In fact, the *Kaluga Hag* may have taught its secrets to a cult that worshipped her, or to loyal minions, and the practice grew from there. It is just as likely to have been brought by adventurers or refugees from Africa or Iran, or one of the other Mediterranean countries. Or it may have sprung from the concept of fighting fire with fire, i.e. fight vile supernatural creatures with an equally vile form of magic. We'll probably never know. Suffice it to say that in the last 110 years, necromancy has grown disturbingly popular in Russia. It is a means to power that ruthless humans and D-Bees have embraced.

Approximately half of the Russian Necromancers are members of powerful cults, secret sects, families or ruling bodies. There are scores of villages and the occasional city-state scattered across Russia where a cult or family of Necromancers have risen to the position of ruling power, an accomplishment earned through the might and intimidation of their "Death Magic."

Necromancers are among the most powerful and feared sorcerers in Russia, however, the Warlords have routed the most dangerous and nefarious individuals, cults and ruling families from their Spheres of Influence in northwestern Russia. The Warlords have also outlawed the vile mystic art and put practicing Necromancers to death. While all the Warlords claim to have purged their territories of the Death Magic, some have been much more diligent and effective than others.

Most Necromancers believe the Warlords' campaign to eradicate evil, demon worshippers and the black arts (most notably, necromancy and witchery) is nothing more than a political and military power play. From the Necromancers' point of view, they represented the Warlords' only real opposition. Many were (and still are) tied to crime networks, bandits and influential political families, or were a power unto themselves. Several even ruled over villages and fledgling kingdoms. Consequently, they represented the Warlords' primary obstacles in seizing power and uniting communities under their own "Spheres of Influence." To establish themselves as "the" power in western Russia, the Warlords had to destroy them. To win the people's support, the Warlords successfully disguised their bid for power as a noble crusade to eradicate demon worshipers and the supernatural in all its forms, including the horrible Necromancers and Witches! Since most Necromancers were indeed evil, involved in crime and exploitation of the weak and innocent, cruel and murderous, the people were easy to win over. Most of the Warlords waged a devastating campaign, at least at first, and slaughtered thousands of Necromancers and their supporters. However, once these Death Mages were routed, and their initial threat eliminated, many of the Warlords relaxed their crusade.

The devastating onslaught and continuing persecution has created tremendous resentment and hatred for all the Warlords (except Seriyev) and has bred an ongoing underground movement against them, if not open warfare. Necromancers engage in subtle and overt vendettas, criminal activities, defiance of the Warlords' laws, and invite insurrection as well as taunt and undermine Warlord control and operations. Furthermore, Necromancers are frequently members of gangs, bandits, criminal organizations, mercenary groups, and demon raiders who strike against the War Camps and human communities under the protection of the Warlords.

Warlords Burgasov, Romanov, and **Kolodenko** have waged effective purges in the eradication of necromancy and witchcraft, however, only *Kolodenko* can truly claim that he has completely wiped these two black arts from his Sphere. In truth, *Burgasov* and *Romanov* have successfully destroyed or routed 70% to 75% of the Necromancers in their respective realms, but the rest have gone underground and remain involved in criminal rackets and operations, as well as dangerous cult and underground activities. These two Warlords genuinely believe necromancy is a pestilence and are dedicated to its annihilation. However, their efforts are further thwarted by the sloth and treachery of their neighbors *Alekseyevna, Seriyev, Orloff,* and *Sokolov.*

Old Man Alekseyevna could care less about Necromancers. As long as they stay out of his affairs and represent no threat to his power base, he leaves them alone. Consequently, necromantic cults, criminal kingpins and influential families thrive in his Sphere. He is noticeably more diligent in dealing with Witches because he hates them for personal reasons.

The charismatic and duplicitous Seriyev puts on a good show and has made a genuine effort to rid his sphere of Witches and demon worshipers, however Necromancers are another story. He has found these cunning and ruthless Death Mages to be effective and desirable allies in his secret underworld network, making for some of his very best enforcers and assassins. Consequently, he is effectively the head of the criminal cartel that is the real power within the Seriyev Sphere. A criminal network heavily influenced by numerous necromantic crime families and independent necromancers who serve Seriyev and the cartel as regional crime lords, special agents, spies and thugs. They are loyal to him and he to them. Like the Mafia of old, they simply keep a low profile and smile at the bogus political war claiming to have stamped out necromancy. **Note:** Witches and other evil practitioners of magic (in fact, all sorcerers in general) have a hard time in the Seriyev Sphere because they represent competition or a threat to the current power brokers. Thus, the cartel helps the authorities identify and locate these "villains," as well as take an active, unseen hand themselves — witches and troublemaking outsiders have a nasty habit of "disappearing."

Warlord Orloff is a despicable monster who sees everybody as a potential enemy. Consequently, he has decreed that his War Camps destroy all Necromancers they encounter. However, there is no investigative branch to seek out and uncover these scoundrels. This means that if a Necromancer keeps a low profile, doesn't bring any attention to himself or his sect, and does not defy or try to undermine Orloff or his kingdom, his War Camps ignore him. Furthermore, Warlord Orloff secretly encourages Necromancers to raid, attack and cause trouble for other Warlords, particularly Romanov, Burgasov, Kolodenko and Alekseyevna. Encouragement comes in the form of looking the other way, denial of their existence, and nonhostility from the members of his War Camp. Depending on the Necromancer(s), the Warlord may even extend them the unofficial protection of his troops by making certain that whatever base of operations or hideouts within (or on) the borders of his Sphere of Influence are "inadvertently" protected by troops. Orloff is infamous for playing border games and lending protection to all brigands, terrorists, and raiders who plunder his enemies and take sanctuary within his borders. This is done by officially ignoring, even refuting, their existence and maintaining strong border defenses against rival Warlords and suspicious outsiders.

This means the Orloff Camp will let the Necromancers (bandits, raiders, etc.) pass unscathed by insisting they are but ordinary and innocent citizens of the Orloff Sphere ("you must be mistaken, there are no necromancers or raiders here. In fact we haven't seen anybody pass this way all day," etc.). However, they will attack any members of a rival Warlord's Camp, as well as heroes, mercenaries, adventurers or outside authorities who try to enter their borders. Orloff's men cannot (as a rule) be bribed or dissuaded, and are quick to use deadly force "in the defense of their border" from "roguish and hostile forces." Thus, they effectively stop any incursions by pursuers under the mantle of sovereignty and self-defense.

Warlord Sokolov is a barbaric savage who sincerely believes all supernatural beings and nonhumans should be destroyed. To that end, he actively battles demons, dragons, monsters, witches, and D-Bees. However, when it comes to Necromancers, as long as they don't challenge him (and nobody in their right mind would), or agree to unofficially and secretly work for him on occasion, he leaves them alone. Of course, they must also pay him an exorbitant tribute and keep a low profile or face obliteration.

The Cossacks dislike Necromancers and are always suspicious of them, but do not actively seek their annihilation.

The Russian Necromancer O.C.C.

Player & Game Master Note: First of all, the Necromancer makes a wonderful villain, whether he is an inexperienced acolyte trying to make a name for himself, a criminal, an unscrupulous adventurer, mercenary for hire, lord of a village, or infamous villain of great power. Most will have underworld connections and/or a gang or henchmen at their disposal. Others will have "associates," allies and friends who represent other dark forces, including demons, dragons, monsters, D-Bees and other evil practitioners of magic. Furthermore, those above 4th level will command at least a small legion of animated dead, zombies, mummies and even the undead — high level Death Mages (8th and up) *may* command a small army of such creatures as well as evil henchmen and supernatural minions.

Although common in Russia compared to other parts of the world, a Necromancer is *not* hiding behind every door. Game Masters should use them as cunning and ruthless reoccurring villains, for while they are "Death Mages" and kill others without hesitation or regret, their own lives are most precious and few will fight to the death.

The evil Necromancer is recommended as a Non-Player Character (N.P.C.) villain. Whether the O.C.C. may be available to player characters is left to the sole discretion of the individual Game Master. Players should make an effort to cooperate with G.M.s who don't allow such a character, especially evil player characters. Reasons for not allowing the character may include a concern for game balance, game direction or personal taste. The **Rifts®** role-playing series offers an exciting array of characters to choose from, so please respect the G.M.'s decision and move forward with the game.

The Necromancer as a player character is not recommended. Players who select such a character must be one of the selfish or evil alignments. Necromancers of a good alignment are NOT possible!

Evil player characters are likely to have a difficult time and a short career (or life) trying to work with predominantly good player characters. On the other hand, Unprincipled or Anarchist Necromancer characters *may* be able to adjust their murderous and ghastly rites, magic and behavior to an acceptable level within the player group, but such "adjustments" will limit their overall Death Magic abilities, ruthlessness and effectiveness.

These characters will be considerably less murderous and cruel than the average Death Mage, exhibiting much greater self-control, restraint and respect for life. They will be far more discriminating, careful and cautious about when, where and how they use their magic. Most will avoid the senseless slaughter of innocent beings and may not engage in human sacrifice or use the more dangerous and disgusting spells.

Similarly, the Aberrant character, although evil, has his own twisted code of honor and justice which means he will show discretion toward who is slain and how the dark magic is used. The Aberrant character is also likely to show his victims mercy with a quick and comparatively painless death and is not likely to murder children or innocent people.

From time to time, these characters with a conscience may find their hands tied and powers limited. For example: The unprincipled (and the nicer Anarchist) character will avoid torture, probably use blood sacrifice only when absolutely necessary and is not a brutal or indiscriminate killer. He will especially avoid wanton killing of innocent beings. In addition, most will have some rationale for taking the life of another: self-defense, revenge, justice, the victim was evil, had no honor, and so on. The character might even resort to becoming a scavenger and grave robber, using the remains of already dead creatures. Most will try to avoid resorting to the taking of a life in blood sacrifices (nor hire an assassin to do their dirty work). The Unprincipled necromancer will also avoid dealings with evil beings, supernatural monsters and even fellow necromancers. They will never enter into pacts with supernatural creatures or work with demon lords or evil tormentors of other beings. These sensibilities may limit the availability of P.P.E. and prevent the use of certain unsavory spells.

Evil and cruel necromancers, including many Anarchists, suffer no such restrictions of conscience and will kill whomever, whenever necessary, without hesitation or regret. Most evil necromancers are ruthless, power hungry and despicable. They do whatever it takes to accomplish the task at hand no matter how reprehensible or vile.

Furthermore, few people ever allow themselves to completely trust a Necromancer, so the player character is likely to operate under a constant veil of suspicion. In addition, the reputation of the Necromancer is such that even the most well intentioned and unusually noble and honorable character will be looked upon with great fear, suspicion and revulsion by most ordinary and good people. Meanwhile, crooks, cutthroats and dark creatures of all types will see the character as a kindred evil spirit. Once his good nature is discovered, that player character will be seen as an aberration and traitor.

The Russian Necromancer O.C.C.

Note: Expanded from *Rifts® Africa* with new magic and material added.

Most Necromancers are of an evil or selfish alignment and generally seek power over the living through their manipulation of the dead through magic and supernatural forces.

Characters of a good alignment cannot practice death magic and even an Unprincipled (selfish) character Necromancer is a rarity. The magic frequently requires the manipulation, enslavement, torture and murder of living beings. Many of the rituals are repulsive and either involve blood sacrifices or working with the remains of the dead, insects, and monsters. Most Necromancers use blood sacrifices regularly, including the murder of humans and other intelligent life forms, usually as a means to draw upon the P.P.E. necessary to perform their magic. Evil Necromancers are typically cold, hard-hearted fiends who kill without hesitation or the slightest bit of remorse. They do what they need to do in their quest for power. Death is simply a resource. The killing of living subjects a necessity to get the P.P.E. which is gloriously doubled at the moment of death. The worst of these Death Mages may slaughter dozens or even hundreds of people to get the amount of P.P.E. necessary to accomplish what they desire.

A large part of the Necromancer's powers is the ability to animate, control and draw power from the remains of the dead. Consequently, these loathsome practitioners of magic are almost certain to carry the remains of the dead with them wherever they go. This includes an array of skeletons, bones, and preserved claws, arms, hands, hooves, wings, etc. These items are likely to be carried in a large satchel, suitcase, trunk or sack(s), to crates transported by wagon or vehicle. Extremely rare and/or valuable items such as the claw of a dragon may be concealed in a pouch, sack, or backpack and NEVER leave his side. Large Necromancers such as ogres, trolls, and giants, as well as truly evil and flamboyant mages, may wear the bones and shrivelled remains of creatures as jewelry, belts, necklaces, and weapons, as easy to grab and use components. Travelling Necromancers may use an entourage of skeletons and zombies as animated servants and protectors. This is an alarming but surprisingly common sight in both Africa and Russia where one or more Necromancers wield tremendous power and have little fear of reprisal. Revolting but true.

Those who establish a permanent lair will be surrounded by skeletons, zombies, bones and body parts, with furniture and decorations made from the bones of the dead (which can be animated in times of need). The lair of especially high level Death Mages will be inhabited by zombies, mummies and animated dead who function as guards and servants. Additional scores of skeletons/corpses will be strategically placed throughout the lair, ready for animation whenever needed. The Necromancer may also enslave or employ low level demons, monsters and vampires. Death Mages frequently entertain and associate with (and sometimes serve) powerful supernatural beings, sorcerers, and ruthless individuals who may visit their lairs. It is wise to use extreme caution when exploring the abode of a Necromancer.

Typical racial divisions among known Necromancers in Africa:
24% Humans (65% males)
20% D-Bees (55% males)
12% Ogres (70% females)
41% Other Monster Races (60% males)
 3% Elves (50% males)

Typical racial divisions among known Necromancers in Russia:
60% Humans (70% males)
16% D-Bees (55% males)
 8% Ogres (70% females)
14% Other Monster Races (60% males)
 2% Other (55% males)

Note: Faerie Folk, Spirits of Light, Elementals, and Ki-lin are *never* Necromancers! Dragons also generally avoid the practice of necromancy. However, humans, D-bees, most optional player races, sphinx, scarecrows, Death Weaver Spider Demons, Syvan, Rahu-men, giants, Orcs, Ogres, Trolls, Wolfen and Za, among others, as well as the occasional god, godling and demon lords may master the dark magic. The monsters in this list and many of the optional monster R.C.C.s are found in the pages of the **Rifts® Conversion Book.**

Special Abilities & Powers of the Necromancer O.C.C.

The most terrifying and fundamental power of the Necromancer is his ability to animate and control the dead. This macabre power has three different manifestations: The union transformation, the augmentation/additional appendages, and animate/control the dead (skeletons, corpses, etc).

1. Union with the Dead

This power enables the Necromancer to transform his own hands or feet into the claws of an animal. The transformation is temporary and is accomplished by tying the claw, in skeletal form or recently severed limb, to his own hand and muttering a spell incantation known only to those of the Necromancer O.C.C. His hand and/or forearm is then transformed into the clawed appendage of that particular creature. This union also gives the sorcerer combat bonuses and abilities relative to that creature.

P.P.E. Cost: Varies; see descriptions of the various types.

Range: Self, only by touch. The animal claw must be tied to the body. At fifth level, the necromancer can perform this transformation on others (same process and conditions), only the duration is half.

Duration: 10 minutes per level of the Necromancer. The transformed limb(s) return to normal when the duration of the magic has elapsed or when the mage is killed or rendered unconscious. Of course the Necromancer can cancel the magic at any time. The entire incantation and the tying of the limb(s) to the subject takes about 15 seconds/one full melee round.

Limitations: The union and transformation of the dead works only on the living. It cannot be used to transform the limbs of vampires, skeletons, or corpses.

Notes: The limb(s) is always proportional to the size of the Necromancer, never tiny or oversized. One or both human hands can be transformed. Any combination of limbs can be used, such as the claw of a tiger on the right hand, the claw of a bear on the left, a pair of horse hooves for both feet, and the wings of a bat attached to the back. Each transformed appendage adds to the Necromancer's frightening visage and power.

This transformation provides enhanced combat powers and speed as follows:

- **Tentacle:** P.P.E. cost: 10. Includes the octopus, squid and a variety of unearthly D-Bees and monsters. +1 to strike, +1 to disarm, +20% to climb using suction cups, +3 to damage, and can pin or entangle an opponent. When used as feet, the character can scale walls like an insect and hang upside down, but speed is reduced by half.

- **Rodent claws/feet:** P.P.E. cost: 10. Includes rats, mice, squirrels, rabbits, and other similar small animals. Provides bonuses of +1 to strike and parry, +2 to Hit Point/S.D.C. damage, and +10% to climb. The magical claw has an opposable thumb and fingers so tools and weapons can be used; roughly equal to human hands. When used as *feet* the mage is +5% to climb and can leap 6 feet (1.8 m) high and across, increase by 30% with a running start.

- **Cat and other feline claws:** P.P.E. cost: 20. +1 on initiative, +2 to strike and parry, +8 to H.P./S.D.C. damage, +20% to climb and +10% to prowl. The claws are retractable, but have no opposable thumb, making it impossible to grasp and use weapons or tools. When used as *feet* the mage is +20% to climb, +15% to prowl and can leap 10 feet (3 m) high and across, increase by 50% with a running start.

- **Canine claws:** P.P.E. cost: 10. Provides bonuses of +1 to parry, and +4 to H.P./S.D.C. damage, but has no opposable thumb, making it impossible to grasp or use weapons or tools. These appendages do not make good humanoid hands, however, when the hind feet of a canine are used for *feet*, they double the mage's normal running speed.

- **Bear claws, badger, wolverine and similar large claws:** P.P.E. cost: 15. +1 to strike and +1 to parry, +10 to damage (S.D.C.), and +5% to climb. The claw is excellent for digging but has no opposable thumb, making it impossible to grasp or use weapons or tools. When used as *feet,* the mage is +15% to climb.

- **Bird claws/talons:** P.P.E. cost: 15. Provides bonuses of +1 to strike and parry, +8 to H.P./S.D.C. damage. The claws can grasp tools and use weapons at -1 to strike or parry. When using modern or complicated devices there is a skill penalty of -20%. Claws used as feet enable the mage to use his feet like an extra pair of crude hands, ideal for grasping and holding, but -10% to perform skills. They reduce speed by 30% but inflict +8 to H.P./S.D.C. damage when used in clawing and kicking attacks.

- **Dragon claws (any kind):** P.P.E. cost: 50. Provides bonuses of +2 on initiative, +1 to strike, +1 to parry, +2 to save vs poison and disease. The claw inflicts 4D6 M.D., makes the Necromancer impervious to fire, and gives the character a physical M.D.C. of 1D6+12 from hatchlings and 1D6+30 from adult dragons (on S.D.C. worlds he has an A.R. of 14)! Claws used as feet enable the character to inflict 4D6 M.D. from kick attacks, 1D6 M.D. from stomp attacks, and can leap 20 feet (6 m) high and across, increase by 30% with a running start.

- **Claws from other creatures of magic,** including the Manticore, Sphinx, Za, etc. P.P.E. cost: 35. Provides bonuses of +1 on initiative, +1 to save vs poison and disease. The claw inflicts 2D6 M.D. and provides the Necromancer with 1D4+8 M.D.C. (on S.D.C. worlds he has an A.R. of 10). Claws used as feet enable the character to inflict 1D6+2 M.D. from kick attacks and double his normal running speed.

- **Claws and appendages from demons & supernatural monsters,** including Sowki, Mindolar, Russian Demons, Ghouls, Gargoyles and other so-called demons. P.P.E. cost: 50. Claws (any kind) provide bonuses of +2 on initiative, +1 to strike and parry, inflict 2D6 M.D., make him a minor M.D. being with 1D6+6 M.D.C., and make the Necromancer impervious to normal S.D.C. weapons, except those made of silver (on S.D.C. worlds he has an A.R. of 12). Claws used as feet enable the character to inflict 2D6 M.D. from kick attacks and can leap 10 feet (3 m) high and across, increase by 50% with a running start.

- **Claws from a non-supernatural mega-damage creature** like the Melech, Peryton, Loogaroo and any number of alien creatures. P.P.E. cost: 20. Provide the bonuses of +1 on initiative, +1 to dodge, inflict 1D6 M.D. but do not make the mage an M.D.C. creature.

Claws used as feet enable the character to inflict 1D6+2 M.D. from kick attacks and double his normal running speed.

Hooves and feet transform the Necromancer's feet and legs.

- **Hooves of any kind:** P.P.E. cost: 15. Hooves, including horse, ox, cow, deer, etc., add +20 to the character's speed attribute and give him the ability to leap 10 feet (3 m) high or lengthwise, increase by 30% with a running start.

- **Rhinoceros or Elephant Feet:** P.P.E. cost: 20. Increases the character's normal speed attribute by +10 but can also run for a short period of 30 seconds (two melee rounds) at +40. Kick or stomp attacks inflict 4D6 Hit Point/S.D.C. damage.

- **Ki-lin hooves:** P.P.E. cost: 25. Adds +30 to the speed attribute and can leap 10 feet (3 m) high or lengthwise, increase by 50% with a running start, and kick attacks inflict 1D6 M.D.

- **Unicorn hooves:** P.P.E. cost: 30. +40 to the speed attribute and can leap 20 feet (6 m) high or lengthwise, increase by 50% with a running start, and kick attacks inflict 2D6 M.D.

- **Monkey or ape (or humanoid) hands/feet:** P.P.E. cost: 15. +20% to climb skill, +5% to acrobatics, plus the feet are equivalent to hands and can grasp and use weapons, tools and devices. However, the character's normal speed is reduced by half; hands are not made for walking.

2. Augmentation with additional appendages

This power enables the Necromancer to temporarily attach *additional* limbs of dead creatures, people and animals, to his own body and animate them as if they were part of him! This grisly ability is not unlike that of the Apocalypse Demon, Death.

The Death Mage can attach as many as three additional pairs of arms or two pairs of legs. If so desired, he could also add a pair of wings, a tail and several sets of horns to his body, or any combination thereof. Not only does this magic augment the Necromancer's combat abilities and raw power, but it makes

him a horrifyingly alien and disgusting sight to behold; +2 to Horror Factor.

Just as with the transformation of union, the appendages must be strapped to his body before they become a (temporarily) living part of him.

P.P.E. Cost: Varies; see descriptions.

Range: Self only, by touch. The appendage must be tied to the body. At eighth level, the Necromancer can perform this transformation on others (same process and conditions), only the duration is half.

Duration: Five minutes per level of the Necromancer. The limbs return to normal inanimate body parts when the duration of the magic has elapsed, or when the mage is killed or rendered unconscious. As usual, the mage can stop the magic at any time. The entire incantation and the tying of the limbs to the subject takes about 15 seconds/one full melee round per each set of additional limbs; perhaps faster if assisted by underlings.

Notes: The limb(s) is always proportional to the size of the Necromancer, never tiny or oversized. One or both human hands can be transformed plus a total of six additional appendages (arms or tentacles, etc.) can be *added* to the body. A tail or single horn counts as ONE appendage, a pair of wings or arms counts as two appendages.

Note: The Necromancer can also transform his original limbs as described in number one, without interfering with the six additional appendages. Furthermore, the additional, dead, appendages retain their dead appearance, just animated.

This transformation and augmentation provides additional combat abilities, powers and speed as follows:

- **Additional arms or tentacles:** P.P.E. cost: 10 per pair, 5 for one, 20 for each pair of M.D.C. limbs. Each additional *pair* of arms or tentacles adds one physical attack or action per melee round and a bonus of +1 to initiative, and +1 to strike and parry. Three additional "pairs" of arms and hands or tentacles can be added to the body of the Necromancer. That's a possible total of eight arms (the character's two natural limbs and six skeleton limbs) with accumulative bonuses. The additional limbs can be human, D-Bee, monstrous or animal. Note that attaching one giant limb counts as two normal sized limbs.

    The limbs of a Mega-Damage creature are also empowered with the strength of that particular creature and means that those specific M.D. limbs inflict their usual amount of M.D. as per the supernatural strength of that particular type of creature.

- **Horn(s):** P.P.E. cost: 4 each. Horns are used as a weapon in head-butting and ramming. A single horn inflicts 1D4 S.D.C. while a pair of horns does 2D4 damage plus normal punch/head-butt damage; each adds six points to the character's physical S.D.C.

- **Rhinoceros Horn:** P.P.E. cost: 8. The horn inflicts 3D6 S.D.C. damage plus the usual punch/head-butt damage and instills the abilities of keen hearing (+1 on initiative) and keen sense of smell (55% to track by smell), plus it gives the wearer an extra 20 S.D.C. However, vision is reduced by half and is a bit blurry.

- **Dragon Horn:** P.P.E. cost: 30. One horn inflicts 2D4 M.D. (plus punch/head-butt damage from beings with supernatural P.S.) and turns the character into an M.D. creature with 25 M.D. points. Two or more horns do 2D6+2 M.D. and each additional horn adds another 12 M.D.C. points.

- **Dragon Tail:** P.P.E. cost: 30. Provides one additional attack per melee from the prehensile tail and inflicts 2D6 M.D. plus typical M.D. punch damage from supernatural P.S. per strike.

- **Dragon Skull:** P.P.E. cost: 50. Often worn as a helmet or ceremonial headdress known as the "dragon helm"; very coveted. It instills the following powers: 20 M.D.C. to the wearer, make the wearer able to understand and speak all languages, read and write Dragonese/Elven, and makes the wearer impervious to fire, resistant to cold, and breathe whatever type of breath weapon (if any) the dragon had, i.e. fire, cold, acid, etc. In addition, the mage can cast any of the spells once known by the dragon equal to a 5th level spell caster!

- **Skull of a powerful supernatural monster** such as a god, godling, greater demon or demon lord (elementals, vampires, alien intelligences and energy beings are not applicable): P.P.E. cost: 120.

The skull gives the Necromancer 40 M.D.C., the ability to speak that creature's language and all of the creature's natural and magical powers, plus spell knowledge (only while the skull is activated) equal to half its level of ability when the creature was alive. Thus, if the creature could cast magic at 10th level, the spells derived from the skull are at fifth level power. If sixth level, spells drawn from the skull are at third, and so on.

- **A pair of wings from a bird, bat or large animal, Xiticix, or alien (excluding tiny insect wings) can be attached to provide flight:** P.P.E. cost: 30.

  The wings must be strapped to the back of the Death Mage and can be undersized or oversized, but when the magic is engaged the wings grow or shrink to the appropriate size for the user. Flying speed is limited to 20 mph (32 km) for most bats and birds, but 35 mph (56 km) from the wings of birds of prey. Large monstrous wings from such creatures as the Xiticix, Pegasus, Peryton, Harpy, Gryphon, Gromek, Loogaroo, and similar beasts, provide a flying speed of 45 mph (72 km) and +2 to dodge while flying.

- **A pair of wings from magical or supernatural monsters,** including dragons and supernatural creatures like the Gargoyle, Baal-rog, Night Owl, and similar creatures. P.P.E. cost: 90. Flies at a speed of 60 mph (96 km), becomes a minor M.D. creature with 1D6+10 M.D.C. (the wings have 2D4x10 M.D.C.) and bonuses of +1 on initiative and +4 to dodge while in flight.

3. Animate and Control the Dead

The Necromancer can animate and control dead bodies, skeletons, corpses, severed limbs, etc., like giant puppets. This power is very similar to the common spell, only the power of the Death Mage is considerably greater than the spell.

- P.P.E. cost: 10
- Range: 300 feet (91.5 m) plus 20 feet (6 m) per level of experience.
- Duration: 10 minutes per level of experience.

- **Unicorn Horn:** P.P.E. cost: 10. The horn inflicts 1D6 M.D. (plus punch/head-butt damage from beings with supernatural P.S.) and instills the abilities to see the invisible, nightvision 90 feet (27.4 m), keen color vision, prowl 50%, +1 on initiative, and never tires.

- **Ki-lin Horn:** P.P.E. cost: 10. The horn inflicts 1D4 M.D. (plus punch/head-butt damage from beings with supernatural P.S.) and instills the abilities to see the invisible, nightvision 90 feet (27.4 m), healing touch (four times per 24 hours, restoring 2D4 Hit Points and 4D4 S.D.C.), and sense evil (automatic sensation).

- The Necromancer can control four corpses/skeletons per level of experience. The bodies or skeletons can be humanoid or animal.

- The animated dead to be controlled must be in the spell caster's line of vision in order to animate, but the Necromancer can add more to his army as he spies them, or use slain adversaries.

- The Necromancer can also send his dead puppets on simple missions such as "destroy" or "kill." These minions can be sent them wandering out of his sight, swinging and smashing everything that gets in their way (they don't chase those who flee). The animated dead will try to follow the command until they are destroyed or the duration time of the magic elapses.

- The animated dead can be the skeleton or corpse of a humanoid, animal or monster and has the following stats and abilities:

  Speed 8

  Two attacks per melee round.

  Damage inflicted by punches, kicks, claws, and bites is 1D6 S.D.C., and only the simplest weapons can be used, such as a flaming sword, vibro-blade, etc. — modern weapons/guns cannot be used by the animated dead.

  Double the speed and damage of giant animals and humanoids and add one attack per melee round.

  These robot-like animatrons feel no pain, fear or emotions, and are completely impervious to poison, disease, mind attacks, illusions, heat and cold.

- Only total destruction will stop an animated dead (the only *alternative* is to slay their creator or render him unconscious). S.D.C. of a small skeleton or corpse is 50, a human-sized one is 80, and a giant one is 140. These S.D.C. numbers are turned into M.D.C. if the *Fragile Bone to M.D.C. Bone* spell is used on the things. They can also be clad in M.D.C. body armor.

  Note that bullets and stabbing weapons (knives, swords, spears, etc.) do 1/3 damage, blunt and smashing weapons, energy blasts and explosives do full damage, while fire does double damage.

4. Impervious to vampires!

Necromancers are impervious to the mind controlling bite and mind powers of the vampire. Furthermore, they cannot be turned into a vampire (but can be slain by them), and they know all the legends about vampires and other undead, and how to best combat them.

Some Necromancers use this ability to become vampire slayers and to ingratiate themselves among ordinary people, or to earn a place among Demon Slayers, warriors and adventurers — this power is a valuable commodity. Others use this immunity and knowledge only for self-defense and to eliminate competition from the undead. The most daring use it to enslave vampires and other undead as their servants and slaves.

5. Horror Factor

The Necromancer is frightening and macabre (most are also incredibly cold-blooded and evil), as a result, even the less extreme and well intentioned Death Mages radiate with a Horror Factor! At first level, the horror factor is 6, add one at levels three, five, seven, nine, eleven, thirteen and fifteen.

Other O.C.C. Abilities & Bonuses

1. P.P.E.: Base P.P.E. is 2D4x10 plus P.E. attribute number. Add 2D6 P.P.E. per each additional level of experience.

2. Bonuses: +10 S.D.C., +1 to save vs magic of all kinds (in addition to P.E. bonuses), +2 to save vs Necromancy spells, +6 to save vs Horror Factor. O.C.C. Attribute bonuses from physical training and magic: +1 to M.E., P.E., and P.S., and +4 to spd.

3. Initial Spell Knowledge: In addition to the five special abilities described previously, the Necromancer can select six necromancy spells (regardless of level) and six common/wizard spells associated with necromancy. The list and description of all available spells are found in the section entitled *Necro-Magic*.

4. Learning New Spells: Additional spells and rituals related to necromancy (see lists) can be learned or purchased at any time regardless of the character's experience level. See the section entitled *The Pursuit of Magic* in the **Rifts RPG**, page 164.

5. Bone Magic. This is a separate branch of Necro-Magic especially common to Russian Necromancers. It is the ability to enchant bones with magical properties and to use bones as building materials. All Russian Necromancers start with a fundamental knowledge of this magic and have two specific bone items (non-Russian Death Mages can select three additional Necro-spells).

Stats for the Necromancer O.C.C.

Alignment: Selfish or evil, but most are evil.

Race: Any, but in Russia, the majority are human.

Attribute Requirements: I.Q. 10 and M.E. 10 or higher, and P.E. 12 or higher.

O.C.C. Skills:

  Speaks & is literate in Euro and one additional language (+20%).

  Speaks one additional language (+20%)

  Lore: Monsters & Demons (+20%)

  Basic Math (+20%)

  Wilderness Survival (+5%)

  Skin and Prepare Animal Hides & Bones (+5%)

  Pilot Hover Craft or Horsemanship (+10%)

  W.P. Knife or Sword

  W.P. Energy Weapon of Choice

  Hand to Hand: Basic can be selected as one O.C.C. Related Skill, Hand to Hand: Expert at the cost of two skills, or Martial Arts or Assassin (if an evil alignment) for the cost of three skills.

O.C.C. Related Skills: Select seven "other" skills, plus select two additional skills at level two, and one at levels 4, 8 and 12. All new skills start at level one proficiency.

Secondary Skills: The character also gets to select six secondary skills from those listed, excluding those marked "None." These are additional areas of knowledge that do not get the advantage of the bonus listed in parentheses. All secondary skills start at the base skill level.

  Communications: Any (+5%)

  Domestic: Any (+5%)

  Electrical: None

Espionage: Disguise, forgery and intelligence only.

Mechanical: None

Medical: First Aid only (+5%)

Military: None

Physical: Any except acrobatics, gymnastics, and wrestling.

Pilot: Any (+2%)

Pilot Related: Any (+2%)

Rogue: Any (+5%)

Science: Any

Technical: Any (+10% on lore, literacy, language or writing)

W.P.: Any

Wilderness: Any

Standard Equipment: Robe or cloak, leather gloves, box of 100 surgical gloves, a couple sets of clothing, boots, 2D4 large sacks, large satchel or suitcase, box of 50 large, resealable plastic bags, sleeping bag, back pack, utility/ammo-belt, canteen, sunglasses or tinted goggles, air filter or gas mask, infrared distancing binoculars, two hand shovels, one hand axe, Wilk's laser scalpel, food rations for a week, and personal items.

Weapons include a silver and a wooden knife, sacrificial short sword (usually ornate and gilded in a precious metal), 2D4 wooden stakes, a wooden mallet, palm size mirror, a dozen flares, an energy pistol with 1D6 E-clips and one or two other weapons of choice. The Necromancer tends to prefer magic weapons and devices over technological ones, including Kuznya items, Bone Magic creations and the rare, Techno-Wizard foreign import.

Vehicle is limited to non-military means of transportation, and may include a hover vehicle, motorcycle or riding animal.

Money: Starts out with 2D6x1000 in credits and 3D6x1000 in sellable black market items or Bone Magic creations. The average Necromancer will accumulate a large fortune performing his terrible services for other powerful practitioners of magic, supernatural monsters and powerful people.

Cybernetics: Starts with none and will avoid them because they interfere with magic. Only cybernetic bio-systems for medical reasons will be considered.

Note: Most Necromancers are of anarchist or evil alignment, extremely self-serving, manipulative and dangerous. Few have much regard for the living and seek personal wealth and power.

Insanity: The Necromancer often becomes deranged with the passage of time. Roll once on the following table at levels four, eight, ten, twelve and fifteen. Of course if you want the character to be crazy, pick one or two at level two or three.

Necromancer Insanity Table

Roll percentile dice.

01-30 No insanity.

31-40 Obsession: Likes to torture, hurt and kill others.

41-45 Obsession: Hates the light of day and tries to avoid it.

46-50 Obsession: Danger — loves it; takes needless risks.

51-55 Phobia: Gods of Light.

56-60 Obsession: Hates good druids, especially Millennium druids.

61-65 Obsession: Dead things — loves them; surrounds himself with skeletons, mummies, zombies, and the like.

66-70 Phobia: Ancient Dragons.

71-75 Phobia: High level Shaman, Wisemen and/or priests of light.

76-80 Phobia: Spirits of Light/Angels.

81-85 Roll for random affective disorder.

86-90 Roll for random phobia.

91-95 Roll for random obsession.

96-00 Roll for random insanity.

Necromancy

Bone Magic (new)

By Kevin Siembieda

Bone Magic is a type of Necro-Magic that involves the enchantment of ordinary bones to give them special magical properties, making them stronger, or manipulating them in some way. Human or humanoid bones (i.e. intelligent beings) are preferred, but animal and monster bones can usually be substituted. The secret of enchanting bones and using bone as a building material is exclusive to the Necromancer O.C.C. In fact, 40-60% of most Death Mages' possessions, from furnishings and jewelry to body armor, are made of bone. Bone Magic is presented with the rest of the Necro-Magic. The original Necro-Magic spells from *Rifts® Africa* plus the new Bone Magic and many other new Necro-Magic spells have been collected and presented in the following pages.

Note: Any furniture or items made from bone or bone turned into wood can be animated. This means tables and chairs with feet and legs made of bones can be animated to walk, run and ram opponents. Skeleton hands and claws at the ends of a scepter, chairs, railings or as part of a door or lock can grab and hold people, or slash at them, plus hands included as part of a gate or door design can function as a lock to hold the door or gate shut.

Necro-Magic Descriptions

By Kevin Siembieda with additional text
and ideas by Mark Sumimoto and Randi Cartier

Note: Includes necromancy spells from *Rifts® Africa*.

Level One

Animate Body Parts

Range: 20 feet (6 m) per level of experience.
Duration: Two minutes per level of the Necromancer.
Saving Throw: Not Applicable
P.P.E.: 2
Limitations: One body part per level of the Necromancer.

The inexperienced Necromancer is able to animate the appendages and parts of the dead, such as hands and arms, feet, legs, tail, wings, mouth (to bite or mouth words), etc., but not the entire body. Also ideal for manipulating dismembered limbs. If connected to an entire body, one body part (per level of the spell caster) can be animated and controlled. Thus, the hand and arm of a corpse or skeleton could be made to reach out and grab or hit somebody, but little more. Dismembered limbs can be made to move along the ground by crawling, jumping or sliding; speed of 5. The Necromancer has complete mental control over the body parts he can manipulate. Each motion/action of the body part(s) counts as one of his melee actions.

If the Necromancer is rendered unconscious or slain, the spell is immediately broken and the limb/part slumps lifelessly to the ground. A successful Turn the Dead will instantly cancel the spell.

Assemble Bones

Range: Touch or within 60 feet (18.3 m) +20 feet (6 m) per level of experience.
Duration: Permanently assembled, although the bone can be easily moved or knocked apart.
Saving Throw: Not applicable, enchantment is used on the bones of the dead.
P.P.E. Cost: Two points

This spell magically assembles loose bones in one melee round (15 seconds). As much as two complete, human-sized skeletons can be pieced together (roughly 80 lbs/36 kg of bones). If the bones are a loose pile of incomplete skeletons, the spell will assemble what it can and then gather the rest of the bones by type, i.e. all rib bones in one row, femurs in another, etc.

Bone & Joint Bonding

Range: Touch or within 60 feet (18.3 m) +20 feet (6 m) per level of experience.
Duration: Permanent, although the bones and joints can be chopped apart.
Saving Throw: Not applicable, enchantment is used on the bones of the dead.
P.P.E. Cost: Two points

This spell creates permanent, sinewy-like bonds and a flexible adhesive to hold bones together and create bendable joints. This is part of the magic involved in animating skeletons and crawling bones; how else could a skeleton stay together and move without real cartilage and muscle? This magical compound is virtually undetectable.

The equivalent of one entire human-sized skeleton can be assembled and bonded together, with bendable joints.

Rattling Bones

Range: Touch or within 60 feet (18.3 m).
Duration: 10 minutes per level of experience.
Saving Throw: Not applicable, enchantment is used on the bones of the dead.
P.P.E. Cost: 2 points

A Necromancer spell used to unnerve people and create an air of fear. In this case, the magic can make a skeleton or equivalent amount of loose bones tremble. This causes the teeth of a skull to chatter and bones to rattle against each and/or on the floor. The rattling nose combined with seeing a skeleton or bones moving, even though restricted to one place, is frightening. The effect is equal to a Horror Factor of 15. Superstitious people and children are -4 to save vs H.F. All others who fail to save suffer the usual penalties for H.F. for one melee round, but the initiative penalty remains in effect for the entire time the bones rattle. Those who successfully save suffer no penalties.

Talking Bones

Range: Touch or within 60 feet (18.3 m).
Duration: 10 minutes per level of experience.
Saving Throw: Not applicable, enchantment is used on the bones of the dead.
P.P.E. Cost: 3 points

This is more of an unnerving trick, a sort of magical ventriloquism, than a powerful magic. The Necromancer can make the skull of any creature seem to talk. The words are his, but the voice is different, raspy and husky, and clearly comes from the skull. The initial words spoken by the skull are startling and frightening; equal to a Horror Factor of 13. Superstitious people and children are -4 to save vs H.F. and likely to flee the area. All others who fail to save suffer the usual penalties for H.F. for one melee round. As a magical form of ventriloquism, even if the Necromancer is within view, his mouth does not seem to move, and sound will not seem to be coming from him. In addition, the mage can leave the area and have the skull repeat one simple six word phrase over and over for the duration of the magic, even if he is miles away. This can be a menacing howl, moaning, wailing, or diabolical laughter, or words like, "go no further," or "beyond that door awaits death," or "now you die," or "beware, beware, beware ..." and so on.

Note that while most frequently used to frighten and intimidate, this magic can also be used to deliver warnings or information, fake seances, and so on, without the Necromancer revealing his true identity.

Level Two

Crawling Bones

Range: Touch or within 60 feet (18.3 m).
Duration: Five minutes per level of experience.
Saving Throw: Not applicable, enchantment is used on the bones of the dead.
P.P.E. Cost: 5 points

This is a simple and limited form of animate dead, except in this case the Necromancer can only manipulate the severed limbs of a corpse or skeleton. This means he can make one finger, hand, hand and forearm, arm, foot, or prehensile tail crawl or snake to him or do his bidding. This animated appendage can be used to frighten (H.F. 12) or distract people by skittering across the floor or a table, or made to retrieve a small object (key ring, knife, cup, jewelry, etc.), or to attack (grab a leg or throat, claw, punch, or stab, etc.). The animated appendage can also be used as an extension of the mage's own hand. For example, the mage could hold an animated appendage such as a forearm and hand by the end of the forearm to touch, move, turn, grab, etc., something out of his normal reach. Skills that require manual dexterity are performed at -20% when a severed hand is used as an extension.

- The number of appendages that can be animated at a time is limited to one per every two levels of experience, rounding up, so that's one at levels 1 & 2, two at levels 3 & 4, three at levels 5 & 6, and so on.
- Attacks/actions per melee round by the crawling bones are limited to three per round.
- Damage by the appendage is 1D6 H.P./S.D.C. damage.
- Speed is 15 for a hand or foot, 10 for all others.
- Equivalent P.S. is 9.
- Typical S.D.C. is as follows:

Finger — 2
Hand — 12
Hand & Forearm — 24
Forearm only — 12
Upper Arm only — 15
Forearm and Upper Arm (no hand) — 27
Foot — 15
Foot & Lower Leg — 30
Lower Leg only — 15
Upper Leg (Femur) — 25
Tail (small/monkey) — 10
Tail (large) — 20

Fragile Bone to Wood

Range: Touch or within 60 feet (18.3 m).
Duration: One hour per level of experience.
Saving Throw: Not applicable, enchantment is used on the bones of the dead.
P.P.E. Cost: 5 points; 30 P.P.E. to make the transformation permanent.

The Death Mage can turn the equivalent of one human-sized skeleton, or equivalent pile of bones (roughly 40 lbs/18 kg), from ordinary bone to the consistency of wood suitable for building. The "wood" bones are 20% stronger and heavier, so if the bone had 15 S.D.C. it now has 18 S.D.C. The wooden bones are a strong, reliable building material with properties nearly identical to wood. They can be nailed, lashed, glued, polished, sanded, etc., and used to make weapons, furniture, baskets, boats, doors, fences, gates, and even entire houses, although the latter is a rarity. Most Necromancers keep the original bone look for dramatic effect and personal preference (most Death Mages like the color and look of bones and skulls). **Note:** Ordinary bone and bone magically made into wood can be bent and molded via use of the Shape Bone spell in order to curve, bend, twist and adjust the shape of bones for use as building materials; ideal for shaping the handles of weapons, the legs for tables and chairs, pieces for head-wear, jewelry, and so on, as well as to get a consistent size, shape, look and symmetry.

The temporary transformation of bone into wood is typically used on simple items when the strength of wood is helpful but long term use is not. For example, the mage might turn a bone to wood in order to use it as a cudgel/club that won't shatter when it hits. Likewise, he might turn bones into wood to use as a brace or pole to jam a door open or closed, or to prop up a wagon to change a wheel, and so on. The Necromancer can also temporarily turn the bones of animated dead into wood, temporarily increasing their S.D.C. by 20% (See *animated dead* under Special O.C.C. Powers for details on animated skeletons). Bones are made into permanent wood for long term use.

Stench of the Dead

Range: 100 feet (30.5 m) plus 10 feet (3 m) per level of experience.
Duration: 2 minutes per level of experience.
Saving Throw: Standard
P.P.E. Cost: 6

A magic mist covers the area when this spell is cast. The mist stinks of rotting meat and decay. The sickening smell causes all who enter its area of affect to cough and retch twice per melee round (15 seconds), plus the eyes water and no other odors can be smelled while in the overwhelming mist. Penalties: Reduce speed, number of attacks per melee and combat bonuses by half. The mist can be cast up to 100 feet (30.5 m) or further with experience.

Hide Among the Dead

Range: Self or self and one other by touch.
Duration: Five minutes per level of experience.
Saving Throw: None
P.P.E. Cost: 5

Like the Chameleon spell, this magic allows the mage or one other to blend in with his background, only in this case, the background is limited to the remains of the dead. This means the Necromancer can hide among any types of corpses, skeletons, and even animated dead and appear to be just another corpse or skeleton. Even the most advanced modern medical and detection devices are fooled, as are magical and psionic means of detection (see aura, sense magic, presence sense, etc.). This magical concealment only works when there is at least one other corpse or skeleton, and if the Necromancer stays still.

98% undetectable if unmoving.

70% undetectable if moving two feet (0.6 m) per melee or slower.

20% undetectable if moving any faster.

Yes, by the way, if the other bodies are removed (he's the last one), the magic is destroyed and the mage will suddenly appear as his real, obviously living self ("How did we miss that guy?"). The same occurs if he is picked up and carried away from the other corpses.

Level Three

Accelerated Decay

Range: Touch
Duration: Permanent results, with decay happen before one's eyesing with each melee round (15 seconds) equal to the effects of one day of decay.
Damage: Decays the equivalent of two days per level of the spell caster. Fresh fish, prepared vegetables or fruit, stew, or any food prepared for consumption that day is inedible after the equivalent of two days of decay, fresh meat after four days, and fresh fruit and vegetables after the equivalent of six days. A fresh corpse can be turned to bits of flesh and bare bone after the equivalent of 60 days of decay. It is unrecognizable after 20 days, and stinks something terrible after four days. High level spell casters can regulate the level of decay in two day increments.
Saving Throw: None, however if protected by a magic circle, sanctum spell, or against "spoiling," the food or deceased is impervious to this spell.
P.P.E. Cost: 8 per corpse or 200 pounds (90 kg) of organic material.

This magic accelerates the decaying process of organic material, from processed meat and prepared food to the body of a corpse. The level of decay and deterioration is equivalent to sitting in the hot sun (even if the actual food or corpse is refrigerated).

An especially useful spell for covering up foul play by turning a fresh corpse into a withered husk. This means that investigators and pathologists are likely to overestimate the time of death by days and have trouble identifying the victim or have trouble determining the cause of death. The spell will also turn freshly prepared food, meat, cut fruit and vegetables into spoiled mush.

Object Read the Dead

Range: Touch
Duration: Instant
Saving Throw: None
P.P.E. Cost: 8

This spell gives the character a power similar to the psionic ability of object read, only this power is limited to divining things about the dead. Information can be gathered from a corpse, animal carcass, skeleton, skull, or a single large bone. The data is limited but helpful:

- General cause of death: old age, disease, plague, accident or murder.

- Race or animal type.

- Whether the creature suffered or not before dying.

- Whether or not magic was involved.

- The length of time the creature has been dead: immediate (a few minutes), recent (a few hours), quite a while (a few days), a long time (several months), years, or decades (over 20 years).

Recognize the Master

Range: Within 10 feet (3 m) of the mage or by voice command of the mage within 100 feet (30.5 m).
Duration: One hour per level of experience, or permanent.
Saving Throw: Not applicable, enchantment is used on the bones of the dead.
P.P.E. Cost: 8, or 30 P.P.E. to make the enchantment permanent.

This feature is typically used in conjunction with permanent bone gates and doors. The spell enables the bone door, gate and any locking mechanisms built into it (even if the lock itself is not made of bone) to recognize the Necromancer who made it and to respond by opening and closing like a modern door with an electronic eye. It will not open to anybody but the Necromancer. To force open a normal door or gate, meaning it has no special key locks, sliding bolts on the inside or magical locking hands, one needs a combined P.S. of 20 or must break the door knob/handle (typically 15 S.D.C., or 4 M.D.C. if made of M.D.C. material). Once broken, the door can be pushed open with ease.

If the Necromancer is within 100 feet (30.5 m), he can also command the enchanted bone doors or gates to automatically open and close whenever anybody approaches, but he can verbally rescind that order, effectively closing and locking all doors/gates under this enchantment. All doors under this enchantment will respond to the Necromancer's voice commands.

Recognize the Undead

Range: Self
Duration: 10 minutes per level of the Necromancer.
Saving Throw: Standard
P.P.E. Cost: 8

The spell caster is given the ability to instantly and automatically recognize all types of undead, including zombies, mummies, animated corpses, vampires and Vampire Intelligences, no matter how human or innocent they may appear. This knowledge enables the character to better prepare himself for conflict with these monsters (or to avoid such conflicts).

Level Four

Command Ghouls

Range: Self
Duration: 15 minutes per level of experience.
Saving Throw: -2
P.P.E. Cost: 10

This incantation makes 2D4 ghouls per level of the spell caster's experience fear and obey the necromancer. This spell will affect grave ghouls, the dybbuk and similar creatures, but has no affect on dimensional ghouls or ghoulish demon lords. Also note that the dybbuk doesn't appreciate mind control and is likely to seek revenge on the person responsible, unless the mission was an enjoyable one. Grave ghouls are too timid to consider retribution.

Eyes of the Dead

Range: Self
Duration: Five minutes per level of experience.
Saving Throw: None for the user. Standard for victims.
P.P.E. Cost: 8

With this enchantment, the eyes of the Necromancer become black and lifeless. Besides looking creepy and enhancing his already frightening appearance (+2 to Horror Factor), these dark eyes will protect the Necromancer from hypnotic suggestion and any mind control which involves eye contact. The enchantment also enables him to recognize ghouls, animated dead, and the undead. Furthermore, the necromancer's own gaze will unnerve any who look into it, sending a chill running down his spine and a penalty of -1 to all combat skills for one melee round.

Funeral Dirge

Range: Self or other by touch.
Duration: Five minutes per level of the spell caster.
Saving Throw: Not applicable.
P.P.E. Cost: 6

Note: Has no effect unless somebody has died, although it can be played for added affect during a Mock Funeral or as a warning.

Upon recitation of this spell, the Necromancer (or another person, enchanted by touch) can play a recognizable mournful funeral dirge/death or funeral march on any type of horn, piano, drum, or string instrument. The music has foreboding and dark undertones and can be heard for one mile (1.6) per level of the spell caster. To ghouls, grave-robbers, demons, and other Necromancers and death cultists, it is sweet music that may mark the death of an enemy, and, to those creatures who feed on or use corpses, signals to them that a fresh corpse is available. All living creatures who hear it know that it marks the passing of a living being and may spark a moment of reflection and/or sorrow. Juicers, Crazies and Old Believers will feel so sad that they are -3 on initiative, -3 to strike, parry, and dodge, and -1 attack per melee round. These penalties remain in force while the music is played and for 2D6 minutes after it stops.

Kill Plants

Range: Touch
Duration: Instant.

Saving Throw: None, unless an intelligent life form, then standard. Millennium Trees are impervious to this spell.
P.P.E. Cost: 10

This death touch inflicts 1D4x10 S.D.C./Hit Point damage to plants per level of the spell caster's experience. The killing touch is usually performed as an act of vandalism, vindictiveness, or cruelty.

Maggots (insects)
Range: Touch
Duration: 2 days unless killed.
Saving Throw: Standard
P.P.E. Cost: 20

A destroying touch in which the Necromancer can touch food or a dead animal and infest it with maggots and worms that feed on the dead. If people act quickly they can kill the larvae and save 2D4x10% of the food by boiling, deep frying, smoking, microwaving and similar measures to kill the bugs and any possible disease.

Necro-Armor
Range: Self or one other by touch.
Duration: One minute per level of the spell caster.
Saving Throw: None for the user; onlookers must save vs a Horror Factor of 13.
M.D.C. of the Armor: 13 points per level of the spell caster.
P.P.E. Cost: 16

Within seconds, the character is covered with a mass of bones, skeletal fragments and putrid remains. This disgusting coating does not appear sturdy, but is, in fact, a barrier of Mega-Damage protection. Aside from that, the sight of this armor as it envelops its wearer is frightening to watch; roll to save vs Horror Factor 13. The armor also exudes a horrid stench, which will impair anyone within 100 feet (30.5 m) unless they have a separate oxygen supply, no sense of smell, or are supernatural predators. Penalties from the stench are -1 to all combat maneuvers (strike, parry, etc.). At the spell's end, the armor sloughs right off and is quickly reabsorbed into the earth. If cast upon another person, the recipient must roll a successful saving throw vs Horror Factor 13 to fight without impairment. Failure means a penalty of -3 to all combat maneuvers for the duration of the armor.

Summon the Dead
Range: One mile (1.6 km) radius per level of the spell caster.
Duration: 4D6x10 minutes.
Saving Throw: None
P.P.E. Cost: 10

This magic is similar to the *Animate and Control Dead* spell, except that this magic is more limited, because the spell caster doesn't actually control the dead but brings the dead to him. This is especially useful when the Necromancer needs corpses in a hurry, but can't take the time to go out and, um ... dig them up.

1D4 corpses/skeletons, +1 per every other level of experience, will rise from their graves (or wherever) and march on a straight path to their summoner. This can take anywhere from a few minutes to a couple hours, depending on how far away the corpse is. Once the dead makes it over to the Necromancer, it collapses. To animate the thing further, the mage must use the *Animate and Control Dead* spell. Summon the Dead simply brings the dead to the Death Mage, exactly how he uses them later depends on the character.

Alternately, the mage can elect to summon one specific dead to come to him. For this to work, the Necromancer must either have personally known the deceased or have a personal belonging, or sample of his or her blood, hair, or skin. This is often done to discover what has happened to a missing ally who is feared to be dead, or to desecrate a specific grave. Only one of the specific dead can be summoned in this manner, but the range is doubled. The same limitations as the general summoning still apply.

Level Five

Consume Power & Knowledge
Range: Self
Duration: Varies.
Saving Throw: Not applicable.
P.P.E. Cost: 20 per each item.

This repulsive magic requires that the necromancer remove the tongue, brain or organ of a dead being, boil or cook it while reciting the magic incantation, and breathe the fumes from the prepared meat. Necromancers who are monsters may tear out the organ and eat it raw (or cooked) with the same magic results. The basic concept behind this magic is the belief by many cultures, both human and monster, that eating the organs of one's vanquished enemies will give the eater his courage or abilities. Different organs offer different powers. No powers are gained from animal organs. More than one item (maximum three) can be cooked up with accumulative effect.

Heart: Courage and strength. The mage is +3 to save vs horror factor, is not easily unnerved or intimidated, gets an additional 10 S.D.C. and can lift and carry twice as much as normal. Duration: One hour per level of experience.

Liver: Sobriety. No matter how much alcohol is consumed, the character cannot get drunk. Duration: One hour per level of experience.

Kidneys: Impervious to poisons and +2 to save vs non-lethal drugs. Duration: One hour per level of experience.

Intestines: Breathing the fumes provides physical nourishment. The character does not need to eat nor does he feel hungry for 48 hours.

Tongue: Can understand and speak all languages. Duration: Two hours per level of experience.

Eyes: The necromancer will recognize the people, places and items once known by the deceased. He will also know basic things about those people, places or items. For example, the necromancer will recognize the deceased's friends, parents, family, lover, wife, enemy, murderer, home, favorite tavern, car, gun, clothes, etc. Duration: One hour per level of experience.

Brains: Provides the mage with all of that person's skills at 60% proficiency. Duration: One hour per level of experience.

Death Mask
Range: Self
Duration: Four minutes per level of experience.
Saving Throw: All who see the death mask must roll to save vs Horror Factor of 13.
P.P.E. Cost: 12

The spell creates a frightening looking death mask that completely covers the spell caster's face. The mask provides the following:

- Disguises the character's normal facial features.
- Frightening visage evokes fear equal to a Horror Factor of 13.
- Wearer is impervious to all normal disease, poisons, and magic sicknesses and curses.
- Prowl at 55%

Divining Tombs & Graves
Range: Self
Duration: 5 minutes per level of the spell caster.
Saving Throw: Standard
P.P.E. Cost: 10 or 35

This magic requires the use of a wishbone from a large bird. The bone is held in both hands, vibrates and pulls the character in the direction of graves or tombs. When a grave has been located the wishbone stops vibrating. For the cost of an extra 25 P.P.E. the divining spell can locate a specific grave or tomb from among many.

Fragile Bone to Stone
Range: Touch or within 60 feet (18.3 m).
Duration: One hour per level of the spell caster.
Saving Throw: Not applicable, enchantment is used on the bones of the dead.
P.P.E. Cost: 10 points; 60 P.P.E. to make the transformation permanent.

The Death Mage can turn the equivalent of one human-sized skeleton, or equivalent pile of bones (roughly 40 lbs/18 kg), from ordinary bone to the consistency of stone. The "stone" bones are twice as strong (double S.D.C.) and twice as heavy. Both ordinary bone and bones already permanently turned to wood (including those turned into weapons, furniture, doors, fences, and other items) can also be turned into stone. Real wood cannot. Additional P.P.E. will need to be expended to make larger bone items into stone.

The Necromancer can also temporarily turn the bones of animated dead into stone, temporarily doubling their S.D.C. (roughly equivalent to two M.D.C.) and punch damage (becomes 2D6 S.D.C.), but weight is also doubled (approx. 80-100 lbs/36-45 kg depending on the size of the skeleton) and speed is reduced to 4 (See *animated dead* under Special O.C.C. Powers for details on animated skeletons). **Note:** Bones cannot be bent or shaped by the *Shape Bone* spell once they are turned into stone. Bones are made permanent for long term use.

Grip of Death
Range: A 10 foot (3 m) diameter up to 100 feet (30.5 m) away.
Duration: Two minutes per level of experience.
Saving Throw: Horror Factor of 13 and dodge of 16.
P.P.E. Cost: 13

This magic causes 1D4+1 hands and arms of skeletons and corpses to erupt from the ground to grab and ensnare everybody in the radius of influence. First, each character in the area of affect must make a successful saving throw vs Horror Factor 13.

A failed save will inhibit the character's ability to dodge and is automatically ensnared by 1D4+1 of the hands risen from the grave (plus the usual penalties).

Those who successfully save vs Horror Factor can attempt to dodge in order to escape the clutches of the flailing hands of the dead. The character must make two consecutive dodges of 16 or higher (uses up two melee attacks) to get out of the area of affect. If even one dodge is missed, the character is ensnared by 1D4+1 of the hands.

Those ensnared are shook and pulled down on their knees, so they cannot simply ignore the clutching hands in an attempt to launch attacks at those outside the area of affect. Such attacks can be attempted but are done without benefit of any attribute, skill or combat bonuses — straight, unmodified die rolls. The same applies for trying to parry or dodge attacks leveled at them while in the Grip of Death! This penalty remains in effect the entire time the characters are trapped by this magic.

Only a strength of 35 or higher (or supernatural P.S. of 20 or higher) can pull free of the hands, but one melee action is burned up for each hand that has a hold. Others can help in the effort, but they may also become ensnared by the hands from the grave as well. Chopping or blasting the grasping hand off at the base of the arm is another possibility but each arm has 13 M.D.C. and will use up the character's melee attacks (the hand vanishes once destroyed). In either case, the character must then roll two consecutive dodges of 16 or higher in order to escape other hands of the dead trying to grab victims. **Note:** Negate Magic and Dispel Magic Barrier *may* offer a means to eradicate the entire magic spell. Anti-Magic Cloud automatically dispels it.

Locking Hand
Range: Touch or within 60 feet (18.3 m); not applicable when permanent.
Duration: One hour per level of experience or permanent.
Saving Throw: Not applicable, enchantment is used on the bones of the dead.
P.P.E. Cost: 10 points per each locking hand; 30 P.P.E. per each to make the enchantment permanent.

The hand of a corpse or skeleton can be made to grab and hold tight with an equivalent P.S. of 24 (a P.S. of 25 or higher is needed to pry it open). This feature is typically used in conjunction with permanent bone gates and doors to be used as a locking mechanism or defense. As a lock, the hand automatically clenches onto a parallel bar or handhold as a tight, grasping fist to effectively lock/hold a door, gate, or grille shut. Anybody trying to pry the hand open will be clawed (2D6 S.D.C. damage) or grabbed and held until the Necromancer arrives. The hand opens when the mage who created it arrives, unless it is holding an intruder in its grasp, then it lets go only upon the command of the mage.

When used strictly for defense, the hand (typically several hands or hands connected to a moveable forearm for an extended reach or leverage) will grab the intruder and hold him tight. If there are several hands, they will try to grab and hold each of the person's arms and legs to prevent escape, and/or try to grab anybody who tries to free its captive or press forward with trying to open the door. Victims who have their hands/arms grabbed are helpless to pull free or perform any skills unless they have a P.S. of 25 or higher. Kicking and using the legs for leverage is of minimal value. If all appendages are held, the character is completely helpless. This locking feature can also be incorporated into chairs, thrones, beds, prison manacles, torture tables or sacrificial altars to hold victims in place and similar.

Note: This enchantment can be used on skeletal hands that have been transformed into wood, stone or M.D.C. materials, provided the hand was once made of genuine bone.

- P.S. of each hand is 24.
- Magically Enhanced S.D.C.: Bone: 24, Wood: 48, Stone: 75, M.D.C.: 30.

Level Six

Poison Touch
Range: Self or one other by touch.
Duration: One minute per level of the spell caster.
Saving Throw: 12 or higher, but victims are -2 to save.
P.P.E. Cost: 15

This spell enables the touch of the Death Mage to secrete a dangerous poison that is transmitted by touch. Each touch requires a separate saving throw, and damage is accumulative. Bare skin must be available. Each touch inflicts 4D6 Hit Point/S.D.C. damage, unless the victim makes a successful save vs poison. A successful save means he suffers only 1D6 H.P. damage. A failed roll to save means the 4D6 damage plus the victim feels feverish, dizzy and nauseous (-1 on initiative, and reduce speed and skill performance by 30%; penalties linger for 1D6 minutes per each poisonous touch). The effects are immediate and cumulative.

The magic Negate Poisons spell or potion will negate the symptoms and penalties, but not the damage inflicted. Those who are impervious to poison are not affected. Mega-Damage creatures only suffer one point of damage and -1 on initiative as they feel a little light headed, and suffer no effects on a successful save.

Wear the Face of Another
Range: Self
Duration: One hour per level of the spell caster.
Saving Throw: Not applicable, victim is dead.
P.P.E. Cost: 15

This grotesque magic enables the Necromancer to quickly (30 seconds/two melee rounds) remove the skin from the face or entire head (including hair) from the skull of a corpse and magically adhere it to his own. The face of the dead man appears completely natural and alive, as if it were the mage's real face. It can make for a completely undetectable physical disguise, unless somebody knows the deceased is dead. Of course the voice, memories, and body remain those of the Necromancer. **Note:** The corpse cannot have been dead for more than 24 hours.

Level Seven

Curse: Death Wish
Range: Touch or 10 feet (3 m) per level of the Necromancer.
Duration: One hour per level of the spell caster.
Saving Throw: Standard, unless a willing subject, Juicer or Crazy, in which case the character is -3 to save.
P.P.E. Cost: 20
Limitations: One victim per spell casting.

This instills the recipient with no fear of death and suicidal tendencies that result in foolish, death-defying risk-taking, fights to the death, and unthinking courage. Unbeatable odds and overpowering opponents will not give them the least bit of hesitation. In fact, the victim will go out of his way to take unnecessary risks or challenge others to the point of making Juicers and Crazies look like sane and reasonable people. Speaking of Juicers and Crazies, their natural tendencies make them especially susceptible to this magic and are -3 to save.

The enchantment gives those affected a bonus of +5 to save vs Horror Factor, +4 to save vs possession and mind control, and +2 on initiative, but it also gives them a penalty of -3 to parry, -6 to dodge, -6 to disarm, and -6 to roll with punch, fall or impact and have no bonuses to save vs coma/death. In fact, the victim rarely even attempts to dodge attacks, preferring to stand his ground against his opponents and fight like a man who doesn't care whether he lives or dies.

Level Eight

Death Bolt
Range: 200 feet (61 m) +20 feet (6 m) per level of the Necromancer.
Duration: Instant, plus effects linger for one minute per level of the spell caster.
Damage: 1D6 damage direct to Hit Points per level of experience! If the opponent is supernatural or some other Mega-Damage creature, it suffers 1D6 M.D. per level of experience of the spell caster.
Saving Throw: Special; potential victims are -2 to save, but cyborgs are +4 to save. Those who save take one third damage and suffer no penalties.
P.P.E. Cost: 30

This magic unleashes a multi-tendrilled bolt of black lightning that erupts from the Death Mage's palm and completely bypasses body armor (or natural A.R.) to inflict damage direct to the target. Damage is S.D.C. or M.D. depending on the nature of the victim. In addition, unless the victim rolls a successful save vs magic, he will suffer from the following penalties: -4 to initiative, -1 to parry and dodge, and Spd is reduced by 25% for one minute/four melee rounds. The bolt can pass through full environmental body armor and even light power armor, but not heavy power armor, medium to heavy Cyborg armor, walls, or heavy vehicles. It has no effect on robots or machines.

Against undead creatures, the bolt has an energizing effect. Vampires, Dybbuk, Zombies, and all other sorts of undead will find its Hit Points or M.D.C. increased (or restored if injured) by 4D6 points the instant bolt the strikes it. Used repeatedly, a Necromancer mage can increase an undeads hit points or M.D.C. by a maximum of 60 points. The duration of the increased durability is two minutes per level of the spell caster, or until additional damage reduces it.

Death Strike

Range: Self; melee attack directed at others.
Duration: One minute (four melee rounds) per level of experience.
Saving Throw: Opponents are -1 to save.
P.P.E. Cost: 25

Every punch, kick, or strike inflicted by bare hands/feet or by hand-held weapons such as a club or sword (excluding guns) inflicts double damage. Furthermore, if the opponent is a Mega-Damage being the doubled damage is Mega-Damage!

Fragile Bone to M.D.C. Bone

Range: Touch or within 60 feet (18.3 m).
Duration: 30 minutes per level of experience.
Saving Throw: Not applicable; the enchantment is used on the bones of the dead.
P.P.E. Cost: 40 points; 160 P.P.E. to make the transformation permanent.

The Death Mage can turn one human-sized skeleton, or equivalent pile of bones, from fragile bone (or permanent wood bone) to Mega-Damage materials! If the bone had 15 S.D.C., it now has 15 M.D.C., if it is an entire animated skeleton, the thing is now an M.D.C. skeleton (S.D.C. converted to M.D.C.). See animated dead under Special O.C.C. Powers for details on animated skeletons. Necromancers sometimes make a suit of armor, weapons, furnishings or decorations out of bone and then permanently transform them into Mega-Damage Structures — has the light weight of bone, but Mega-Damage resilience.

22 M.D.C. for armor that covers chest and shoulders only (weighs 15 lbs/6.8 kg), 22 M.D.C. for skull helmet (weighs 5-8 lbs/2.3 to 3.6 kg), 45 M.D.C. for a half-suit and helmet that protects the upper body, arms and head (weighs 22 lbs/10 kg), and 80 M.D.C. for a full body suit made predominately from bones and/or the exoskeleton of alien beings. The full suit may incorporate padding and other, non-bone materials. Average weight is 40 lbs (18 kg). **Note:** Additional P.P.E. may be needed to make M.D.C. armor or to turn larger quantities of bone into M.D.C. material. One or more blood sacrifices are often needed to acquire the necessary amount of P.P.E. Bones cannot be bent or shaped by the *Shape Bone* spell once they are turned into M.D.C. material, and this magic can only be used on ordinary bone or bone transformed to wood, not stone.

Mock Funeral (curse)

Range: Line of vision.
Duration: 24 hours +12 hours per level of the Necromancer, starting with level two.
Saving Throw: 16 +1 per every three levels of the Necromancer's experience, so if the Death Mage is 3rd level, potential victims must roll a 17, if 6th level they need 18, at 9th level they need 19, and if 12th level or higher they need to roll either a natural 20 or 21 or higher with bonuses.
Limitation: Only *one* curse can be placed on an individual at a time.
P.P.E. Cost: 40 for one individual, +20 for each additional member of a group or family included in the curse.

A powerful method of unnerving (sometimes frightening away) an enemy by placing a "death curse" on the individual and leaving a coffin with his effigy as a warning. This ritual magic involves making an effigy (often a scarecrow) of the character to be cursed and the participants (Necromancer and at least one other person) wailing, mocking, cursing, laughing and scoffing at the individual, group or family characterized by the effigy. In the case of cursing an entire group or family (six people maximum), the effigy is the head of the family or group with small rag dolls laid in the coffin with him or her to signify each family or group member.

The person(s) being "laid to rest" in effigy must, at some point, see himself in the coffin for the magic curse to work. To this end, the coffin is left in some obvious, often unavoidable place, like an entrance way, doorway, front room, bedroom, in or on top of a vehicle, etc. If the coffin is spied from a distance, the character(s) is inexorably drawn to it to see who is inside. The coffin can be elaborate and fancy or a simple wooden box (typically the latter).

Note: This death curse is especially dangerous and effective, because the Necromancer who inflicted it knows exactly what his victim's (temporary) fears and weaknesses are, and *will* exploit them. So if the character is vulnerable to poison or fire, the mage or his henchmen will use that against him. Likewise, if vulnerable to a particular creature, like a water spirit, fire demon, dragon, etc., the villain will try to pit one or more against the character. These curses are designed specifically to intimidate, terrify and undermine the Necromancer's enemies.

Types of Mock Funerals & their Curses

If the coffin is filled with dirt, the cursed individual will feel trapped, pressed upon, buried by responsibility and worry. All skills are performed at -20% and initiative is -2.

If the effigy is torn or chopped apart, the cursed character will feel lost and confused. Sense of direction/land navigation and navigation skills are -70%, all other skills are -10%; becomes easily lost even in familiar surroundings.

If the effigy is holding a dagger & blood stains run down from the mouth/lips, the cursed character suffers from a Death Wish, same as the spell described under 7th level Necro-Magic, only for the longer duration that comes from a Mock Funeral ritual curse.

If burned, the cursed individual will suffer double damage from fire.

If a metal spike is driven into the chest, the cursed individual will suffer double damage from lightning and electricity.

If laid upon or wrapped in a banner of one the Warlords, Sovietski, or other power, the individual will be hounded by members of that group — wanted dead or alive for crimes he may or may not have committed. The latter will require the Necromancer having false accusations made against the individual or frame him for something he didn't do.

If filled with snakes, the cursed individual cannot save vs poison and suffers double damage from poison, plus he is -1 to save vs magic cast by dragons.

If filled with rats or mice (dead or alive), the cursed individual cannot save vs disease and suffers double damage from illness.

If drowned (the casket is either filled with water or dumped in water — river, lake, pond, pool, etc.), the cursed character forgets how to swim, making him vulnerable to drowning, and water based attacks by water demons, water spirits and water elementals do double damage.

If the casket is overturned and the effigy is dumped onto the ground, the cursed individual cannot save vs punch, fall or impact and takes full damage from such attacks, including explosions. Furthermore, the character is -50% on the skills climb, acrobatics and gymnastics.

If left on a doorstep, or wherever the character is currently living or an establishment he/she frequents, it is a *warning* that the individual or family is marked (usually by a Necromancer or his friends or associates), and that the individual or family member must cease his activities against them or be destroyed. Often a note will be attached to the effigy to clarify exactly whom should be left alone.

Level Nine

Curse of Hunger
Range: Touch or 10 feet (3 m).
Duration: 24 hours per level of experience.
Saving Throw: Standard
P.P.E. Cost: 50

This magic instills an unreasoning feeling of hunger in its victim, similar to the Starvation Touch of the Horseman of the Apocalypse, Famine. The feeling of hunger is so strong that even when stuffed to the gills, the victim will think of nothing but eating. While hungry, the victim is -2 on initiative and all combat abilities. After eating, he will be fine for the next 2D6 minutes, but will quickly become hungry again. If he eats again when he's already full, he will become extremely sick and vomit 1D4 times in the next twenty minutes. Penalties are the same as when hungry, except that vomiting will fully impair the victim for one melee round (15 seconds); this means only one melee action and no combat bonuses (the act of vomiting takes up all other melee actions that round). Supernatural creatures and creatures of magic are immune to the effects of the spell.

Death's Embrace
Range: Touch or up to 30 feet (12.2 m) per level of experience; line of sight.
Duration: Effects last for 1D6 minutes per level of the spell caster.
Damage: Special
Saving Throw: Standard saving throw vs magic, however, psychics with *sensitive* powers are -2 to save.
P.P.E. Cost: 35

A powerful force of arcane energies is summoned and directed toward one particular living target. The energies are take the form of a black, ghostly apparition that swirls around and embraces the victim. For the duration of the spell, the apparition softly weeps and moans. The effect is that the character embraced by the thing feels defeated and lost to the point that he simply stands or sits, unable to take any initiative whatsoever. The victim will not attack, perform skills, or even shout a warning to a friend. The only action he can take is in self-defense. Once gone or dispelled, the character instantly snaps out of his stupor and takes action. **Note:** This debilitating energy can be dispelled by sorcerers via Negate Magic, Dispel Magic Barrier, and Reality Flux.

Funeral Pyre
Range: 20 foot (6.1 m) radius per level of the spell caster.
Duration: 1D4 minutes
Saving Throw: None
P.P.E. Cost: 35

This spell causes all corpses and dead bodies within range to burst into flame, and only those quickly doused with a vial of holy water or embraced (held) by the living will not be consumed. After 1D4 minutes, the remains will be burnt down to a pile of bones. This is very useful for cleaning up after a big battle or destroying evidence of a slaughter, although the surviving skeletons will raise questions.

Note: This spell has no affect on animated dead, mummies, zombies, or the undead.

Greater Animated Dead
Range: 800 feet (244 m); line of vision.
Duration: 10 minutes per level of experience.
Saving Throw: None
P.P.E. Cost: 50

Virtually identical to the *Animate and Control Dead* spell, except the range and duration are all doubled (as noted above), the number of dead one can animate is doubled (4), and the *animated dead* are twice as fast (spd 14). They are also stronger (P.S. 20; inflicting 2D6+5 S.D.C./H.P. damage), have 50% more S.D.C. (75-210 depending on size) and each has four attacks per melee round (instead of two).

Shadows of Death
Range: Self or 20 feet (6 m)
Duration: 24 hours per level of experience.
Saving Throw: Standard
P.P.E. Cost: 45

This spell creates strange and monstrous shadows but has two different applications. If cast on himself, the Necromancer's own shadow will seem to have a life of its own, move independent of the mage, make sudden or threatening movements, and generally look frightening and unnatural. This adds +2 to the horror factor of the mage and makes opponents -2 on all combat bonuses because the movements of the shadow are startling and distracting.

Alternately, the shadows of death can be cast on others. In this case, the spell is considered a curse. Victims have a constant feeling that they are being watched and/or in danger. They constantly catch glimpses of movement and strange shadows from the corners of their eyes. This makes the character paranoid and jumpy, plus they have trouble sleeping. Penalties: Tired from lack of sleep and constantly being on edge, reduce speed and endurance/fatigue levels by 20% and all combat bonuses are -1.

Shadow of Doom (curse)
Range: Touch or 20 feet (6 m)
Duration: 48 hours per level of experience.
Saving Throw: Standard
P.P.E. Cost: 45

This spell should be considered a magic curse. The cursed character is depressed and feels like the sword of doom is about to drop on him. Penalties: -2 on initiative, -1 on all other combat bonuses and -20% on all skill proficiencies.

Level Ten

Command Vampires
Range: Self and 50 feet (15.2 m) per level of experience
Duration: One hour per level of experience or less
Saving Throw: Special
P.P.E. Cost: 100

This spell imbues the spell caster with the ability to impose his will over vampires as if he were a Master Vampire of the same level of experience. Effects are identical to the *Mind Control: Vampire over Vampire* ability listed on pages 21-22 of **Rifts® World Book One: Vampire Kingdoms™**, except that only one vampire per level of experience can be controlled this way. Only Wild and young Secondary Vampires are affected. Masters, Ancient Secondary Vampires, and, of course, the Vampire Intelligences, are immune.

As stated in **Vampire Kingdoms™**, a Secondary Vampire that fails to resist will remain under control for 1D4 hours. A Wild Vampire will remain subservient for 2D6 hours. After the time period elapses, the vampire can try again to resist the mind control. Should a vampire manage to resist or otherwise break free of the mind control, it can attack the Death Mage, but not necessarily. Vampires are evil creatures who like doing evil, so they may enjoy the tasks that are asked of them while under the Necromancer's influence. They may even volunteer to assist the Necromancer in his evil tasks after the spell elapses (this won't happen if the mage abuses or tortures the creatures or fellow undead). Otherwise, the mage can keep trying to enforce his will over vampires for one hour per level of his experience or until an hour before sunrise. Vampires do need their sleep, after all.

Curse of Wasting
Range: Touch or 10 feet (3 m).
Duration: 24 hours per level of experience.
Saving Throw: Standard
P.P.E. Cost: 80

WILSON '98

No matter how much the victim eats, his body begins to waste away as if he hasn't eaten in days. After 24 hours the victim's eyes are sunken and grey, the body unnaturally thin and sickly looking and the character feels tired and weak. P.S., P.P., Spd and attacks per melee round are all reduced to half (also reduce any attribute bonuses appropriately). In addition, skill performance is -20%.

The character gets thinner and weaker with each passing day, reduce the following every 24 hours: -1 on all combat maneuvers (initiative, strike, parry, etc.), -1 on all saving throws, -10% on skill performance, -1 on Spd; all penalties are cumulative.

Supernatural creatures and creatures of magic can also be affected by the curse, but only for two hours per level of the spell caster's experience (so only the initial penalties appear after one hour). Vampires and other undead are not affected.

Strength of the Dead
Range: Self, must touch the dead creature.
Duration: 2 minutes per level of experience.
Saving Throw: None
P.P.E. Cost: 60

Temporarily draws and gives to the Necromancer half the S.D.C. and Hit Points (or M.D.C. if a mega-damage creature!) that the creature had while it was alive!

Summon Insect Swarm
Range: 1000 miles (1600 km)
Duration: 12 hours per level of experience.
Saving Throw: None
P.P.E. Cost: 80

This ritual magic will cause 1000 flying insects (per each level of experience of the summoner) to amass in a gigantic, blinding cloud. The swarm covers a 100 foot (30.5 m) radius per level of the Necromancer.

Blinding cloud of flying insects: Thousands of flying insects fill the air as a massive, living cloud. The swarm interferes with accurate radar readings, creating false readings, and reduces visibility to about 10 feet (3 m). The bugs are also very distracting, noisy and annoying, covering or splattering themselves on windshields and visors, impairing vision even more. The insect swarm may also clog engines, air intake valves, vents, and joints of bots, borgs and vehicles, causing varying damage and problems, such as engines overheating, cutting off air supplies, etc.

Characters not protected inside environmental body armor, power armor or a vehicle will be pelted and covered by the bugs. Even though most of the insects in this swarm are harmless, they will crawl in the ears and nose, fly into the mouth and eyes, crawl under clothes and so on. The overall sensation is disgusting and debilitating. Penalties: Characters caught in the cloud lose half of their melee actions, can barely see or hear, completely lose initiative and all combat bonuses, and speed is reduced by half.

Level Eleven

Bone Scepter
Range: As per spell or as melee weapon.
Duration: As per spell (3rd level potency) or until destroyed.
Saving Throw: As per spell.
P.P.E. Cost: 160 points; creates a permanent magic item.

Typically a scepter or rod made entirely of bone and which ends with a skull, skeletal jaw with teeth, or hand, claw or taloned foot (bird-like). The permanent enchantment turns it into a low-powered magic weapon with the powers to cast three different spells once each per 24 hours: Select three from the following:

Repel Animals	Fear
Negate Poison	Spoil
Turn Dead	Sickness

It is considered a magic weapon with 50 M.D.C. (on S.D.C. worlds it has 500 S.D.C.). The weapon suffers damage only when an adversary deliberately tries to destroy it by direct attacks at the weapon only. When used as a blunt weapon it inflicts 3D6 H.P./S.D.C. damage to mortal S.D.C. beings and 2D6 M.D. to demons and other Mega-Damage creatures, including those clad in full M.D.C. body armor, cyborgs and robots.

Bone of Invisibility
Range: Wearer or holder; must be worn or held in one's hand to be effective.
Duration: 15 minutes. The bone is so empowered until it is destroyed.
Saving Throw: As per spell.
P.P.E. Cost: 180; creates a permanent magic item.
   Note: Requires one single, small bone from a rat.

Typically a small enchanted bone that fits in the palm of the hand or worn as a simple necklace. This bone can turn the holder/wearer invisible as often as six times per 24 hours. To activate its magic, the user must close his hand around it and say, "make me invisible." This magic item has 30 M.D.C. (on S.D.C. worlds it has 300 S.D.C.), but only suffers damage when an adversary deliberately tries to destroy it by directing his attacks at it only.

Summon Vampire
Range: 1000 miles (1600 km)
Duration: 24 hours per level of experience.
Saving Throw: None
P.P.E. Cost: 150

This ritual magic will cause 1D4 vampires within a 1000 mile (1600 km) radius to come to the Necromancer within 12 hours (at night, of course). If there are no vampires in the area, none will come. Only wild vampires and/or secondary vampires must heed the mystic summons. The master vampire and old secondary vampires are not affected.

Most vampire(s) see the Necromancer as a kindred spirit and a potential ally, so they will gladly work with the death mage. The magic requires the undead to stay for 24 hours per level of experience of the summoner. However, they can decide to stay longer if that is what they desire, the only difference is the vampire is no longer obligated to obey the Necromancer. This means a free vampire may continue to work with the sorcerer, especially if there is a lot of bloodshed or if the creature likes the mage's scheme. Otherwise, the vampire is free to do as he pleases.

Transfer Life Force
Range: 10 feet(3 m) per level of experience.
Duration: 24 hours per level of the spell caster.
Saving Throw: None
P.P.E. Cost: 150

This spell enables the Necromancer's life essence to inhabit and animate skeletons, corpses, mummies, zombies and even puppets, like a robot. The possessed dead thing has all the mental and physical powers of the Necromancer, however magic spells and psionic powers cannot be used, because the corpse has no P.P.E. or I.S.P.!

The body is dead so it is impervious to pain, hunger, thirst, fatigue, disease, drugs, poisons, gases, heat and cold. However, the sense of smell is lost and the sense of touch is about half of normal. Vision and hearing are provided by mystic means. If the body is destroyed, it is no big deal, the spell caster simply returns to his real living body and can always inhabit another dead body if so desired. The spell can be used as an offensive measure or a subtle means to spy or confuse. The spell caster can disguise himself completely by inhabiting a recently deceased individual or conceal his identity by inhabiting a corpse or skeleton. **Note:** The dead body looks ... well ... dead and continues to discolor and decay. After a while, the dead body will smell pretty terrible and parts may drop off.

Level Twelve

Bone Staff
Range: As per spell or as melee weapon.
Duration: As per spell (3rd level potency) or until destroyed.
Saving Throw: As per spell.
P.P.E. Cost: 210 points; create permanent a permanent magic item.

A staff made entirely of bones. It may have a skeletal jaw with teeth, one or more skulls, hands, claws, taloned foot, horns, giant teeth, or feathers at the top or on each end. The permanent enchantment turns it into a low-powered magic weapon with the powers to *turn the dead* (equal to a 3rd level spell), *hold vampires at bay* as if it were a holy symbol and inflicts *double damage to animated dead* — corpses, skeletons, crawling hands, and mummies (but not the undead or zombies). It is considered a magic weapon with 80 M.D.C. (on S.D.C. worlds it has 800 S.D.C.). The weapon suffers damage only when an adversary deliberately tries to destroy it by directing his attacks at the weapon only.

When used as a blunt weapon it inflicts 4D6 H.P./S.D.C. damage to mortal S.D.C. beings and 3D6 M.D. to demons and other Mega-Damage creatures, including those clad in full M.D.C. body armor, cyborgs and robots.

Necklace of Bat Skulls
Range: Wearer; must be worn to be effective. Can be worn as a necklace or bracelet.
Duration: The necklace is so empowered until it is destroyed.
Saving Throw: As per spell.
P.P.E. Cost: 290; creates a permanent magic item.

Note: Must have at least four skulls.

An amulet that gives the wearer perfect hearing (+1 on initiative) and enables him to see in non-magical darkness (nightvision 200 feet/61 m) as long as the item is worn. The amulet is considered a magic item with 50 M.D.C. (on S.D.C. worlds it has 500 S.D.C.), but only suffers damage when an adversary deliberately tries to destroy it by directing his attacks at it only.

Necklace of Bird Skulls
Range: Wearer; must be worn to be effective. Can be worn as a necklace or bracelet.
Duration: The necklace is so empowered until it is destroyed.
Saving Throw: As per spell.
P.P.E. Cost: 290; creates a permanent magic item.

Note: Must have at least four skulls.

An amulet of clear sight that gives the wearer perfect 20/20 vision (no need for eyeglasses) and exceptional long-distance vision, plus enables him to see into the ultraviolet spectrum of light as long as the item is worn. The amulet is considered a magic item with 50 M.D.C. (on S.D.C. worlds it has 500 S.D.C.), but only suffers damage when an adversary deliberately tries to destroy it by directing his attacks at it only.

Necklace of Dragon Teeth
Range: Wearer; must be worn to be effective. Can be worn as a necklace or bracelet.
Duration: The necklace is so empowered until it is destroyed.
Saving Throw: As per spell.
P.P.E. Cost: 320; creates a permanent magic item.

Note: Must have at least three teeth.

An amulet of clear sight that gives the wearer the ability to *see the invisible* as long as it is worn or held in one's closed hand. The amulet is considered a magic item with 80 M.D.C. (on S.D.C. worlds it has 800 S.D.C.), but only suffers damage when an adversary deliberately tries to destroy it by directing his attacks at it only.

Necklace of Snake Skulls
Range: Wearer; must be worn to be effective. Can be worn as a necklace or bracelet.
Duration: The necklace is so empowered until it is destroyed.
Saving Throw: As per spell.
P.P.E. Cost: 300; creates a permanent magic item.

Note: Must have at least four skulls.

An amulet of healing and protective magic that makes the wearer impervious to disease that causes fever, snake bites, and poison, plus provides a +2 bonus to save vs all types of *magical* illnesses. The amulet is considered a magic item with 50 M.D.C. (on S.D.C. worlds it has 500 S.D.C.), but only suffers damage when an adversary deliberately tries to destroy it by directing his attacks at it only.

Summon Worms of Taut
Range: Not applicable
Duration: 24 hours per level of experience.
Saving Throw: Standard
P.P.E. Cost: 210

This ritual plucks one or more demonic worms of Taut from its native dimension and magically places it before the summoning Necromancer. The creature is automatically under the spell caster's control and will obey him without question.

Not all worms can be summoned, only the Nippers, Fire Worms and Tomb Worms. As many as one per level of experience can be summoned.

The problem with this spell is that after the duration time has elapsed, the necromancer's control over the worms is gone but they remain. All Worms of Taut are extremely aggressive and dangerous predators. See **Rifts Conversion Book** or **Palladium's Monsters & Animals** for descriptions.

Level Thirteen

Skull with Flaming Eyes

Range: 300 feet (91 m) as a lantern, or by touch.
Duration: Will function indefinitely or until destroyed.
Saving Throw: As per spell.
P.P.E. Cost: 300 points; creates a permanent magic item.

A magical creation that permanently enchants the skull of a human or other intelligent creature with the powers of light, warmth and fire. It is considered a magic item with 100 M.D.C. (on S.D.C. worlds it has 1000 S.D.C.). The skull suffers damage only when an adversary deliberately tries to destroy it by directing his attacks at it only.

- Flaming eyes that provide light like a lantern and which can fire beams of light like a high-powered flashlight or lantern; 300 foot (91.5 m) range.
- The light from the eyes magically extinguishes during the day and in brightly lit rooms, and automatically appears with the coming of dusk or in darkness.
- The flaming eye sockets burn like hot coals and can be used to light wicks or branches to build a fire by placing one end of the item into the glowing eye socket. Putting a finger into the eye socket will burn, inflicting 3D6 H.P./S.D.C. damage and setting any flammable items (like gloves) on fire; 1D6 M.D. to angels/Spirits of Light, Faerie Folk, Elementals and spirits.
- Provides warmth equal to a large campfire or fireplace.
- Skull can fire Bolts of Fire six times per 24 hours: 5D6 M.D., double damage to angels/Spirits of Light, Faerie Folk, Elementals and spirits; range: 300 feet (91 m).

Skull of Knowledge

Range: As per spell; range of vision is 1000 feet (305 m).
Duration: As per spell (3rd level potency) or until destroyed.
Saving Throw: As per spell.
P.P.E. Cost: 320 points; creates a permanent magic item.

Each of the following magic spells or abilities can be performed once per 24 hours and the skull relates/speaks about what it has seen or learned. All spells are equal to 3rd level in potency and duration, non-magical abilities are limited to 30 minutes.

See the Invisible
See Aura
Second Sight
Eyes of Thoth
Cipher: Count & perform basic mathematical calculations 98%
Identify plants and fruit 98%.
Translate for one particular language 90%

Note: The skull itself can understand and speak all languages at all times at 90% proficiency, and responds in the language by which it was addressed. The skull never speaks or does its magic without being addressed with the opening words, "O' Skull of Knowledge, tell me ..." whatever — "what invisible beings you spy," "what words you read," "what of my future can you see," etc.

Necklace of Goblin Skulls

Range: Wearer; must be worn to be effective. Can be worn as a necklace or bracelet.
Duration: The necklace is so empowered until it is destroyed.
Saving Throw: As per spell.
P.P.E. Cost: 340; creates a permanent magic item.

Note: Must have at least two skulls.

A macabre amulet that gives the wearer the ability to understand and speak Gobblely and Faerie Speak, as well as nightvision (100 feet/30.5 m) as long as the item is worn. The amulet is considered a magic item with 50 M.D.C. (on S.D.C. worlds it has 500 S.D.C.), but only suffers damage when an adversary deliberately tries to destroy it by directing his attacks at it only.

Curse: To Hell & Back

Range: Touch or up to 10 feet (3 m).
Duration: One melee round (15 seconds) for the initial voyage to hell, but the effects linger for one hour per level of the spell caster.
Saving Throw: -1 to save vs magic.
P.P.E. Cost: 180

Unless the targeted individual rolls a successful save vs magic, this spell sends him on a mental and emotional trip through the darkest corners of his mind. In a span of only a few seconds, the victim will re-experience every loss he has ever felt and every injury he has ever inflicted. During this mental assault, the character is oblivious to everything around him and cannot take any action. The experience is humbling to even the strongest spirit and shattering to all others. After this moment of torture, vestiges of the experience will continue to haunt the victim for up to one hour per level of the spell caster. The effects are half for those with an M.E. attribute of 20 or higher.

For the duration of this haunting, the victim is obviously shaken and emotionally feeble. During this period, the character

is distracted and despondent. If nothing demands his immediate attention, the character will want to curl up into the fetal position and be left alone. The victim suffers from emotional shell-shock with the following penalties: -6 to initiative, -4 to parry and dodge, -6 to save vs Horror Factor, and -4 to save vs mind control. In addition, the speed attribute, skill performance, and attacks per melee are reduced by half, and only one offensive move can be taken per round, all others are defensive only. Even 1D4 days after the experience, the victim will be -1 on initiative.

Summon Magot (monster)

Range: Not applicable
Duration: 12 hours per level of experience.
Saving Throw: Standard
P.P.E. Cost: 320

This impressive ritual actually plucks one hideous Magot demon from its native dimension and magically places it before the summoning necromancer to do his bidding. The Magot is automatically under the spell caster's control and will obey him without question. The creature's time on Earth is limited and it warps out after the duration time of the summoning magic elapses, or when the summoner bids it to leave, or when it is slain.

The Average Magot

M.D.C.: 1D4x1000
Horror Factor: 13
Attacks per Melee Round: 8
Damage: 4D6 M.D. swat with eye stalk, 6D6 M.D. punch, or 2D6x10 M.D. bite. Each of the three eye stalks fire a beam that causes temporary petrification for 3D6+2 minutes. Victims need a 13 or higher to save.
Magic & Psionics: None
Notes: Average I.Q. 5, P.S. 43, Spd 90, 20 feet (6 m) tall. See **Rifts Conversion Book** pages 214 & 215 for complete details.

Level Fourteen

Return from the Grave

Range: Self only
Duration: Special
Saving Throw: None
P.P.E. Cost: Special; a total of 60 P.P.E. and 24 hit points are permanently spent.

This magic is less of a ritual and more like a full-time commitment. One evening, once a week, before going to rest, the Necromancer must conduct a ritual which requires reciting a series of arcane verses, ceremonial bloodletting (human or large animal sacrifice), and the temporary expenditure of 25 P.P.E. by the mage. Furthermore, an involved ritual must be conducted every full moon, during which the mage permanently sacrifices three P.P.E. and two Hit Points. After a full year of conducting both rituals, the magic is complete and the Necromancer must only recite a mantra every night.

The purpose of the magic is not obvious at first. But when its effects are realized, they are very apparent. If the year-long ritual is done properly, without missing any of the nightly rituals (if so, P.P.E. and H.P. expended are lost; start again), it will enable the Death Mage to "return from the grave" as a member of the undead. The willing subject of this magic will forever walk the Earth as a vampire, at least until someone destroys him. He is very powerful, thoroughly evil, and even more dedicated to death than before. This magic is one of the only ways for someone to become a member of the undead (equal to a Master Vampire) without being reliant on some other source of power, such as a Vampire Intelligence. **Note:** Supernatural creatures and creatures of magic, like dragons, cannot use this magic, but mortals and D-Bees can.

The basic powers and weaknesses of this creature are as follows:

- Hit points are equal to twice the amount of the Necromancer's base P.P.E. at the time of his death. They do not increase with further experience as an undead, since it is locked at the highest level he had attained before death.

- P.S. attribute is increased to 26 or +4, whichever is higher, and is considered to be supernatural.

- P.P. and Spd are identical to what the mage had during his life.

- P.E. is no longer applicable as the creature never tires and is immune to poisons, disease, cold and many forms of magic.

- P.B. attribute is reduced to 1D6.

- All mental attributes are reduced by -1D4.

- Horror Factor is 3, plus one per level of experience he achieved in life.

- Attacks per melee are four, plus one for every four levels of experience in life.

- New combat bonuses are +3 to initiative, +4 to strike and parry, +2 to dodge, +3 to roll with punch/impact, +1 to entangle, and +2 to disarm, in addition to any P.S. or P.P. attribute bonuses.

- The powers of necromancy remain, but in a diminished capacity. All *Special Abilities & Powers of the Necromancer O.C.C.* (1-5) remain intact, but O.C.C. *bonuses* do not apply.

Furthermore, the Death Mage's usual P.P.E. level is reduced by half, making spell casting limited. Moreover, reborn as a vampire, the character only turns to magic when it amuses him or when desperate, otherwise the character relies on his vampiric abilities.

- Half the O.C.C., O.C.C. Related and Secondary skills the mage knew in life are retained, the others are forgotten. All skills that remain are permanently frozen at the level they were at the time of death.

Summary of natural Vampire combat abilities (as they apply to undead created by this sorcery):

The undead creature is no longer vulnerable to normal weapons. Only magic, psionics, wood or silver weapons and physical attacks or strikes from a supernatural creature will inflict damage to the undead. In addition, weapons made of or plated with silver (the bane of all undead) inflict double damage.

Damage is regenerated at the rate of 1D6 Hit Points per melee round. The undead creature can function even if reduced to -20 Hit Points, albeit at half speed. Even when reduced to -40 Hit Points, he will be immobile/comatose, but will survive, recover 1D6 H.P. per melee round, regaining consciousness at zero.

Otherwise, the Undead Necromancer has all the basic abilities, bloodlust and desires of a classic vampire (see **Rifts® Vampire Kingdoms™** for details). The only way to permanently destroy the creature is the same way as to kill a vampire.

Available Common Spell Magic

The Necromancer is a spell caster so he or she can learn any spell, however, except for those listed as follows, the P.P.E. cost to perform a spell is two times the normal amount. For example the Armor of Ithan spell normally costs 10 P.P.E., but will cost the Necromancer 20, befuddle (normally 3) will cost six and so on. Most of these death wizards focus on spells that are directly applicable to necromancy and don't learn a wide range of many other spells.

Likewise, necromancy spells can be learned by other spell casters such as the Line Walker and Shifter, but to execute them, the cost is double. Techno-Wizards and mystics NEVER learn Necro-Magic. All spells are described in the **Rifts® RPG** or **The Federation of Magic™**.

Level One
Death Trance (1)
Globe of Daylight (2)
Lantern Light (2)
Sense Evil (2)
Sense Magic (4)

Level Two
Cloak of Darkness (6)
Concealment (6)
Detect Concealment (6)
Fear (5)
Turn Dead (6)

Level Three
Breathe Without Air (5)
Fuel Flame (5)
Ignite Fire (5)
Life Source (2+)

Level Four
Fireblast (8)
Ley Line Transmission (30)
Magic Net (7)
Repel Animals (7)
Shadow Meld (10)
Trance (10)

Level Five
Aura of Death (12)
Circle of Flame (10)
Death Curse (special)
Horrific Illusion (10)
Horror (10)

Level Six
Fire Ball (10)
Mask of Deceit (15)
Tongues (12)

Level Seven
Animate & Control Dead (20)
Constrain Being (20)
Life Drain (25)

Level Eight
Commune with Spirits (25)
Exorcism (30)
Luck Curse (40)
Minor Curse (35)
Sickness (50)
Spoil (30)
World Bizarre (40)

Level Nine
Aura of Doom (40)
Dessicate the Supernatural (50)
Protection Simple (45)
Purge Self (70)

Level Ten
Armorbane (100)
Banishment (65)
Control/Enslave Entity (80)
Deathword (70)
Restore Limb (80)
Level Eleven
Create Mummy (160)
See in Magic Darkness (125)

Level Twelve
Create Zombie (250)
Ensorcel (400)
Soultwist (170)

Level Thirteen
Sanctum (390)
Shadow Wall (400)

Level Fourteen
Restoration (750)

Level Fifteen
Transformation (2000)

The cost of specific components

Some average costs for basic key components

Brain: Cyclops — 500,000+ credits
Brain: Dragon — 750,000+ credits

Brain: Operator — 45,000+ credits
Brain: Scholar — 25,000+ credits
Brain: Scientist — 35,000+ credits
Brain: Warrior — 35,000+ credits
Brain: Practitioner of Magic — 200,000+ credits

Claw: Animal — 1D6x100 credits
Claw: Bird (large) — 1D4x100 credits
Claw: Creature of Magic (sphinx, etc.) — 250,000+ credits
Claw: Dragon Hatchling — 200,000+ credits
Claw: Dragon Adult — 600,000 to a million credits
Claw: Lesser Supernatural Beings/Demon — 50,000 to 100,000 credits
Claw: Greater Supernatural Beings — 200,000 to 500,000 credits
Claw: Ogre, Troll, Giant — 2D6x100 credits

Eye: Dragon — 50,000+ credits
Eye: Humanoid — 2,000+ credits
Eye: Supernatural Being — 40,000+ credits

Horn: Animal — 2D4x100 credits
Horn: Supernatural Being — 2D4x1000 credits
Horn: Dragon — 30,000+ credits
Horn: Ki-lin — 20,000+ credits
Horn: Unicorn — 40,000+ credits

Hooves: Animal — 1D4x100 credits
Hooves: Ki-lin — 30,000 credits
Hooves: Unicorn — 50,000 credits

Tail: Dragon — 70,000+ credits
Tail: Manticore — 18,000 credits
Tail: Malignous — 45,000 credits
Tail: Monkey — 1D4x100 credits

Tongue: Supernatural Creatures — 150,000+ credits
Tongue: Dragon — 500,000+ credits
Tongue: Faerie Folk — 50,000 credits
Tongue: Humanoids (D-Bees, elves, etc.) — 2D6x100 credits

Wings: Animal (gryphon, dragondactyl, etc.) — 1D6x1000 credits
Wings: Bird (large) — 1D6x100 credits
Wings: Creatures of Magic (Sphinx, etc.) — 275,000+ credits
Wings: Dragon Hatchling — 200,000+ credits
Wings: Dragon Adult — 850,000 to 1D6 million credits
Wings: Lesser Supernatural Beings — 250,000 to 800,000 credits
Wings: Greater Supernatural Beings — 500,000 to 1D6 million credits.

Note: The cost can be as much as four times greater depending on the demand, situation and exactly who the deceased was.

The costs to Necromancers is usually 50% higher because the component has greater value to the character and shop owners take advantage of that. However, charging more than 50% above common market value is rare for fear of retribution from the sorcerer.

Selling such items to a magic shop is likely only to command 10% of the average selling price.

Born Mystic O.C.C.

The Born Mystic is also known as the Mystic Wiseman, as well as the Russian Mystic or simply a Sage or The Born. These characters are fundamentally Mystics as presented in the **Rifts® RPG**. However, their range of magic knowledge is specifically attuned to the needs, traditions and superstitions of Russia. Consequently, their range of abilities is different from the Mystic found in North America and other parts of the world — for their spell casting and magic knowledge is limited to what is euphemistically called Russian Magic.

In addition, the Born Mystic can also select 1D4+1 Living Fire Magic spells (any from levels 1-7) *or* 1D4+1 Bone Magic of choice (Bone Magic spells are listed under the Quick Find contents, and are generally the Necromancer spells that include the word "bone" in the name of the spell).

As a Mystic, they possess both psionic and magical powers. Both are abilities that simply appear. They are often acclaimed advisors and prophets who see the world differently and can glimpse the future. The intuitive nature of the Born Mystic's power is such that they simply accept suddenly knowing something and have learned to trust their feelings. This also means that most disregard formal education in favor of following their own cosmic path. Most believe that too much education creates walls that block one from the natural psychic emanations and deaden one to the true world around them. They also believe that too much reliance on technology and physical objects will have the same effect. Consequently, a Born Mystic will avoid cities, bionics, the Warlords and technology. Since most wander the world as adventurers, sages and advisors, most don't amass too many tangible possessions, other than those that uplift the spirit like works of art, musical instruments, books, magic items and similar things.

While there are hours of mediation and training to focus their thoughts, most Born Mystics will tell you that one does not learn to become a mystic, but is born with the "gift."

The Powers of the Born Mystic:

The abilities of the Born Mystic are a combination of psychic and magic powers. Because Russia and the surrounding lands are plagued by supernatural menaces, much of the Born Mystic's powers and bonuses are oriented toward countering and fighting demons.

1. Psionic Powers: At level one the Born Mystic automatically has the powers of Mind Block, Exorcism, Commune with Spirits, Sixth Sense, and Meditation. He also gets to select three powers from the Sensitive category *or* one from the Super Psionic Category. Also select two from either the Physical or

Healing category (note that this is the psychic's only chance to take Healing).

Additional psionic abilities: The character gets to select one additional psionic power from the categories of Sensitive or Physical at levels 3, 5, 7, 9, 11, 13 and 15.

2. I.S.P.: To determine the character's amount of Inner Strength Points, take the number of M.E. as the base, roll 2D4x10, and add it to the base number. The character gets another 10 I.S.P. for each additional level of experience, starting at level one. Considered to be a Master Psionic.

3. Magic Powers: The Born Mystic spends years pondering about the mysteries of life, his place in it, and how magic might help him find his place in the world. When he is ready to find or make his place by exploring it as an adventurer, the character enters into a meditative trance that lasts six days. At the end of that period, the character intuitively knows how to cast seven specific spells. The nature of the spells will typically reflect the character's alignment and current view of life.

At first level, select a total of *three* spells from common Wizard magic levels one and two. Also select a total of *four* Nature Magic spells of choice selected from levels 1-3.

These are part of the Born Mystic's permanent spell casting abilities and cannot be changed. Nor can the character learn new spells like a Line Walker, because his magic abilities must come from meditation and cosmic awareness.

Additional Magic: The Born Mystic will intuitively sense whenever he or she has reached a new metaphysical plateau (new level of experience). At each new junction in life (experience level), the character will find time to meditate on life, his goals and magic. As a result, he can select a total of two new magic spells from any level up to his own level of experience (i.e. a fourth level Born Mystic can select his spells from levels 1-4). Spell selections can be made from Wizard spells found in the *Rifts® RPG* and *Federation of Magic™*, or from Nature Magic (described under the *Old Believer* in this book).

4. P.P.E.: A die roll of 1D6x10 +P.E. attribute number determines the character's initial base P.P.E. Add another 2D6 points to the P.P.E. for each level of experience. The Born Mystic can also draw on ambient P.P.E. from ley lines and blood sacrifices the same as the Line Walker or any sorcerer.

5. Bonuses: As a master psionic, the Born Mystic needs to roll a 10 or higher to save versus psionic attack (plus any M.E. attribute bonuses). +2 to save vs mind controlling drugs, potions, and magic charms, +5 to save vs possession, and +2 to save vs Horror Factor.

6. Dowsing (Special): This is the psychic ability to locate fresh water whether it be with a divining rod or by more scientific and logical means. The percentage number indicates the success ratio of locating fresh water. A person can roll once every melee round to sense water, but must roll *two consecutive* successful rolls to actually locate it. **Base Skill:** 20% +7% per level of experience.

Born Mystic P.C.C.

Also known as the Born, Sage, Mystic Wiseman and Russian Mystic.

Alignments: Any

Racial Restrictions: None, although the vast majority (70%) are human.

Roll The Eight Attributes as normal for that race.

Average Level of Experience (N.P.C.): 1D4+4 or as required by the Game Master.

Attribute Requirements: None, other than psionic ability. However a high I.Q. and M.A. (10 or higher) are strongly suggested.

O.C.C. Skills:
Basic Math (+10%)
Speaks Russian at 98%
Speaks Euro and one other language of choice (+20%)
Lore: One of choice (+10%)
Horsemanship: General
Land Navigation (+15%)
W.P.: Two of choice
Hand to Hand: Basic
Hand to hand: basic can be improved to expert at the cost of two "other" skills, or martial arts (or assassin, if an evil alignment) for the cost of three "other" skills.

O.C.C. Related Skills: Select six other skills at level one, plus select one additional skill at levels three, six, nine and twelve. All new skills start at level one proficiency.

Communications: Radio Basic only.
Domestic: Any (+5%)
Electrical: None
Espionage: Escape Artist, Disguise & Intelligence only (+5%)
Mechanical: None
Medical: First Aid only.
Military: None
Physical: Any, except Boxing, Wrestling and Acrobatics.
Pilot Skills: Any, except robots, power armor, military vehicles, ships and aircraft.
Pilot Related Skills: Any
Rogue Skills: Any, except Computer
Science: Any (+5%)
Technical: Any (+10%)
W.P.: Any
Wilderness: Any (+5%)

Secondary Skills: The character also gets to select four Secondary Skills from the previous list at level one, and one additional skill at levels four, eight and twelve. These are additional areas of knowledge that do not get the advantage of the bonus listed in the parentheses. All Secondary Skills start at the base skill level. Also, skills are limited (any, only, none) as previously indicated in the list.

Starting Equipment: Light suit of M.D.C. body armor, an S.D.C. dagger (1D6), one M.D. weapon of choice, wooden cross, two sets of clothing, a nice cloak or cape (with or without hood), leather boots, belt, blanket, backpack, satchel, bedroll, two medium-sized sacks, two small sacks, a water skin, food rations for 1D4 weeks, a pocket mirror, flashlight, hair comb, and some personal items.

Vehicle: Starts with a good quality horse.

Secret Resources: None per se.

Money: Starts with 3D6x100 credits or Rubles, and 2D4x1000 in tradeable goods.

Cybernetics: None, and avoids them like the plague, because any cybernetics or other forms of physical augmentation interferes with psionics and magic. However, cybernetic prosthetics and bio-systems for medical reasons will be considered if necessary.

Russian Fire Sorcerer O.C.C.

Many people mistake the Russian Fire Sorcerer with Fire Warlocks. While it is true that both command power over fire, and they share a handful of similar spells, both are actually quite different. The Fire Sorcerer has no link to or reverence for elemental beings. The sorcerer's powers come from an ancient, nearly forgotten, tradition of Russian spell casting that focuses on fire and smoke.

Special Powers & Abilities of the Fire Sorcerer

1. Immune to smoke. The Fire Sorcerer can see clearly through smoke and is not affected by even the thickest choking clouds of smoke and falling ash — can breathe smoke without penalty or discomfort.

2. Impervious to normal fire & heat. The Fire Sorcerer feels comfortable even in blast furnace heat; no penalties or damage. He can walk on hot coals, sift through hot ash and stir boiling water with his finger, as well as drink boiling water. However, Mega-Damage and magic heat and fire do full damage, unless additional magic is used for superior protection.

3. Impervious to brilliant light. The mage can see through glare and is unaffected by bright or harsh light (can not be blinded by light).

4. P.P.E.: Like all practitioners of magic, the Fire Sorcerer is a living battery of mystic energy that he can draw upon at will. *Permanent Base P.P.E.:* 2D4x10 +P.E. attribute number. Add 1D6 P.P.E. per level of experience. Additional P.P.E. can be drawn from ley lines and blood sacrifices (see **Rifts® RPG**, page 162, *Taking P.P.E. from the living*). However, most Fire Sorcerers tend to avoid human sacrifices to acquire the doubled P.P.E. released by the victim at the moment of their death. Of course, the most evil don't have any qualms about killing.

5. Initial Spell Knowledge: Select three Fire Magic spells from levels 1-4. Each additional level of experience, the character will be able to figure out/select one new spell equal to his own level of achievement. Make selections from Living Fire Magic or common Wizard spells found in the **Rifts® RPG** or **Federation of Magic™**.

6. Learning New Spells. Additional Living Fire Magic spells or common Wizard spells of any level, can be learned and/or purchased at any time regardless of the character's experience level. *See the Pursuit of Magic* in the **Rifts® RPG**.

7. O.C.C. Bonuses: +3 to save vs Horror Factor, +1 to save vs possession, +2 to save vs magic, +4 to save vs magic fumes, +1 to spell strength at levels 3, 7, 11 and 15.

Russian Fire Sorcerer O.C.C.

Also known as the Fire Lord.

Alignment: Any, but most common is anarchist (35%).

Racial Restrictions: None, although the vast majority (80%) are human.

Roll The Eight Attributes as normal for that race.

Average Level of Experience (N.P.C.): 1D4+2 or as required by the Game Master.

Attribute Requirements: I.Q. 9, M.E. 9 or higher.

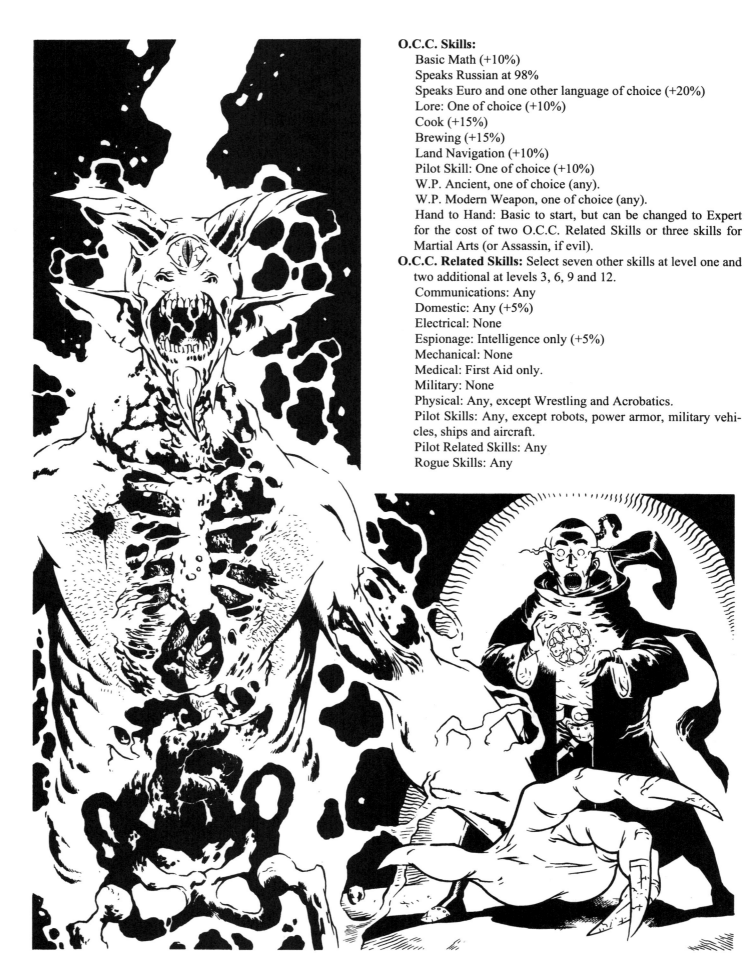

O.C.C. Skills:
    Basic Math (+10%)
    Speaks Russian at 98%
    Speaks Euro and one other language of choice (+20%)
    Lore: One of choice (+10%)
    Cook (+15%)
    Brewing (+15%)
    Land Navigation (+10%)
    Pilot Skill: One of choice (+10%)
    W.P. Ancient, one of choice (any).
    W.P. Modern Weapon, one of choice (any).
    Hand to Hand: Basic to start, but can be changed to Expert for the cost of two O.C.C. Related Skills or three skills for Martial Arts (or Assassin, if evil).

O.C.C. Related Skills: Select seven other skills at level one and two additional at levels 3, 6, 9 and 12.
    Communications: Any
    Domestic: Any (+5%)
    Electrical: None
    Espionage: Intelligence only (+5%)
    Mechanical: None
    Medical: First Aid only.
    Military: None
    Physical: Any, except Wrestling and Acrobatics.
    Pilot Skills: Any, except robots, power armor, military vehicles, ships and aircraft.
    Pilot Related Skills: Any
    Rogue Skills: Any

Science: Any (+5%)
Technical: Any (+10%)
W.P.: Any
Wilderness: Any

Secondary Skills: The character also gets to select four Secondary Skills from the previous list at level one and one additional at levels 2, 4, 6, 8 and 12. These are additional areas of knowledge that do not get the advantage of the bonus listed in parentheses. All secondary skills start at the base skill level. Also, skills are limited as previously indicated.

Standard Equipment to Start: Light suit of M.D.C. body armor, an S.D.C. dagger (1D6), Vibro-Knife (1D6 M.D.), one M.D. weapon of choice, one silver knife, silver cross, mallet and six wooden stakes, two medium sacks, one large sack, backpack or satchel, bedroll, canteen or water skin, belt, boots, flashlight, language translator, note pad, 2D4 markers or pencils, a robe or cloak, travelling clothes, and a handful of personal items. Additional weapons, special items and magic items may be acquired over time.

Vehicle: Starts with none.

Secret Resources: None per se.

Money: Starts with 3D6x100 credits or Rubles, and 2D4x1000 in tradeable goods.

Cybernetics: None, and avoids them like the plague, because any cybernetics or other forms of physical augmentation interferes with magic. However, cybernetic prosthetics and bio-systems for medical reasons will be considered if necessary.

Spell Descriptions for Living Fire Magic

Note: Other than the few spells that are also common Wizard spells (from **Rifts®** or **Rifts® Federation of Magic™**, and reprinted for the gamers' convenience), Russian Living Fire Magic is exclusive to the Fire Sorcerer O.C.C. This unique O.C.C. is exclusive to the geographic locale of Russia, and is typically passed on from parent to child; occasionally from teacher to student. Its mystic secrets are closely guarded.

Level One

Cloud Of Smoke
Range: 90 feet (27.4 m)
Duration: One minute per level of experience.
Saving Throw: None
P.P.E: 2

This magic enables the arcanist to create a cloud of dense, black smoke (30x30x30 feet/9 m maximum size) up to ninety feet (27.4 m) away. Victims caught in the cloud will be unable to see anything beyond the cloud, and their impaired vision allows them to see no more than three feet (0.9 m) inside it, and only blurry shapes. While in the cloud, victims will be -5 to strike, parry and dodge. The smoke may make people cough, but does not cause damage and once out of the cloud, people recover in a few seconds.

Finger Sparks
Range: Self
Duration: The ability lasts for one melee round (15 seconds) per level of the caster. The small flurry of sparks lasts about one second.
Saving Throw: Not applicable.
P.P.E. Cost: 2

Note: This is considered "used" fire. Each snap of the fingers counts as one melee action.

The sorcerer can cause sparks to fly every time he snaps his fingers. This can be done to entertain (like a magic trick or sparklers) or to attempt to light a fire. Sparks hitting highly combustible material (nylon, gasoline, turpentine, lamp oil, gunpowder, etc.) a 0-80% likelihood of igniting it. Sparks hitting moderately combustible materials like a cigarette, cigar, candle wick, clothing, rags, hair, wood, paper, etc.) A 0-40% chance of starting it on fire. Zero chance of starting human flesh, meat, healthy grass or plants on fire.

New Fire
Range: Touch and requires two sticks
Duration: Results in one melee round (uses up all melee actions for that round); the fire lasts as long as it is nurtured.
Saving Throw: Not applicable.
P.P.E. Cost: 1

This spell enables the sorcerer to flawlessly create magic fire by rubbing two sticks together; i.e. using friction to create a new, pure fire "born of wood," rather than getting it from another fire or some other means. The new fire generated from the rubbing of two sticks will light a fire (torch, campfire, fireplace, bonfire, etc.) without fail, even in a strong wind. Once started, the fire must be normally maintained. This fire born of wood is considered "chistyi" (pure) for use in purification rites and magic, as well as for building normal fires.

Pluck & Handle Flame
Range: Self/touch.
Duration: One minute per level of the spell caster.
Saving Throw: Not applicable.
P.P.E. Cost: 4

Note: This is "used" or second-hand fire.

The spell caster can pluck the flame from a candle, torch or lantern, or snatch a small tongue of flame from a fireplace, campfire or other large fire, and handle it as if it were a substantive thing. The tiny to small tongue of fire continues to burn on the sorcerer's finger or hand without injury to the mage and without any apparent energy source. The mage can carry the fire around on his finger or hand, place it on his shoulder or head, and even put it in his pocket without it spreading. This can be continued for the full duration of the spell. Before the spell elapses, the flame must be returned from whence it came or placed on a new source of energy (i.e. another candle, lantern, piece of wood, fireplace, etc.), otherwise it will simply vanish; magically extinguished.

While in hand, the flame can be used like a candle or torch to light the way, or to light a different candle, torch, oven, etc. However, when used to light something else, the entire "plucked" flame goes to that new place or item to burn (the item where the fire originated is undamaged and can be relit by hand to get it going again). The sorcerer can even make the tongue of flame leap from one hand to the other, or from the top of his head or shoulder back to his hand, but it cannot jump out of his hand onto something or someone else; the mage must physically place it there. Cupping the flame in both hands or putting it inside his mouth and closeing it, extinguishes it.

Smoke Smell
Range: Can be cast up to 100 feet (30.5 m) away.
Duration: Two minutes per level of experience.
Saving Throw: None
P.P.E: 1

This magic creates the unmistakable smell of something burning. The smell can be made to come from one particular object (oven, box, computer, engine, generator, wall socket, etc.) or to permeate one particular room or vehicle. This is a distraction and confusion causing spell that should get everybody who smells it looking around in search of the cause in order to prevent a fire. While distracted, the spell caster and his companions are +15% to prowl/sneak past the people searching for the cause of the burning smell, plus those searching are slow to react, -2 on initiative.

Level Two

Bright Sun
Range: Can be cast up to 300 feet (91 m) away and has a radiance that fills a 100 foot (30.5 m) diameter with bright light.
Duration: Lasts five minutes per level of the spell caster.
Saving Throw: Not applicable.
P.P.E. Cost: 5

A spell that creates a brilliant light radiating from a small magical sphere. Despite its brightness, those looking into it are not blinded or harmed, unless they are demons. Vampires, undead and other demonic supernatural beings are blinded by the light (-9 to strike, parry and dodge for 1D6 melee rounds) and recoil from it. Il'ya demons, the Unclean, ghouls, Succubus or Incubus and others vulnerable to the light of day are forced to assume their true demonic form and retain only the P.S. and M.D.C. they have during the day. This spell is effectively a more powerful Globe of Daylight, except the sphere of light cannot be moved once it appears.

Column of Smoke
Range: Up to 90 feet (27.4 m) away.
Duration: Two minutes per level of experience.
Saving Throw: None
P.P.E: 3

The sorcerer can create a narrow, spiralling column of white smoke that rises up into the air 12 feet (3.6 m) per level of his experience. This smoke is typically used like a ladder for climbing. It can also be used as a signal. *See the Climb Smoke spell.*

Extinguish Fire
Range: 20 foot (6 m) area, up to 80 feet (24.4 m) away.
Duration: One minute (4 melee rounds) per level of experience.
Saving Throw: None
P.P.E.: 4 (putting in 8 P.P.E. doubles the range and duration).

The mage can instantly put out up to a 20 foot (6 m) diameter of fire 80 feet away (24.4 m). A total of 40 feet (12.2 m) can be extinguished every 15 seconds (one melee).

Locate & Identify Fire
Range: Self, but sensing range is 1000 feet (305 m) per level of experience.
Duration: Five minutes per level of the spell caster.
Saving Throw: Not applicable.
P.P.E. Cost: 4

The spell caster can sense if fire is within the radius of his sensing range. He can also tell if there is one, a few, several, or many (the latter two probably indicating a town), and the general direction of the fire(s), as well as whether the fire is burning out of control. This power also enables the mage to accurately determine the heat emitted by a fire, estimate how long ago a fire burned and whether it was natural, magical, or deliberately set, by examining the remains of a fire.

Toxic Smoke Cloud
Range: 90 feet (27.4 m)
Duration: One minute per level of experience.
Saving Throw: None
P.P.E. Cost: 5 for the standard cloud, 10 P.P.E. to double the size and or range.

This magic enables the sorcerer to create a billowing cloud of burning and choking grey and black smoke (30x30x30 feet/9 m maximum size) up to ninety feet (27.4 m) away. Victims caught in the cloud will find it difficult to breathe. Unless protected by an air filter and goggles, or environmental armor, those caught in the smoke suffer 2D6 Hit Point/S.D.C. damage for every melee round they are trapped in the smoke, and can barely see (no initiative, no sense of direction, -1 melee attack/action and -6 to strike, parry, and dodge); can not see outside the cloud. **Note:** The penalties from the toxins remain for 1D4 melee rounds after the victims manage to find their way out of the toxic cloud. Mega-Damage creatures will not suffer damage but will have difficulty seeing (roughly equal to the previous Cloud of Smoke spell) and suffer half the penalties. People who see the smoke from a distance will assume there is a fire.

Level Three

Circle of Flame
Range: 10 feet (3 m) around self.
Duration: 2 minutes per level of experience.
Saving Throw: None
P.P.E.: 6 for Fire Sorcerers, 10 for other magic O.C.C.s.

The mage can create a circle of flame around himself. No combustible material is required. The flame is five feet (1.5 m) tall and inflicts 6D6 S.D.C. damage or 1D4 M.D. to anybody who tries to pass through the fire.

Fire Fists
Range: Empowers self only. Inflicts damage by touch.
Duration: One melee round per level of the spell caster.
Damage: 1D6 M.D. +1 additional M.D. per level of experience (no P.S. damage applies unless it is from supernatural P.S.). In the alternative, the mage can will the flames to inflict S.D.C. damage in increments of 2D6 up to 6D6 S.D.C.
Saving Throw: Dodge punch.
P.P.E. Cost: 8

The hands of the spell caster appear to be engulfed in fire, however, the flames only burn targets the sorcerer desires to damage.

Insect Chaser

Range: Affects a 100 foot (30.5 m) diameter per level of the spell caster.

Duration: Instant results; the fumes and its magic linger for 30 minutes per level of the spell caster.

Saving Throw: None

P.P.E.: 5 for Fire Sorcerers, 10 for other magic O.C.C.s.

A nice smelling wood or incense is lit with a "New Fire" and the Insect Chaser spell cast. The pleasant, light aroma keeps biting insects and crop devouring bugs away. Affects a 100 foot (30.5 m) diameter per level of the spell caster.

Ignite Fire

Range: 40 feet (12.2 m)

Duration: Instant results (counts only as one attack; fire lasts until it is put out).

Saving Throw: None

P.P.E.: 3 for Fire Sorcerers, 6 for other magic O.C.C.s.

Note: This is not "New Fire."

A magic that cause spontaneous combustion. The magic will ignite any material that can burn. This means the mystic could set a chair on fire, a jacket, hair, and so on. **Note:** Volatile substances that are *contained in something,* like gasoline in the gas tank of a car, can NOT be ignited. The target to be set on fire must be clearly *visible.* Maximum area of affect is 3 feet (0.9 m). If somebody's clothes or hair are set on fire, they have two melees (30 seconds) to get it off or put the fire out before damage is inflicted; no other combat or action is possible. Damage from the small fire is 2D6 S.D.C. per melee (beginning after the first 2 melees).

Impervious to Fire

Range: Self or one other up to 60 feet (18.3 m) away; line of sight.
Duration: 5 minutes per level of experience.
Saving Throw: None
P.P.E.: 5

A magic invocation that makes the individual temporarily impervious to all types of fire. M.D. plasma, napalm, and normal and magical fires do no damage to the person or to anything he is wearing/on his person.

M.D. Torchfire

Range: Touch; close, hand to hand combat.
Duration: Two minutes per level of experience.
Damage: 2D6 M.D.
Saving Throw: Not applicable.
P.P.E. Cost: 8

The spell transforms an ordinary, lit S.D.C. torch into a fire that does Mega-Damage. The torch can be used as a jabbing or clubbing weapon, with the fire doing 2D6 damage to whomever is struck. The fire stays at the top of the torch and does not set anything on fire. When the magic is over, it returns to being an ordinary torch.

Level Four

Blessing from Svarozhich

Range: A blessing cast on a particular individual who must be present when the magic is performed or within a half mile (0.8 km).
Duration: One hour per level of the spell caster.
Saving Throw: Not applicable.
P.P.E. Cost: 8

The spell is cast and a sheath of corn is tossed into a fire where it burns and brings luck. The luck can be cast upon the spell caster or one character of his choice. Those endowed with the Blessing of Svarozhich can handle or work around fire without fear of injury or misfortune (no accidental fires, burns, mistakes, etc.). Furthermore, M.D. fire attacks leveled against the blessed individual do half damage, and the blessed one is impervious to normal fire and heat, and +3 to save vs illnesses that cause fever.

Climb Smoke

Range: Self or one other by touch.
Duration: Four minutes per level of the spell caster.
Savings Throw: Not applicable.
P.P.E. Cost: 8

This spell enables the spell caster (or one other enchanted by touch) to climb up billowing clouds or strands of smoke as if it were as solid as earth. The climbing skill is 85%/80%.

Fireblast

Range: 50 feet (15.2 m)
Duration: Instant
Damage: 3D6 M.D.
Saving Throw: Dodge
P.P.E.: 10

Fireblast is a simple offensive spell in which the mage shoots mega-damage flames from his or her hands. The blast is only one foot (0.3 m) wide, but extends for the full 50 feet (15.2 m).

Everything in its path will take damage unless those in its path can dodge. The blast can be stopped by doors, walls, etc., but only if the spell's damage does not destroy the object. Otherwise, the flames keep going. This is a great spell for clearing out passageways.

Fire Bolt

Range: 100 feet (30.5 m) +5 feet (1.5 m) per level of experience.
Duration: Instant
Damage: 4D6 M.D.
Saving Throw: Dodge
P.P.E.: 7

The mage can create and direct a bolt of fire. Bonus to strike is +4. Damage is normally 4D6 M.D., or 1D6x10 S.D.C. (the mage can adjust the damage to be S.D.C. or M.D.).

Fire Shield

Range: Hand to hand combat.
Duration: Three melee rounds per level of experience.
Damage: 1D4 M.D. by touch.
Saving Throw: Dodge
P.P.E. Cost: 10

The sorcerer creates a shield of living flame. The shield can be used like a physical object to parry attacks, but is so hot and intimidating that the attacker(s) is -2 to strike and parry. Furthermore, unless a hand-held weapon is large and the attacker does not lean into the flames of the Fire Shield, the attacker will take

1D4 M.D. from the heat and flame of the shield. In addition, the user of the shield is impervious to normal flame, while magic fire and M.D. flames do half damage.

Fire Meld
Range: 60 feet (18.3 m) +10 feet (3 m) per level of experience.
Duration: One minute per level of the Fire Sorcerer.
Saving Throw: Not applicable.
P.P.E. Cost: 10

The spell caster can make himself completely disappear by stepping into a fire. The concealing flame must be at least as big as a campfire, with bonfires and larger being ideal. Inside the sheltering fire, no form of magical or man-made detection can detect or locate the mage. Furthermore, shooting through or stabbing into the flame has no effect on the mage who is now part of the living fire. However, the sorcerer within can not take action, speak, or attack without stepping out of the fire. Waiting silently and patiently can be difficult, especially when the fire also obscures the vision and hearing of the one hidden inside the fire. Stepping out of the fire makes that individual reappear. Dowsing the fire with water, putting out the flame, will reveal the sorcerer drenched in water.

Level Five

Armor of Svarozhich
Range: Self
Duration: One minute per level of the spell caster.
Saving Throw: Not applicable.
M.D.C. of the Armor: 12 points per level of the spell caster.
P.P.E. Cost: 15

Within seconds, the character is covered with a suit of chain mail armor that appears to be made of molten metal that is still red hot. The wearer is impervious to heat and fire, including M.D. plasma and magical fire, plus the suit offers M.D. protection from physical attacks. Those who touch the armor will be burned, suffering 4D6 S.D.C. damage.

Bonfire of Purification
Range: Touch and requires "New Fire."
Duration: Results in one melee round; the fire lasts as long as it is nurtured (i.e. wood is added, the fire stoked, etc.), up to 48 hours.
Saving Throw: Not applicable.
P.P.E. Cost: 15

First a *New Fire* must be made (uses up all the melee actions for one round). Once the "pure" flame is created, it is used to light a bonfire while the sorcerer casts his second spell to create a *Bonfire of Purification*. The magic causes the wood for the bonfire to ignite immediately and completely into a raging (but controlled) fire.

This spell creates a magical, purifying fire in which any corpse thrown into it is incinerated in one minute; only ash remains! Furthermore, any disease the bodies may have harbored is completely destroyed, and the bodies of victims of a vampire's bite (before they are reborn as a vampire) can be destroyed without fear of them returning as the living dead.

Furthermore, any food cooked in the fire or water or beverage boiled by the fire will be made clean of any disease, including food or drink magically "spoiled."

Fire Ball
Range: 90 feet (27.4 m) — +20 feet (6 m) per level of experience for Fire Sorcerers.
Duration: Instant
Damage: 1D4 M.D. per level of the spell caster.
Savings Throw: None except dodge, but the victim must know the attack is coming and must roll an 18 or higher.
P.P.E. Cost: 6 for Fire Sorcerers, 10 for other magic O.C.C.s.

The spell caster creates a large fire ball which hurls at its target at an awesome speed, inflicting 1D4 Mega-Damage points of damage per each level of the spell caster. The fire ball is magically directed and seldom misses.

Fumigate: Insects
Range: Touch; close, hand to hand combat.
Duration: Two minutes per level of experience.
Damage: Kills insect pests.
Saving Throw: Not applicable.
P.P.E. Cost: 12

This spell creates a thick grey cloud of smoke that has a tinge of sulfur to it. Indoors, the cloud will fill and cover a 1000x1000 foot area (305x305 meters). Outdoors, the cloud hangs low to the ground and is blown by the wind, brushing over 10 times the area it covers indoors, but dissipates twice as fast. Everything the cloud covers for more than 15 seconds will see the fumes kill insect pests, including fleas, lice, mites, ticks, locusts, and crop eating bugs.

Spiral Fire Blast
Range: 60 feet (18.3 m) +10 feet (3 m) per level of experience.
Duration: Instant
Damage: Varies.
Saving Throw: Dodge at -2.
P.P.E. Cost: 15

A conical blast of fire that appears in the shape of a spiralling coil of fire that is tapered at the hands of the sorcerer, but enlarges to end in a diameter of eight feet (2.4 m) at the point of impact. Everything that touches at the edge of the fire takes 1D6 M.D. but the main target at the end and center of the spiral blast takes 3D6 M.D. plus 1D6 M.D. per level of experience!

Level Six

Fire Blossom
Range: Touch; appears above the open palm of the mage's hand.
Damage: Varies
Duration: One month per level of the spell caster, but burns out within 1D6 minutes after it is activated.
Saving Throw: None
P.P.E. Cost: 20

This is a unique spell in which the mage creates a Fire Blossom — a small tongue of flame (about three inches tall). It flickers but does not burn and can be held, put in one's pocket or placed in a bag or backpack without fear of starting a fire. The fire does not burn until the mage or the recipient of the Fire Blossom (it can be created and given as a gift) activates it. Once done, the Fire Blossom bursts into a raging fire three feet (0.9 m) tall and two feet (0.6 m) wide. It will burn without combustibles (wood, rags, coal, etc.) for 1D6 minutes and then vanishes.

If placed on or stoked with combustibles, these items will immediately catch fire and burn, thus the Fire Blossom can be used to create a campfire, light torches, or to start a fire.

Fire Sword

Range: Touch; close, hand to hand combat.
Duration: One minute per level of experience.
Damage: 4D6 M.D. (only 1D6 M.D. to foes impervious to fire).
Saving Throw: Not applicable.
P.P.E. Cost: 20

The spell transforms an ordinary S.D.C. sword of any size or type into a magical blade of steel and flame! After creating it, the spell caster can give the sword to someone else, if he so desires. The weapon functions as a magical sword by stabbing and cutting as usual. Creatures vulnerable to fire will suffer double damage. When the magic elapses, the weapon returns to its normal S.D.C. form.

Healing Fire

Range: Touch; those to be healed must slowly pass through the fire.
Duration: The healing property of the fire lasts for one minute per level of the spell caster. Approximately 20 people can pass through the healing fire per minute.
Preparation Time: At least 3D4 minutes to prepare the bonfire and light it with "new fire."
P.P.E. Cost: 20

First a *New Fire* must be made (uses up all the melee actions for one round). Once the "pure" flame is created, it is used to light a bonfire while the sorcerer casts his second spell to create a *Healing Fire*. The magic causes the wood for the bonfire to ignite immediately and completely into a raging (but controlled) fire.

When the fire is roaring, and the edges of the flame are a greenish color, the magic is ready. People who enter the fire pause for a couple of seconds, and continue to pass through it in a forward direction (never back the same way they entered, or the magic has no effect). Those passing through the fire are not burned, but instantly healed of 3D6 Hit Points and 2D6 S.D.C. The same individual can only pass through the same Healing Fire twice. The second time only 1D6 H.P. and S.D.C. are restored. After that, the flame, while tinged with green, does not burn, but neither does it heal.

Those sick from disease can also be helped: 2D6 H.P. are restored, symptoms are reduced by half and the duration of the disease (and remaining penalties) is reduced in half. A sick individual can only be helped once. Afterward, the flame does not burn, but neither does it heal. **Note:** Has no effect on magical illnesses, illness caused by magical spoiling, or curses.

Animals can also be chased through the flame to heal them of injury or to purge them of disease (completely kills disease in animals).

Humans and mortal D-bees possessed by a supernatural force scream as they pass through the flame and a demonic image will, for an instant, appear in the fire around them. These individuals receive no healing, but if held in the fire for one minute, an exorcism will occur with a +20% chance for success (otherwise equal to the Exorcism spell).

Perun's Celestial Fire Bolt

Range: Up to 900 feet (274 m) +100 feet (30.5 m) per level of the spell caster; line of vision.
Duration: Instant.
Damage: To man-made things and mortal beings, the bolt does 3D6 M.D. +1 M.D. per level of the spell caster, but to supernatural beings (demons, Deevals, entities, ghosts, angels, deities, alien intelligences, etc.) the damage is 1D6x10 M.D. +2 additional M.D. per level of experience! Vampires suffer only 3D6 Hit Points, but supernatural creatures vulnerable to lightning take double damage, plus the lightning flash will reveal the true nature of the Unclean, Il'ya and other monsters who are revealed by lightning (the same is true of the Call Lightning spell).
Saving Throw: Dodge at -5!
P.P.E. Cost: 20

A large, fiery lightning bolt that rockets from the hand of the spell caster and said to be similar to those hurled by the ancient God of War, Perun.

Level Seven

Ballistic Fire

Range: 1000 feet (305 m) +10 additional feet (3 m) per level of experience.
Damage: 1D6 M.D. per fiery missile
Duration: Instant
Saving Throw: None
P.P.E. Cost: 25

Ballistic Fire is an anti-infantry spell designed to mow down large numbers all at once. The spell creates one fiery missile per level of the spell caster which can then be directed and fired simultaneously at whatever multiple targets the mage desires. Actually, these missiles can be directed at several different targets (as few as one target per missile) as volleys of several missiles directed at two or more targets, or all concentrated as one large volley to all hit the same target. The balls of fire are magically guided and never miss! Regardless of the missiles created and the way they are distributed, the attack of Ballistic Fire takes only a single spell attack (approximately 7 seconds).

Bonfire of Expulsion

Range: Touch and requires "New Fire."
Duration: Results in one melee round; the fire lasts as long as it is nurtured (i.e. wood is added, the fire stoked, etc.), up to 48 hours.
Saving Throw: Supernatural beings, Faerie Folk and Woodland Spirits are all -1 to save per level of the spell caster.
P.P.E. Cost: 35

First a *New Fire* must be made (uses up all the melee actions for one round). Once the "pure" flame is created, it is used to light a bonfire while the sorcerer casts his second spell to create a *Bonfire of Expulsion*. The magic causes the wood for the bonfire to ignite immediately and completely into a raging (but controlled) fire.

All *lesser demons, sub-demons, entities, Faerie Folk* and *evil Russian Woodland Spirits* who fail to save vs magic (note the substantial penalty to save) fear the pure fire and must flee the area — running at least 2D6 miles (3.2 to 19 km) away. They will not come any closer for the next 1D4 days +12 hours per level of the spell caster, or as long as the bonfire burns. More-over, many will become so frightened or bored from the wait that they will leave the immediate area in search of easier fun. This magic is typically used to at least temporarily purge evil spirits and minor demons from a farmstead or village. The Bon-fire of Expulsion, when used as a campfire, will also keep such creatures away from camp, and serves to notify such superhuman beings that a Fire Sorcerer, Old Believer, or Born Mystic protects this place. Unfortunately, it also puts them on notice and may invoke their ire.

Note: The magic fire has no effect on other magical creatures, including Demon lords, vampires, demigods, gods, angels, or elementals. Nor are greater demons of 5th level experience or higher, affected. Inexperienced greater demons must save vs magic but at half the penalty noted previously.

Lesser supernatural creatures that successfully save vs magic cannot come within 1200 feet (366 m) of the bonfire but can try long-range attacks or cause trouble in the surrounding area. Greater demons who save vs the magical bonfire are *not* held at bay, but are -1 on initiative and -1 attack per melee round.

Fire Gout

Range: 30 feet (9 m) per level of experience.
Duration: Instant
Damage: 6D6 M.D. +1 per level of experience.
Saving Throw: Dodge
P.P.E. Cost: 20

The caster can magically conjure and direct a stream of fire similar to a flamethrower, only wider and can be fired straight up into the sky. It can be directed with a wave of the hands — point and shoot. The fiery stream extends the full length of its range (stopped or blocked only by large obstacles in its path) and is about three feet (0.9 m) in diameter. The intended target can attempt to dodge but is -3 to do so. There is a 01-70% likelihood that combustible materials will be set on fire.

Perun's Fire Scourge

Range: By touch or up to 100 feet (30.5 m) +30 feet (9 m) per level of experience.
Duration: The blast is instant, the continuing fire varies.
Damage: 1D4 M.D. per level of experience against mortal creatures and S.D.C. objects.

Against the supernatural, the magic is devastating: The initial blast does 1D6 M.D. per level of the spell caster, but the demon is also set on fire for one full melee round per level of the spell caster, inflicting 6D6 M.D. damage per round; double damage against Alien Intelligences and their avatars or life essences.

Note: Supernatural creatures of fire and lightning, including elementals and fire demons, take only half damage from the initial blast and are *not* set on fire.

Only completely immersing oneself in water or using the magic spells Extinguish Fire, Negate Magic and Anti-Magic Cloud can extinguish the magic fire before its duration of damage expires. Of course, the spell caster can extinguish it at will.

Saving Throw: Dodge at -3.
P.P.E. Cost: 25

This magic creates a small, fiery lightning bolt that shoots from the hand and is truly effective against demons, Deevals and other supernatural beings. Creatures of magic, like the dragon, sphinx and Faerie Folk, only suffer 1D6 M.D. +1 M.D. per level of experience of the spell caster.

Level Eight

The Torch & Wheel

Range: Varies
Duration: 24 hours or as long as it takes to complete the ritual.
Saving Throw: Not applicable.
P.P.E. Cost: 40

A purification ritual magic used to dispel illness on people or crops.

A pole is put in the center of a wagon wheel with two torches attached to it. The wheel is then and rolled around the village without stopping until the circle is completed. The pace can be fast or leisurely, depending on the spell caster and the urgency of the situation. If both torches stay lit the entire time, it means that the village and all within the circle (including animals, food, stored grain, etc.) are free of disease or magic spoiling. The completing of this ritual also makes all within +3 to save vs disease and magical spoiling for 48 hours.

If one torch goes out before the circle is completed it means spoiling magic and/or disease or blight is present. The wheel, with its one lit torch, will magically roll to each food or place of contamination.

If both torches go out, it is a sign that either demons or a powerful witch (6th level or higher) is somewhere within the circle. However, the wheel does not locate such supernatural or magical pestilence.

Level Nine

Desiccate the Supernatural

Range: One up to 50 feet (15.2 m) away per level of experience, or two by touch.
Damage: 2D4x10 M.D. (or Hit Points, whichever is appropriate).
Duration: Instant
Saving Throw: -1 to save
P.P.E. Cost: 50

Desiccate is a vicious spell designed for use against *supernatural* monsters. It will not work against any opponent in full environmental armor (body armor or power armor), or safely locked in an armored M.D.C. vehicle or room. Likewise, it will *not* work against ordinary mortals, human or D-bee, only *supernatural beings*, good or evil, including spirits in physical form, sub-demons (Gargoyles, Brodkil, etc.), demons, deevils, elementals, Spirits of Light (elementals), demigods, gods, avatars (the life essences of alien intelligences, including vampires), angels, and others. It is important to note that the sphinx, dragons, unicorns, faerie folk and a handful of other superhuman beings possessing supernatural strength and abilities, but known as "Creatures of Magic," are *not* true supernatural creatures (they are more magical than supernatural, or at least not in the same way as demons and gods) and are immune to this magic.

The spell works by drawing moisture out of the target, killing it in a matter of 2D4 seconds, and hopefully reducing it to a withered husk. Regenerating creatures will be unable to bio-regenerate damage caused by this spell until they replenish their body's water supply. Creatures that do not incorporate water in their bodies (i.e. pure energy) will not be harmed by this spell. Water Elementals suffer double damage. A successful save vs magic means the creature suffers half damage.

Dragonfire
Range: 100 feet (30.5 m)
Duration: One melee round per level of experience.
Damage: 1D4x10 M.D.
Saving Throw: None except dodge, but the victim must know the attack is coming and must roll a 16 or higher.
P.P.E. Cost: 20 P.P.E. for the Fire Sorcerer, 40 for other magic O.C.C.s.

This spell allows the caster to temporarily breathe fire just like an adult Fire Dragon. Every melee round that the spell is in effect, the mage is able to breathe as many as two searing blasts of fire that each inflict 1D4x10 M.D. The Dragonfire blasts are magically directed and seldom miss. For the spell to work, there can be nothing blocking the caster's mouth, no helmet, gas mask, etc.

Level Twelve

Metamorphosis: Smoke
Range: Self
Duration: 20 minutes per level of the spell caster.
Saving Throw: Not applicable.
P.P.E. Cost: 220

Said to be one of the most powerful of all the metamorph magics, the mage can transform himself into a swirling cloud of smoke. As such, no physical or energy attacks can harm him. No locked door can stop him, for he can slip through the tiniest crack or keyhole. Although the mage can not communicate or cast magic in this form, he can hear and see events around him as would a normal human being. Of course, he can materialize (naked) with but a thought.

The smoke moves at a maximum speed of 14. Prowls (natural, innate ability) at an 80% skill proficiency, is completely silent, can hover up to 200 feet (61 m) high and can be carried by the wind. The smoke resembles the grey smoke that rises from burning wood or charcoal. The vision of those who step into the smoke cloud is obscured (-2 on initiative, -2 to strike, parry and dodge), but the smoke is not as dense as real smoke, and does not cause people to cough or choke on its fumes.

Mystic Kuznya O.C.C.

"Kuznya" is Russian for "smith." Mystic Kuznya are men and women with supernatural powers and the ability to forge superior metal weapons, as well as the ability to make a number of magic weapons. However, these are not "Techno-Wizard" weapons, but melee weapons of metal and magic said to be empowered by *Svarog the Divine, Highest of the Gods*, the first Mystic Kuznya.

The Magic Smith possesses supernatural strength, is invulnerable to all fire except magical ones (they do normal damage), and is a lesser Mega-Damage creature with skin like steel. All are master metal workers able to forge weapons, armor, plows, tools, utensils and similar metal works (jewelry, goblets, horseshoes, nails, chains, etc.). Furthermore, they can forge any metal object from nails and horseshoes to swords and chalices of the finest quality in one tenth the time it would take an ordinary smith to make a comparable low quality item. The Mystic Kuznya also has a rudimentary understanding of building construction and fortifications.

When not making M.D. materials, tools, melee weapons, armor and other metalworks, the Mystic Kuznya is out enjoying himself (firm believers of working hard and playing hard) or adventuring. Males and females possess supernatural strength and exceptional knowledge in ancient weapons, making them extremely formidable warriors in their own right.

The Mystic Kuznya's ability to make M.D.C. materials and magical items, even low or minor ones, makes them a mega-hot commodity, and something of travelling heroes or celebrities. They are welcomed in most towns, treated like royalty and begged to "bless" most people with some offering (even a small one) of their great magical powers. Remember, in the impoverished and low-tech civilization that represents 80-90% of Russia, the Mystic Kuznya's ability to transform ordinary metal into M.D.C. metal (let alone give select items magical properties) is both a godsent miracle and a blessing. Consequently, these smiths are often swarmed like movie stars with thronging multitudes begging for their help, and others just wanting to glimpse or touch these legendary sorcerers.

This celebrity can actually be a problem. For one, it destroys any chance of coming and going unnoticed, forcing many of these smiths to hide their giant sledgehammer and travel in disguise to avoid the pressures of their status. Second, it can be tiring, frustrating and annoying to be constantly pestered and have people falling all over themselves to win your favor, even when the cause is a good one, and the people deserving. Third, it can make some Mystic Kuznya become cocky playboys or glory seeking party animals revelling in their status. Worse, some become snide and bossy snobs who use the desperate people around them by demanding the sun and the moon just for being in their presence. However, these are comparatively uncommon occurrences (only 15% of the Kuznya are creeps).

Most Mystic Kuznya realize they fill an important need in hard and dangerous times, so they try to be patient, understanding and kind. This means most will spend at least a day or two, sometimes several weeks (depending on their own situation, needs, concerns, and responsibilities), working in the village foundry or blacksmith, cranking out often ordinary metal sup-

plies (nails, spikes, horseshoes, chain links, metal sheeting, pots, pans, tools and other things) in quick order to give the people a helping hand.

The Mystic Smiths are very serious about their craft and are completely aware of the power their magic items represent. Consequently, they are very stingy when it comes to doling out even minor magic items and M.D.C. materials. This has caused some people to see them as callous and not truly caring at all. Of course, such foul sentiments are whispered for fear that the smith might hear and not give them anything at all. Anything is better than nothing.

What few people know is that the Mystic Kuznya's powers are dangerous and deliberately limited. The Mystic Smiths understand that the items, especially magic horseshoes, magic weapons and armor, and M.D. weapons and material can change the balance of power in a region or bring tragedy instead of prosperity. Their power of magical creation is a double-edged sword that can cut for good and beneficial ways or for evil, war and disaster. Their power is one of tremendous responsibility that sometimes weighs upon them. The Mystic Kuznya must think long and hard about making magic and M.D. items for people. He must try to look at the big picture and imagine the possibilities of what such a gift might bring. To this end, he must try to learn as much as he can about the person or people of that village and the surrounding region. Who are their rivals, competitors and enemies? What brigands or dark forces operate in the region and how might they react? How do these people conduct themselves (are they kind, compassionate and sharing, or aggressive and haughty, or zealots, etc.)?

Many a young, generous Kuznya has wept when he discovered the "gifts" he left at a village filled with good and honest people lead to their subjugation or slaughter. Pillaged by a faction from one of the many War Camps, or by bandits, rivals or monsters who either coveted the magical and M.D. weapons and items, or who feared such items would give "sheep" the teeth of a lion and instigate rebellion or independence among the villagers. And that's just one possible scenario. Warlords and members of their War Camps covet the creations of the Mystic Kuznya and often demand them (when discovered) as tribute. Meanwhile, Reavers and the greedy or wicked soldiers within the War Camps simply steal or kill to get their hands on them. Bandits, demons, dragons, foreign invaders, mercenaries, sorcerers, and adventurers can be just as bad, or worse.

This situation is compounded by the fact that *all* Mystic Kuznya are sworn — in a dream visitation by their patron god, Svarog the Divine — to serve no king, nation, people or army. That the children of Russia must make their own place in the world, and that the gifts the Mystic Kuznya have to offer are meant only to inspire and help, not empower any one man or nation. For if left unchecked, the things they can make could give an army the power to vanquish their enemies and conquer the land. And, if things go the way they so often do, breed envy and contempt, and give life to inhumanity, war, hatred and evil. Of course, this is not true of all men, but even the gods cannot clearly see what the future holds or how any man will respond to greatness, power and glory, or what his heirs will do when he is gone. Thus, rather than give birth to inequity and evil, the Divine God forbids his Mystic Children to serve any such power. Instead, he allows them to give just enough to help and inspire their fellow mortals to survive, find their own place, and strive for greatness on their own.

To enforce this decree, the Mystic Kuznya are inhibited from making mass quantities of weapons and M.D. material for any king, warlord, nation, people, or army. Moreover, the Mystic Kuznya can only make M.D. and/or magical items of his own free will — so when placed under torture, the threat of death, mind control, or extorted ("do it or these innocent people die"), the smith automatically becomes unable to make anything other than normal S.D.C. items. The Mystic Kuznya insist it is the power of Svarog that prevents them from doing otherwise, but scholars and scientists suspect it is a mental block that comes with the smiths' magical belief and focus — basically mind over matter — that makes their magical creation powers vanish. Whatever the cause, the fact is that the Mystic Kuznya cannot be forced to make magic or M.D. items nor willingly make them for any one power. Thus, they make and give out their magical metal works carefully, being stingy with magic items, giving the occasional creation to a struggling farmer, village champion, priest or wise man, but more often to valiant Bogatyrs, monster slayers, heroes and adventurers who fight so that all people, humans and D-Bees, may live free of oppression, monsters and demons so that they may find their place in the world. And, with luck, make it a better place.

Note: When stripped of his magical creation powers (can't make anything but normal S.D.C. items at the normal rate of speed), the Mystic Kuznya retains his supernatural P.S., physical M.D.C. and other O.C.C. abilities. Also note that 8 out of 10 villages and towns, and even most modern cities throughout Russia and Asia, will have a blacksmith or foundry where the Mystic Smith can ply his trade. The character must have access to blacksmith and metal working facilities, even if they are crude and primitive. Heck, they love primitive, just give them a forge, fire and an anvil, and they are ready to go.

Special Powers & Abilities of the Mystic Kuznya

1. The Mettle of Kuznya Sorcery. The magic of the Mystic Smith transforms them into creatures "not unlike metal" — lesser M.D.C. beings with P.E. x3 as the base M.D.C. plus 2D6 M.D.C. per level of experience. On the down side, their skin is as hard and cold as steel.

2. Limited Invulnerability. The Kuznya's hard M.D.C. bodies are impervious to S.D.C. weapons, and natural cold, heat and fire, but magical fire does full damage and magical cold does half damage. All M.D. weapons, explosives, energy blasts, etc., inflict full damage.

3. Supernatural P.S.: When creating the character, roll for the P.S. attribute as usual but then add 1D6+12 to the number rolled, and make it supernatural P.S. This means punches and kicks inflict M.D. and the smith can carry 100x his P.S. in pounds.

Supernatural P.S. Damage Table:

P.S. 15 or less: Only inflicts 1D6 S.D.C. on a restrained punch, 4D6 S.D.C. on a full strength punch or 1D4 M.D. on a power punch (counts as two melee attacks). P.S. bonuses are added to S.D.C. attacks.

P.S. 16 to 20: Inflicts 3D6 S.D.C. on a restrained punch, 1D6 M.D. on a full strength punch, or 2D6 M.D. on a power punch (counts as two melee attacks). P.S. bonuses are added to S.D.C. attacks.

P.S. 21 to 25: Inflicts 4D6 S.D.C. on a restrained punch, 2D6 M.D. on a full strength punch, or 4D6 M.D. on a power punch (counts as two melee attacks). P.S. bonuses are added to S.D.C. attacks.

P.S. 26 to 30: Inflicts 5D6 S.D.C. on a restrained punch, 3D6 M.D. on a full strength punch, or 6D6 M.D. on a power punch (counts as two melee attacks). P.S. bonuses are added to S.D.C. attacks.

P.S. 31 to 35: Inflicts 5D6 S.D.C. on a restrained punch, 4D6 M.D. on a full strength punch, or 1D4x10 M.D. on a power punch (counts as two melee attacks). P.S. bonuses are added only to S.D.C. attacks.

P.S. 36 to 40: Inflicts 6D6 S.D.C. on a restrained punch, 5D6 M.D. on a full strength punch, or 1D6x10 M.D. on a power punch (counts as two melee attacks). P.S. bonuses are added only to S.D.C. attacks.

P.S. 41 to 50: Inflicts 1D6x10 S.D.C. on a restrained punch, 6D6 M.D. on a full strength punch, or 2D4x10 M.D. on a power punch (counts as two melee attacks). P.S. bonuses are added only to S.D.C. attacks.

P.S. 51 to 60: Inflicts 1D6 M.D. on a restrained punch, 1D6x10 on a full strength punch, or 2D6x10 on a power punch (counts as two melee attacks). P.S. bonuses not applicable.

P.S. 61 to 70: Inflicts 2D6 M.D. on a restrained punch, 1D6x10+10 on a full strength punch, or 2D6x10+20 on a power punch (counts as two melee attacks). P.S. bonuses not applicable.

Monster Note: Some supernatural creatures will have a greater or weaker damage range than the above table provides. These are exceptions to the general rule. **Biting attacks** typically inflict half the M.D. as a punch unless the maw is especially large or powerful, then a bite could inflict the same damage or more. **Tails and tentacles** typically inflict the same amount of M.D. as a punch. Power punches are not usually possible with a tail, but are possible with a tentacle. Kicks usually inflict the same M.D. as a punch, but in some cases the kick may inflict 1D6 more Mega-Damage.

4. Special O.C.C. Skills of the Mystic Kuznya:

Gemology: The ability to identify and appraise the nature and value of precious metals (silver, gold, etc.) and stones (jade, ruby, sapphire, diamond, etc.). This ability also enables the character to identify fakes, but at a penalty of -10%. A failed roll means the character cannot tell whether or not the item is fake or real, or its value is grossly under or overestimated. **Base Skill:** 50% +5% per level of experience.

Metalwork and Forge: An expertise in the ancient craft of forging, shaping and working metal to create all manner of metal items, from tools and utensils to weapons, armor, chain mail, silverware, etc. The percentile number indicates the quality of technique and appearance. All Mystic Kuznya are highly skilled professionals. A successful skill roll means a superior, high quality product.

In the case of silverware and other items, it means beautiful craftsmanship that commands 50%-100% more money (5-10x more if exquisitely detailed). In the case of an ordinary S.D.C./H.P. weapon, it means the weapon has exceptional balance and a fine edge or other feature that makes the weapon +1 to strike, +1 to parry and +1D6 to damage. In the case of metal S.D.C. armor, the suit gets +1 to Armor Rating and has 40% more S.D.C. than is standard without additional weight. All Kuznya weapons and armor are worth 100%-200% more than the standard price. **Note:** The use of Kuznya Magic can transform a normal S.D.C. weapon, tool or armor into an M.D.C. one; see magic elsewhere in this section. **Base Skill:** 60% +3% per level of experience. A failed roll means an average quality item without the extra bonuses or value (and a disappointment to the Mystic Smith).

Shape, Engrave, Etch & Emboss Metal: The skill of decorating, detailing and manipulating metal to create fancy designs, artwork, frills, etchings, engravings, embossing, colorful inlay of gold, silver, chrome, etc., insetting gems, adding fins, spikes or studs, high polish, and other artistic work done with metal — all metal, from iron and steel to silver and gold. The percentile number indicates the quality of technique and appearance. All Mystic Kuznya are highly skilled professionals. **Base Skill:** 70% +3% per level of experience.

5. Initial Spell Knowledge: The Mystic Kuznya doesn't actually know spell magic or cast spells, other than a handful of weapon related ones. Their true power is their ability to create magic weapons and select items made from metal.

Spells are limited to the following: Ignite Fire, Fuel Flame, Extinguish Fire, Superhuman Strength, and the following described in The Federation of Magic: Manipulate Objects, Deflect, Ricochet Strike, Implosion Neutralizer, Create Steel, Power Weapon, Speed Weapon, and Enchant Weapon.

No other spells can be learned.

6. P.P.E.: Like all practitioners of magic, the Mystic Kuznya is a living battery of mystic energy that he can draw upon at will. Permanent Base P.P.E.: 1D4x10+25, but add 1D6+15 P.P.E. per level of experience. The more experienced the character, the greater his raw ability. Additional P.P.E. can be drawn from ley lines and P.P.E. willingly offered, (see the **Rifts® RPG** for details), but no Kuznya can draw P.P.E. from blood sacrifices; the magic won't work with "death" energy.

7. No Psionics: Any psychic abilities that might have developed are used to fuel Kuznya magic and superhuman abilities noted above.

8. O.C.C. Bonuses: +1D4 on M.E., +1D4 M.A., +2 on P.E., +1 on initiative, +1 to strike and parry, +1 to disarm, +6 to pull punch, +2 to save vs Horror Factor, +2 to save vs possession. Also see superhuman P.S.

Magical Equipment of the Mystic Kuznya:

All Mystic Kuznya have the following magical items which are used both as weapons and for making magic metal items.

1. An indestructible, giant sledgehammer. It is considered a lesser magic item that is used both as a tool in forging metal items and as a weapon. The head of the hammer alone weighs 100 pounds (45 kg) and is mounted on an iron handle six feet (1.8 m) long. As a weapon, the sledgehammer requires two hands to wield it skillfully and does 6D6 M.D., double damage to supernatural beings and creatures of magic, and is +1 to strike and +2 to parry or disarm (no bonuses apply if used one-handed). It is -2 to strike when thrown. **Note:** The giant sledgehammer requires a normal P.S. of 35 or a supernatural

P.S. of 19 to use it. Characters with insufficient P.S. require the use of both hands, are -6 to strike, parry and dodge, have no initiative, and each strike of the hammer uses up two melee attacks. Characters with a P.S. under 22 can't even lift it.

2. Three indestructible hammers made of gold. They are considered lesser magic items crucial as tools in the forging of magic metal items. Without them, the Magic Smith cannot forge magical creations. As a weapon, each of the small gold hammers inflicts 2D6 M.D., is +1 on initiative, +2 to strike and parry and is a well balanced precision instrument. **Note:** Striking two of the hammers together causes a spark that can be used to build a fire.

3. Three indestructible tongs made of gold. They are considered lesser magic items crucial as tools in the forging of magic metal items. Without them, the Magic Smith cannot forge magical creations. They are impervious even to magic fire and are said to be able to hold a burning star. As a weapon, the gold tongs or pincers inflict only one M.D., but they can be used to parry or grab magic weapons, including flaming swords; +2 to parry and +2 to disarm when used against melee weapons, even magic ones.

4. M.D.C. Chain Mail. A full suit of chain mail (typically steel, silver or gold) with protective helmet, and arm and leg plates. 400 M.D.C., but surprisingly light and flexible.

Russian Mystic Kuznya O.C.C.

Also known as the Hands of Svarog.
Alignment: Any except miscreant or diabolic, and even anarchist is rare (5%). Most are principled (32%), scrupulous (31%), unprincipled (23%) or aberrant (9%).
Racial Restrictions: Humans only, 35% of which are females.
Roll The Eight Attributes as normal but see bonuses and supernatural P.S. as noted previously. Don't roll for Hit Points or S.D.C.
Average Level of Experience (N.P.C.): 1D4+4 or as required by the Game Master.
Psionics: None!
Attribute Requirements: I.Q. 9, M.E. 12, P.E. 14 or higher.
O.C.C. Skills:
Basic Math (+30%)
Speaks Russian at 98%
Speaks Euro and one other language of choice (+20%)
Lore: One of choice (+10%)
Armorer (Field Armorer; +30%)
Recognize Weapon Quality (+30%)
General Repair/Maintenance (+15%)
Find Contraband (+10%)
Cook (+10%)
Art (+10%)
Prospecting (+10%)
Land Navigation (+10%)
Pilot Skill: One of choice (+10%); may select Horsemanship.
W.P. Ancient: Blunt
W.P. three Ancient of choice (any).
W.P. Modern Weapon, one of choice (any).
Hand to Hand: Expert to start, but can be changed to Martial Arts (never Assassin) for the cost of two O.C.C. Related Skills
O.C.C. Related Skills: Select six other skills at level one and one additional at levels 3, 6, 9 and 12.

Communications: Any
Domestic: Any
Electrical: None
Espionage: None
Mechanical: Basic and Automotive Mechanics only (+5%)
Medical: First Aid only.
Military: Any
Physical: Any, except Gymnastics and Acrobatics.
Pilot Skills: Any, except robots, power armor, military vehicles, ships and aircraft — Horsemanship is most likely.
Pilot Related Skills: Any
Rogue Skills: None
Science: Any (+10% on chemistry skills)
Technical: Any (+10%).
W.P.: Any
Wilderness: Any (+5%)
Secondary Skills: The character also gets to select four Secondary Skills from the previous list at level one and one additional at levels 2, 4, 6, 8 and 12. These are additional areas of knowledge that do not get the advantage of the bonus listed in parentheses. All Secondary Skills start at the base skill level. Also, skills are limited as previously indicated.
Standard Equipment to Start: The hammers, tongs and armor noted earlier plus a silver S.D.C. dagger (1D6), silver M.D. knife (2D6 M.D.), magic scissors (1D4 M.D.), magic M.D. bolt cutter (2D6 M.D.), one man-made M.D. weapon of choice, gold cross, metal etching tools, tool kit, wire cutter, two medium sacks, one large sack, backpack or satchel, bedroll (plus saddlebags if he has a horse), water skin, belt, boots, flashlight or lantern, language translator, note pad, 2D4 markers or pencils, a couple sets of clothes, including one set of dress clothes, and a handful of personal items. Additional weapons, special items and magic items may be made or acquired over time.
Vehicle: Starts with none.
Secret Resources: Even first level Mystic Kuznya are highly regarded and welcomed at most farmsteads, villages, and even modern cities. This is largely because people will plead for the smith to make them (usually simple) magical items, ordinary metal smith items (but in a tenth of the time) and for general assistance in metalwork and construction. Mystic Kuznya are also regarded as heroes and monster slayers, which also makes them welcome. As a rule, they are treated like visiting royalty, given the finest accommodations, food, drink and courtesy either free of charge or at cost, even if the smith doesn't agree to do any work or make any magic for them! They want him to remember them favorably, and, perhaps the next time he passes through, to think kindly of them and maybe offer some of his or her amazing services. Such royal treatment does not usually extend to the smith's travelling companions unless he agrees to do some work for the village, church or local business.
Money: Starts with 3D6x1000 credits or Rubles, and 3D6x1000 in tradeable goods, not to mention invaluable abilities that can be traded for vast amounts of wealth.
Cybernetics: None, and avoids them like the plague, because any cybernetics or other forms of physical augmentation interferes with magic. However, cybernetic prosthetics and bio-systems for medical reasons will be considered if necessary.

The Magical Metal Creations of the Mystic Kuznya

The Drain of Creation

Every time the Mystic Smith makes a *Greater Magic Item* or a weapon with a feature that makes it a Greater Magic Item, he is temporarily drained, because part of his life force is used to supplement and create the magical weapon. The mage will recover, but it takes 2-5 weeks.

Penalties of Creation: Reduce the Mystic Kuznya's M.D.C., P.P.E., speed, all bonuses, and the number of attacks per melee round by half for *4D6+12 days* after the creation of one of the *Greater Magic Items* or the installation of one feature that makes the weapon a *Greater Magic Item*. Penalties and lost M.D.C. and P.P.E. can not be replenished through meditation, magic or psionics and remains unavailable until the period of weakness comes to a natural end. Giving a weapon more than one *Greater Feature* has a cumulative effect and will reduce the character more with each such feature. No other major creations can be done until the P.P.E. and character's strength returns. This physical and magical drain makes the character vulnerable and weak and is another reason the Mystic Kuznya is sparing in the creation of *Greater Magic Items*.

Note: The creation or installation of each feature that counts as a *Greater Magical Item* requires a minimum of 2D6 hours of magical crafting and has the lasting debilitating effect noted above. Each *Greater Feature* has an accumulative effect in draining the Mystic Kuznya. This means only one such feature can be added to the weapon or item when the Mystic Kuznya has sufficient P.P.E. and may mean it will take 2-6 months to create an item with multiple Greater Magical Features. As many as four Greater Magical features can be instilled in a single weapon or armor, two for all other items. The specific magical creations described under *Greater Metal Magical Items* may be exceptions to this rule, but that's because they have been allegedly designed by the god, Svarog, and follow an exact and unalterable blueprint (i.e. other features can *not* be added, nor can features be left out or substituted).

Magical Weapon Features

The following features (up to a total of four per item) can be magically imbued in any weapon, tool or simple item made entirely of metal. Only the Mystic Kuznya is capable of such transformations. All transformations are permanent, but M.D.C. items can be destroyed by attacks directly leveled at the weapon or item, and the Mystic Kuznya has the power to destroy supposedly *indestructible* weapons and items created by a fellow Kuznya by re-forging it and turning it back into S.D.C. material. This process or reversion costs the same amount of P.P.E. to destroy it as it did to make it, plus it also has the same effect and penalty as making a *Greater Magic Item*.

Note: Only those items indicated as counting as a *Greater Magic Item* causes the smith to suffer from long-lasting and debilitating side effects. Features that do not mention this side effect can be cast without penalty other than the momentary loss of P.P.E. which recovers as normal.

Each "feature" is a separate P.P.E. Cost.

Fair market cost varies dramatically. Most are considered priceless, with the least powerful garnering 40,000-80,000 credits and the most powerful getting 250,000 to 500,000 credits, sometimes more.

Features ...

- **Impervious to Fire**: Makes any S.D.C. metal tool or weapon impervious to fire, even M.D. fire. P.P.E. Cost: 20

- **Combat bonuses:** A weapon that is exceptionally well balanced, +1 to strike and +2 to parry and disarm. P.P.E. Cost: 70

- **Quick Strike**: A special "quick draw and strike" combat bonus that gives the user +1 on initiative and +1 to strike when thrown for that particular well balanced and comfortable weapon. P.P.E. Cost: 50

- **Make any Metal M.D.C.:** The magic turns any type of metal, from soft metal like lead, gold and silver to hard metal like iron and steel, and even light, flimsy alloys like aluminum and tin, into M.D.C. materials. Commonly used to make a tool or an ancient style melee weapon (axe, pick, knife, mace, ball and chain, hammer, war hammer, knife, sword, pole arm, staff, etc.) into a Mega-Damage weapon. Tools made of M.D.C. material but used for S.D.C. applications never wear out or break, unless exposed to M.D.C. force.

  Forged in Silver. This is crucial in making sturdy, M.D.C. weapons made of solid (and incredibly pure) silver. The purity of the silver is so high because the magic makes the soft metal harder than steel. Normal S.D.C. silver weapons and items often require the mixture of other alloys to make it harder and more durable, or, in the case of weapons, requiring a hard steel alloy weapon to be silver coated/plated (a coating that can be scratched or removed). Magic eliminates such practical needs and considerations.

  Note #1: Weapons made of "pure silver" inflict an extra 1D6 points of damage (S.D.C. or M.D. as the case may be) to creatures like vampires and the Unclean who are vulnerable to the metal.

  Note #2: Just because a metal weapon is turned into an M.D.C. material does *not* mean it inflicts Mega-Damage — it does not (except possibly to certain supernatural beings). It still does S.D.C. and Hit Point damage unless the smith also gives it the power to inflict Mega-Damage.

  P.P.E. Cost: 30 P.P.E. per every 50 M.D.C. points put into the melee weapon; with 500 M.D.C. being the maximum. Can also transform metal sheets or parts into M.D.C. material at a cost of one P.P.E. per pound (0.45 kg).

  In the case of arrows and bullets (any caliber), 30 P.P.E. will turn 30 of the small objects into M.D.C. items (one point each) — silver objects if the client provides the silver.

- **Inflict Mega-Damage.** The P.P.E. cost to make a magical weapon capable of inflicting Mega-Damage varies with the amount of M.D. the weapon inflicts. First, however, the weapon must be a Mega-Damage Structure (has at least 50 M.D.C.) itself. **Note:** Hammers are the Mystic Kuznya's specialty, so they can add an extra 1D6 M.D. to "hammers" without P.P.E. cost (maces, morning stars, clubs and other blunt weapons are *not* considered hammers).

Arrows can not inflict more than 1D6 M.D. unless a special magic arrow (described elsewhere), small weapons like knives, maces, short swords and small hammers can not inflict more than 3D6 M.D.; large weapons like war hammers, sledgehammers, large swords, pole arms, lances, etc., can range from 1D6 to 1D6x10 M.D. depending on the desire of the smith and the amount of P.P.E. spent.

1D6 M.D. costs 50 P.P.E.

2D6 M.D. costs 100 P.P.E.

3D6 M.D. costs 150 P.P.E.

4D6 M.D. costs 225 P.P.E.

5D6 M.D. costs 300 P.P.E.

1D4x10 M.D. costs 350 P.P.E. and is restricted to large swords and pole arms only. Counts as a *Greater Magical Item* with the usual side effects and penalties for its creation.

1D6x10 M.D. costs 500 P.P.E. and is restricted to large swords and pole arms only. Counts as a *Greater Magical Item* with the usual side effects and penalties for its creation.

- **Indestructible.** Makes any metal melee weapon magically indestructible even to magical and M.D. attacks, and makes it an M.D. weapon that automatically does 1D6 M.D. (additional M.D. can be added). Being indestructible also means the blade never dulls. P.P.E. Cost: 200, and counts as a *Greater Magical Item* with the usual side effects and penalties for its creation.

- **Double damage against supernatural beings.** P.P.E. Cost: 50 P.P.E. per die of damage (i.e. a weapon that normally does 3D6 M.D. costs an extra 150 P.P.E. to do 6D6 to the supernatural, 200 P.P.E. to do 4D6 = 8D6, and so on), but counts as a *Greater Magical Item* with the usual side effects and penalties for its creation.

- **Variable Damage: S.D.C. to M.D.** Does 1D6 to 4D6 S.D.C. (the Mystic Kuznya sets the exact amount of damage) to mortal creatures but does an equivalent number of dice in M.D. to supernatural beings (1D6 to 4D6 M.D. depending on what the S.D.C. damage is). P.P.E. Cost: 100 P.P.E., and counts as a *Greater Magical Item* with the usual side effects and penalties for its creation. Add another 100 P.P.E. to include creatures of magic and any Mega-Damage opponent.

- **Variable Damage: Low M.D. to High M.D.** The weapon normally does 1D6 or 2D6 M.D. to most opponents (the Mystic Kuznya sets the exact amount of damage) but does 4D6 or 5D6 M.D. to supernatural beings and Mega-Damage opponents. P.P.E. Cost: 250 or 300 P.P.E. depending on the level of damage that can be inflicted, and counts as a *Greater Magical Item* with the usual side effects and penalties for its creation.

- **Flaming Weapon.** The weapon bursts into magical fire upon command by the wielder. Adds 3D6 M.D. to the weapon's usual damage capacity. P.P.E. Cost: 200, but counts as a *Greater Magical Item* with the usual side effects and penalties for its creation.

- **M.D.C. Metal Armor** of any type, from chain mail to full plate. P.P.E. Cost: 50 P.P.E. per 50 M.D.C. points put into the armor. Maximum M.D.C. is 300 for chain mail, 400 for scale mail or plate and chain, and 500 M.D.C. for full plate. The armor is surprisingly comfortable and comparatively light considering the protection it offers, but is not a full environmental suit. Typically 10%-15% skill and movement penalties.

- **Silent Armor.** Makes a barely detectable sound no louder than the rustling of a cloth jacket; reduce prowl penalty by half. P.P.E. Cost: 80

- **Featherweight Armor:** Regardless of what type of metal the armor is made of, it has a maximum weight of six pounds (2.7 kg); reduce prowl and movement penalties by half. P.P.E. Cost: 110

- **Fast Forge.** To completely forge any magical weapon, tool or chalice in 24 hours costs an extra 100 P.P.E., but is the equivalent of having made a *Greater Magical Item* (even though the item may not be one) with the usual side effects and penalties for its creation. Fast Forging body armor takes 4D6+48 hours and 200 P.P.E. in addition to the normal cost of making the armor.

Magic Bonuses from Different Types of Metal

Various types of metal in the hands of the Mystic Kuznya, have special traits and bonuses when applied to weapons. In a few cases, the traits and bonuses are innate and don't require additional P.P.E. to activate. In others to get one or more of their special properties, additional P.P.E. must be applied. In all cases the innate nature of the metal keeps the additional P.P.E. cost low.

Gold: Symbol of wealth, purity and quality. When used as a weapon, it adds +1 on initiative, +2 to strike and parry and is an impeccably well balanced and precision instrument. P.P.E. Cost: 30.

Silver: Namely a metal that can hurt a large number of otherwise invulnerable or semi-invulnerable supernatural beings even in S.D.C. form. Such S.D.C. silver weapons inflict the equivalent S.D.C. damage as M.D. (i.e. a silver sword that inflicts 2D6 S.D.C. would inflict 2D6 M.D.). If the metal is 90% (or better) in purity, the weapon inflicts an additional 1D6 damage to beings vulnerable to it. Also known as the "moon sliver metal." P.P.E. Cost: Zero.

Bronze: Represents the power of the sun. The weapon itself is automatically impervious to all types of fire (no P.P.E. necessary). Its highly polished surface can also reflect sunlight as easily as a mirror. P.P.E. Costs: 15 P.P.E. enables the weapon to cast a blinding flash six times per 24 hours; 45 P.P.E. enables the weapon to fire a bolt of concentrated light, similar to a laser, once per melee round — effectively adds one melee attack and does 3D6 M.D.; range 1200 feet (366 m).

Copper: The fire metal. The weapon is automatically impervious to fire (no P.P.E.). P.P.E. Cost: 15 points can make the weapon wielder resistant to M.D. fire (does half damage), or 30 P.P.E. makes him impervious to all fire as long as the weapon is in his possession. 60 P.P.E. makes a copper weapon able to become a flaming weapon that can inflict an additional 3D6 M.D. and does half damage to supernatural creatures linked to fire (when normally, flaming weapons do no damage). Furthermore, no evil creature can pick it up without getting burnt and taking half the damage that's normally inflicted when struck by the weapon. Yet good and innocent beings find the weapon harmless.

Iron: A magical ground that inflicts its normal damage to otherwise impervious energy beings, ghosts and spirits (no P.P.E. necessary). P.P.E. Cost: 20 points to make the weapon user resistant to electricity and lightning (half damage), or 60 P.P.E. to make the wielder impervious to it. Pure Iron also does additional damage to some supernatural beings.

Steel: An iron alloy (combined with nickel and other trace elements) that represents strength and a hard edge. P.P.E. Cost: 15 points make the weapon +1 to strike, 30 P.P.E. adds 1D6 M.D.

Notable Lesser Magic Items

Unbreakable (M.D.) Plow

This is pretty much what it sounds like, a strong, M.D.C. plow that can cut through earth and hit tree roots, stumps and rock without breaking. Very popular among farmers. P.P.E. Cost: 100

Magic M.D. Scissors

Mega-Damage blades that can stab or cut through M.D.C material under an eighth of an inch thick (does 1D4 M.D. per cut or stab). Can cut through most S.D.C. material that is thinner than one inch. P.P.E. Cost: 90

Magic M.D. Bolt Cutters

Magic M.D. Bolt Cutters that can cut M.D.C. chain, cable or rods that are less than two inches in diameter (1D6+6 M.D.). Can cut through S.D.C. material up to four inches in diameter like butter. Note that bolt cutters are designed to cut metal bolts, links, rods and cable and cannot cut like scissors in a straight line. They have a pair of long handles and a large, short head and resembles large, plier-style wire cutters. P.P.E. Cost: 120

Magic Hammer

A super-strong but lightweight hammer that never wears out and never breaks. Still an S.D.C. item (does 2D6 S.D.C. damage as a weapon). P.P.E. Cost: 30

Magic M.D. Arrows

Three metal arrows can be turned into M.D. dealing projectiles per expenditure of 30 P.P.E.; does 1D6 damage.

The metal an arrow is made of will give it different properties at no extra charge.

Gold — +2 to strike
Silver — The usual effect on many supernatural creatures.
Bronze — Flies twice as far as normal.
Copper — Bursts into flame, is +2 to damage and will set combustibles on fire.
Iron — inflicts damage to otherwise impervious energy beings, entities, Midnight Demons, ghosts and spirits.
Steel — +1 to strike and inflicts 2D6 M.D. instead of 1D6 M.D.

Greater Magical Metal Items of the Mystic Kuznya

Angel Horseshoes

Enables the horse or similar riding animal to run 30% faster and leap 50% higher and farther, without additional stress or fatigue. Furthermore, the animal fatigues at half the usual rate (i.e. can run twice as long without tiring) and the horseshoes themselves last three times longer than ordinary ones. P.P.E. Cost: 60 per set of four.

Dragon Armor

A suit of metal scale armor (also know as Jazeraint armor) that is impervious to Dragon's breath (any), and heat and fire of all kinds, including Mega-Damage plasma blasts and magical fire.

The upper body and the majority of this suit of armor (70%) must be scale armor, but can also include pieces that are full metal plate, like forearm vambraces or gauntlets, or chain mail or other comparatively light and flexible materials (leather, M.D.C. plastics or ceramics, etc.) to cover parts of the arms, legs, or groin area.

- M.D.C. Range: 200-300
- Weight: 20-25 pounds (9 to 11.2 kg).
- Fair mobility; a penalty of -10% applies to the skills prowl, climb, swim, acrobatics, and gymnastics.
- Market Cost: 50,000-70,000+ credits. Rare.
- P.P.E. Cost: 210

Angel's Armor

The armor itself is traditional looking plate and chain armor. The chest plates are made of polished gold, as are the shoulders and tops of the arms. The forearms are covered in metal vambraces, but the undersides of the arms are covered in silver chain mail. A large symbol of the sun radiating light, or an angel with the sun or rays of light generating from behind it, or a cross with rays of light radiating from it, is always part of the design of the chest plating.

Angel's Armor gives the wearer the ability to fly at will. In addition to the wearer's own body and armor weight, he can carry up to 200 lbs (90 kg). Plus the wearer can cast Globe of Daylight and Turn Dead 3x per 24 hours. The chest design functions as a holy symbol that will both warn creatures of darkness that they face a champion of light, and keep creatures such as lesser vampires and others repelled by holy symbols at bay.

- M.D.C. Range: 300-400
- Weight: 30-35 pounds (13.6 to 15.7 kg).
- Fair mobility; a penalty of -15% applies to the skills prowl, climb, swim, acrobatics, and gymnastics.
- Market Cost: 85,000 credits and up. Rare.
- Limitations: Only characters of a good alignment can draw on the armor's magical powers of flight, turn dead and daylight.
- P.P.E. Cost: 280

Dragonblade

A sword made of bronze, copper or red metal. It does 1D6 M.D. to most opponents, but 4D6 M.D. against dragons, fire elementals and other supernatural creatures of magic (fire demons, etc.). Plus the weapon's wielder is resistant to M.D. fire (takes half damage). **Note:** If adapted to non-M.D.C. environments like the Palladium Fantasy World, any sword strike above eight penetrates the dragon, elemental or demon's natural A.R. and does damage. P.P.E. Cost: 200

Spiritblade

A blue-grey sword made of iron. It does 3D6 M.D. to most opponents, but 5D6 M.D. against energy beings, ghosts, spirits, entities, elementals and all ethereal beings, including life es-

sences and Astral Travelers. **Note:** If adapted to non-M.D.C. environments like the Palladium Fantasy World, any sword strike above six penetrates the "spirit" and does damage, provided the character doesn't dodge or parry. P.P.E. Cost: 300

Serpent Rod

An iron staff that is surprisingly lightweight and useful as both a weapon and magic item, (it is depicted in the illustration of the Born Mystic).

It does 2D6 M.D. to most opponents, but 4D6 M.D. against supernatural beings, and double damage (8D6 M.D.) to "serpents," including dragons, the demonic Serpent Hound, Wolf-Serpent and Worms of Taut. **Note:** If adapted to non-M.D.C. environments like the Palladium Fantasy World, any strike above 10 penetrates the creature's Armor Rating and does 1D6x10 damage to "serpents" (3D6 damage to mortals).

In addition, the Serpent Rod makes the wielder impervious to snake venom (including magical creations of the Snake to Sword spell), +3 to save vs any type of poison (spoiling and disease *not* included), and snakes will not bite this character for any reason. Worms of Taut are reluctant to attack (no initiative) and all combat bonuses and bite damage is half when directed at the character with the Serpent Rod.

P.P.E. Cost: 380

Metal Claw Wand

The wand somewhat resembles a fireplace poker with a long, thin metal rod ending in an open, clawing animals' paw, typically that of a bear, tiger or monster, or talons of an eagle. It is used to stoke fires (impervious to M.D. fire), a tool in metal working and as a weapon. In the former capacity, the taloned claw can open and close to grasp, hold and carry items beyond the reach of the smith. As a weapon, the claw does 4D6 M.D., +1D6 M.D. if made of steel, +1 to strike if made of gold, +1 to parry if made of copper, and can grab and hold energy beings, entities and ghosts if made of iron. P.P.E. Cost: 160

Russian Line Walker

The term sorcerer is usually applied to the Russian Ley Line Walker. However, "sorcerer" is used to describe all types of practitioners of magic, just as the term "wizard" is the common catch-all term used in the West. The Russian Line Walker is one of the most feared because their spell casting abilities are very diverse and powerful.

The Russian Line Walker, or Sorcerer, is the traditional "wizard" type spell caster. He is fundamentally the same as the North American version described in the **Rifts® RPG**, page 83. The only substantive difference is the selection of spells. Instead of using #8 in **Rifts®**, use the one below.

8. Initial Spell Knowledge. In addition to the ley line powers, the Russian Line Walker is a master of spell magic (they tend to avoid ritual magic, but can perform rituals when needed). At level one experience, players may select *two* common Wizard spells from spell levels 1, 2, 3 and 4 (that's a total of eight). Selections are made from spells found in the **Rifts® RPG**, starting on page 167, and/or Wizard spells described in **Rifts® World Book 16: The Federation of Magic**, starting on page 129.

The Russian Line Walker also selects a total of *four* spells from either Nature Magic or Bone Magic; any spells under 8th level can be selected.

Each additional level of experience, the character will be able to figure out/select one new "wizard" spell equal to his own level of achievement/experience. Additional spells can be learned or purchased as usual.

Russian Shifter/Summoner

The Russian Shifter is more of a monster summoner who summons, controls and commands numerous supernatural monsters. They also associate with members of the underworld, criminals, witches, necromancers and evil practitioners of magic. The original description for the Shifter is found in the **Rifts® RPG**, page 87. I had intended to explore and explain this O.C.C. in greater detail but time and space limitations prevent my doing so. Perhaps in some future sourcebook.

The Old Believer O.C.C. & Nature Magic

The Old Believer is the keeper of the old faith. A combination shaman, sage and sorcerer who knows and understands all the old superstitions, folk tales, and lost Russian Magic (knots, bones, nature, etc.) and lives by the "old ways." In addition to knowing the secrets of the old Nature Magic, the Old Believer is a wise man versed in lore, legend, superstition and folk tales from throughout the ages, going back to pre-Christian era Russia, and some say, before recorded history. As such, they know about animal husbandry, planting, demons, monsters, magic and healing. They are welcomed and respected by common folk, especially peasants and farmers living far from civilization or the protection of the Warlords. The Old Believers are also accepted by most Woodland Spirits, and feared by witches and Russian demons. Most roam the land helping people along the way as best they can. While some charge high fees for their services (livestock, horses, gold, diamonds, credits, etc.), the majority are gentle, kind and compassionate, willing to take a warm bed, bowl of porridge, some basic supplies and a thank you as payment for most of their services and magic.

On the mundane end of the spectrum, Old Believers will work in the fields, help harvest crops, offer advice, act as a judge to resolve disputes and/or assign restitution, spread news, deliver (verbal) messages and tell folk tales. However, most consider their principle duty as healers (of the body and spirit) and Monster Chasers. They usually use the term "chaser" rather than "slayer," because most Old Believers are just as glad to identify and drive away evil spirits, demons, witches and other dark forces as they are to destroy them. It's not that they are lazy or cowards, it's just that driving supernatural creatures away can be just as effective as killing them, and usually easier and without risk of bloody retribution. Old Believers are nothing if not pragmatic and practical.

The Warlords regard these rather paradoxical and enigmatic men and women with suspicion, concern, and a little bit of fear.

The reason is that the Believers swear allegiance to no king or nation, wield ancient magic and arcane knowledge, won't share their secrets (many an Old Believer has died under torture without teaching the secrets of the old ways), and insist they live to

serve *all* men and Moist Mother Russia. They are often suspected of being spies or in league with dangerous Woodland Spirits, consequently, they are watched closely, but even the War Camps turn to the Old Believers for their counsel and unique magic, from time to time.

Special O.C.C. Abilities & Bonuses

1. Empathy with animals. Whether this is a strictly magical or psionic power is unclear (not even the Old Believers know), but all have an affinity with animals similar to Psi-Stalkers and Simvan. Domesticated animals will always take an immediate liking to them and will do their best to please the mage. This empathy automatically gives the character the ability to ride any horse (wild or tame) or any other non-predatory animal at a +15% bonus and/or work with any domestic animals.

Wild animals, with the exception of felines and mutant or alien predators, will react to the Old Believer as if he was a fellow woodland creature and allow him to walk among them without fear. This ability enables the character to operate in the wild without causing animals to react to his presence — birds do not fly away, animals do not run, and therefore, do not indicate the approach of an intruder. Even watchdogs will not sound a bark of alarm at his presence. **Note:** The affinity with animals means that the character will hunt and eat meat only for food, never for pleasure, and feels sadness whenever he sees an animal in distress. Supernatural predators see the Old Believer as a threat. Psi-Stalkers and Simvan (the latter can be found in Germany, Romania, Poland and western Russia) will also see the Old Believer as a kindred spirit.

2. Animal Familiar. At level two the Wise Man automatically gets an animal familiar via the Familiar Link spell (see *Rifts® RPG*, page 182).

3. The Staff of Moist Mother Earth. Most Old Believers use a walking stick or staff from the very beginning, but at fourth level, the mage can create the Staff of Moist Mother Earth. This is done by preparing an ordinary piece of wood by whittling and carving it into a staff (the Old Believer must do all the work making it), going to a remote area of the wilderness (typically a tree or boulder in the Steppe, a mountain peek or deep forest), placing the staff on the ground and fasting (no food) and meditating for seven days without interruption. On the dawn of the eighth day, the staff will crackle and glow with green energy. The Old Believer must immediately pick up the staff while it still glows, and the two are bonded together and the magic completed.

Powers of the Magic Staff: Only the Old Believer can draw upon the staff's powers.

- Becomes an indestructible M.D.C. structure. However, 16 days after the Old Believer dies, it turns into a fragile rod of rotting wood.
- It does 1D6 M.D. to most opponents, but 4D6 M.D. against supernatural beings and creatures of magic (dragons, Faerie Folk, Woodland Spirits, etc.) of all kinds. However, if anybody except the Old Believer uses the staff it only does 3D6 S.D.C.! **Note:** If adapted to non-M.D.C. environments like the Palladium Fantasy World, any strike above 10 penetrates the supernatural creature's Armor Rating and it does 2D6+4 to mortal opponents and 5D6 damage to supernatural beings and creatures of magic. Anybody other than the mage using the weapon can only inflict 1D6 damage to any type of living being.

- Woodland Spirits, Faerie Folk and elemental beings recognize the staff as a symbol of Earth and life, and know that the person who wields it is a kindred spirit. They will consider the Old Believer to be a friend and brother and will not harm him unless attacked first or commanded to do so by a higher power.

- The Old Believer can raise the staff up so that the top is above his head and pump 6 P.P.E. into it to turn it into a holy symbol. Duration: 10 minutes per level of the mage. When used as a holy symbol, the head of the staff glows with a dim, pale light. It will frighten and hold vampires, other undead and similar creatures at bay with the same effect that any holy symbol would have on these misbegotten creatures.

- While holding or touching the staff, the Old Believer can understand all languages perfectly, including Elementals.

4. Special O.C.C. Skills of the Old Believer:

Gemology: The ability to identify and appraise the nature and value of precious metals (silver, gold, etc.) and stones (jade, ruby, sapphire, diamond, etc.). This ability also enables the character to identify fakes, but at a penalty of -10%. A failed roll means the character cannot tell whether or not the item is fake or real, or its value is grossly under or overestimated. **Base Skill:** 50% +3% per level of experience.

Masonry Expert: A complete understanding of the principles of bricklaying and stone construction. The percentile number indicates the success ratio of recognizing deterioration, improper construction, the intended purpose of construction, locate foundations and load bearing walls, recognize styles of masonry, estimate the approximate age or period of construction, and identification of different styles. The Old Believer can also lay bricks to repair or build walls and houses, or assist in their construction or tearing down. **Base Skill:** 40% +5% per level of experience. The masonry skill adds a bonus of +5% to locate secret compartments when both skills are known.

Rope Works: This is a skill that takes into account the various needs and uses of rope. The character knows a variety of ways to tie knots, the advantages to various types of ropes and cords, their tensile strength and how to weave/make rope. A failed roll to tie a knot means that it is loose and sloppy and easy to untie, slip out of, or likely to unravel or snap when strained. **Base Skill:** 60% +3% per level of experience. Characters bound/tied by this character are -10% to escape/slip knots.

Sculpt, Carve & Whittle Wood: The art of cutting, carving and whittling staves, walking sticks, weapons (bows and arrows, wooden knives, stakes, clubs, etc.), jewelry and three dimensional figures and other objects out of wood. The percentile number indicates the quality of technique and appearance. All Old Believers are woodworkers of professional quality. **Base Skill:** 70% +3% per level of experience.

5. Initial Spell Knowledge: Starts with 1D6+6 Nature Magic spells of choice selected from any level, and the following common wizard spells found in the *Rifts® RPG*, Globe of Daylight, Sense Evil, Sense Magic, Climb, Turn Dead, Purification (food and water), plus the following spells found in *Federation of Magic*: Cleanse, Create Wood, Mystic Fulcrum and Life Blast.

6. Learning New Spells by Communing with Nature: Unlike the Ley Line Walker and most other practitioners of magic, the Old Believer learns new Nature Magic by communing with nature. Once, every time a new level of experience is acquired, the Old Believer can go to a ley line where he fasts and meditates for seven days. On the morning of the eighth day, he magically knows 1D4 new magic spells.

Spell selection is limited to either common Wizard spells (see *Rifts® RPG* and/or *Federation of Magic™*) or Nature Magic. Selections from Wizard Spells can range up to two levels higher than the Old Believer's current level of experience. Nature Magic can range up to three levels higher than the Old Believer's current level of experience. For example, a 2nd level Old Believer can select Nature Magic spells from levels 1-5, a 3rd level mage from levels 1-6, and so on.

7. P.P.E.: Like all practitioners of magic, the Old Believer is a living battery of mystic energy that he can draw upon at will. *Permanent Base P.P.E.:* 2D4x10 +P.E. attribute number. Add 2D6 P.P.E. per level of experience. Additional P.P.E. can be drawn from ley lines and blood sacrifices (see **Rifts® RPG**, page 162, *Taking P.P.E. from the living*). However, Old Believers avoid human and animal sacrifices and even the rare evil ones often avoid it.

8. Bonuses: +1D6 to M.A. attribute, +1D4 to P.E. attribute, resistant to normal cold (half damage, but suffers full damage from magical cold), +6 to save vs magical spoiling, sickness and curses, +3 to save vs poison, +7 to save vs disease, +9 to save vs possession, and +4 to save vs Horror Factor. All are in addition to possible attribute or other bonuses. +1 to spell strength at levels 2, 5, 8 and 11.

Old Believer O.C.C.

Also known as Monster Chasers or the Believers.

Alignment: Any, but most are of good alignments (55%).

Racial Restrictions: Since the secrets of the ancient magics known collectively as Nature Magic are closely guarded and passed on from generation to generation, the vast majority (97%) are human.

Roll The Eight Attributes as normal for that race.

Average Level of Experience (N.P.C.): 1D4+3 or as required by the Game Master.

Psionics: Psionic abilities are not a requirement, but approximately 18% possess minor or major psionics.

Attribute Requirements: I.Q. 10, M.E. 10, or higher.

O.C.C. Skills:

Basic Math (+20%)

Speaks Russian at 98%

Speaks Euro and one other language of choice (+20%)

Lore: Demons & Monsters (+30%)

Lore: Three of choice (+10%)

Holistic Medicine (+15%)

Animal Husbandry (+15%)

Brewing (+15%)

Botany (+15%)

Identify Plants & Fruits (+20%)

Carpentry (+10%)

Cook (+20%)

Preserve Foods (+20%)

Land Navigation (+10%)

Horsemanship: General & Exotic (+10%)

W.P. Ancient, one of choice (any).

W.P. Modern Weapon, one of choice (any).

Hand to Hand: Basic to start, but can be changed to Expert for the cost of two O.C.C. Related Skills or three skills for Martial Arts (or Assassin, if evil).

O.C.C. Related Skills: Select five other skills at level one and two additional at levels 3, 6, 9 and 12.

Communications: Radio Basic only.

Domestic: Any (+10%)

Electrical: None

Espionage: Intelligence only.

Mechanical: None

Medical: Any (+10%)

Military: Camouflage only (+10%)

Physical: Any, except Boxing and Acrobatics.

Pilot Skills: Any, except robots, power armor, military vehicles, ships and aircraft.

Pilot Related Skills: Any

Rogue Skills: None

Science: Any (+10%)

Technical: Any (+15%)

W.P.: Any

Wilderness: Any (+10%)

Secondary Skills: The character also gets to select one Secondary Skill from the previous list at levels 1, 3, 5, 7, 9, 11 and 13. These are additional areas of knowledge that do not get the advantage of the bonus listed in parentheses. All Secondary Skills start at the base skill level. Also, skills are limited as previously indicated.

Standard Equipment to Start: In addition to the magical staff, the character will have a light suit of M.D.C. body armor, an S.D.C. dagger (1D6), a pair of silver knives (1D6 S.D.C.; often hidden in the boots), small whittling knife (1D4 S.D.C.), small hatchet (1D6 S.D.C.), woodworking tools, a trowel and putty knife for mason work, grinding bowl, 1D4+2 small jars or plastic containers (with lids), 1D4+1 eight ounce vials (with lids), a small pot, 2D4 food coloring dies, one M.D. weapon of choice, small silver cross worn around the neck, mallet and six wooden stakes, two medium sacks, four small sacks, saddlebags, large satchel, backpack, bedroll, 50 feet of rope, water skin, belt, boots, flashlight, note pad, 1D4 markers, 2D4 pencils, 1D4 pieces of chalk, 1D4 pounds (0.45 to 1.8 kg) of bee's wax, a cape or cloak, travelling clothes, and a handful of personal items. Additional weapons, special items and magic items may be acquired over time.

Vehicle: Starts with a horse of good quality.

Secret Resources: None to start, but makes many acquaintances and friends on his or her travels.

Money: Starts with 1D6x100 credits or Rubles, and 1D4x1000 in tradeable goods. However, the Old Believer's knowledge and magic is usually a tradeable commodity to get him food, a safe place to sleep, supplies and basic equipment.

Cybernetics: None, and avoids them like the plague because any cybernetics or other forms of physical augmentation interferes with magic. However, cybernetic prosthetics and bio-systems for medical reasons will be considered if necessary.

Spell Descriptions for Nature Magic

Level One

Crunching Egg Shell
Range: Can be heard up to 12 feet (3.6 m) away per level of the spell caster.
Duration: One hour per level of the spell caster.
Saving Throw: Not applicable.
P.P.E. Cost: 2

Note: Requires real egg shells.

The mage sprinkles crushed egg shells on the ground, usually in a circle around him, his bed, campsite, etc., or in front of an entrance way, on a window ledge, in front of a chest or cabinet, and so on. When anybody other than the spell caster steps on the shattered shells it makes an impossibly loud crunch as if magnified by a megaphone or loudspeaker, with every step. Everybody within earshot will hear the noise. A simple safeguard to alert the mage to the presence of intruders. Anybody attempting to prowl is -50%; roll for every two steps.

Melt Bee's Wax
Range: Touch
Duration: Results are immediate; melting ability lasts one melee round per level of experience.
Saving Throw: Not applicable.
P.P.E. Cost: 2

Note: Ancient and rare Beekeeper's Magic.

The mage can instantly melt hardened bee's wax held in his hand or bee's wax in a container that is held in his hand or touched. The melted wax is used as an important ingredient in numerous spells. This spell can also be used to warm honey.

Sacred Oath
Range: Self only.
Duration: Instant
Saving Throw: None
P.P.E. Cost: None

To swear an oath on the sanctity of "Damp (or Moist) Mother Earth" is a solemn vow made before the ancient goddess of the Earth. The Old Believer cannot lie or break his word when he swears on "Moist (or Damp) Mother Earth" or in the name of "Mokosh," another name for Moist Mother Earth. If he does, all his magic powers and spells are reduced by half (half range, half damage, half duration, etc.). Break his oath a second time, and he loses all magical abilities except for his staff and familiar! The halved or lost powers cannot be restored unless the Old Believer begs the goddess of the Earth for forgiveness and a second chance. This requires seven days of fasting from food, 10 hours or more a day of meditation and repentance and, on the morning of the eighth day, mentally transferring, by force of will, 2D6 Hit Points and 2D6 P.P.E. permanently into the Earth — H.P. and P.P.E. are lost forever! If a pine sapling suddenly appears where the mage has focused his energy, he knows he is forgiven and his powers are restored to full (minus those sacrificed to the Earth). If no sapling appears, he must spend the next six months helping others, protecting the Earth from supernatural evil and dark magic, and repeat the process. **Note:** Mokosh usually forgives. The G.M. can make a random roll if he or she desires; 01-97 means the mage is forgiven and his powers restored.

Level Two

Glue with Bee's Wax
Range: Touch
Duration: Results immediate.
Saving Throw: Not applicable.
P.P.E. Cost: 4

Note: Ancient and rare Beekeeper's Magic.

The spell caster can use hot, melted bee's wax like a powerful adhesive to glue and mend broken items. This "glue" will work on most types of material (paper, plastic, wood, stone, glass, metal, etc.). Equal to a strong, high quality adhesive.

The Bee's Friend
Range: Self only.
Duration: Five minutes per level of experience.
Saving Throw: Not applicable.
P.P.E. Cost: 4

Note: Ancient and rare Beekeeper's Magic.

This spell makes Honey Bees and all bees regard the mage as a friend so they won't sting him. It also allows him to crack open their hive without injury to the hive or bees, remove up to two pints of honey or one pound (0.45 kg) of wax, and magically reseal the hive without the bees attacking him.

Make Honey & Syrup Candy
Range: Touch or up to 10 feet (3 m) away; line of sight.
Duration: Results are immediate.
Saving Throw: Not applicable.
P.P.E. Cost: 6

Note: Ancient and rare Beekeeper's Magic.

The mage can pour honey or syrup into any basic shape or several small to medium droplets of circles and magically turn them into candy. Up to one pound (1.6 kg) of honey or syrup can be turned into candy per level of experience. The sweet candy is firm but chewable, melts in the mouth, soothes sore throats and tastes delicious.

Sustained by the Earth
Range: Self only.
Duration: Results immediate.
Saving Throw: Not applicable.
P.P.E. Cost: 5

The spell caster can eat a handful of dirt and gain the sustenance of a complete meal. Unfortunately, it still tastes like dirt.

Level Three

Bake Magic Kulich
Range: Touch
Duration: Immediate results upon eating.
Saving Throw: Not applicable.
P.P.E. Cost: 7

A ritual involving the making and baking of "kulich," a Russian sweet bread. Two slices of this bread provides the nourishment and feeling of having eaten an entire meal. One loaf can be made per level of the spell caster. Each loaf can be cut into 20 slices. **Note:** Requires the ingredients and facilities to make the bread.

Bless Food
Range: 12 feet (3.6 m)
Duration: Immediate results, that last until the food is eaten.
Saving Throw: Not applicable.
P.P.E. Cost: 8

A short prayer or mantra that protects prepared food and drink, or stored food from the "spoiling" magic of witches and the "decay" spell of the Necromancer. Seven pounds (3.2 kg) of food or one gallon of liquids (3.8 liters) can be "blessed" and made impervious to spoiling magic per level of the spell caster. **Note:** The food is still vulnerable to natural decay and spoiling.

Seal a Wound with Bee's Wax
Range: Touch
Duration: Results immediate.
Saving Throw: Not applicable.
P.P.E. Cost: 7

Note: Ancient and rare Beekeeper's Magic.

The Old Believer pours hot bee's wax over a cut, opened wound or ulcer. The wax does not burn and seals the wound as if it had been sutured closed. The bleeding and pain stop immediately and the injured character heals an extra one Hit Point per 24 hours. When the wound is completely healed (all H.P. restored) the wax falls off, revealing a barely noticeable scar.

Level Four

Bee's Wax Disguise
Range: Touch
Duration: Five minutes per level of experience.
Saving Throw: Not applicable.
P.P.E. Cost: 10

Note: Ancient and rare Beekeeper's Magic.

The spell caster can use hot wax on his own face or body, or on a willing participant, and mold it into a disguise. The hot wax does not burn as it is applied, in fact it feels soothing, and can be built up, sculpted and molded like makeup putty. Being hot wax, hair and even fur is easily applied to the skin, as are horns and other cosmetic features. After the desired features are is finished, the spell caster says one final phrase and the wax features transform to look like real, flexible flesh, bone and hair. The false face will remain in place as a real looking disguise until the spell elapses or the character is blasted by M.D. or magical heat. Magic fire will melt the disguise. The quality of the disguise is equal to the Disguise Skill at 62% +2% per level of the spell caster.

Colored Egg
Range: Touch
Duration: Immediate results upon eating.
Saving Throw: Not applicable.
P.P.E. Cost: 10

A ritual involving the making of a hard-boiled egg that is then dyed one or more different colors, like an Easter Egg. Eating the egg quells hunger for 24 hours and provides the nourishment and sustenance of three daily meals (breakfast, lunch and dinner). One colored egg can be made per level of the spell caster. The entire egg (minus the shell) must be eaten for the magic to work. **Note:** Requires the ingredients and facilities to make the egg; i.e. fresh chicken or duck eggs, boiling water and food dye. The egg will remain fresh and edible for one week per level of the spell caster and is impervious to Spoiling Magic.

Hold Tight with Bee's Wax
Range: Touch
Duration: Results are immediate, duration varies.
Saving Throw: Not applicable.
P.P.E. Cost: 5 for preserving purposes, 10 to seal a window, door or large container like a crate or trunk.

Note: Ancient and rare Beekeeper's Magic.

The Old Believer can pour hot bee's wax around the edges of the lid or cover to any container (jar, bottle, barrel, etc.) to seal it airtight. This magic is typically used to preserve canned and bottled food and drinks, increasing the life of the preserved food, drink or specimen 10 times longer than usual (years). 10 small containers (each holding no more than one gallon or 7 pounds/3.2 kg of material) can be sealed tight per level of the mage's experience. They can be opened by either warming the wax seal or with a P.S. of 15.

A magical bee's wax seal can also be applied to windows, doors, and large containers such as trunks and coffins to hold them tight. This magic is used to momentarily keep the lid shut, or window or door closed in an effort to keep people in or out. To break the bee's wax seal and open the item, a character needs a combined P.S. of 40 or supernatural P.S. of 20 or higher! The magic lasts for 20 minutes per level of the spell caster. Once the spell duration elapses, a P.S. of 12 can force it open. Note that the Old Believer who cast the spell can open the wax sealed door (or whatever) normally, as if the wax wasn't there. Other mages with the same power can open it with a P.S. of 15 or by melting the wax by running their finger over it and casting the Melt Wax spell (counts as four melee actions).

Make Honey Medicine
Range: Touch or can cast the magic on a piece of honey candy or spoonful of honey up to 20 feet (6 m) away; line of sight.
Duration: Results are immediate.
Saving Throw: Not applicable.
P.P.E. Cost: 8 or 12

Note: Ancient and rare Beekeeper's Magic.

The mage can turn a spoonful of honey into a magical elixir that, when taken orally, straight or poured into hot tea or other drink, will instantly soothe a sore throat and stop coughing for 2D4 hours. It can also Cure Minor Disorders as quickly as the common wizard spell of the same name (see *Rifts® RPG*, page 172) — basically cures non-magical hiccups, indigestion, gas, heartburn, minor nausea, motion sickness, slight headaches, minor muscle aches and low fever. P.P.E. cost is 8 points.

The Honey Medicine can also be poured and rubbed on the skin to stop the itch, irritation and pain of a rash or burn. P.P.E. cost is still 8 points.

To stop/negate poison, a somewhat more potent Honey Medicine must be enchanted, requiring 12 P.P.E. This medicine immediately stops the illness and penalties caused by poison and restores 1D6 Hit Points. **Note:** This magical "medicine" has no effect on magic illness, curses or potions.

Negate Spoiling Magic

Range: By touch or 10 feet (3 m) away; line of sight.
Duration: Immediate effect.
Saving Throw: Not applicable.
P.P.E. Cost: 10

The sorcerer can negate the damage and danger created by Spoiling Magic, restoring one pound (0.45 kg) of food or a pint of liquid per level of experience.

Level Five

Glimpse of the Future

A Wood & Water Divination

Range: On behalf of another person, family or a community.
Duration: Immediate results.
Saving Throw: Not applicable; unwilling recipients are immune.
P.P.E. Cost: 15

After participating in a cheerful, circle dance, throwing a garland made from a birch tree into a river imparts some tiny measure of divination. If thrown in by a girl/young woman and it floats, it means she will be wed within the next two years and that her prospective fiance can be found in the direction the garland floated away (the magic can defy the natural current of the water). If the garland sinks, the girl can expect tragedy to befall her or her family, perhaps even her own death.

When performed by the Old Believer on behalf of a community or family, floating with the current means prosperity in the coming year. Floating in a spinning motion means things are good and safe now, but there are forces afoot that may change this. Sinking means tragedy (disease, crop failure, fire, a grievous loss, etc.) or that dark forces lurk in its future. Unfortunately, exactly what this tragedy might be is not indicated. If the garland bursts into flame the moment it hits the water, it indicates the presence of great supernatural or magical evil (typically a high-powered practitioner of magic, terrible monster, greater demon or demon horde). For a few minutes the flaming garland will bob and move in the general direction where the evil lives or will come from, then sinks, indicating danger and possible tragedy.

Rope of Steel

Range: Touch or from 10 feet (3 m) away per level of the spell caster.
Duration: 15 minutes per level of the spell caster.
Saving Throw: Not applicable
P.P.E. Cost: 12

This spell turns ordinary S.D.C. hemp cord, horse hair rope, or any rope made of natural fibers into a Mega-Damage steel. It retains the feel, weight and flexibility of ordinary rope, but has a tensile strength of two tons and it takes 12 M.D. to cut it! Prisoners bound with the enchanted rope require a combined *supernatural P.S.* of 50 of higher to break it or pull free (-30% penalty to Escape Artist skill). **Note:** This spell does not work on string, yarn, thread, rags, wire, chain, metal or plastic. Also see Magic Knots. Affects up to 50 feet (15.2m) of rope per level of the caster.

Level Six

Magic Knots

Range: Touch. The mage must make the knot(s) while casting the spell.
Duration: Results are immediate. Duration of the knot varies.
Saving Throw: -2
P.P.E. Cost: Varies

The spell caster can make one or more magic knots. Each type of knot has a special meaning and magic.

Fake Knot: A knot that looks tight and strong, but which is easily worked loose in one melee round (15 seconds). P.P.E.: 4

Four Winds Knot: When combined with this magic, ordinary rope, leather strips, wire or chains will hold ethereal spirits, including the Midnight demon, entities, ghosts and vampires (they can not turn into mist when bound by this magic knot). P.P.E.: 20.
Duration: Five minutes per level of the spell caster.

Hangman's Knot/Noose/Choker: A sliding knot that tightens from being pulled, weight and tension. A simple nonmagical use is hanging criminals or restraining animals or prisoners (tightens and chokes the person or animal that pulls on the rope).

When enchanted, the Hangman's Noose can be used to hang Mega-Damage Creatures! P.P.E.: 50; Duration: Three minutes per level of the spell caster.

When worn around the neck as a cord or necklace that ends in a small, symbolic hangman's noose, the character is +2 to save vs disease and the effects of Spoiling Magic and spoiled foods. P.P.E.: 60; Duration: 24 hours per level of the spell caster (can be made a permanent protective charm with the expenditure of 230 P.P.E.).

It can also be used to tie charms and jewelry. When used to tie a cluster of 1D4+1 tiny bones, or a little pouch of bones to a cord or chain worn around the neck, it protects the wearer from all Death Curses and magic that does damage direct to Hit Points; +6 to save. Even if the save fails, damage and penalties are half. P.P.E.: 75; Duration: 12 hours per level of the spell caster, but can be made a permanent protective charm with the expenditure of 330 P.P.E.

Knotted Skull: If worn, the skull is likely to be that of a small animal tied to string and held by 2-3 knots. This serves as a charm that protects any food carried by the character from Necromantic Decay or Maggots spells, and is +2 to save vs Magic Spoiling. P.P.E.: 45; Duration: 12 hours per level of the spell caster, but can be made a permanent protective charm with the expenditure of 300 P.P.E.

If a skull is hung from a tree, post or pole in the four corners of the wind (north, south, east, west) in a crop field, it brings good fortune and reduces damage from disease, frost and vermin by 15%. Moreover, the area is impervious to spoiling unless two of the skulls are cut down and smashed. An easy thing to accomplish, but a clear indication of foul intent and the possible presence of black magic and probably a witch or demon. P.P.E.: 80; Duration: 24 hours per level of the spell caster, but can be made a permanent protective charm with the expenditure of 290 P.P.E.

Sheepshank Knot: When combined with this enchantment the knot can strengthen rope and hold or pull two times the weight the rope can normally accommodate. P.P.E.: 6; Duration: One hour per level of the spell caster.

Simple Knot: When enchanted, the knot is strong, reliable and will not come undone unless untied or cut. P.P.E.: 3; Duration: Until untied.

Slip Knot: This enchantment is used to bind two pieces of rope together. Once the knot is finished, it can be slipped or pulled to the end of the rope and right off, making the two pieces one strong, single, unknotted piece of rope! P.P.E.: 7; Duration: Permanent results.

Half Hitch Knot: When combined with this enchantment, any boat tied to a dock will not slip loose unless somebody undoes the knot. P.P.E.: 6; Duration: Until untied.

Strength of the Earth
Range: Self only.
Duration: Two minutes per level of the spell caster.
Saving Throw: Not applicable.
P.P.E. Cost: 12

The expenditure of P.P.E. and eating a pinch of earth temporarily turns the character's P.S. into supernatural strength and his natural S.D.C. (not H.P.) into M.D.C. In addition, fire and cold based magic inflicts half damage. **Note:** The punches and kicks from supernatural P.S. inflict M.D. and the character can lift and carry weight 100x his P.S.

Level Seven

Living Bones of Stone
Range: Self or another character by touch.
Duration: Five minutes per level of the spell caster.
Saving Throw: Not applicable; unwilling recipients are immune.
P.P.E. Cost: Self 24; transforming another costs 50.

This is not a literal transformation, but a magical enchantment that makes the bones roughly as strong as stone and the body a Mega-Damage Structure with 6D6x2 M.D.C. +3 points per level of experience. Also double the character's weight. Bones are virtually impossible to break (requires a supernatural P.S. of 55 or greater or a fall from more than 500 feet/153 m).Falls under 500 feet (152 m) do no damage, those from higher up only inflict 1D6 M.D. per every 1000 feet (305 m), and the enchanted character's punches and kicks inflict 1D6 M.D. Explosions, and cold and fire based magic do only half damage, but energy blasts and magic weapons do full damage.

If M.D.C. is reduced to three points or less, the spell is broken and the character is exhausted, weak and injured, his S.D.C. reduced to zero and Hit Points down to 3D4. The spell cannot be repeated for at least one hour and until at least 75% of the character's Hit Points are restored. **Note:** This magic only affects the body of the character, and not anything he may be wearing. The transformed character can will himself back to normal at any time; counts as one melee action.

Level Eight

Living Bones of Air
Range: Self or another character by touch.
Duration: Five minutes per level of the spell caster.
Saving Throw: Not applicable; unwilling recipients are immune.
P.P.E. Cost: Self 28; transforming another costs 60.

This is not a literal transformation, but a magical enchantment that makes the body, and any clothes or possessions on it at the time of the invocation, as light as a feather and temporarily insubstantial, becoming semi-transparent like a ghost. In this form, the character can walk and run at three times his normal speed, walk or run across water, leap into the air and float 10 feet (3 m) high or across per level of the spell caster, and is impervious to heat, cold, and all physical attacks! Only psionic attacks and magic that affects the mind or emotions (including illusions) can hurt the transformed character.

Unfortunately, spell casting is impossible in this form because speaking or making any sound is impossible. Moreover, the intangible character can not touch, carry, operate or strike anything in the physical world except via psionic powers (if any). Despite being intangible, the ghostly figure cannot walk through solid walls and objects. However, he can squeeze through narrow openings like a partially open window and bars that are at least two inches apart. **Note:** The transformed character can will himself back to normal at any time; counts as one melee action.

Demon's Mock Funeral
Range: Self or other.
Duration: Immediate Results; 24 hours +12 per level of the spell caster.
Saving Throw: Standard save vs illusion with a penalty of -8; any bonuses to save vs illusion do not apply to this ritual.
Note: Only effective against the select supernatural beings.
P.P.E. Cost: 40 for one individual, +20 for each additional member of a group or family included in the funeral as dead.

An unusual and strange magical ritual that creates a convincing illusion designed to trick supernatural beings (good and evil), Russian Woodland Spirits, Faerie Folk, Witches (all types) and their *willing* minions into believing a particular person is dead. This is usually done to stop the creature from following, troubling or seeking revenge upon the individual portrayed as dead. It can also be used to lower the creature's guard concerning old enemies or famed heroes (i.e. thinking his enemy or opponent is dead, the creature comes out in the open and reestablishes its operations/activity without worrying about interference or attack from the deceased).

Interestingly, this illusion only affects those beings noted previously, anybody else looking into the coffin sees the obviously artificial effigy. Consequently, any (fake) mourners and visitors paying their respects should wail and mourn to keep the illusion convincing. However, all Russian peasants (including children), Reavers, Gypsies and Russian people in general, recognize and understand exactly what this mock funeral is all about and act accordingly — kneeling or bowing, and crossing themselves as they pass the coffin, placing a flower on the coffin, weeping, etc.

Note: Any mortal removing the effigy from the coffin breaks the spell; supernatural beings and all those listed earlier won't touch the body.

Swords to Snakes

Range: 60 feet (18.3 m)
Duration: One melee round (15 seconds) per level of the spell caster.
Damage: None, other than temporarily disarming one's foe.
Saving Throw: None, however, magic weapons are immune to this magic.
P.P.E. Cost: 25

This powerful magic spell temporarily turns knives and swords (including Vibro-knives and swords, but not other types of weapons) into seemingly ordinary, nonpoisonous snakes! They don't do anything but squirm and deprive a warrior of his weapon.

One sword/dagger can be transformed per level of the spell caster.

Level Nine

Enchant The Mighty Rooster

Range: Touch or 10 feet (18.3 m); line of sight.
Duration: One melee round (15 seconds) per level of the spell caster.
Damage: None
Saving Throw: Not applicable. Undead must save vs H.F.
P.P.E. Cost: 45

The Rooster is a traditional *Harbinger of the New Day* and announces the dawn and rising of the morning sun, thus it is an enemy of creatures of darkness. When in the hand of the Old Believer and enchanted by his magic, the Rooster becomes a weapon against vampires and the Unclean.

While enchanted, the bird can be used to identify *vampires, Dybbuk,* or any undead, as well as metamorphed *Unclean,* by crowing, clawing and pecking at the hell-spawned creatures whenever within 20 feet (4.6 m) of one. Furthermore, the crow of the rooster hurts the ears of the undead and Unclean and strikes fear into the black hearts of these fiends equal to a Horror Factor of 16. A failed roll means the creature loses one melee action for that round and is -1 on initiative and -1 to parry and dodge, namely because the demons are so frightened and unnerved by its crowing. The penalties last for one minute, but if the rooster continues crowing every 30-60 seconds (and the animal will as long as these creatures are nearby) the penalties remain in place until the bird stops making noise. **Note:** If the vampires or Unclean know that dawn will be approaching soon (within the next 1-30 minutes) the penalty is doubled and a failed H.F. roll means the demon flees from the approaching light of day, even though it may be 30 minutes away.

The enchanted rooster can also track such creatures like a bloodhound to their current location, lair, or hiding place. Tracking skill is 79% +1% per level of the spell caster.

Magic Egg

Range: By touch.
Duration: The duration of the magic released varies.
Saving Throw: Varies, if it applies at all.
P.P.E. Cost: 70

A large egg that has had its yolk removed through a tiny hole and the shell colorfully decorated with paint and bits of glued sparkles or seashells, bone and tiny gems and/or feathers. This enchantment turns the egg shell into a magic container with one M.D.C. To release the magic inside, one simply cracks the egg open.

The magic inside the egg always affects the person who opens it, and may contain any of the following:

- 1D4+1 Honey Bees per level of the spell caster are released. If the opener is of a good alignment (including unprincipled), they will circle the character's head for a moment. If he is injured, each bee will land on him and sting (a symbolic gesture so the magic will work through body armor). Each sting restores one Hit Point (or M.D.C. if a Mega-Damage creature). If healthy, the bees vanish, but in so doing, leave the character with a psychic premonition about some event in the immediate future, or about a friend or loved one in danger (i.e. that the person is in danger, the desperateness of the situation, and his general whereabouts). Duration: Approx. 1D4 melee rounds.

The bees attack any evil creature and, at least momentarily frighten and obscure vision until they can be killed. The individual plagued by the bees is -2 on initiative, -1 on all combat maneuvers and -15% to perform any skill. Furthermore, he is very conspicuous because of the swarm of buzzing bees around his head, making prowl and any stealthy action (pick pocket, seduction, etc.) impossible. Those seeing the strange occurrence are frightened or startled (H.F. 12) and likely to move out of his way. The bees are ordinary and can be killed from 1D4 S.D.C. points of damage, however, they are small and fast so attacks (other than fumigation) are -5 to strike per each bee. Duration: The bees swarm around the head of the evil individual for five minutes per level of the spell caster.

- An egg-shaped sphere of mystic energy; 10 P.P.E. points per level of the spell caster. This energy can be used within the next minute (four melee rounds) in the performance of magic, but only by the character who cracked open the egg.
- Armor of Ithan or Living Bones of Stone is cast upon the opener of the egg. Equal to the level of the spell caster.
- Calm Storm is cast equal to the level of the spell caster.

Speed of the Snail (50 P.P.E.)

Identical to the spell found on page 183 of **Rifts®**.

Level Ten

Healing Water

Range: 10 feet or by touch.
Duration: One minute per level of the spell caster.
Saving Throw: Not applicable.
P.P.E. Cost: 50 for healing pool, 200 to restore life.

The mage can temporarily transform a tub, barrel of water or pond into "healing waters." Anybody placed in the water while it is enchanted will be physically restored. This means broken bones are magically knitted back together, cuts and bruises healed, and internal bleeding stopped and repaired; 4D6 Hit Points (no S.D.C.) are restored. As many as five people per minute can be healed; must immerse themselves completely for 6-10 seconds each.

If 200 P.P.E. is spent, and one pint of the spell caster's own blood added to the water, it can restore the life of the dead, provided that the body of the deceased is whole and has not been dead for more than three hours. As many as one character can be brought back to life (2D6 H.P. above zero) per minute. **Note:** The mage is temporarily drained as part of his life force is used to supplement and revive the deceased; reduce the spell caster's Hit Points, S.D.C., speed, all bonuses, and the number of attacks per melee round by half for 24 hours.

Snakes to Swords
Range: Touch and hand to hand combat range.
Duration: One minute per level of experience.
Damage: Varies with snake type.
Saving Throw: 18 or higher for normal snakes and 14 or higher for Worms of Taut. Victims of magic venom need to roll a 14 or higher to save vs magical poison.
P.P.E. Cost: 25 for small nonpoisonous snakes, 50 for non-lethal venomous snakes, 100 for lethal snakes and constrictors, and 140 for select Worms of Taut.
Note: By Mark Sumimoto with Kevin Siembieda.

This magic amplifies and combines with the snake's essence to reshape the serpent into a magic blade. The design of the weapon varies with the serpent being used. The handle or hilt retains the same color or color pattern as the snake and has the feel of snake skin (or worm skin as the case may be). The blade is silver and engraved with a design that looks like the serpent it was created from.

The damage and size of the blade also varies with the type of snake being used.

- Nonpoisonous snakes become daggers or short swords that inflict 3D6 H.P./S.D.C. or one M.D., depending on the nature of the target (meaning H.P./S.D.C. creatures take S.D.C. damage, while Mega-Damage creatures suffer M.D.).

- Constrictors (nonpoisonous), like pythons or boas, become large swords, that inflict 5D6 S.D.C. or 1D6 M.D.

- Snakes with nonlethal venom become broad swords or other large swords that inflict 6D6 H.P./S.D.C. or 2D6 M.D. depending on the nature of their opponent.

- Lethal venomous snakes (i.e snakes who often kill with a single bite, including most vipers) become large swords that inflict 1D4×10 S.D.C. or 3D6 M.D., plus the victim struck by the weapon must roll to save vs poison (14 or higher). A failed roll means an additional 2D6 damage (S.D.C. or M.D.) plus the victim suffers from a burning sensation and light-headedness (-10% on all skills for 24 hours).

- Small Worms of Taut can also be transformed by this magic. *Fire Worms* are turned into flaming swords that inflict 1D4×10+8 M.D. (sorry, M.D. only). *Nippers* become large swords that inflict 3D6 M.D. (sorry, M.D. only), plus the victim struck by the weapon must roll to save vs poison (14 or higher). A failed roll means double damage (and -10% on all skills for 24 hours)! *Tomb Worms* become daggers or short swords that inflict 2D6 M.D. (sorry, M.D. only).

Note: Shifters or other mages who have snakes or Worms of Taut as their familiars will find this spell to be particularly useful. They will also be able to cast this spell at the standard P.P.E. cost, instead of the doubled cost required for those who do not practice necromancy.

Level Eleven
Circle Dance
Range: Varies, but no more than a five mile (8 km) diameter.
Duration: Results are immediate and last for 12 hours per level of the spell caster.
Saving Throw: Not applicable.
P.P.E. Cost: 200, but note that 10 P.P.E. can be drawn from each participant without their noticing or caring because they are all willing participants in the ritual.

The "khorovody," or circle dance, is a ritual magic disguised as a cheerful and festive event that involves singing and nurtures laughter, fun and good feelings in the participants (a few to over a hundred) and all observers, which can number over a thousand. This happy and positive feeling combined with the magic makes everybody who participates, watches or listens confident, positive and cheerful. It also makes them all +2 to save vs all magic with evil intent for the next 24 hours +4 hours per level of the spell caster. Furthermore, the detestable merriment sends lesser demons, evil Woodland Spirits, Faerie Folk, witches and evil beings retreating to sulk and grumble in their dark and dingy lairs for the next 48 hours (coming out only if drawn out).

Protective Magic Ring
Range: Varies with the current need, maximum of one mile (1.6 km) diameter per level of experience.
Duration: Results are immediate and last for 12 hours per level of the spell caster.
Saving Throw: Not applicable.
P.P.E. Cost: 140

This ritual magic can be used in one of two ways:

Circling a farm or homestead before sunrise and either sweeping around the area three times in a circle with a newly made (not yet used) broom, or by encircling the place and laying small charms and icons along the path of the circle to: 1) prevent illness, lesser demons, and evil Woodland Spirits from penetrating the protective magic circle for the next 24 hours +1 hour per level of the spell caster; or 2) to send lesser demons and evil Woodland Spirits and Faeire Folk running from inside the enchanted circle and stay gone for 8 hours per level of the spell caster.

Summon Fog (140 P.P.E.)
Identical to the spell found on page 186 of **Rifts®**.

Level Twelve
Bee's Wax Effigy
Range: Touch to make the effigy, but the effects of its magic are good up to five miles (8 km) away.
Duration: Results are immediate and last for 12 hours per level of the spell caster. Takes 20 minutes to make the figure and perform the magic.
Saving Throw: Not applicable.
P.P.E. Cost: 280
Note: Ancient and rare Beekeeper's Magic.

A ritual magic that involves the mage making a small wax figure out of bee's wax and applying to it a lock of hair or fingernails of the character to be protected. The wax figure is then put in a safe (often secret) place. Once the ritual is completed, the magic is in place.

The Bee's Wax Effigy is a form of protection magic that endows the person it represents with *one* of the following:

- Impervious to fire, including M.D. plasma and magic fire.
- Impervious to cold, including magic cold and ice shards (harmlessly bounce off the character although they sting a bit).
- Impervious to poison and disease, including magical illness, spoiling and toxins (like the poison pimples of the Kaluga Hag), but not curses.
- Impervious to mind control and possession.
- Resistant to Witches — +3 to save vs all spells, curses, spoiling and psionic attacks from any type of witch.
- The Blessing of the Good Earth — this protection comes in the way of increased strength and endurance making the recipient +6 to P.S., immune to fatigue, and +1 to save vs magic, poison, and disease.

Calm Storms (200 P.P.E.)

Identical to the spell found on page 186 of **Rifts®**.

Summon Rain (200 P.P.E.)

Identical to the spell found on page 187 of **Rifts®**.

The Slayer O.C.C.

The Demon and Serpent Slayer, more commonly known simply as The Slayer, is dedicated to exterminating evil supernatural beings, dragons, dangerous Woodland spirits, and "monsters" of all sorts, including witches, Necromancers and evil practitioners of magic. However, they specialize in exterminating demons and serpents.

The character can cast magic spells, yet he has little interest in the pursuits of magic, except as they might apply to ridding the world of demons and all manner of supernatural horrors. Each has his own reasons for hating the supernatural, but all are dedicated to ridding the Earth of such monsters. Most are hard-boiled investigators and ruthless fighters relentless in their battle against the supernatural. When it comes to fighting demons and monsters, the Slayer takes no chances and shows no mercy. They fight to kill and don't rest until their quarry is dead at their feet. There is no compromise unless it is to let an enemy go in order to protect or save the lives of innocent humans or D-Bees. The warrior's first goal may be freeing the world of demons, but his next is protecting and preserving human life and Mother Russia from the monsters, thus even the most bloodthirsty of The Slayers will not jeopardize a single human life in their pursuit to destroy evil. Demons often view this as a weakness and use it against the mighty warriors by holding innocent mortals, particularly women and children, hostage, or as bait in a trap. Like their Chinese cousin, the *Demon Queller*, most Slayers have a weakness for beautiful members of the opposite sex. However, unlike the Quellers, these warriors seldom "party" and their demeanor is almost always tight-lipped, grim and serious. Even when with a woman or part of a celebration, they are wary and ill at ease, fully aware of the treachery and shapechanging abilities possessed by so many supernatural be-

ings and witches. Some go so far as to swear off sex for fear that it might lead them astray, into danger, or distract him from other matters.

The Demon and Serpent Slayer may travel alone or ride with other heroes, demon slayers, and adventurers, but rarely are more than two or three Slayers seen travelling together. How many of these fierce, determined warriors exist in the world is completely unknown. The Slayers call no man master, and owe no allegiance to any one nation. This makes the Warlords uneasy. Most members of the War Camps see the Slayers as arrogant hotshots and loose cannons who see themselves as too good for them. They are not alone, the Slayers' business-like attitude puts off most people who either find these warriors to be cold and condescending or frightening and brooding killing machines.

Demon and Serpent Slayers are usually large, muscular men of Russian, Mongolian, Chinese or mixed heritage (Russian and some other). Most are clean shaven, wear light to heavy armor and use both magic, magic weapons and modern weapons. Among their favorites are pump guns and shotguns with silver ammunition. Many also use the bow and arrow or a cross bow, and are well versed in the methods of slaying vampires, Russian Demons, Woodland Spirits, and dragons. Most Slayers are quiet and soft-spoken, quite a contrast to the bombastic Demon Queller, Russian Hunter-Trapper and bragging Exo-Hunter. Slayers tend to be men of few words and strong action. However, when they speak, they are confident and direct, and never timid. Yet despite their reputation, most can be surprisingly compassionate, gentle and warm, especially toward women and children.

When resting between hunting and slaying evil, they enjoy peace and quiet, and beautiful things (be it a woman or an inspiring view), drink vodka, indulge in eating treats, and may even dance or play a musical instrument and enjoy friends and people around them. However, such quiet times are short and few between, because the Russian Demon and Serpent Slayer is constantly on the prowl looking for supernatural evil that needs destroying.

Special Slayer O.C.C. Abilities and Bonuses

The first four "abilities" are the result of part training and part magic — the warrior's desire to destroy supernatural evil is so strong and focused that it has magically transformed him to some degree, making him more than human.

1. Recognize Supernatural Shapechangers, particularly Russian Demons, Woodland Spirits, Demon Familiars, werebeasts, vampires, and witches. Part of this ability draws on the character's expansive knowledge and understanding of demons and magic, which enables him to recognize common forms taken on by various demons. However, this ability goes beyond this and into the realm of some sort of sixth sense.

Whenever the Slayer is touched, even brushed, by a demon or spirit in a different form, the character instantly feels its demonic essence, although the exact nature of the beast will remain unknown until he can see the eyes. By looking an animal or person in the eye (10 feet/3 m maximum distance), the Slayer can tell exactly what type of supernatural creature it is, as well as its approximate level of power (within one level). **Base Skill:** 56%+3% per level of experience (-20% to recognize witches). A

failed roll means he knows the thing is more than human but can't tell exactly what it is.

2. Impervious to Vampires. The Slayer can not be turned into a vampire nor mind controlled by them in any way. Additionally, the character is +3 to save vs all types of mind control, hypnosis, and mind altering chemicals, and the act of seduction is -30% when used on the Slayer.

3. Nightvision & See the Invisible are a regular and constant part of the Slayer's sharp vision. Nightvision 500 feet (152 m).

4. Ley Line Healing/Rejuvenation: The Slayer can absorb or channel ley line energy to double the rate of natural healing. This is done by resting at a ley line for several days of recovery. Once every 48 hours, the character can also do an instant healing. This is accomplished by meditating while sitting on a ley line. After 15+1D6 minutes, 2D6 Hit Points and 2D6 S.D.C. are restored.

5. Initial Spell Knowledge (limited): The Slayer mostly (90%) knows combat and offensive spells useful in battling the supernatural and really isn't interested in learning more.

Initial spells include: Globe of Daylight, Turn Dead, Armor of Ithan, Fire Bolt, Fire Ball, Call Lightning, Magic Net, Magic Pigeon, and Tongues, plus the following described in *Federation of Magic:* Magic Shield, Fists of Fury, Deflect, Targeted Deflection, Ricochet Strike, Frostblade and Lightblade.

6. Learning New Spells. At best, every two levels of experience the character will learn one or two spells to add to his demon fighting repertoire. Additional spells from common Wizard spells of any level can be learned and/or purchased at any time regardless of the character's experience level. *See the Pursuit of Magic* in the **Rifts® RPG**.

7. P.P.E.: The Slayer has a strong understanding of magic and is a modest spell caster. As such, he is a living battery of mystic energy which he can draw upon at will. *Permanent Base P.P.E.:* 1D4x10+10 +P.E. attribute number. Add 2D4+1 P.P.E. per level of experience. Additional P.P.E. can be drawn from ley lines and blood sacrifices (see **Rifts® RPG**, page 162, *Taking P.P.E. from the living*). However, most avoid blood sacrifices unless their victim is an evil supernatural being.

8. O.C.C. Bonuses: +1 on initiative at levels 2, 4, 8 and 12, +4 to pull punch, +3 to save vs possession, +1 to save vs magic, +4 to save vs disease, +1 to spell strength at levels 3, 7, 11 and 15. +1 to save vs Horror Factor at levels 1, 3, 4, 5 7, 8, 10, 12 and 14. All bonuses are in addition to any possible attribute and skill bonuses. The warrior has a Horror Factor of 13 to lesser demons and 9 to greater demons.

9. The Slayer's Code is simple: Destroy supernatural evil before it can kill you or hurt an innocent. The only good demon is a dead one. They are *never* to be trusted, and any apparent good they offer is either tainted or part of a trick or trap. Beware of them in all their guises, for the visage of evil has many faces.

As for "serpents" — the dragon's capacity for evil is equal to its capacity for knowledge and power. Beware the serpent for it is ancient, cunning and wise. Luckily for dragons, most (although not all) Slayers make the distinction between good and honorable "serpents" and wicked ones.

Slayer O.C.C.

Also known as the Demon and Serpent Slayer, Demon Hunter, and sometimes confused with the Demon Queller.

Note: Demon Quellers, described in **Rifts® Japan**, are also found in Russia, particularly the southern and eastern portions.

Alignments: Any, but typically scrupulous (33%), unprincipled (24%), anarchist (20%), aberrant (8%) and other (15%).

Attribute Minimum Requirements: M.E. 14 and P.S. 12 or higher. A high I.Q. and P.P. are also helpful but not a requirement.

Racial Requirements: None; although predominately human males.

O.C.C. Skills:
Basic Math (+10%)
Speaks Russian at 95%
Speaks Chinese and one other language of choice (+20%)
Lore: Demons & Monsters (+30%)
Lore: One of choice (+20%)
Intelligence (+10%)
Tracking (+15%; humans and demons)
Land Navigation (+10%)
Wilderness Survival (+10%)
Pilot Skill: One of choice (+10%)
Climbing (+5%)
Swimming
Boxing
W.P. Ancient, three of choice (any).
W.P. Automatic and Semi-Automatic Rifles (including shotguns)
W.P. Modern Weapons, two of choice (any).
Hand to Hand: Expert to start, but can be changed to Martial Arts or Assassin for the cost of one O.C.C. related skill.

O.C.C. Related Skills: Select five other skills at level one and two additional at levels 4, 8 and 12.
Communications: Any
Domestic: Any (+5%)
Electrical: None
Espionage: Any
Mechanical: None
Medical: First Aid only.
Military: None
Physical: Any, except Gymnastics.
Pilot Skills: Any, except robots, power armor, military vehicles, ships and aircraft.
Pilot Related Skills: Any
Rogue Skills: Any
Science: Any (+5%)
Technical: Any (+10%).
W.P.: Any
Wilderness: Any

Secondary Skills: The character also gets to select three Secondary Skills from the previous list at level one, and one additional skill at levels 3, 7, 9 and 13. These are additional areas of knowledge that do not get the advantage of the bonus listed in the parentheses. All Secondary Skills start at the base skill level. Also, skills are limited (any, only, none) as previously indicated in the list.

Standard Equipment: One suit of light M.D. armor, one suit of heavy M.D. armor, travelling clothing, silk robe, boots, gloves, 30 feet (9 m) of rope, 1D4 large sacks, 1D4 small sacks, backpack, bedroll, two canteens or a large water skin, and 4D4 days of rations.

Weapons include a large Vibro-Sword (or two), a survival knife, silver plated knife or sword, 10 shot riot control shotgun with an interchangeable 50 shot drum, 200 rounds of silver shot (does 4D6 S.D.C. to mortals, but 1D6x10 to vampires and were-creatures and 4D6 M.D. to demons vulnerable to silver), plus a Triax TX-5 Pump Pistol (4D6 M.D. rounds and silver rounds), 50 extra M.D. rounds, plus three weapons of choice (usually reflective of W.P. skills), six wooden stakes and a mallet, small silver cross and a medium wooden one. The Slayers absolutely love magic weapons, vibro-blades, rifles and heavy weapons. Magic items may be acquired over time and through role-playing.

Vehicle: Starts with a horse or rickety old hovercycle or similar vehicle with only half its M.D.C.

Secret Resources: None to start, but makes many acquaintances and friends (and enemies) on his or her travels.

Money: 2D4x1000 in credits or Rubles and 1D6x1000 in tradeable goods to start.

These characters can make large amounts of money, but most don't care about money (or fame) provided they have enough to keep hunting. This doesn't mean they'll work for a bowl of borscht and a soft bed, quite the contrary, demon hunting is exhausting and expensive. Consequently, if a village elder, local lord, wealthy individual or Warlord offers money, gold, silver (especially silver), vehicles, riding animals, armor, ammunition, etc., in trade or in appreciation, the Demon and Serpent Slayer will take it. Likewise, they aren't shy about demanding "fair pay" in the way of necessary supplies even from poor villages. Most will share the wealth with friends and the poor, plus most will have secret caches scattered across Russia, especially if the warrior travels a particular circuit.

Cybernetics: None, and avoids them like the plague, because any cybernetics or other forms of physical augmentation interferes with magic. However, cybernetic prosthetics and bio-systems for medical reasons will be considered if necessary.

Russian Gypsies

Note: All material presented on Gypsies is an entirely fictional and fanciful portrayal of these historically nomadic and enigmatic people. We make no attempt to portray the Gypsy in any "real" or "historical" way. These portrayals are *not* meant to present any real-life race, people, society, organization, or culture. Nor does anybody at Palladium Books encourage the exploration of the occult or use of magic. All magic and powers are fictional. We hope we have not offended anybody.

Russian Gypsies

The Gypsies, as a people, are believed, by some ancient scholars, to have originated from northern India in ancient times long before the Great Cataclysm. They have always been a nomadic people and are said to see all of Earth as their birthright, but no one place their home. With the Coming of the Rifts, that "birthright" may have been expanded to include the Megaverse.

Gypsies have always embraced secrets, passion and magic. They have been willing to dare to glimpse the future, go where few others dare to tread, and make their own way in the world. They are cunning, resourceful, artful in language (i.e. fast-talkers and superb liars), but their real strength lies in their strong identity as a homeless, wandering, but cheerful people, and their connection to their family clan for unity and strength of numbers. Gypsies work magnificently as part of a team, and Gypsy bands work together in such subtle ways that one may not realize what they are up to until it is too late.

On Rifts Earth, they are universally considered scoundrels, thieves, confidence artists, dangerous sorcerers and troublemakers known to roam throughout the world. They are especially strong and numerous in Eastern Europe, Russia, Iran and India — largely because the collapse of civilization has demolished political and national barriers (giving them the freedom and simple nomadic lifestyle that they so cherish) and made the region (a traditional roaming territory) a land of opportunity for those bold enough to exploit it.

Without debate, there are Gypsy clans that are amoral, despicable and evil, with long traditions as criminals or association with witches and/or demonic forces. However, many Gypsies are not evil, or criminals, although most are regarded as outlaws.

The reason for their outlaw status in Rifts Russia (and most places) is because most Gypsy clans and enclaves (sub-groups or small bands) are a lively, free-wheeling people with minds open to adventure, exploration (of magic and other people and dimensions, as well as the world), and a broad tolerance for the inhuman and magical that many Rifts societies find frightening, dangerous, abhorrent or blasphemous. Gypsies tend to accept everybody from D-Bees to aliens, and more often than not, will even deal with supernatural beings and creatures of magic. Part of this comes from the Gypsies' own unique view of a world without boundaries and where great personal freedom is valued above most everything else. Another part comes from the necessity of being able to adapt, adjust and survive in any and every environment. Thus, centuries of accepting change and using cunning and guile has made the Gypsies incredibly adaptable.

Yet another part of this is their outward facade. Their ability to seem wiser and bolder than they may really be. The ability to *appear* nonchalant, unimpressed, savvy, wise and unfettered even in the face of the unexpected, bizarre or deadly — even when inwardly shocked, horrified or frightened. This bold, tough-guy image is carefully nurtured and expertly played. It is part of their coping and survival mechanism. On top of that, most deliberately create an air of mystery around themselves and their people. This too is a survival mechanism to keep their rivals and enemies guessing and off balance, and perhaps even a little frightened. This means a Gypsy won't balk when confronted by a Woodland Spirit or maniacal demon, and may exchange pleasantries, information and even goods and services with the monster, even though the man or woman may be as frightened or repulsed as anybody. Their open-mindedness and sense of freedom also makes them more accepting of D-Bees and alien beings from other worlds. Some Gypsies even study Temporal Magic and have traveled to other dimensions.

Unfortunately, all of this tends to work against them nearly as much as it does for them. Most ordinary folk, especially farmers and peasants, are more than a little bit afraid of Gypsies. At best, most regard them as amoral sorcerers, fortune-tellers, thieves, con artists and people of ill-repute. At worst, they are regarded as thieving brigands, kidnappers, murderers, witches, demon worshippers and evil sorcerers who consort with the demonic, willingly sell their souls, and wield dark magic for their own selfish and evil purposes.

The Warlords and their War Camps buy into the worst of this crap (hey, it's human nature to believe the worst and be tantalized by the mystical, mysterious and dangerous). Thus, Gypsies are regarded as a dangerous and corrupting force — nomadic bandits, villains, spies and agents of evil (from wicked humans and enemies of the Warlords to demons and hell-spawned monsters). Consequently, the Warlords' troops harass, threaten, search and steal from Gypsies constantly. If they suspect one or more to be responsible for raids against a War Camp, or in cahoots with demonic forces troubling the troops or villages in the region, the members of a gypsy band may be interrogated, tortured, the women raped, and some to all murdered without a formal trial or evidence of wrongdoing. Remember, the Warlords represent martial law, and Gypsies are fair game because they are lawbreakers (if for no other reason than they associate with nonhumans), practice forbidden magic (namely the craft of the Hidden Witch, but occasionally other types of witchery and ancient Russian magic), and are not even true Russians! After all, they are self-proclaimed "people of the world" ... Megaverse, even.

A lone Gypsies or small groups (2-4), will frequently go out in the world to find adventure away from the family clan. Some may even be outcasts, tossed from a clan or band because their views didn't conform, or they are seen as some sort of misfit. Actually, it is more likely that a Gypsy or Gypsy band comes to accept other player characters who are the real misfits. Gypsies tend to accept everybody and welcome fellow misfits, outcasts and outlaws. Thus, a Gypsy character can join a diverse group

of player characters, or the player characters can become part of a Gypsy band. Gypsies are especially fond of practitioners of magic, mystics and psychics, Old Believers, Huntsmen-Trappers, Slayers, Demon Quellers, Travelling Story Tellers, Cossacks, Simvan, dragons, mercenaries, thieves/raiders, spies, vagabonds, and free-spirited adventurers in general.

They hate the cocky Exohunter and most Warlord troops, especially bloodthirsty Reavers, War-Knights, Cyborg Shocktroopers and most demons. Most (not all) dislike demonworshipers, Pact Witches, Night Witches, Necromancer and other practitioners of evil. The Mystic Kuznya is viewed with mixed feelings and a certain amount of contempt. While a Gypsy will accept a gift from one, they *never* ask or beg a Mystic Kuznya for anything. In fact, few gypsies will "beg" anybody for anything, they'd rather win it or steal it first. Most other people and occupations are viewed with indifference.

Common O.C.C.s among Gypsies other than the specific Gypsy O.C.C.s include (in no particular order):

Bandit/Raider/Highwayman (*see Rifts® New West*)
Professional Thief (*see Rifts® Mercenaries*)
Professional Spy (*see Rifts® Mercenaries*)
Smuggler (*see Rifts® Mercenaries*)
Safe Cracker (*see Rifts® Mercenaries*)
Wilderness Scout (*see Rifts® RPG®*)
Vagabond (*see Rifts® RPG®*)
Ley Line Walker (*see Rifts® RPG®*)
Rogue Scholar (*see Rifts® RPG®*)
Healer/Body Fixer (*see Rifts® RPG*)
Traveling Story Teller (*see Warlords of Russia®*)
Born Mystic
Old Believer
Hidden Witch

Note: Most avoid artificial augmentation.

The Gypsy Code

Gypsies have no home or dream of a homeland ... all the world (Megaverse?) is theirs.
Utopia is no place.
The past is naught but a haunted memory. Live for the present and look to the future.
Celebrate life and yearning for it gives birth to passion and adventure.
Life is an adventure.
Change is good. Adapt and keep moving or lose sight of freedom.
Be loyal to true friends, never betray a friend, willingly die for a friend, for true friends are the greatest of life's gifts.
Do not lie, embellish. Make the world colorful, cheerful and full of wonder and surprises.

Note: Gypsies lie a great deal, and do so cheerfully, although not necessarily to cheat or deceive. They like to embellish upon real events. It's part of their storytelling legacy, in which a tale is spun not simply to relate the facts but to enthrall, impress and entertain. Of course, this penchant to enhance and playfully misguide makes them masters at the art of lies. Most can weave convincing tales, explanations, plausible excuses or reasons, pretend to be somebody else, and so on, at the drop of a hat. The more subtle and sincere sounding, cleverly mixing truth, (seemingly genuine) emotion and sharp observation with falsehood, the better. For many, telling lies and convincing (but untrue) stories really is an art to be proud of. **Player Note:** This should all be part and parcel of role-playing the character. If your Gypsy can spin wondrous tales and talk the tail off a monkey, do it — play it. Conversely, not all Gypsies are good at lies and deception. Unfortunately, since the reputation of Gypsies is otherwise, his teammates and associates are likely to "assume and expect" that he can. This can get the character into all kinds of interesting or tight situations where he is expected to talk or fake his way in or out of a situation, giving the player (or G.M. using an N.P.C.) the opportunity to bungle, stutter and perhaps get the group into trouble because he can't do it. Besides, it's always good to have fun with, play, tease and confound the "gadji" or "gadjikano" — non-Gypsy.

The Gypsy Language

The Gypsy Language (spoken and written) is a unique and separate *secret* language known only to Gypsies. It is never taught to outsiders and strangers, not even the best of friends and those they consider to be blood-brothers. Only those born Gypsy may know the secret language, a language that borrows words, parts of words and elements from a dozen different languages (Romanian, Polish, Russian, Indian, Chinese, etc.) and combines it with their own codes, different meanings, strange combinations and variations. Gypsies jokingly refer to those who don't comprehend their language as having a "wooden ear." **Base Skill (for Gypsies):** 60% +3% per level of experience; all outsiders are -60% to even have a vague understanding of the tongue and -90% to decode the written form.

The Gypsy's secret language is mainly a spoken one, but it does have a dozen simple symbols that mean one of following: Danger, hide, safe/good, moved/travelling, valuable, steal, magic, friend, enemy, monster, vampire and illusion or false/shapechanger. Only a Layer of the Law and other Elders can read and write in the complete secret language. Most other Gypsies can recognize the writing as being their secret tongue, but cannot read it except for a word here and there. However, they know to take it to an Elder to get such writing translated. Whether the Elder does so accurately is up to the character and the content of the message. Often, the contents of such writings are meant to be known only by the Layer of the Law and/or Elders. All Gypsies accept this. **Note:** Gypsies also speaks Euro and two or more others languages fluently, but only 20% are literate in any language.

The Gypsy Wagon

The Gypsy Wagon is much more than a traditional and colorful mode of transportation and might be considered a small mobile home or large camper. It is a Gypsy groups' home, meeting place, lair and sanctuary — a safe haven protected by magic.

The typical Gypsy Wagon is an ornate vehicle covered with elaborate carvings, inlay, and fancy frill and detailing. While most may appear to be made of wood and shingles, the majority are constructed of M.D.C. materials. Approximately 18%-25% are hitched and pulled by a modern, M.D.C. tractor, truck cab, land rover (hover or wheeled) or other strong, all-terrain vehicle, but most are drawn by horse or, more often, Mega-Steeds (the true Megahorse is the most coveted, but 99% use one of the other alien animals; 41% Horned Steeds, 22% Ursan Forest

Steeds, 12% Burkov Mastodon, 9% Bionic Horses, 4% Hell Horses, 1% Serpent Hounds, 1% Mega-Horse and 10% other creatures).

Inside, the wagon typically has 4-6 folding bunk-beds with space on the floor where 2-6 more people can pull up a pillow or bedroll to rest or sleep. If the Wagon has a hung ceiling and a classic concave roof, there is likely to be storage or sleeping space between the sturdy, interior ceiling and the actual outer roof. In one corner is a trunk (serves as a storage compartment and seat that can accommodate 2-3 people comfortably) and typically a wall cabinet with locking doors. Across from the trunk is a stove with a pipe leading up through the ceiling to release smoke. The stove can be of any variety from wood burning to a modern, high-tech one with its own generator and microwave. Near the stove will be hooks and pegs for hanging sacks of grain and supplies. A barrel bolted to the floor or an actual, modern sink and water dispenser is also in this area.

There is typically a door or hatch in the front where the driver sits (there is room for three if the wagon is drawn by animals), one in the back and sometimes, one in the side. Somewhere on the floor (or in the roof), will be one or two secret trap doors allowing Gypsies to sneak in or out. There will also be a handful of secret compartments built into the floor, wall and/or ceiling/roof. The rear quarter of the Gypsy Wagon is typically a separate small room with plush sofas on either side of the walls (covered in pillows), and a table in the middle. The chair at the head of the table is a tall backed one with a cushioned seat, the others are either bean bags, pillows or stools. The exterior door is solid M.D.C. material with strong locks and a sliding bolt. Outside, an awning, flags and/or sign may be raised to invite people to take notice. This back room is usually for meetings where fortunes are told, snake oil, love potions and herbs are sold, healing are performed and deals are made with *gadji*.

The outside of the wagon, high and low, is likely to have decorative railings, posts, charms, statuary, and other extending objects that are more than mere decoration. They also serve as strong hand-holds and posts from which extra horses and livestock can be tethered or pulled, additional carts or wagons can be towed (most wagons have a front and rear hitch; as many as four wagons can be hooked together and pulled), sacks of goods and loot can be hung or tied, and for comrades to grab hold of a moving wagon to make a quick getaway or to hang outside and battle pursuers.

M.D.C. by Location: The exact amount of M.D.C. will vary somewhat depending on the individual clan, sub-group, available resources, the amount of combat the group and vehicle has seen lately, etc.

Chimney/Smokestack (1; small, metal) — 10-20
Windows (2-6) — 10-30 each
Doors (2-3) — 50-120 each
Trap Door (1 or 2) — 35-50 each
Wheels (4-6) — 20-100 each
Hitch for Horses or Cab (1 set) — 90-150
Roof — 100-250
* Cab/Pulling Vehicle (when applicable) — 250+
Wagon (main body) — 225-450

* The exact amount will vary dramatically with the type of vehicle, from tractor or semi-truck style cabin to Land Rover, hover vehicle or even a tank. Note that the means of locomotion

is much more likely to be a team of 2-4 Mega-Steeds or even a cyborg or monster (the latter two being willing associates, indentured servants or slaves).

Magical Protection: The following are common means of magical protection incorporated inside or on the Wagon itself; this is in addition to any Gypsies or guard animals being present. **Note:** A Gypsy Wagon is rarely left unattended. There is usually at least one elder (typically a female) left behind, but more likely, the elder, 1-3 children, a male guardian and 1-2 others.

Permanent Sanctum spell
Circle of Protection: Lesser or Superior
Circle of Travel (*Federation of Magic*)
Watchguard (*Federation of Magic*)

Speed: Varies with the type of locomotion, from horse drawn to hover vehicle. Average speed of animal-drawn wagons is about 10-15 mph (16 to 24 km), with a maximum speed of around 30-40 mph (48 to 64 km), depending on the animals. Motorized conveyances can go as fast as 80 mph (128 km), but seldom faster for fear the wagon will tip and roll.

Size: Small: 12-15 feet (3.6 to 4.6 m) long. Medium: 20-25 feet (6 to 7.6 m) long. Large: 30-40 feet (9 to 12 m) long.

Width: Small: 8-10 feet (2.4 to 3 m). Medium: 12-15 feet (3.6 to 4.6 m). Large: 16-20 feet (4.9 to 6 m).

Height: Typically 8-14 feet (2.4 to 4.9 m) tall, regardless of size.

Cargo: The stout and sturdy wagons can typically carry 20-40 tons without fear of breaking a wheel or axle, and pull twice that weight.

Game Master Note: The rules for travelling shows and carnivals found in **Rifts® World Book One: Vampire Kingdoms**, can be a valuable and fun aid when incorporating gypsy troublemakers and villains. Also note that vampires plague parts of Europe (like Romania) and may work with unscrupulous Gypsies and prey upon more reputable clans.

Russia's Link to North America

Gypsies are the few people who know about the existence of dimensional gateways that link Russia to Africa, India, China and North America. The two most famous portals to North America are a constant dimensional rift located at the edge of the Moskva Crater, that is connected to the *Calgary Rift* (southwestern Canada), and a nexus junction located in the middle of the Ural Mountains that randomly opens to the Saint Louis Archway, better known as the *Devil's Gate*. The Coalition States have troops stationed at the Devil's Gate who constantly monitor this portal and capture or destroy any living thing that emerges from it.

A lesser known ley line nexus junction at the southeastern tip of the Altay Mountains opens randomly and connects to the haunted ruins of *Old Detroit* (Michigan, of course), as well as randomly to Atlantis (bad news) and the Ethiopia Rift in Africa. Gypsy sorcerers and elders know of these places.

Gypsy O.C.C.s

Russian Gypsies are a little different than their Gypsy kin in Germany and other parts of Europe and the Mediterranean. Russian Gypsies tend to be predominantly humans, with only 25% being D-Bees. They also tend to be more traditional and superstitious, with many following the Mystic Arts and thieving rather than men at arms; none will submit to Juicer, Crazy or Bionic conversions. This means there *may* be some differences between Russian Gypsies and the traditional Gypsy Occupational Characters Classes first described in **Rifts® Triax & The NGR**. Note that the German O.C.C.s, with slight modification, are presented here for the convenience of the gamer.

Gypsy O.C.C.s
Gypsy Thief
Gypsy Wizard-Thief
Gypsy Seer or Sorcerer
Gypsy Fortune Teller
Gypsy Witch
Gypsy Beguiler/Shapechanger
Gypsy Healer: The Gifted
Gypsy Elder: Layer of Laws
Gypsy Enforcer/Warrior

Traditional Gypsy Thief O.C.C.

The Gypsy thief is a cat-burglar, pick-pocket, con-man and thug, all rolled into one. Some are slimy little weasels or mean looking punks. Others are suave and debonair or seductive beauties. According to Gypsies, all men can be like God (good and kind) or like the devil (evil). It's a matter of "baxt," or luck. Regardless of how the thief may look or act, timid or bold, crude or sophisticated, cocky or seductive, male or female, all are masters of their craft.

Gypsy Thief

Alignment Limitations: Unprincipled, anarchist or any evil. A thief cannot be of a good alignment.

Racial Restrictions: None, although the vast majority (70%) are human.

Roll The Eight Attributes as normal for that race.

Average Level of Experience (N.P.C.): 1D4+4 or as required by the Game Master.

Psionics: Psionic abilities are not a requirement.

O.C.C. Bonuses: +1D4 to M.A., +1 to P.P., +1D6 to speed, +2 on initiative, +1 to dodge, +1 to roll with punch, fall or impact, +3 to pull punch, and +1 to save vs Horror Factor.

Attribute Requirements: P.P. 12 or higher. A high I.Q., M.A. and P.E. are helpful but not a requirement.

O.C.C. Skills:
Basic Math (+20%)
Speaks Gypsy (starts at 63%)
Speaks Euro and two of choice (+20%)
Streetwise (includes Streetwise: Drugs, both are +14%)
Horsemanship: General (+20%)
Horsemanship: Exotic
Play Musical Instrument: one of choice (+10%)
Dance (+15%)
Concealment (+10%)
Palming (+20%)
Pick Locks (+15%)
Pick Pockets (+15%)
Find Contraband (+14%)
Escape Artist (+20%)
Acrobatics
Climbing (+10%)
Prowl (+10%)
W.P.: Choice of two (any)
Hand to Hand: Basic to start, but can be changed to Expert for the cost of one O.C.C. Related skill or two skills to pick Martial Arts (or Assassin if evil).

O.C.C. Related Skills: Select five other skills from any of the available skill categories. Plus select one additional skill at levels 3, 6, 9 and 12. All new skills start at level one proficiency.
Communications: Radio: Basic, Scramblers & Optics and Surveillance only (+5%)
Domestic: Any (+10%)
Electrical: None
Espionage: Disguise, Forgery, Intelligence, and Wilderness Survival only (+10%)
Mechanical: None
Medical: First Aid only (+5%)
Military: None
Physical: Any, excluding Wrestling and Gymnastics.
Pilot: Any (+10%), except Robots, Power Armor, Military Vehicles, Ships and Aircraft.
Pilot Related: Any
Rogue: Any (+10%, particularly Card Sharp and Seduction)
Science: None
Technical: Any (+10%; languages +15%)

W.P.: Any

Wilderness: Any (+10%)

Secondary Skills: The character also gets to select three Secondary Skills from the list, excluding those marked "None," at level one and one additional skill at levels 4, 7, 10 and 13. These are additional areas of knowledge that do not get the advantage of the bonus listed in parentheses. All Secondary Skills start at the base skill level.

Standard Equipment: Flashy clothes, including leather jackets, boots and gloves, light mega-damage body armor or Triax T-40 "plainclothes" armor, bright colored bandanna, bright colored scarf, sunglasses or tinted goggles, energy rifle, energy pistol, pair of knives, lock picking tools, knapsack, backpack, 1D4 small pouches or sacks, canteen, binoculars, magnifying glass, pocket flashlight, large flashlight, 50 feet (15.2 m) of light cord and grappling hook, note pad or sketch book, 1D4 pens/markers or pencils. **Note:** All gypsies are snappy and stylish dressers. Thieves tend toward black and dark blue colors with splashes of golds and reds. They love leather.

Vehicle: A horse, robot horse, hovercycle or land buggy are the character's choices for a vehicle (pick one).

Secret Resources: Most Gypsies regard each other as members of one big family or elite brotherhood, so one Gypsy will usually help another unless there is some history of rivalry or enmity (feuds and trouble between clans do exist). Help can be giving a fellow Gypsy sanctuary, hiding or smuggling him away, sharing information, trading or fencing goods, to giving him a place to sleep and a hot bowl of food — 96% will help even a hated rival or enemy avoid the even more hated Warlords and their troops, but such help will be minimal and fleeting. With time and experience, most Gypsies develop underworld connections and "associates" (good guys and criminals) scattered everywhere.

Notable Additional Equipment that a thief may want to acquire includes special clothing with concealed pockets, weapons and items with false (hollow) handles and bottoms, disguises, a better or alternative vehicle, jet pack, magic items, additional weapons, Vibro-Blade, laser scalpel, signal flares, smoke grenades, tear gas grenades, mini-tool kit, multi-optic band, handcuffs, surveillance items, pocket mirror, pocket laser distancer, pocket digital disc recorder/player for recording his observations, and a hand-held computer.

Money: Starts with 1D4x1000 in credits or Rubles and 2D4x1000 in trade goods (most of it stolen). The Gypsy enjoys the good life and tends to spend money quickly and freely on life's many pleasures and extravagances.

Cybernetics: Starts with none. Most gypsies will avoid getting cybernetics except for medical reasons.

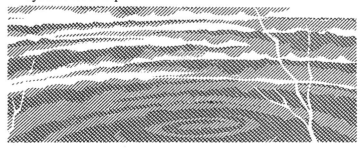

Traditional Gypsy Wizard-Thief O.C.C.

The Wizard-Thief is fundamentally a ley line walker with an emphasis on magic that is useful in thievery. Unlike the traditional line walker, the Wizard-Thief usually has much less understanding of magic and a narrower band of spell knowledge. This is because the character is a thief first and a wizard second. The art of mystic thievery is traditionally passed down from father to son (or daughter). Since the main interest is stealing, the focus of the magic is almost entirely aimed in that direction. The Wizard-Thief seldom even considers acquiring other areas of magic. Consequently, their spell knowledge will reflect their thief orientation and is limited to what poppa could teach. Typically, most of the character's spells will be of the type that cause illusion, deception, confusion and concealment. The Wizard-Thief progresses in experience at a slower pace because the character is fundamentally a split-class and focuses much of his training and attention on thievery and streetsmarts rather than magic.

Special Wizard-Thief O.C.C. Abilities

1. Sense ley lines and magic energy: The ability to sense whether a ley line or nexus is nearby. Identical to the line walker O.C.C.; see **Rifts® RPG,** page 83.

2. Read Ley Lines: The power to instantly know the direction, length, nexus locations, and similar things about the ley line. Identical to the line walker O.C.C.; see **Rifts® RPG**, page 83.

3. Ley Line Transmission: The ability to send a verbal and/or visual message along a ley line. Identical to the line walker O.C.C.; see **Rifts® RPG,** page 83.

4. Ley Line Phasing: The power to instantly teleport from one place to another on the same ley line. Identical to the line walker O.C.C.; see **Rifts® RPG,** page 83.

5. Initial Spell Knowledge: At level one experience, the character knows the following spells:

Blinding Flash
Globe of Daylight <u>or</u> Lantern Light (*Federation of Magic*)
Manipulate Objects (*Federation of Magic*)
See the Invisible
Chameleon
Concealment
Detect Concealment
Charismatic Aura <u>or</u> Chromatic Protection (*Fed. of Magic*)
Mask of Deceit
Fool's Gold
Escape
Energy Disruption
Levitation <u>or</u> Mystic Fulcrum (*Federation of Magic*)
Armor of Ithan <u>or</u> Armor Bizarre (*Federation of Magic*)
Repel Animals
Reduce Self
Teleport: Lesser

The character can also select a total of four additional spells. The spell selections can be made from levels 1-4 wizard spells

ramón pérez mcmxcviii

or Nature Magic. The character should be able to figure out/select one new spell equal to his own level of achievement with each new level of experience attained.

6. Learning New Spells: Additional spells and rituals of any magic level can be learned and/or purchased at any time regardless of the character's experience level, but are limited to the common wizard spells described in the **Rifts® RPG** and **Federation of Magic™** (*See the Pursuit of Magic in the Rifts® RPG, page 164*). Just remember that the Wizard-Thief specializes in robberies so spell selections are limited to those that help his carreer as a "Thief." That having been said, the Wizard-Thief is not likely to learn more than a handful (2-8) additional spells in his lifetime.

7. P.P.E.: Like all practitioners of magic, the Wizard-Thief is a living battery of mystic energy that he can draw upon to create magic. The character's permanent P.P.E. base is 2D4x10 plus the P.E. number. Add 2D6 P.P.E. per level of experience.

8. Bonuses: +2 to save vs Horror Factor, +2 to save vs possession, +1 to save vs magic, +1 spell strength at levels 3, 7, 10 and 13.

Note: The Gypsy Wizard-Thief does not have the Line Walker's powers of line drifting, ley line rejuvenation, or ley line observation ball.

Gypsy Wizard-Thief O.C.C.

Alignment Limitations: Unprincipled, anarchist or any evil. A thief cannot be of a good alignment.

Racial Restrictions: None, although the vast majority (80%) are human.

Roll The Eight Attributes as normal for that race.

Average Level of Experience (N.P.C.): 1D4+2 or as required by the Game Master.

Psionics: Psionic abilities are not a requirement.

Attribute Requirements: I.Q. 10, M.E. 12 or higher; a high P.P. (12 or better) is ideal but not mandatory. Only 50% of the wizard-thieves are literate in any language.

O.C.C. Skills:
Basic Math (+20%)
Speak Gypsy (+10%)
Speaks Euro, Russian and three languages of choice (+30%)
Lore: Demons & Monsters (+20%)
Lore: Faeries (+15%)
Dance (+15%)
Play Musical Instrument: one of choice (+5%)
Streetwise (+10%)
Palming (+10%)
Pick Pockets (+5%)
W.P. One of choice
Hand to Hand: Basic to start, but can be changed to Expert for the cost of one O.C.C. Related skill or two skills to pick Martial Arts (or Assassin if evil).

O.C.C. Related Skills: Select five other skills from any of the available skill categories. Plus select one additional skill at levels 3, 6, 9 and 12. All new skills start at level one proficiency.
Communications: Any (+5%)
Domestic: Any (+10%)
Electrical: None
Espionage: Disguise, forgery, intelligence, and wilderness survival only (+10%)
Mechanical: None
Medical: First aid only (+5%)
Military: None
Physical: Any, excluding boxing, wrestling and acrobatics.
Pilot: Any (+10%), except robot combat elite, tanks & APCs, jets, jet fighters, and ships.
Pilot Related: Any
Rogue: Any (+5%)
Science: Any (+10%)
Technical: Any (+10%; literacy and languages +15%)
W.P.: Any
Wilderness: Any (+5%)

Secondary Skills: The character also gets to select two secondary skills from the list, excluding those marked "None," at levels 2, 5, 8 and 12. These are additional areas of knowledge that do not get the advantage of the bonus listed in parentheses. All secondary skills start at the base skill level.

Standard Equipment: Cloak or cape (with or without a hood), a set of clothing, a set of traveling clothes, light mega-damage body armor or Triax T-40 "plain clothes" armor, bright colored bandanna, bright colored scarf, stylish gloves, sunglasses, energy rifle or pistol, pair of knives, knapsack, backpack, 1D4 small pouches or sacks, six wooden stakes and a mallet, wood or silver cross, canteen, binoculars, magnifying glass, pocket flashlight, large flashlight, 50 feet (15.2 m) of light cord note pad or sketch book, a dozen pens, markes or pencils. **Note:** All gypsies are colorful and stylish dressers.

Vehicle: A horse, or bionic or robot horse, or hovercycle or land buggy are the character's choices for a vehicle.

Notable Additional Equipment that a Wizard-Thief may want to acquire includes magic weapons, magic items, magic potions, magic equipment, scrolls, Vibro-Blade, laser scalpel, signal flares, smoke grenades, tear gas grenades, mini-tool kit, multi-optic band, handcuffs, surveillance items, pocket mirror, pocket laser distancer, pocket digital disc recorder/player for recording his observations, and a hand-held computer.

Special Resources: Same as the Gypsy Thief.

Money: Starts with 1D6x1000 in credits or Rubles and 3D4x1000 credits worth of tradeable goods (probably stolen). The Gypsy enjoys the good life and tends to spend his money quickly and freely on life's many pleasures and extravagances.

Cybernetics: Starts with none and will avoid getting cybernetics except for medical reasons. He may consider Bio-Wizard items.

Traditional Gypsy Seer O.C.C.

The Gypsy Seer is are a variation on the Mystic. Exactly why variant Mystics are so common among the Gypsies of Europe and the oracles of China remains a mystery (also see the *Gypsy Fortune Teller, Beguiler* and *Born Mystic*; the latter is not exclusive to Gypsies, but an O.C.C. common among them). Like the traditional Mystic, and Born Mystic, this character possesses both psionic and magic powers. The character is born with these powers so the Seer needs no formal education and does not study magic. Psychic powers may start to manifest themselves as young as age five. After puberty, around age 14, the Gypsy Seer will suddenly know some spell magic, including the Oracle spell.

The Seer just accepts his powers as a gift of nature. The intuitive nature of the character's powers tends to give him or her a spiritual or metaphysical perspective on life. They trust feelings and dreams, see signs of good luck or bad omens, read palms, see the future and sense danger.

The Psionic Powers of a Gypsy Seer

1. Sense Supernatural Evil: The Seer is keenly aware of the supernatural world around him/her. As a result, the character can sense the presence of supernatural evil forces. **Range:** 300 feet (91.5 m) plus 20 feet (6 m) per level of experience.

The Seer can also sense the approach of great evil, including a supernatural, alien intelligence, gods, demon lords, and an invading army of monsters or humans. The ability will come as a feeling of dread and a prophetic dream at least 72 hours in advance of the real danger. Frequently, the warnings and dreams come weeks in advance.

2. Read Palms: The Seer can tell a lot about a person by looking at the character's palms. In many respects, this power is a sort of acute clairvoyance and see aura rolled into one.

By looking at a person's palm, the seer can see the following:

- Estimate the person's alignment.
- Tell if the character is filled with hate or happiness.
- Tell whether he or she is troubled by something or afraid.
- Tell whether or not the character is sick or addicted.
- Tell whether or not the character is hunted.
- Tell whether or not the character is in love.
- Whether he or she is possessed.
- Recognize the sign of evil; i.e. recognize vampires, werebeasts, and demon shapechangers like the Succubus, Incubus, Dybuk, and other supernatural beings who can perform metamorphosis into human form. This ability does not include humans transformed by metamorphosis spell magic, Changelings or dragons.
- Estimate age within 2D4 years. This means the seer can recognize creatures who are hundreds or thousands of years old even though they may look completely human.
- Sense the presence of psionic powers.
- Sense high P.P.E. (20 or more points)
- Estimate the general level of experience. Low (1-3), medium (4-7) high (8 and up).
- Estimate the general alignment, i.e. good, selfish, or evil.

Note: By using his power of clairvoyance while holding the person's palm, the Seer may glimpse that person's possible future. The impression is usually vague, like, "I sense danger" or good fortune, or "you will find what you are looking for," or "you will be challenged," or "you will have to make an important decision." The Seer's insight is usually based on events already in motion and that are likely to transpire within the next eight weeks. Occasionally, the Seer will actually see an image of some future event involving the character (G.M.'s discretion).

3. Psionic powers of the Gypsy Seer: Clairvoyance, Object Read, Presence Sense, Sixth Sense, See Aura, Mind Block Auto-Defense and Hypnotic Suggestion.

At experience levels 2, 4, 7, 10 and 13 the character can select one additional psionic power from the categories of Sensitive or Healing.

4. I.S.P.: Roll 1D6x10 plus the character's M.E. number to determine the base Inner Strength Points (I.S.P.). The Seer gets an additional 10 I.S.P. per level of experience.

5. Saving throws versus psionic attack: The Gypsy Seer is considered to be a master psionic and saves on a roll of 10 or higher.

6. Other Bonuses: +4 to save vs Horror Factor, +2 to save vs magic, +5 to save vs possession and insanity, and +1 spell strength at levels 3, 7, 10 and 13.

Magic Powers

1. Initial Spell Knowledge: At level one experience, the character knows the spells Oracle, Exorcism, See the Invisible, and Death Trance.

2. Learning New Spells: The Seer intuitively knows a couple of new spells as he reaches each new level of experience.

At second level he learns Tongues and one common wizard spell of choice from levels one and two.

At third level he learns Eyes of Thoth and one spell of choice from levels one and two wizard spells.

At fourth level he learns Commune with Spirits and one wizard spell of choice selected from levels 1-3.

At fifth level he learns Calling and one wizard spell of choice selected from levels 1-4.

At sixth level he learns Protection Circle: Simple and Superior, plus one wizard spell of choice selected from levels 1-5.

At seventh level he learns Dispel Magic Barrier, Santum and one wizard spell of choice from levels 1-6.

At eighth level and each subsequent level of experience, the character can select two new wizard spells with selections made from levels 1-8.

3. P.P.E.: Like all practitioners of magic, the Seer is a living battery of mystic energy that he can draw upon to weave magic. The character's permanent P.P.E. base is 1D6x10 plus the Seer's P.E. attribute number. Add 1D6 P.P.E. per level of experience.

Gypsy Seer O.C.C.

Also known as the Gypsy Sorcerer.

Alignments: Any, although most are unprincipled, anarchist or any evil.

Racial Restrictions: None, although the vast majority (80%) are human males.

Roll The Eight Attributes as normal for that race.

Average Level of Experience (N.P.C.): 1D4+2 or as required by the Game Master.

Attribute Requirements: M.E. 14 or higher; a high I.Q. and M.A. are helpful but not mandatory. Only 10% of the gypsy seers are literate in any language.

O.C.C. Skills:

Basic Math (+20%)

Lore: Demons & Monsters (+20%)

Lore: Faeries (+15%)

Dance (+15%)

Sing (+10%)

Play Musical Instrument: Two of choice (+10%)

Speaks Gypsy (+6%)

Speaks Euro & Russian (+30%) and 2 languages of choice (+20%)

Wilderness Survival (+20%)

Streetwise (+16%)

Palming (+10%)

Concealment (+6%)

W.P. One of choice

Hand to Hand: Basic to start, but can be changed to Expert for the cost of two O.C.C. Related skills or three skills to pick Martial Arts (or Assassin if evil).

O.C.C. Related Skills: Select four other skills from any of the available skill categories. Plus select one additional skill at levels 3, 6, 9 and 12. All new skills start at level one proficiency.

Communications: Any (+5%)

Domestic: Any (+10%)

Electrical: None

Espionage: Any (+5%)

Mechanical: None

Medical: First aid or Holistic Medicine only (+5%)

Military: None

Physical: Any, excluding Boxing, Wrestling, Gymnastics & Acrobatics.

Pilot: Hover vehicles, automobiles, horsemanship, and boats (+10%)

Pilot Related: Any

Rogue: Any (+4%)

Science: Any (+10%)

Technical: Any (+10%)

W.P.: Any

Wilderness: Any (+5%)

Secondary Skills: The character also gets to select two Secondary Skills from the list, excluding those marked "None," at levels 2, 5, 8 and 12. These are additional areas of knowledge that do not get the advantage of the bonus listed in parentheses. All Secondary Skills start at the base skill level.

Standard Equipment: Hooded cloak or robe, a set of clothing, a set of traveling clothes, light mega-damage body armor, Millennium Tree leaf armor, or Triax T-40 "plainclothes" armor, bright colored bandanna, bright colored scarf, energy rifle or pistol, walking stick or staff, a knife or sling, knapsack, backpack, 1D4 small pouches or sacks, six wooden stakes and a mallet, a silver cross, squirt gun filled with water, a canteen filled with holy water, canteen for drinking water, pocket flashlight, note pad and sketch book, pocket digital disc recorder/player for recording his dreams and observations, 1D4 writing implements. **Note:** Of all the Gypsies, the Seer dresses the most demure. However, the character is likely to wear 2D4 rings, bracelets, necklaces, pins, earrings and other jewelry.

Vehicle: A horse, car or hover vehicle but only if the character has a driving or riding skill, otherwise none.

Notable additional Equipment that a Seer may want to acquire includes magic jewelry/crystals, staves and wands, magic potions, herbs, demon slaying weapons/magic, and other types of exotic jewelry, weapons and objects. Sensory equipment, hand-held computer, language translator, cameras and recording equipment may also be of interest.

Secret Resources: Standard fare, same as the Gypsy Thief.

Money: Starts with 2D6x1000 in credits or Rubles and 3D4x1000 credits worth of gold, jewelry and tradeable goods. The Gypsy enjoys the good life and tends to spend money quickly and freely on life's many pleasures and extravagances.

Cybernetics: Starts with none and will avoid getting cybernetics except for medical reasons. The character may consider bio-wizardry items.

Russian Gypsy Fortune Teller O.C.C.

Unlike the Traditional Seer, the "Fortune Teller" is more of a true "medium." Somebody through whom psychic and mystical energies flow, and with that individual having little true understanding of how or why things happen, but accepting them nonetheless. The Gypsy Fortune Teller or Medium is a bit less powerful and polished, but instinctive and intuitive on a more primal, gut level. Her psychic and magical powers focus on glimpses of the future and sensing the supernatural. Perhaps because women tend to be more intuitive and social by nature, 78% of all Gypsy Fortune Tellers are human females.

The *Russian Gypsy Fortune Teller* has all the basic abilities of her Western cousin (described previously), plus a few unique talents and leanings unique to the Russian Gypsy.

The Psionic Powers of the Fortune Teller

1. **Sense Supernatural Evil:** Same as the Gypsy Seer.

2. **Read Palms:** Same as the Gypsy Seer.

3. **See through metamorphosis/shapechangers.** The Gypsy Fortune Teller can detect and identify metamorphed Dragons, Woodland Spirits, Demons and other supernatural shapechangers. This clairvoyant power comes in the form of recognizing omens and strange shadows that identify the true nature of the metamorphed creature.

A Gypsy Fortune Teller who unwittingly sees a supernatural creature disguised in its human or animal form will suddenly, without trying or willing it to happen, catch a shadow out of the corner of her eye — a shadow that reflects the true, natural shape of the creature before her eyes. This can be startling as the shadow could come from anywhere: the shadow caused by the light of a passing vehicle or opened door, clouds passing over the moon, a moth or bird flying past a light, the movement of tree branches in the wind, or seemingly out of nowhere. In the alternative, an omen might appear. An omen can be a particular animal suddenly running by or making noise, or an incident such as a flower falling from the stem when gently brushed by a disguised demon of death, or a baby suddenly awaking, screaming and crying when the shadow of a disguised Kaluga Hag falls upon it, suddenly noticing a cracked or broken egg (indicating a Deathless One), and so on.

The Gypsy psychic is trained to notice and recognize such things, but if distracted, busy or consumed with other thoughts and pressing matters, she *may* miss the signs. The omen typi-

cally happens only once or twice. Once, the very first time the Gypsy Fortune Teller *sees* him/it — I use the word "see" because she doesn't need to be introduced to the shapechanger, but see him at a distance up to 200 feet (61 m) +50 feet (15 m) per level of experience. And a second time, if the shapechanger makes its first threatening approach to her directly. **Note:** In the light of the moon, the Gypsy Fortune Teller sees the personal shadows of The Unclean and Il'ya demons in the form of their true demonic selves (only the Fortune Teller sees this aberration).

4. **Sense the presence of a Witch's Spoiling Magic.** The Fortune Teller can sense whether or not sickness or spoiling is natural or caused by a witch. She can also sense if this was a malicious act of anger not likely to be pursued with more trouble, or whether it is the first of several vindictive acts in a campaign of retribution or vendetta that will continue into the days, weeks, or months ahead.

5. **Commune with Woodland Spirits.** The Gypsy Medium is somehow on the same wavelength as Russian Woodland Spirits. What this means is that these creatures of magic regard her as a kindred spirit and potential comrade. They may share information, news and food, lend a helping hand, and come to each other's defense — this must be a two-way relationship, with the Gypsy doing favors and acts of kindness for the spirit(s) as well. Even the more sinister and murderous Russian Spirits treat these women as equals and never attack them without good reason. Furthermore, when around these Woodland Spirits, the Fortune Teller can often (but not always) pick up random thoughts from them, like, "I hate him," "... attack at midnight," "... I know where ..." "this will be good,"'"... when the demons come ..." and so on. These are only random, often partial phrases, thoughts or, sometimes, just emotions and impressions.

6. **Psionic powers of the Gypsy Fortune Teller:** Clairvoyance, Dowsing, Object Read, Remote Viewing, See Aura, See the Invisible, Commune with Spirits, and Mind Block.

At experience levels 2, 4, 7, 10 and 13 the character can select one additional psionic power from the categories of Sensitive or Physical.

7. **I.S.P.:** Roll 2D4x10 plus the character's M.E. number to determine the base Inner Strength Points (I.S.P.). The Fortune Teller gets an additional 10 I.S.P. per level of experience.

8. **Saving throws versus psionic attack:** The Gypsy Medium is considered to be a master psionic and saves on a roll of 10 or higher.

9. **Other Bonuses:** +1D6 to M.A., +1D4 to P.B., +1 on initiative, +1 to save vs illusions, +3 to save vs possession and insanity, +2 to save vs Horror Factor, +1 to save vs magic, and +1 spell strength at levels 3, 8 and 12.

Magic Powers of the Fortune Teller

1. **Initial Spell Knowledge:** At level one experience, the character knows the spells: Second Sight, Glimpse of the Future (Nature Magic), See the Invisible, Object Read the Dead (Necro-Magic) and Turn Dead.

2. **Learning New Spells:** The Mystic Fortune Teller/Medium intuitively knows two new spells each new level of experience. Spell selections can be made from common wizard spells up to one level higher than her own current level of experience.

At second level she knows Divining Tombs & Graves (Necro-Magic) and one common wizard spell of choice.

At third level she learns Negate Spoiling Magic (Nature Magic) and one spell of choice.

At fourth level she learns Commune with Spirits and one wizard spell of choice selected from levels 1-3.

At fifth level she knows Watchguard (Federation of Magic) and one wizard spell of choice.

At sixth level she knows Bonfire of Purification (Fire Magic), plus one wizard spell of choice.

At seventh level she knows Oracle and one wizard spell of choice.

At eighth level she knows Negate Magic and one wizard spell of choice.

At ninth level she knows Locate & Identify Fire (Fire Magic) and one wizard spell of choice.

At tenth level and each subsequent level of experience the character knows one additional new wizard spell of choice.

3. P.P.E.: Like all practitioners of magic, the Fortune Teller is a living battery of mystic energy that she can draw upon to weave magic. The character's permanent P.P.E. base is 1D6x10 plus the Medium's P.E. attribute number. Add 1D6 P.P.E. per level of experience.

Gypsy Fortune Teller O.C.C.

Also Known as a Gypsy Medium.

Alignments: Any, although most are scrupulous, unprincipled, or anarchist.

Racial Restrictions: None, although the vast majority (78%) are human females.

Roll The Eight Attributes as normal for that race.

Average Level of Experience (N.P.C.): 1D4+3 or as required by the Game Master.

Attribute Requirements: M.A. 14, M.E. 14 or higher; a high I.Q. and P.B. are helpful but not mandatory. Only 6% of the Gypsy Mediums are literate in any language.

O.C.C. Skills:
Basic Math (+15%)
Lore: Demons & Monsters (+25%)
Lore: One of choice (+10%)
Dance (+20%)
Sing (+20%)
Play Musical Instrument: One of choice (+15%)
Speaks Gypsy (start at 63%)
Speaks Euro, Russian and two languages of choice (+20%)
Find Contraband (+6%)
Palming (+5%)
Card Sharp (+12%)
Streetwise (+10%)
Seduction (+20%)
Imitate Voices/Impersonation (+10%)
Ventriloquism (+10%)
W.P. One of choice
Hand to Hand: Basic to start, but can be changed to Expert for the cost of two O.C.C. Related skills or three skills to pick Martial Arts (or Assassin if evil).

O.C.C. Related Skills: Select four other skills from any of the available skill categories. Plus select one additional skill at levels 3, 6, 9 and 12. All new skills start at level one proficiency.

Communications: Any (+10%)
Domestic: Any (+10%)
Electrical: None
Espionage: Intelligence and Escape only (+5%)
Mechanical: None
Medical: First aid only (+5%)
Military: None
Physical: Any, excluding boxing and acrobatics.
Pilot Skills: Any, except robots, power armor, military vehicles, ships and aircraft.
Pilot Related Skills: Any
Rogue: Any (+4%)
Science: Any
Technical: Any (+10%)
W.P.: Any
Wilderness: Any

Secondary Skills: The character also gets to select two Secondary Skills from the list, excluding those marked "None," at levels 2, 5, 8 and 12. These are additional areas of knowledge that do not get the advantage of the bonus listed in parentheses. All Secondary Skills start at the base skill level.

Standard Equipment: Silk robe, silk dress, wool cloak, a set of clothing, a set of traveling clothes, light mega-damage body armor, Millennium Tree leaf armor, bright colored bandanna, bright colored scarf, energy rifle or pistol, a survival knife, silver dagger (hidden in boot), scrying skull or crystal ball, several decks of playing cards (one marked deck for cheating at cards), large purse/handbag, knapsack, backpack, 1D4 small pouches or sacks, a silver cross, canteen filled with holy water, a waterskin for drinking water, pocket flashlight, pocket digital disc recorder/player for recording her dreams and observations, note pad and sketch book, box of chalk, box of crayons, and 1D4 other writing implements. **Note:** The Fortune Teller is one of the most flamboyant of the gypsies, and dresses in brightly colored clothing, ornate silk, and wears a lot of rings, bracelets, earrings, and jewelry.

Vehicle: None to start.

Notable Additional Equipment that a Fortune Teller may want to acquire includes magic jewelry and crystals, staves and wands, magic potions, herbs, magic weapons, magic items, exotic jewelry, and artifacts, riding animal or vehicle, and perhaps a language translator, cameras, recording equipment and other odds and ends.

Special Resources: Pretty much the same as the Gypsy Thief, except she also has a special relationship with Woodland Spirits.

Money: Starts with 1D6x1000 in credits or Rubles and 3D6x1000 credits worth of gold, jewelry, and tradeable goods. The Gypsy enjoys the good life, but tends to be a bit more frugal with her money than most.

Cybernetics: Starts with none and will avoid getting cybernetics except for medical reasons. The character may consider bio-wizardry items.

The Gypsy Witch

A good number of Gypsy women are attracted to the seemingly quick and easy power of the Hidden Witch (most avoid becoming Pact Witches and Night Witches). The bold and cunning nature of most Gypsies gives the woman the notion that she'll be able to conquer the magic, and not have the magic conquer her. Thus, headstrong, brazen and anxious to earn their place in their clan, many a young maiden chooses to become a Hidden Witch.

The Hidden Witch O.C.C. is described in the Witch section.

The Gifted One O.C.C.

"The Gifted" or "The Gifted Ones" are Gypsy Psi-Healers. This character will have both psionic healing abilities and knowledge in the ways of medicine and herbology. They are among the most revered of the gypsy and often hold a high place among the clans. The Gifted tend to be the least violent and have few thief/rogue skills.

The Psionic Powers of The Gifted Ones
Randomly roll or select one of the following:

01-25 Major psionic: Select a total of six powers from any two psionic power categories (limited to Healing, Sensitive, and Physical). I.S.P.: 1D4x10 plus M.E. number. Add 1D6+1 I.S.P. for each level of experience. Bonuses: +2 to save vs disease and poison, +1 to save vs magic, +1 to save vs magic sickness and curses, and +2 to save vs Horror Factor.

26-50 Major psionic: Select eight powers from the Healing category. I.S.P.:1D4x10 plus M.E. number. Add 1D6+1 I.S.P. for each level of experience. Bonuses: +3 to save vs disease and poison, +1 to save vs magic, +2 to save vs magic sickness and curses, and +3 to save vs Horror Factor.

51-75 Master psionic: Select five Healing powers, two Sensitive powers, two Physical powers, and the Super Psionic power of Bio-Regeneration and one Super Psi-Power of choice. At levels 4, 7, 10 and 13, the character can select one additional super psionic power or two lesser psi-powers from any of the three categories. I.S.P.: 2D6x10 plus M.E. number. Add 10 I.S.P. for each level of experience. Bonuses: +2 to save vs disease and poison, +1 to save vs magic, +1 to save vs magic sickness and curses, and +3 to save vs Horror Factor.

76-00 Master psionic: Select *all* Healing powers and four Super Psionic powers of choice. At levels 2, 4, 6, 9 and 12, the character can select one additional Super Psionic Power or two lesser psi-powers from any of the three categories. I.S.P.: 2D6x10 plus M.E. number. Add 10 I.S.P. for each level of experience. Bonuses: +4 to save vs disease and poison, +1 to save vs magic, +2 to save vs magic sickness and curses, and +4 to save vs Horror Factor.

The Gifted One O.C.C.
Also known as The Gifted and Psychic Healer.
Alignment: Any
Racial Restrictions: None, although the vast majority (80%) are human males.
Roll The Eight Attributes as normal for that race.
Average Level of Experience (N.P.C.): 1D4+4 or as required by the Game Master.
Attribute Requirements: M.E. 14 or higher; a high I.Q. and P.P. are also ideal but not mandatory. Less than 5% of The Gifted are literate in any language.
O.C.C. Skills:
  Basic Math (+10%)
  Speaks Gypsy (+9%)
  Speaks Euro and Russian (+30%) and two of choice (+20%)
  Streetwise & Streetwise Drugs (both are +20%)
  Dance (+20%)
  Cook (+20%)
  Preserve Food (+20%)
  Identify Plants & Fruits (+20%)
  Biology (+20%)
  Pathology (+20%)
  Medical Doctor (+15%)
  * Holistic Medicine (+30%)
  W.P. Knife
  W.P. Targeting (typically throwing knives and sling)
  Hand to Hand: Basic to start, but can be changed to Expert for the cost of two O.C.C. Related Skills or three skills for Martial Arts (or Assassin, if evil).

  * **Note:** With the Game Master's approval, in this case the Holistic Medicine skill can include the skills and powers of the herbalist/herbology skill as presented in **Rifts® World Book Three: England**, including making curative teas and potions. The character also relies on his or her psionic healing powers and abilities.

O.C.C. Related Skills: None if a Master Psionic. Select four "other" skills from any of the available skill categories if a Major Psionic, plus select one additional skill at levels 3, 6, 9 and 12. All new skills start at level one proficiency.
  Communications: Any (+5%)
  Domestic: Any (+10%)
  Electrical: None

Espionage: Any (+5%)
Mechanical: None
Medical: See O.C.C. skills
Military: None
Physical: Any, excluding boxing, wrestling, gymnastics & acrobatics.
Pilot: Hover vehicles, automobiles, horsemanship, and boats only (+10%)
Pilot Related: Any
Rogue: Any
Science: Any (+10%)
Technical: Any (+15%)
W.P.: Any
Wilderness: Any (+10%)

Secondary Skills: The character also gets to select two Secondary Skills from the list, excluding those marked "None," at levels two, four, eight and twelve. These are additional areas of knowledge that do not get the advantage of the bonus listed in parentheses. All Secondary Skills start at the base skill level.

Standard Equipment: Hooded cloak or robe, medical gown, a set of fancy clothing, a set of traveling clothes, light mega-damage body armor, Millennium Tree leaf armor or Triax T-40 "plainclothes" armor, bright colored bandanna, bright colored scarf, weapon of choice, a pair of throwing knives, large silver knife, small hand axe, scalpels, knapsack, backpack, small pouches or sacks, silver cross, mirror, magnifying glass, binoculars, pen flashlight, pocket digital disc recorder/player for recording his diagnoses and observations, 1D4 writing implements.

Medical kit with soap, disposable towels, bandages, suture tape, antiseptics, protein healing salve, aspirin, painkillers, antibiotics, sedatives, anesthesia, hypodermic gun, stethoscope, pen flashlight and portable compu-drug dispenser. As well as another bag of holistic herbs, teas, salves and potions.

Surgical kit includes a variety of scalpels, one laser scalpel, needles, clamps, sutures, suture tape, suture gun, several IRMSS/Internal Robot Micro-Surgeon Systems, RMK/Robot Medical Kit, hand-held blood pressure machine (computerized), 3D4 thermometers, six unbreakable specimen containers, 100 pairs of disposable surgical gloves, two pair of reusable surgical gloves, and other basic items.

Vehicle: A horse, car or hover vehicle, but only if the character has a driving skill.

Special Resources: Pretty much the same as the Gypsy Thief, except he is likely to known other healers, psychics and witches.

Money: Starts with 1D6x1000 in credits or Rubles and 3D4x1000 credits worth of gold, jewelry, and tradeable goods. The Gypsy enjoys the good life and tends to spend money quickly and freely on life's many pleasures and extravagances.

Cybernetics: Starts with none and will avoid getting cybernetics except for medical reasons. This character will never consider bio-wizardry items.

The Layer of Laws

The Layer of Laws is an Elder who serves as the leader of a band or one of the wise men, counsellors and leaders of a clan. The Layers of the Law can be male or female (about a 50/50 split) and are the keepers of secrets, knowledge and lore. This entails settling disputes, passing out judgement, meting out justice, enforcing Gypsy laws and traditions, advising the members of the group, keeping records (often in his or her head), and generally guiding and aiding their band. They are also excellent story-tellers and terrible gossips with their noses in everybody's business.

The Layer of Laws knows a little bit about many things, but is seldom arrogant or condescending, except to gadje. Most are patient, understanding and good listeners and teachers. Many look like kindly old grandparents, but most are still as sharp as a whip, quick thinking, astonishing fast talkers, convincing liars, master thieves and — though slowing down physically (reduce P.S. P.P., P.B. and Spd by 20% for old age) — they are worldly, experienced, confident and capable.

Layer of Laws O.C.C.

Also known as the Wise Elder, and Good Mother or Good Father.

Alignment: Any, but most are unprincipled, anarchist or aberrant.

Racial Restrictions: 100% human, with a Gypsy lineage that can be traced back at least four generations, often much farther.

Average Level of Experience (N.P.C.): 1D6+5 or as required by the Game Master. Player Characters start out at 4th level and are at least 50 years of age.

Psionics: Psionic abilities are not a requirement.

Attribute Requirements: I.Q. 9, M.E. 13, or higher.

O.C.C. Skills:

Basic & Advanced Math (+30%)

Speaks the secret Gypsy language at 98%

Literate in the complete Gypsy language at 91%

Literate in one language of choice (+15%)

Speaks Euro, Russian and two others of choice (+20%)

Cook (+20%)

Horsemanship: General

Animal Husbandry (+10%)

* Holistic Medicine (+10%)

Land Navigation (+15%)

Astronomy (+5%)

Botany (+5%)

Law (+20%)

Knows all Lores (three favorites are +10%)

Interrogation (+10%)

Palming (+10%)

Pick Locks (+5%)

Card Sharp (+10%)

W.P. Ancient, one of choice (any).

W.P. Modern Weapon, one of choice (any).

Hand to Hand: Basic (no other is available)

* Note: With the Game Master's approval, in this case the Holistic Medicine skill can include the skills and powers of the Herbalist/Herbology skill as presented in **Rifts® World Book Three: England**, including making curative teas and potions.

O.C.C. Related Skills: Select three other skills at level one and two additional at levels 3, 6, 9 and 12.

Communications: Radio: Basic only.

Domestic: Any (+5%)

Electrical: None

Espionage: Intelligence only (+10%)

Mechanical: None

Medical: Any

Military: None

Physical: Any, except Boxing, Wrestling and Acrobatics.

Pilot Skills: Any, except robots, power armor, military vehicles, ships and aircraft.

Pilot Related Skills: Any

Rogue Skills: Any

Science: Any (+5%)

Technical: Any (+10%).

W.P.: Any

Wilderness: Any (+5%)

Secondary Skills: None.

Standard Equipment: Comparatively simple clothing suitable for their station and age, although they still tend to wear a lot of gold and jewelry. One suit of light modern or magic Mega-Damage body armor, bright colored scarf, sunglasses, pair of silver knives (one in the belt, the other in a boot), energy pistol and one weapon of choice, cane or walking stick (may be magical), lock picking tools, gold cross worn as jewelry, 1D6+2 vials of holy water, mirror, knapsack, backpack, 1D4 small pouches or sacks, water skin, binoculars, magnifying glass, pocket flashlight, large flashlight, 50 feet (15.2 m) of light cord, 1D4+4 note pads or sketch books, a dozen pens/markers and/or pencils, a box of chalk.

Vehicle: Has his/her own Gypsy Wagon and two Horned Steeds or Ursan Forest Steeds to pull it.

Notable Additional Equipment that an Elder may want to acquire includes valuable gems, jewelry and artifacts, fine wine and brandy, magic items and information ... always information.

Secret Resources: In addition to the standard fare, the Layer of Laws will know many other people, including elders in other bands, informers among the Warlords, "friends" in various villages, smugglers, fences, witches, Necromancers, heroes and adventurers. Furthermore, they know most every (supposed) secret in their own group. Thus, they will know about most every secret occupation, alliance or secret dealing and goings-on in the group.

Money: Starts with 1D6x1000 in credits or Rubles and 3D6x1000 in trade goods. Like all Gypsies, Elders enjoy the good life and tend to spend their money quickly and freely on life's many pleasures and extravagances, but they manage to ferret away a nice amount for rainy days, sometimes a small fortune.

Cybernetics: Starts with none and will avoid getting cybernetics except for medical reasons.

Gypsy Beguiler O.C.C.

The Beguiler is always an attractive woman or man of uncommon beauty or handsomeness. They too are Mystics, human beings with both psionic and magical powers, only the magic power of the Beguiler is not spell casting but the ability to change their shape at will.

The act of shapechanging requires concentration to perform and maintain, which means skill performance and attacks/actions per melee round are halved while in the altered shape (always round up). Being rendered unconscious or suffering severe injury (lose S.D.C. and more than 80% of Hit Points) will also make it impossible to keep its unnatural appearance and revert back to its true human form. Ironically, it is assuming a different human form that is the most difficult to maintain. Animal forms are much easier to keep.

The Special Powers & Bonuses of the Beguiler

1. Human Metamorphosis: The ability to change one's human appearance or impersonate another living person — often used for seduction, infiltration, spying, sabotage and assassination.

The P.P.E. Cost is 60 points per hour of transformation, however the more experienced the Beguiler becomes, the easier it is to perform and maintain the false appearance. Reduce the P.P.E. cost by five points per each level of experience and double the number of hours the form can be maintained (for a geometric increase in duration; i.e. two hours at 2nd level, four hours at 3rd level, eight hours at 4th level, 16 at 5th, and so on).

- Can make oneself appear as much as 50 years older or as young as a six year old child.
- Can make oneself appear 50% more beautiful or less attractive (adjust P.B. appropriately).
- Can make self appear to be the opposite sex.
- Can make oneself appear to be thin, wizened, sickly or buff and healthy.

- Can make oneself appear frighteningly inhuman, D-Bee-like or demonic, with a Horror Factor of 10 +1 per every two levels of experience.

2. Metamorphosis into an animal. The Gypsy Beguiler can also transform into *large* wild animals — animals no smaller than a house cat (dogs, wolves, bears, deer, eagles, etc.). The animal form is easier to assume so the P.P.E. cost is lower and the duration longer than the initial ability to change human shape.

The P.P.E. Cost is 10 points per hour of transformation. The animal shape can be maintained for up to six hours +4 per level of experience. The transformation takes two full melee rounds (30 seconds).

3. Minor Mega-Damage Creature: Hit Points and half S.D.C. are turned into M.D.C. +1D6 M.D.C. per level of experience.

4. Bio-Regeneration: 1D4 M.D.C. per hour.

5. P.P.E.: The character's permanent P.P.E. base is 2D4x10 +P.E. attribute number, and 2D6 P.P.E. per level of experience.

The Psionic Powers of the Beguiler

1. Psionic powers of the Beguiler: Detect Psionics, Suppress Fear, Empathy, Telepathy, Resist Fatigue, Resist Hunger, Resist Thirst, Mind Block Auto-Defense and Hypnotic Suggestion.

At experience levels 3, 6, 9, 12 and 15 the character can either select one Super Psionic power or two lesser psionic powers from the categories of Sensitive or Physical.

2. I.S.P.: Roll 2D4x10 plus the character's M.E. number to determine the base Inner Strength Points (I.S.P.). The Beguiler gets an additional 8 I.S.P. per level of experience.

3. Saving throws versus psionic attack: The Beguiler is considered to be a Master psionic and saves on a roll of 10 or higher.

4. Other Bonuses: +1D4 to M.A., +1D6+3 to P.B., +3 to save vs possession and insanity, +3 to save vs Horror Factor, +1 to save vs magic.

When in animal form the character has the basic abilities of that animal, and is +2 on initiative, +1 to strike, +2 to dodge, +2 to roll with punch, fall or impact, +2 to save vs poison and disease, and +10% to track by smell.

Gypsy Beguiler O.C.C.

Also Known as a Gypsy Shapechanger.

Alignments: Any, although most are selfish or evil.

Racial Restrictions: None, although the vast majority (78%) are human females.

Roll The Eight Attributes as normal for that race.

Average Level of Experience (N.P.C.): 1D4+3 or as required by the Game Master.

Attribute Requirements: M.E. 13, P.E. 13, P.B. 15 or higher; a high I.Q. and P.S. are helpful but not mandatory. Only 3% of the Gypsy Beguilers are literate in any language.

O.C.C. Skills:
Basic Math (+5%)
Lore: One of choice (+10%)

Dance (+10%)
Sing (+10%)
Play Musical Instrument: Two of choice (+15%)
Speaks Gypsy (start at 63%)
Speaks Euro, Russian and two languages of choice (+10%)
Find Contraband (+6%)
Palming (+5%)
Pick Pockets (+15%)
Pick Locks (+10%)
Streetwise (+10%)
Seduction (+20%)
Interrogation (+15%)
Intelligence (+10%)
Imitate Voices/Impersonation (+10%)
Boxing
W.P. Two of choice (any)
Hand to Hand: Expert, but can be changed to Assassin for the cost of one O.C.C. Related skill.

O.C.C. Related Skills: Select three other skills from any of the available skill categories. Plus select one additional skill at levels 3, 6, 9 and 12. All new skills start at level one proficiency.

Communications: Radio: Basic and Surveillance only
Domestic: Any
Electrical: None
Espionage: Any (+5%)
Mechanical: None
Medical: None
Military: None
Physical: Any
Pilot Skills: Any, except robots, power armor, military vehicles, ships and aircraft.
Pilot Related Skills: Any
Rogue: Any (+4%)
Science: Any
Technical: Any (+10%)
W.P.: Any
Wilderness: Any

Secondary Skills: The character also gets to select two Secondary Skills from the list, excluding those marked "None," at levels 2, 5, 9 and 13. These are additional areas of knowledge that do not get the advantage of the bonus listed in parentheses. All Secondary Skills start at the base skill level.

Standard Equipment: Flashy clothes, including leather garments, light mega-damage body armor, bright colored bandanna, bright colored scarf, sunglasses or tinted goggles, two weapons of choice, pair of knives, lock picking tools, knapsack, backpack, 1D4 small pouches or sacks, canteen, binoculars, magnifying glass, mirror, pocket flashlight, sketch·book, 1D4 pens/markers or pencils.

Vehicle: None to start.

Notable Additional Equipment: Covets magic items, magic weapons, exotic jewelry, and artifacts.

Special Resources: Pretty much the same as the Gypsy Thief, except Woodland Spirits take a natural dislike to this character.

Money: Starts with 2D4x1000 in credits or Rubles and 2D6x1000 credits worth of gold, jewelry, and tradeable goods. Spends money like water; loves to dance, sing and party.

Cybernetics: Never!

Gypsy Enforcer O.C.C.

The Russian Gypsy Enforcer is one of the few warrior O.C.C.s among the Gypsies. The character is usually male and serves the clan and/or group as its protector, defender and enforcer. As a protector/defender, the warrior keeps an eye out for everybody in his group, stands watch, makes defensive strategies and tactics, picks the (safe) location for camp, hand picks and assigns other guards, and protects the wagon(s), women and children. As an "enforcer" he helps to carry out any threats and acts of retribution against enemies and rivals.

The character has magic weapons, "acquired" Kuznya items along with modern weapons and body armor. As a sign of their station, all wear beards and mustaches, and most have long hair pulled back into a ponytail.

Gypsy Enforcer

Alignment Limitations: Unprincipled, anarchist or any evil. A thief cannot be of a good alignment.

Racial Restrictions: None, although the vast majority (70%) are human.

Roll The Eight Attributes as normal for that race.

Average Level of Experience (N.P.C.): 1D4+4 or as required by the Game Master.

Psionics: Psionic abilities are not a requirement.

O.C.C. Bonuses: +1D6 to P.S. +1 to P.P., +2 to P.E., +1D6 to speed, +3D6 to S.D.C., +3 on initiative, +4 to pull punch, and +3 to save vs Horror Factor.

Attribute Requirements: P.S. 14 or higher. A high I.Q., M.A. and P.E. are helpful but not a requirement.

O.C.C. Skills:
Basic Math (+10%)
Speaks Gypsy (starts at 63%)
Russian and two of choice (+20%)
Streetwise (includes Streetwise: Drugs, both are +14%)
Horsemanship: General (+10%)
Horsemanship: Exotic
Pilot: One of choice (+10%; typically, small and fast).
Land Navigation (+10%)
Dance (+10%)
Palming (+5%)
Pick Locks (+5%)
Boxing
Climbing (+10%)
Prowl (+10%)
W.P. Ancient: Two of choice (any)
W.P. Modern: Two of choice (any)
Hand to Hand: Expert to start, but can be changed to Martial Arts or Assassin for the cost of one O.C.C. Related skill.

O.C.C. Related Skills: Select three Military skills and three other skills from any of the available skill categories. Plus select one additional skill at levels 3, 6, 9 and 12. All new skills start at level one proficiency.

Communications: Any (+10%)
Domestic: None
Electrical: None
Espionage: Any (+5%)
Mechanical: Basic and Automotive only (+5%)
Medical: First aid only (+5%)
Military: Any (+10%)

Physical: Any

Pilot: Any (+10%), except robots, power armor, military vehicles, ships and aircraft.

Pilot Related: Any

Rogue: Any (+5%)

Science: None

Technical: Any (+5%; language and lore +15%)

W.P.: Any

Wilderness: Any

Secondary Skills: The character also gets to select three Secondary Skills from the list, excluding those marked "None," at level one and one additional skill at levels 4, 7, 10 and 13. These are additional areas of knowledge that do not get the advantage of the bonus listed in parentheses. All Secondary Skills start at the base skill level.

Standard Equipment: Military garb, boots and gloves, set of "plain clothes," a suit of light mega-damage body armor, a suit of heavy or magic or Kuznya M.D.C. body armor, one Mystic Kuznya magic weapon, sunglasses or tinted goggles, two ancient weapons of choice, two modern weapons of choice (with 2D6 extra E-Clips), a box of 144 silver bullets, six wooden stakes and a mallet, pair of silver knives, gold cross worn as jewelry, lock picking tools, knapsack, backpack, 1D4 small pouches or sacks, two canteens, binoculars, medium-sized flashlight, pocket mirror, pocket laser distancer, 60 feet (16.3 m) of light cord and grappling hook, and some personal items.

Vehicle: Starts with a Mega-Steed or fast combat bike or hovercycle.

Secret Resources: The usual fare, plus one or more arms dealers to get ammunition and combat supplies, and probably knows a handful of mercenaries and Warlord Reavers.

Notable Additional Equipment that an Enforcer may want to acquire includes all the magic weapons and armor he can lay his hands on, M.D. weapons, grenades and other explosives, and combat gear.

Money: Starts with 2D6x100 in credits or Rubles and 1D4x1000 in trade goods. The Gypsy band he serves provides for most of the Enforcer's needs, including a place to sleep, food, magic healing, basic supplies, ammunition and even the occasional weapon and mode of transportation. Like most Gypsies, he enjoys the good life and tends to spend money quickly and freely on life's many pleasures and extravagances.

Cybernetics: Starts with none, but will consider getting the occasional implant and partial bionics (arms, legs).

More on the Sovietski

War Machines

The old Soviet Empire was known for its diverse tanks and missile systems, and the Sovietski have taken their lessons from the past. Missile launching 'Borgs and armored vehicles are the backbone of the *Armiya Sovietski*, "New Soviet Army." They provide a swift and deadly response to flying targets the size of a Wing-Rider or Gargoyle to that of a dragon or airship, as well as devastating effect pounding on ground troops. In fact, many believe it is the Sovietski's superiority in heavy combat vehicles that has enabled it to avoid being conquered and integrated by one of the Warlords. The Sovietski and its strong defenses lend a calming and stabilizing affect to northeastern Russia.

The following are some notable Sovietski combat vehicles that got squeezed out of **Warlords of Russia™** due to space limitations.

Features Common to Russian M.D.C. Vehicles

1. Cyber-Link: The Warlords' pervasive use of cybernetics and cyborg warriors means most *small vehicles*, particularly combat and wilderness types, have jacks and hook-ups to link the cyborg pilot directly to the vehicle. This means a direct and instant feed of information to and from on-board computers, sensors, communication systems and weapons, making the vehicle a fast-responding extension of his own body (+5% to piloting skill, +1 on initiative, etc.; see the *Cyber-Link* description in the Cybernetics Section of **Warlords of Russia™** for complete bonuses and details).

2. Gromeko Battlefield Computers: Takes care of communications, visual data and internal cybernetic systems (monitors personal damage). All communications are automatically encrypted/decrypted by the sender/receiver units without their operators having to specify it. This can be turned off if desired, but rarely is (unless you want to "leak" some information).

It also features "Enemy Profiling" for up to 600 different cyborg designs, styling, and armor, 1000 identifying insignias and marks, as well as 2000 monsters and demons — each rendered in full color with schematics of known weaknesses, armor, weapons, etc., capable of rotation and zoom to x25 magnification. The Gromeko functions as a kind of passive *Friend or Foe Identification system*, flashing words, or symbols for the majority who cannot read, on the monitor and HUD display. This vehicle model of the Gromeko is larger, has a more powerful computer and larger memory compared with the bionic version tied into the cyber-optics of many 'Borgs. Visual Range: 6,000 feet (1828 m). Requirements: A video camera with telescopic capabilities (otherwise reduce range to 2000 feet/610 m).

3. Enviro-Sensors: An external and internal sensor system that monitors the environment outside and inside the vehicle. This is done on a molecular level and used to detect and measure impurities, chemical, germ/biological and other dangerous agents (toxic gases, smoke, pollution, spores, radiation, etc.) in the immediate area surrounding the vehicle. It can identify 6000 elements, gases and agents as well as measure temperature,

wind speed, humidity, barometric pressure and similar air and environmental aspects.

The same is true inside the vehicle, with links to the life support system to monitor conditions and warn of breaches and dangers inside. When exposed to gases, oxygen masks drop from concealed compartments in the ceiling (similar to those in 20th Century airplanes) to protect crew and passengers.

4. Cyber Harness: A metal harness normally kept tilted up over the pilot, co-pilot, sensor operators and gunners. These pull down over the user, and have cyber-jacks that link into the cyborg, to pilot the vehicle. The computer controls the vehicles functions, and is controlled cybernetically by the user. While in this condition, a cyborg *may not move* or take any effective action.

The most incredible thing about this setup is that the cyborg can simultaneously fire a number of weapons systems equal to his level of experience! Warlords sitting in their Warthrones can usually access almost all their weapons at once!

5. Cybernetic Locking Mechanisms: Hatches and doors to sensitive areas, like engines, may be fitted with a cyber lock, which means the individual must link with the lock for it to open. While linked, the lock accepts information to open based on the Warlords "Symbol," a recognition pattern built into every Warlords cyborgs. Other systems, like energy weapons, rail guns, ignition switches and more, have this feature.

6. Cyborg Containment Slings (CCS's): Most larger Russian vehicles come standard with cyborg containment slings, which are connected to the ceiling of the main troop compartment near the sides. 'Borgs may rest in these harness slings while a vehicle is in motion, for Russian vehicles tend to be on the rough and bouncy side. Without the slings, there is a 50% chance every few minutes the vehicle is in motion (I'm thinking battlefield conditions) that anyone standing in the main compartment(s) area will be thrown around and/or lose their footing. The CCS's can be exited immediately through a buckle release.

7. Other Common Sensor Systems: Perfect, crisp, 20/20 digital vision optics relay, video camera, Infrared/Ultraviolet 1,000 feet (304 m), Passive Nightvision 2,500 feet (762 m), and Digital Recorder (16 hours maximum data).

8. Long-Range Radio Communication System: Approx. 500 mile (800 km) range in the steppes and tundra, 300 miles (482.7 km) in the forests and around cities (interference) and 100-200 (160 to 320 km) in the mountains (**Note:** The interference from the latter two is common to all ground vehicles, not just Russian designs).

9. Radar: Can identify and track up to 56 aerial targets simultaneously at a range of 30 miles (48 km).

10. Power Source: Most large vehicles are nuclear powered, but many smaller vehicles are available with a choice of liquid fuel engines or electrical/solar powered engines. The average life of a small nuclear powered vehicle is 10 years, while large vehicles typically have 20 years.

11. Full environmental pilot and crew compartment: Russian robot vehicles typically contain enough room to seat 2-4 cyborgs (4-8 human-sized passengers), and are sealed airtight and pressurized when in use. They are suitable for use in all hostile environments and can even survive underwater for a few hours (300 -400 feet/91-122 m maximum depth). However, un-

less stated otherwise, the vehicle cannot propel itself underwater nor move along the bottom of a lake or sea floor.

The following features are common on all larger Russian vehicles.

- Computer controlled life support system. In Russian vehicles, this constantly monitors the status of the vehicles interior. It checks air quality, presence of harmful gases or radiation, excessive heat and cold and so on. Any suspicious conditions will be instantly red-lighted in the cockpit and all control stations of the vehicle.

- Automated blast doors. These will close and lock without being given a signal in the presence of high levels of radiation (cracked fusion power plant for example), nerve gas or any other toxic element. They will not open until overridden by a special code, electronically picked or blown apart. Blast doors all have 100 M.D.C. **Note:** Small vehicles don't have blast doors, and may not have an environmental compartment.

- Internal cooling and temperature control.

- Air purification filters and circulation system, and gas filtration, humidifier/dehumidifier (which is often in disrepair), all of which automatically engage in low oxygen or contaminated air environments. 36-48 hour oxygen supply units in most vehicles.

- Insulated, high temperature resistant shielding for up to 400 degrees centigrade. Normal fires do no damage. Nuclear, plasma, and magic fires do full damage.

- Radiation shielded to at least 1,000 rads (enough to make a character ill almost instantly).

- Polarized and light sensitive/adjusting tinted observation windows (when applicable).

- Heads Up Display (HUD).

Design Note: Most (although not all) Russian vehicles tend to look big, heavy and clunky.

Thunderbolt Assault Truck

The Thunderbolt is a medium-sized half-track cargo vehicle that has been modified to accommodate a pair of the big cannons identical to the ones used by the Thunderstorm Artillery Cyborg.

The cannons are built into the bed of the truck using a sturdy hydraulic system to both lower and raise the cannons and to absorb the recoil. The cab section of the truck accommodates a driven and CGO Gunner (Cannon Guidance Operator — the guy who activates, aims and fires the cannons). The driver's compartment has a sliding roof panel on the passenger's side giving the CGO access to a mounted Cyclone Pulse Laser Rifle. The Thunderbolt is an important part of the mobile artillery defense network that defends the cities of the Sovietski. They are positioned and move to strategic locations as they are needed, and their mobile nature and frequently changing position prevents enemies from targeting their (changing) locations.

Thunderbolt Artillery Truck
Model Type: ZSU 13/14
Crew: Two; a driver and CGO gunner.
Capacity: One additional passenger can be squeezed into the

cab of the vehicle but as many as a half dozen can ride out-side, on top of the cannons (when the guns are not in use, of course).

M.D.C. by Location:

Forward Windows (4; cab) — 25 each
* Headlights (2) — 2 each
* Rear Lights (2) — 2 each
Roof Hatches (1; top) — 30
Doors (2; side) — 50 each
Tractor Treads (2) — 75 each
Front Tires (2; cab) — 20 each
Reinforced Pilot's Compartment — Not applicable
Forward Laser Weapon (1; cab) — 50
Cannon Barrels (2) — 180 each
Cannon & Missile Housing — 300
** Main Body: Forward Cab Section — 175
** Main Body: Truck Bed — 180

* Locations marked with a single asterisk are small and/or difficult targets to hit. Thus, they can only be hit when a character makes a *called shot* and even then, the attacker is -3 to strike.

** Depleting the M.D.C. of the entire main body will destroy the vehicle.

Height: 6 feet, 5 inches (1.9 m) with guns lowered. 15 feet (4.6 m) at maximum elevation.

Width: 7 feet (2.1 m) with cannon housing (otherwise 6 feet/1.8 m).

Length: 18 feet (5.5 m)

Weight: 22 tons fully loaded.

Power Source: Nuclear.

Speed: Top: 70 mph (112 km), with a typical cruising speed of 40 mph (64 km). Deep snow and treacherous terrain may re-duce speed to under 20 mph (32 km).

Life Support: Air circulation and cleaning system with gas fil-tration and toxic warning system. The vehicle's cab can be sealed independently and has an air purification, purge and circulation system (with a two hour supply of oxygen) that can clean and recycle breathable air for approximately eight hours.

Sensors: Digital HUD with auto-range-finding, radar and all large vehicle sensors and features.

Sovietski Cost: 600,000 Universal credits for a basic half-track vehicle without cannons (fuel engine), 3.5 million credits with cannon artillery unit and nuclear power system, but the equivalent elsewhere would cost 5-7 million.

Weapon Systems

1. Artillery Unit: A self-loading, double-barrelled Howitzer plus mini-missile launch system. The twin cannons can raise and lower and tilt in a 45 degree arc of fire, and rotate side to side 45 degrees.

On the side of each cannon is a sliding panel that conceals five mini-missile launch tubes (shown closed in the illustra-tion, open in the Thunderstorm Cyborg illustration on page 222 of *Warlords of Russia*). These are used for both defense and offense and are especially effective against light flying targets.

Primary Purpose: Tactical bombardment of the enemy.

Secondary Purpose: Anti-Armored Vehicles and Infantry Support.

Mega-Damage: Cannons: 2D4x10 M.D. per single round, 4D4x10 per double, simultaneous blast (two rounds). A simultaneous twin blast counts as one melee attack.

Mini-Missiles: Varies with missile type.

Range: Cannon: 8,300 feet (2530 m); about a mile and a half.

Mini-Missiles: One mile (1.6 km).

Rate of Fire: Each single or double blast counts as one melee attack.

Payload: 20 cannon shells total, for 10 double blasts or 20 single ones. A three man team with two wearing MM-61 Explorer Exoframe (see page 176, in Warlords of Russia™) or two being Light or Heavy Machines, can reload four shells per melee round.

Mini-Missile Payload: A total of 40 missiles, four per each of the 10 launch tubes (five tubes per side); identical to the weapon system used by the Thunderstorm Cyborg.

2. Manned S-500 "Cyclone" Pulse Laser Rifle (mounted): A modified, mounted S-500 heavy laser weapon is built into a housing on the passenger side of the half-track. The passenger (typically the CGO) slides open the ceiling panel, stands up on the seat, straps into a support harness and fires away. The weapon can rotate 180 degrees side to side and can tilt up and down in a 30 degree arc of fire. The weapon has an independent power pack so in case the cannon power system is knocked out, the S-500 can still fire.

Primary Purpose: Anti-Personnel.

Secondary Purpose: Assault & Defense.

Mega-Damage: 1D6x10 M.D. per pulse blast. A switch can make the weapon fire one, single, precision shot doing 2D6 M.D.

Rate of Fire: Each blast counts as one melee attack.

Maximum Effective Range: 3,000 feet (914 m).

Payload: 60 from an E-Pack; two are standard issue; four shots from a standard E-Clip (inserted in the side in case of emergencies).

"Bulldog"
All Weather Tracked Vehicle

The Bulldog is a comparatively small, multi-purpose, four-tracked, military ground vehicle designed with rough terrains and Russian winters in mind. Its wide, independent track system enables it to ride on top of deep snow or to plow through it — 75% are fitted with a wide, "V" shaped, heavy M.D.C. plow that can double as a battering ram or bulldozer. It is a multi-purpose military vehicle used for troop transport, exploration, light assault, civil defense, hauling, snow removal and battering ram. Light assault capabilities include a pair of low-profile, heavy laser turrets in the front, a manned rail gun turret above the pilot compartment and a mini-missile launcher on the top toward the rear. A side port bubble is located on each side and can be used to look outside, or the glass panel slid out and used as a gun port by shooters from inside (obstructed view so shooters are -3 to strike). A heavy-duty winch and cable is built into the rear.

Bull Dog Armored Tracked Combat Vehicle

Model Type: ZSU 17/18

Class: Multi-purpose, all-terrain, armored assault and transport vehicle.

Crew: Four: One driver/pilot, one co-pilot/communications and two gunners. A fifth and sixth crewman can be accommodated with cramping space.

Troop Capacity: 20 troops comfortably, 30 cramped; half if Heavy Cyborgs. A dozen troops can also ride on the exterior in case of emergency.

M.D.C. by Location:

    Tracks (4) — 100 each

    * Rail Gun Turret (1; top, front) — 55

    * Forward Laser Turrets (2) — 50 each

    Mini-Missile Launcher (1; rear) — 90

    * Headlights (6) — 4 each

    Main Bay Hatch (1; rear) — 140

    * Doors (2) — 90 each

    * Top Hatch (1; rear roof) — 80

    Windows (4; large) — 30 each

    * Small Windows (2; sides) — 12 each

    * Winch (2, front and rear) — 90 each

    Reinforced Pilot's Compartment — 65

    ** Main Body — 340

    * Locations marked with a single asterisk are small and/or difficult targets to hit. Thus, they can only be hit when a character makes a *called shot* and even then, the attacker is -3 to strike. Destroying one of the four tracks/tread units slows the vehicle by 20%; destroying two slows it by 70%. Losing three to all treads reduces speed to 5% of normal.

    ** Depleting the M.D.C. of the entire main body will destroy the vehicle.

Speed

Land: Has a top speed of 80 mph (128 km) on relatively flat surfaces, but travel over difficult terrain is typically a more cautious 40 to 50 mph (64 to 80 km). In very mountainous and/or treacherous conditions, best speed is 25 mph (40 km), and reduce speed an additional 10% in deep snow or icy conditions.

Underwater: Travel in or underwater is not possible — the Bull Dog sinks like a rock — but its airtight compartment has enough air to last three hours and can tolerate a depth of up to 300 feet (91 m).

Statistical Data

Height: 6 feet (1.8 m) tall to the deck/roof, another 5 feet (1.5 m) for the guns and missile launcher, for a total of 11 feet (3.3 m).

Width: 7 feet (2.1 m)

Length: 20 feet (6 m) for the vehicle itself, but the plow adds another four feet (1.2 m).

Weight: 10 tons but can carry an additional 20 tons and pull 40.

Cargo Bay: Minimal in the cab: Small arms and other items can be stored inside. Most are designed for troop transport with removable bench seats, so the seats can be removed when needed to haul supplies. Crated and sturdy items can be tied on top or pulled from behind — can pull up to 40 tons, but reduce speed 5% for every ten tons.

Power System: Nuclear fusion; average energy life is 10 years.

Sovietski Cost: 2.2 million Universal credits for a Bull Dog complete with weapons and missiles. It is *seldom* sold by the Armiya Sovietski, but a few hundred have fallen into the hands

of outsiders over the years and the Poles have recently released a knock-off they call the "Mighty Little Hound" (this knock-off is 10% slower and has 20% less M.D.C. at a cost of 2.5 million credits. They also offer a gasoline version for 1.1 million; 120 mile/192 range).

Weapon Systems

1. Foward Mini-Laser Turrets (2): Mounted in the forward section are a pair of single barreled, heavy lasers built into ball-turrets. Each has a 60 degree arc of fire up and down and can turn side to side 180 degrees. They can be fired independently of each other or simultaneously at the same target. Typically operated by the pilot and/or co-pilot/communications officer.

Primary Purpose: Defense

Secondary Purpose: Anti-Personnel

Mega-Damage: 4D6 M.D. per single blast or 6D8 per simultaneous double blast at the same target.

Rate of Fire: Equal to the hand to hand attacks of the gunner/pilot.

Maximum Effective Range: 2,000 feet (610 m).

Payload: Effectively unlimited, runs off the nuclear power system.

2. Rail Gun Turret (top): This weapon is located in the forward section and rests in an elevated seat between the pilot and co-pilot, making the gunner recessed and a low profile target. All targeting is done via sensors and computer generated screen images. In the alternative, the gunner can look out of a narrow viewing slit.

Primary Purpose: Anti-Personnel.

Secondary Purpose: Defense.

Mega-Damage: A burst is 16 rounds and inflicts 1D4x10 M.D.C.

Rate of Fire: Only fires 16 round bursts, and each counts as one melee attack.

Maximum Effective Range: 4,000 feet (1200 m)

Payload: A 9600 round drum for 600 bursts is standard issue. A second ammo-drum is usually carried along and can be installed in one minute (4 melee rounds).

3. Mini-Missile Launcher: A missile launcher is mounted on the top toward the rear of the vehicle.

Primary Purpose: Anti-Vehicle & Anti-Aircraft.

Secondary Purpose: Anti-Personnel & Defense

Mega-Damage: Varies with missile type, but a typical payload is Armor Piercing (1D4x10 M.D.) or plasma (1D6x10 M.D.), but others can be substituted or mixed for a variety.

Rate of Fire: Volleys of 2, 4 or 8 missiles.

Maximum Effective Range: About one mile (1.6 km).

Blast Radius: Varies

Payload: 32 total, with an additional 64 stored inside. Takes one minute to reload.

4. Standard Sensor Cluster System: Communications rig 25 miles (40 km, double at high elevations), targeting computer, VR Remote Control System Computer, passive nightvision 2,000 feet (610 m), infrared/ultraviolet scanning 1,500 feet (457 m), telescopic to 6,000 feet (1828 m), and loudspeaker 300 feet (91.5 m). It also has spotlight with a range of 600 feet (183 m); plus all systems standard for large vehicles.

Note: Does not have a Cyber-link feature.

Life Support: Air circulation and cleaning system with gas filtration and toxic warning system. The vehicle's cab/pilot's section and rear cabin can be sealed independently and have an air purification, purge and circulation system (with an 8 hour supply of oxygen) that can clean and recycle breathable air for approximately 14-18 days. Can withstand up to 400 Rads of radiation.

Thundersword Multi-Combat Platform

An incredible armored personnel carrier (APC) nicknamed the "Centipede" that is also a phenomenal all-terrain ground vehicle and weapon platform. It was designed before the Great Cataclysm to offer troops maximum transport protection and then follow up with heavy and versatile field support. The feature that makes the Thundersword such an ideal all-terrain vehicle and earns it the nickname "Centipede" is the sliding, accordion-style plates that make up its *flexible* mid-section. The Thundersword can *bend* in the middle 45 degrees in all directions, enabling it to make tight turns that a long vehicle could not make easily, turn half of the vehicle to face an enemy while leaving the other half behind cover, crawl up and down uneven terrain, and, if absolutely necessary, break in two — both sections, but only the forward half can drive. It is a deadly front-line combat unit with excellent firepower, mobility, heavy armor, and multiple weapons.

The Front Section. The forward half has a long, narrow view strip in the front and a battery of optical, computer and sensor systems. There is a heavy-duty, airtight hatch on both sides, toward the rear of that half, plus too roof hatches for the disembarking of troops in the forward section. The very front is operated by a pilot, co-pilot/gunner, two gunners, two communications officers, Medical Officer, and Field Commander Officer or War Knight. This section serves as a mobile field command center with independent radar, combat computers, and sensors linked to the rear sensor cluster and back-up communications. The rest of the forward section holds human troops and light to medium cyborgs.

Its weapons are limited to a forward laser turret mounted in the front bumper, a high-powered rail cannon, and pop-up mini-missile launcher, plus its complement of 18-24 troops.

The Rear Section. The rear half is primarily a troop transport and weapon platform. It can accommodate 40 human-sized troops (50 cramped), or 30 Heavy Machines or 20 Thunderhammer or Thunderstrike Shocktroopers, perhaps even 2-4 hovercycles. Troops can disembark from the large bay door in the rear, but the entire roof section that holds the two heavy laser cannons slides open so troops can fly or climb out en masse. The two plate shields extend out to the side of the vehicle for such disembarkment and provide cover fire. This can be done even while the vehicle is moving.

In addition to the pair of heavy lasers (triple barrels protected by an outer cannon-like covering), a pair of medium-range missile launchers are located in the rear.

The Mid-Section. The middle section is a system of heavy, overlapping shields designed for flexibility of movement.

Hidden Treads. The "Centipede" has two tread or track systems in the front and rear sections. However, if one or more of these are destroyed, a second pair of concealed treads toward the middle of each section drops down and takes over. Their location makes them -5 to strike, even with a "Called Shot," unless the attacker is running alongside the Thundersword and can level a shot or explosive blast past the destroyed outer tread and at the one beyond it, deep under the vehicle.

Thundersword Multi-Combat Platform

Model Type: APC

Class: Infantry Assault and Transport Vehicle

Crew: Ten: One pilot, a co-pilot, two communications officers, two forward gunners, Medical Officer, Field Commander, and two rear gunners. Can accommodate four more personnel comfortably, typically 1-2 Military Specialists or Field Scientists, and 1-2 paramedics or field doctors.

APC Troops Payload:

Front Section: 18-24 human-sized troops.

Rear Section: 40 human-sized (50 cramped), or 30 Heavy Machines, 20 Thunderhammer or Thunderstrike Cyborg Shocktroopers. Or any combination.

Note: An additional 20 human-sized troops could ride on top of the vehicle in case of an emergency.

M.D.C. by Location:

** Main Body: Front Section — 530

* Window Slit (1; long) — 100

* Forward Headlights (3; lower front) — 5 each

Forward Laser Turret – 80

Main Outer Hatch/Door (2; on sides) — 140 each

Main Inner Hatch (2; on sides) — 80 each

* Roof Hatches (2; top) — 90 each

Rail Cannon (1; top turret) — 140

* Pop-Up Mini-Missile Launcher (1; top) — 110

* Rear Treads (4; two concealed) — 180 each

* Communications Antenna (1) — 10

Concealed Searchlight (lower front) — 50 (cover); 15 light

** Main Body: Rear Section — 600

Rear Missile Housings (2) — 100 each

Laser Cannons (2) — 150 each

Sensor Cluster (1) — 90

Sliding Bay Shields (top lasers) — 220 each

Main Rear Hatch (1; large) — 130

* Concealed Escape Hatch (2; ceiling) — 80 each

* Rear Treads (4; two concealed) — 180 each

* Tail Lights (3) — 5 each

** Mid-Section/Flexible Main Body — 310

* Every item marked by a single asterisk is small and/or difficult to strike. An attacker must make a "called shot" to hit and even then he is -3 to strike.

Destroying the four-sensor cluster in the rear means long-range communications and radar are lost; only has standard systems in place (front section).

** Depleting the M.D.C. of the main body will shut the APC down completely, rendering it useless.

Speed

Land: 80 mph (128.7 km) maximum.

Breaux!

163

Water: 50 mph (80 km), but no deeper than 12 feet (3.6 m).

Flying: None

Statistical Data

Height: Front section 13 feet (4 m); Rear section 16 feet (4.9 m) when accounting for the lasers and sensor cluster.

Width: 14 feet (4.3 m)

Length: 42 feet (12.8 m)

Weight: 40 tons unloaded.

Cargo: Troops, power armor, robots, small vehicles and/or supplies can be carried inside this APC and cargo transport, up to 100 tons, plus an additional 50 tons can be pulled in tow.

Color: Grey with silver, black and red detailing.

Power System: Nuclear; average energy life is 20 years.

Sovietski Cost: 23 million credits. It is exclusive to the Sovietski, nobody has knocked it off, and is not available on the Black Market.

Weapon Systems

1. **S-5050 Rail Cannon:** Designed to be a heavy, long-range, general purpose weapon, it is suitable for assault, anti-armor attacks and cover fire in the support of infantry.

Primary Purpose: Assault

Mega-Damage: A full damage burst is 40 rounds and inflicts 1D6x10 M.D. At the flip of a switch the weapon can fire 10 shot bursts which inflict 3D6 M.D.

Maximum Effective Range: 5000 feet (1524 m)

Rate of Fire: Equal to the combined hand to hand attacks of the gunner (usually 4-6).

Payload: 12,000 round drum feed for 300 long bursts or 1,200 short bursts! Reloading a drum will take about 15 minutes for those not trained, but a mere five minutes by characters with engineering or field armorer skills.

2. **LSU-10 Laser Turret (1; forward section):** A short-range, heavy laser turret is built into the front, lower right hand side of the APC. It points forward but has a 60 degree arc of fire, up and down.

Primary Purpose: Anti-Personnel

Secondary Purpose: Defense

Mega-Damage: 4D6 M.D. per single blast.

Range: 2000 feet (610 m)

Rate of Fire: Equal to the number of combined hand to hand attacks (usually 4-6) of the gunner.

Payload: Effectively unlimited.

3. **Pop-Up Mini-Missile Launcher (1; forward section):** Located next to the Rail Cannon is a Pop-Up Mini-Missile Launcher.

Primary Purpose: Anti-Aircraft and Anti-Armor.

Secondary Purpose: Anti-Personnel

Missile Type: Any type of mini-missile can be used, but standard issue is fragmentation (anti-personnel, 5D6 M.D.) and plasma (1D6x10).

Mega-Damage: Varies with missile type.

Range: About one mile.

Rate of Fire: One at a time, or in volleys of two or four.

Payload: 80 total; self-loading auto-launch system.

4. **SU-L60 High-Powered Tri-Laser Cannons (2; rear section):** The two big guns that slide off to the sides when the ceiling bay door is open are the main guns for the Thundersword. Each cannon can move up and down in a 45 degree arc of fire and the entire turret can rotate a full 360 degrees. As usual, all the weapon systems are powered from the vehicle's nuclear power supply.

Primary Purpose: Anti-Aircraft and Anti-Armor

Secondary Purpose: Defense

Mega-Damage: 1D6x10 M.D. per single blast per cannon.

Rate of Fire: Equal to the number of combined hand to hand attacks of the gunner (usually 3-6). **Note:** Each cannon has its own, independent gunner.

Maximum Effective Range: 6000 feet (1828 m)

Payload: Effectively unlimited

5. **Medium-Range Missile Launchers (2; rear section):** A pair of vertical missile launchers capable of firing short or medium-range missiles (medium are standard issue).

Primary Purpose: Anti-Aircraft and Anti-Armor.

Secondary Purpose: Anti-Personnel

Missile Type: Any type of medium-range (or in an emergency, short-range) missile can be used, but heavy missiles are standard. Mega-Damage: Varies with missile type.

Range: 40-60 miles (64.3 to 96.9 km) for medium-range missiles.

Rate of Fire: One at a time, or in volleys of two or four.

Payload: Eight total; four per each launcher. An additional payload of 8-16 missiles *may* be carried by the APC but reduces troop payload by 6 human-sized troops. Takes 1D4 minutes to reload each by hand.

6. **Sensor System Note:** All the basic features for combat vehicles, plus long-range and enhanced radar and communications via the sensor cluster (rear). Weapon stations have the Cyber-link feature.

Life Support: Air circulation and cleaning system with gas filtration and toxic warning system. The vehicle's cab/pilot's section and rear cabin can be sealed independently and have an air purification, purge and circulation system (with an 8 hour supply of oxygen) that can clean and recycle breathable air for approximately 14-18 days. Can withstand up to 400 Rads of radiation.

SU-52 "Groundthunder" Heavy Tank

The "Groundthunder" was one of the last Pre-Rifts ground assault tanks. It incorporates many of the traditional features of old-style (and less expensive) "tread" tanks. The Sovietski has six A-3 Armored Tank Battalions composed of 600 Groundthunders, 20 Hailstorms and 20 Maelstrom Tanks, that's a total of 3840 tanks in these six battalions alone (3600 Groundthunders)! The tank is not as fast or versatile as the later hover tanks, but is 100% reliable, can take a beating and keep on running, and rarely breaks down in the field. It is also comparatively easy to pilot and has an impressive battery of weapons. Weapon systems include medium-range missiles, mini-missiles, cannon, hatch rail gun, and low profile laser turret.

Plus, the front M.D.C. wheels are spiked and designed for both crushing infantry troops and providing better traction.

The tank itself has a relatively low profile and good speed for a heavy ground vehicle. The heavily armored turret can turn 360 degrees and contains the main gun, medium-range missile

launcher, hatch gun, spotlight, large searchlight, and smoke dispenser. Tucked away in the forward section below the cannon is the mini-missile launcher and laser turret.

"Groundthunder" Heavy Tread Tank

Model Type: SU-52

Class: Assault Tank

Crew: Five: One pilot, a co-pilot/gunner, two gunners and a communications officer, field scientist or intelligence officer. One additional passenger can squeeze into the crew compartment but quarters are cramped.

M.D.C. by Location:

Cannon Turret Housing — 300

Main Cannon (1) — 150

Medium-Range Missile Launcher (1; rear) — 130 each

* Hatch Rail Gun (1; side) — 90

* Low Profile Laser Turret (1; front) — 100

Mini-Missile Launcher (1; front) — 90

Smoke/Gas Dispensers (6; per side) — 5 each

* Main Hatch (1; front, top) — 150

* Sensor Tower (1; rear) — 35

Gunner's Hatch (1; top of turret) — 150

Armor Covered Treads (2) — 120 each

Reinforced Crew Compartment — 170

** Main Body — 375

* Every item marked by a single asterisk is small and/or difficult to strike. An attacker must make a "called shot" to hit and even then he is -3 to strike.

** Depleting the M.D.C. of the main body will shut the tank down completely, rendering it useless. It also exposes the inner, reinforced, crew compartment.

Destroying one of the treads reduces the tank's speed by 50% and inflicts a -20% piloting skill penalty when making sharp turns or special maneuvers. Destroying both treads immobilizes the vehicle.

Speed

Land: 90 mph (144.8 km); excellent speed for a tread-driven tank.

Water: None; the "Groundthunder" is not amphibious, although it can slosh through water up to its turret (roughly five feet/1.5 m) without trouble.

Flying: None

Range: The nuclear power supply gives the tank 20 years of life and indefinite mileage without fear of overheating.

Statistical Data

Height: 10 feet (3 m) overall; the lower main body is only five feet, 3 inches (1.55 m) tall, but the turret with the Medium-Range Missile Launcher and sensor tower adds another five feet (1.5 m).

Width: 11 feet (3.3 m)

Length: 16 feet (4.87 m)

Weight: 21 tons unloaded.

Cargo: None

Color: Typically grey or camouflage.

Power System: Nuclear; average energy life is 20 years.

Sovietski Cost: 18 million credits. It is exclusive to the Sovietski military and is not available on the Black Market.

Weapon Systems

1. **SGT-50 High-Powered Cannon (1):** The big gun is a high-powered, long-range cannon. The gun is built into a swivel housing that offers a 360 degree rotation, but the entire top turret turns. Arc of fire, up and down, is 45 degrees.

Primary Purpose: Anti-Armor

Secondary Purpose: Anti-Personnel & Defense.

Mega-Damage: 1D4x10 M.D. per single blast.

Rate of Fire: Four per melee round.

Maximum Effective Range: 6000 feet (1828 m)

Payload: 60 rounds.

2. **Hatch Rail Gun:** This gun can be fired remotely from inside the tank or manually by a hatch gunner. The gun can rotate 360 degrees and has a 45 degree arc of fire, up and down.

Primary Purpose: Anti-Aircraft

Secondary Purpose: Anti-Personnel and Defense.

Mega-Damage: A full damage burst is 40 rounds and inflicts 1D4x10 M.D. At the flip of a switch the weapon can fire short 10 round bursts which inflict 2D6 M.D.

Maximum Effective Range: 4000 feet (1220 m)

Rate of Fire: Equal to the combined hand to hand attacks of the gunner (usually 4-6).

Payload: 8,000 round drum feed for 200 full bursts or 800 short bursts. Reloading a drum will take about 20 minutes for those not trained, but a mere five minutes by characters with engineering or field armorer skills.

3. **Low Profile Laser Turret (1):** A heavy laser that can rotate 90 degrees side to side and has a 45 degree arc of fire.

Primary Purpose: Anti-Armor

Secondary Purpose: Anti-Personnel

Mega-Damage: 4D6 M.D. per single blast

Range: 1,200 feet (366 m).

Rate of Fire: Equal to the number of combined hand to hand attacks (usually 3-6) of the gunner.

Payload: Effectively unlimited.

4. **Medium-Range Missile Launcher (1):** Located in the rear is a missile launcher capable of firing short or medium-range missiles (medium are standard issue). Typically operated by one of the gunners.

Primary Purpose: Anti-Aircraft and Anti-Armor.

Secondary Purpose: Anti-Personnel

Missile Type: Any type of medium-range (or in an emergency, short-range) missile can be used, but heavy missiles are standard. Mega-Damage: Varies with missile type.

Range: 40-60 miles (64.3 to 96.9 km) for medium-range missiles.

Rate of Fire: One at a time, or in volleys of two or three.

Payload: Six total.

5. **Mini-Missile Launcher (1):** A nine shot mini-missile launcher is located in the front of the vehicle. Operated by one of the gunners.

Primary Purpose: Anti-Aircraft and Anti-Armor.

Secondary Purpose: Anti-Personnel

Missile Type: Any type of mini-missile can be used, but standard issue is fragmentation (anti-personnel, 5D6 M.D.) and plasma (1D6x10).

Mega-Damage: Varies with missile type.

Range: About one mile.

Rate of Fire: One at a time, or in volleys of 2, 3, 6 or 9.

Payload: 36 total.

6. **Smoke Dispensers (12):** Six smoke dispensing units are mounted on each side of the tank. Each unit can release a dense cloud of smoke that will cover an 80 foot (24 m) area behind it, or cover the vehicle if it is stationary. It can also release tear gas.

Payload: 12 total. The usual mix is eight smoke and four tear gas.

7. **Close Combat:** The "Groundthunder" can run over enemy troops and smash through light M.D.C. walls and barriers.

  Hit Damage (bounce off the side) — 2D6 M.D.

  Crush Damage (run over) — 1D6x10 M.D.

  Ram Damage — 4D6 M.D.

8. **Sensor System Note:** All the same basic features as the robot vehicles. Plus enhanced radar, long-range communications, and Cyber-Link feature.

Life Support: Air circulation and cleaning system with gas filtration and toxic warning system. The vehicle's cab/pilot's section and rear cabin can be sealed independently and have an air purification, purge and circulation system (with an 8 hour supply of oxygen) that can clean and recycle breathable air for approximately 14-18 days. Can withstand up to 400 Rads of radiation.

SUH-86 "Hailstorm" Sovietski Hover Tank

The Hailstorm is an unusual pre-Rifts design that makes it a fast hover vehicle that is classified as a tank, but is really a combination APC and tank.

In the capacity of a tank, it has a huge rail cannon, hidden pop-up mini-missile launchers, forward laser turret and a pair of medium-range missile launchers.

As a troop carrier, the tank crew is housed in the compartment with the two spotlights, and the rest of the vehicle is devoted to the high-powered hover system and rear cargo bay which typically carries a squad of six Light Machines and 4-6 Heavy Machines each equipped with jet packs, and 2-6 Thunderstrike Cyborg Shocktroopers — troops who often jettison into combat while the Hailstorm is flying at full speed. They are used as troop support, for troop extraction and rescue, air drops, and surgical strikes.

"Hailstorm" Medium Hover Tank

Model Type: SUH-86

Class: Assault Hover Tank

Crew: 5-6: One pilot, a co-pilot/gunner, two gunners, communications officer and sometimes one other, typically a field scientist or intelligence officer. Two additional passengers can squeeze into the crew compartment but quarters are cramped.

M.D.C. by Location:

  Main Cannon (1) — 280

  Medium-Range Missile Launchers (2; sides) — 130 each

  Forward Laser Turret (1) —100

  Pop-Up Mini-Missile Launchers (2; near cannon) — 80 each

  * Main Hatch (1; front, top) — 150

* Concealed Hatch (1; rear, floor) — 100
* Concealed Door (1; crew compartment) — 100
* Rear Bay Door (1; rear) — 35
* Spotlights (2; crew compartment) — 6 each
* Headlights (7) — 4 each
Bottom Hover Jets (12; six per side) — 120 each
Side Jet Thrusters (2; sides) — 150 each
Reinforced Crew Compartment — 200
** Main Body — 410

* Every item marked by a single asterisk is small and/or difficult to strike. An attacker must make a "called shot" to hit and even then he is -3 to strike.

** Depleting the M.D.C. of the main body will shut the tank down completely, rendering it useless. It also exposes the inner, reinforced, crew compartment.

Destroying four hover jets reduces the tank's speed by 50% and inflicts a -20% piloting skill penalty when making sharp turns or special maneuvers. Destroying more than 6 hover jets immobilizes the vehicle.

Speed
Land & Air: 160 mph (256 km); maximum altitude 2000 feet (610 m). Water: Can jet across the surface of water provided the speed is a minimum of 50 mph (80 km). Cannot go into or underwater.
Flying: See above.
Range: The nuclear power supply gives the tank 20 years of life and indefinite mileage without fear of overheating.

Statistical Data
Height: 24 feet (7.3 m) overall; the main body is 14 feet (4.3 m), but the big gun adds another 10 feet (3 m).

Width: 15 feet (4.6 m)
Length: 38 feet (11.6 m)
Weight: 20 tons unloaded.
Cargo: None
Color: Typically blue-grey or camouflage.
Power System: Nuclear; average energy life is 20 years.
Sovietski Cost: 26 million credits. It is exclusive to the Sovietski military and is not available on the Black Market.
Note: As excellent as this tank is, it is expensive. Approximately 960 are in service.

Weapon Systems
1. SRG-500 High-Powered Rail Cannon (1): The big gun can rotate 360 degrees and has an arc of fire, up and down, of 45 degrees.
Primary Purpose: Anti-Armor
Secondary Purpose: Anti-Aircraft/Dragons.
Mega-Damage: A full damage burst is 80 rounds and inflicts 2D6x10 M.D. At the flip of a switch the weapon can fire 40 round bursts which inflict 1D6x10 M.D.
Maximum Effective Range: 8000 feet (2438 m).
Rate of Fire: Equal to the combined hand to hand attacks of the gunner (usually 4-7).
Payload: 24,000 round drum feed for 300 full bursts or 600 short bursts. Reloading a drum will take about 20 minutes for those not trained, but a mere five minutes by characters with engineering or field armorer skills.
2. Ball-Laser Turret (1): A heavy laser that can rotate 180 degrees side to side and up and down.
Primary Purpose: Anti-Missile and Anti-Armor
Secondary Purpose: Anti-Personnel

Mega-Damage: 4D6 M.D. per single blast

Range: 2000 feet (610 m).

Rate of Fire: Equal to the number of combined hand to hand attacks (usually 4-6) of the gunner.

Payload: Effectively unlimited.

3. Medium-Range Missile Launchers (2): Located on the sides are a pair of missile launchers, capable of firing short or medium-range missiles (medium are standard issue). Typically operated by one of the gunners.

Primary Purpose: Anti-Aircraft and Anti-Armor.

Secondary Purpose: Anti-Personnel

Missile Type: Any type of medium-range (or in an emergency, short-range) missile can be used, but heavy missiles are standard. Mega-Damage: Varies with missile type.

Range: 40-60 miles (64.3 to 96.9 km) for medium-range missiles.

Rate of Fire: One at a time, or in volleys of two or three.

Payload: Six total.

4. Pop-Up Mini-Missile Launchers (2): A pair of six shot mini-missile launchers are located near the main gun. Operated by one of the gunners.

Primary Purpose: Anti-Aircraft and Anti-Armor.

Secondary Purpose: Anti-Personnel

Missile Type: Any type of mini-missile can be used, but standard issue is fragmentation (anti-personnel, 5D6 M.D.) and plasma (1D6x10).

Mega-Damage: Varies with missile type.

Range: About one mile.

Rate of Fire: One at a time, or in volleys of two, three or four.

Payload: 48 total; 24 per each launcher.

5. Sensor System Note: All of the same basic features as the robot vehicles. Plus enhanced radar, long-range communications, and Cyber-Link feature.

Life Support: Air circulation and cleaning system with gas filtration and toxic warning system. The vehicle's cab/pilot's sec-

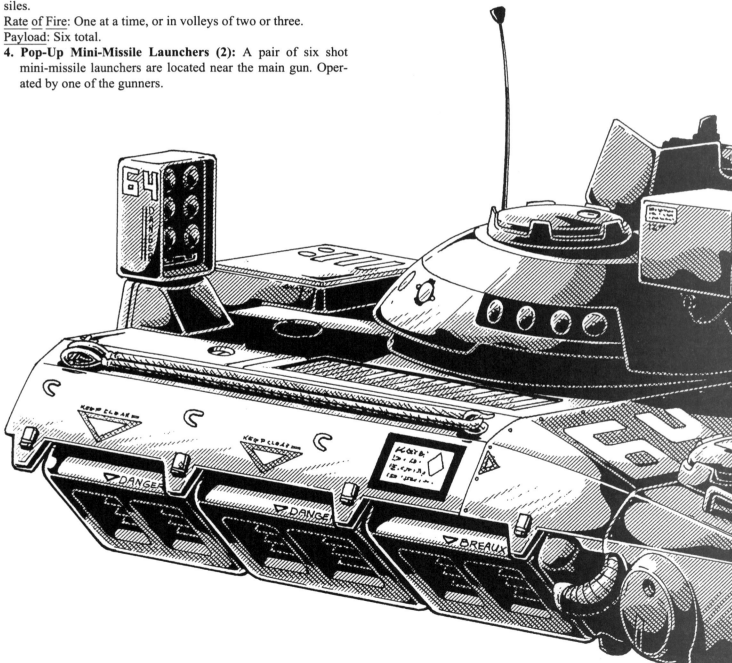

tion and rear cabin can be sealed independently and have an air purification, purge and circulation system (with an 8 hour supply of oxygen) that can clean and recycle breathable air for approximately 14-18 days. Can withstand up to 400 Rads of radiation.

SUH-88 "Maelstrom" Sovietski Hover Tank

The Maelstrom is a compact, low-profile, fast and powerful frontline hover tank. The tank has six large hover jets (three on each side) and three down the middle of the undercarriage. To confound high-tech enemies, the tank uses a stealth system that makes it invisible to radar!

The main weapon is a high-powered plasma cannon, but it also has a rack of medium-range missiles, a forward, drum-style ion-turret, a pop-up mini-missile launcher on top of the main

cannon, and a manned rail gun behind the cannon. There are also 16 concealed mini-missile launch tubes built along the sides and back of the turret. The plasma cannon is something of an experiment for the Sovietski Military. It is based on pre-Rifts designs and took years to develop. The range is inferior to rail guns or cannons but the payload is effectively unlimited.

"Maelstrom" Medium-Heavy Hover Tank
Model Type: SUH-88
Class: Assault Hover Tank
Crew: 5-6: One pilot, a co-pilot/gunner, two gunners, communications officer and sometimes one other, typically a field scientist or intelligence officer. Two additional passengers can squeeze into the crew compartment but quarters are cramped.

M.D.C. by Location:

Main Turret — 360
Main Cannon (1) — 250
* Hatch Rail Gun (1) — 100
Ball-Ion Turret (1; front) — 70
* Pop-Up Mini-Missile Launcher (1; near cannon) — 70
* Mini-Missile Launch Tubes (16; main turret) — 6 each
Medium-Range Missile Launcher (1; rear) — 90
* Main Hatches (2; front & top) — 150
* Concealed Hatch (1; rear, floor) — 100
Box Targeting & Sensor System (1; cannon) — 100
* Secondary Sensor Cluster (1; main turret) — 20
* Spotlight (1; Main Turret) — 8
* Headlights (5) — 4 each
* Bottom Hover Jets (9) — 100 each
Reinforced Crew Compartment — 220
** Main Body — 540
* Every item marked by a single asterisk is small and/or difficult to strike. An attacker must make a "called shot" to hit and even then he is -3 to strike.

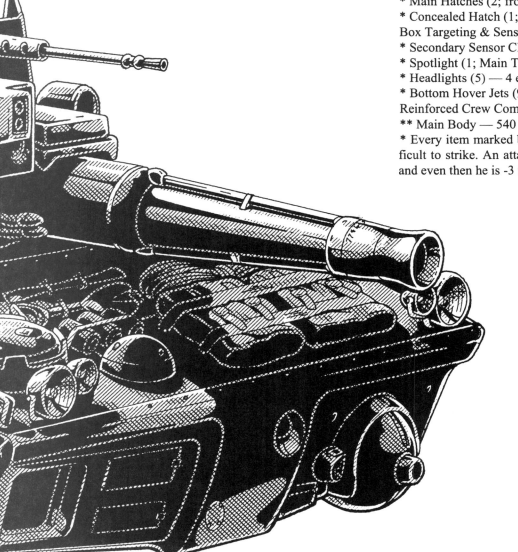

** Depleting the M.D.C. of the main body will shut the tank down completely, rendering it useless. It also exposes the inner, reinforced, crew compartment.

Destroying four of the hover jets reduces the tank's speed by 50% and inflicts a -20% piloting skill penalty when making sharp turns or special maneuvers. Destroying more than six hover jets immobilizes the vehicle.

Speed

Land: 120 mph (192 km). The vehicle typically hovers three to four feet (0.9 to 1.2 m) above the ground, but can raise as high as 20 feet (6 m) and make jumps up to 60 feet (18.3 m) in length.

Water: The "Maelstrom" can also hover across the surface of water at a speed of 100 mph (160 km) and even submerge itself underwater up to an ocean depth of 1500 feet (457 m) and travel at about 25 miles an hour (40 km/21 knots) underwater. However, it cannot open its hatches underwater without flooding and sinking.

Flying: See above.

Range: The nuclear power supply gives the tank 20 years of life and indefinite mileage without fear of overheating.

Statistical Data

Height: Low profile: 11 feet (3.3 m) overall; the main body is 9 feet (2.7 m), but the targeting box and rail gun adds another two feet (0.6 m).

Width: 11 feet (3.3 m)

Length: 20 feet (6 m)

Weight: 18 tons unloaded.

Cargo: Minimal

Color: Typically blue-grey or camouflage.

Power System: Nuclear; average energy life is 20 years.

Sovietski Cost: 32 million credits. It is exclusive to the Sovietski military and is not available on the Black Market.

Note: As excellent as this tank is, it is very expensive, so there are only 480 in service.

Weapon Systems

1. **SPC-100 High-Powered Plasma Cannon (1):** The turret that the cannon is built into can rotate 360 degrees and the cannon itself has an arc of fire, up and down, of 45 degrees.

Primary Purpose: Anti-Armor

Secondary Purpose: Anti-Aircraft/Dragons.

Mega-Damage: 2D4x10+20 M.D. per blast.

Maximum Effective Range: 4000 feet (1220 m).

Rate of Fire: Equal to the combined hand to hand attacks of the gunner (usually 4-7).

Payload: Effectively unlimited.

Note: After 50 blasts without a break the main cannon shuts down for one minute to cool.

2. **Ball-Ion Turret (1):** A heavy ion turret that can rotate 180 degrees side to side and up and down.

Primary Purpose: Anti-Monster

Secondary Purpose: Anti-Personnel & Defense.

Mega-Damage: 6D6 M.D. per single blast

Range: 1400 feet (426.7 m).

Rate of Fire: Equal to the number of combined hand to hand attacks (usually 4-6) of the gunner.

Payload: Effectively unlimited.

3. **Hatch Rail Gun:** This gun can be fired remotely from inside the tank or manually by a hatch gunner. The gun can rotate 360 degrees and has a 45 degree arc of fire, up and down.

Primary Purpose: Anti-Aircraft

Secondary Purpose: Anti-Personnel and Defense.

Mega-Damage: A full damage burst is 40 rounds and inflicts 1D4x10 M.D. At the flip of a switch the weapon can fire short 10 round bursts which inflict 2D6 M.D.

Maximum Effective Range: 4000 feet (1220 m)

Rate of Fire: Equal to the combined hand to hand attacks of the gunner (usually 4-6).

Payload: 8,000 round drum feed for 200 full bursts or 800 short bursts. Reloading a drum will take about 20 minutes for those not trained, but a mere five minutes by characters with engineering or field armorer skills.

4. **Pop-Up Mini-Missile Launcher (1):** Located on the plasma cannon next to the box targeting sensor.

Primary Purpose: Anti-Aircraft and Anti-Armor.

Secondary Purpose: Anti-Personnel

Missile Type: Any type of mini-missile can be used, but standard issue is fragmentation (anti-personnel, 5D6 M.D.) and plasma (1D6x10).

Mega-Damage: Varies with missile type.

Range: About one mile.

Rate of Fire: One at a time, or in volleys of two or four.

Payload: 32 total.

5. **Concealed Mini-Missile Launch Tubes (16):** All are located on the cannon turret. Same stats as #4, except payload and rate of fire. Operated by one of the gunners.

Rate of Fire: One at a time, or in volleys of 2, 3 or 4.

Payload: 32 total; two missiles per launch tube.

6. **Medium-Range Missile Launcher (1):** Located in the rear is a missile launcher capable of firing short or medium-range missiles (medium are standard issue). Typically operated by one of the gunners.

Primary Purpose: Anti-Aircraft and Anti-Armor.

Secondary Purpose: Anti-Personnel

Missile Type: Any type of medium-range (or in an emergency, short-range) missile can be used, but heavy missiles are standard.

Mega-Damage: Varies with missile type.

Range: 40-60 miles (64.3 to 96.9 km) for medium-range missiles.

Rate of Fire: One at a time, or in volleys of two or three.

Payload: Six total.

7. **Smoke Dispensers (2):** A pair of smoke dispensing units are mounted on the rear of the tank. The unit can release a dense cloud of smoke that will cover an 80 foot (24 m) area behind it, or cover the APC if it is stationary. It can also release tear gas. Payload: Four, two each.

8. **Sensor System Note:** All of the same basic features as the robot vehicles. Plus enhanced radar, long-range communications, and Cyber-Link feature.

Life Support: Air circulation and cleaning system with gas filtration and toxic warning system. The vehicle's cab/pilot's section can be sealed and has an air purification, purge and circulation system (with an 8 hour supply of oxygen) that can clean and recycle breathable air for approximately 14-18 days. Can withstand up to 400 Rads of radiation.

Other Sovietski Vehicles

The Sovietski finds such favor with the Kiev based **Novyet Manufacturers**, and there is such demand for their vehicles from both the government/military and businesses, that Novyet has built two factories in New Moscow. The Sovietski gets their vehicles in quantity, at a 30% to 40% discount. Favorites include the Landcrawler, Arctic Hoverbike, Snowshoe Jetsled, and Explorer Sku.

Vehicles, weapons and equipment of NGR/Triax manufacture, Poland and other places can also be found in Russia, particularly in and around the big cities.

Note that the average Soviet citizen does *not* own a vehicle other than a bicycle and/or motorcycle or horse.

Rules clarifications on dodging energy blasts

Rules for dodging gunfire, rail guns and energy blasts: These blasts are so fast that they are difficult to dodge and virtually impossible to parry. Only rare, select O.C.C.s offer superior dodge and parrying abilities against such attacks. To attempt to dodge high speed attacks, the character must realize that he is under attack and see where the attack is coming from (i.e. the sniper in the tree to the right, or the SAMAS flying in at 12 O'clock). In all cases the dodger must roll 1D20 and beat the strike roll of the attacker; defender always wins ties.

The dodging of energy bolts from close range (within approximately 100 feet/30.5 m) is done without the usual dodge bonuses and with a penalty of -10.

To dodge energy bolts from long-range (500 feet/122 m or farther) or when a lot of ground cover is available to dive behind quickly (i.e. trees, ruins, vehicles, other people, etc.), the dodge is done without bonus and with a penalty. of -8.

In either of the cases above, if the character under attack forfeits *all* his attacks that melee round and does nothing but *dodge* the entire round, he is -6 to dodge energy blasts.

Russian Gods

Kevin Siembieda really does suffer from an overactive imagination. We added 16 pages to this book and we still don't have enough space for everything that our wild Cossack Siembieda wants to include. Consequently, the *Russian Gods* have been cut from **Mystic Russia**. But don't despair, they will appear in **The Rifter™ #5 or #6**, complete with the breathtaking artwork of Kent Burles. See the last two pages of this book for more information about **The Rifter™ Sourcebook series**.

Books on Magic

The theme of magic and the supernatural has made **Rifts® Mystic Russia** an exciting book of monsters and magic. For those of you looking for other Palladium titles where *magic* is the focus, check out these ...

Rifts® World Book Two: Atlantis, which includes the legendary Tattoo Magic, Stone Magic and Splugorth Bio-Wizardry (the use of symbiotes) and Rune Weapons.

Rifts® World Book Three: England. which includes Druids, Mystic Herbology, magic potions, the Millennium Tree, Temporal Magic, Ghost Knights, an alien intelligence and more.

Rifts® World Book Four: Africa. The first appearance of the Necromancer, but also includes the African Witch, Medicine Man, Rain Maker, and African Priest, plus D-Bees, stats for Erin Tarn and Victor Lazlo, Egyptian Gods, and the ultimate supernatural horrors: The Four Horsemen of the Apocalypse!

Rifts® World Book Six: South America. With Biomancy, Totem Warriors, Voodoo Priests, gods, mutant animals and more.

Rifts® World Book 15: Spirit West™. Native American myth, legend, magic and spirits brought to life, Rifts style.

Rifts® World Book 16: Federation of Magic™. A detailed look at the infamous *Federation of Magic* and legendary *Magic Zone*, plus over 120 new magic spells, Techno-Wizard devices, Automatons, Magi, Conjurers, Mystic Knights, and more!

Dragons & Gods™: A sourcebook for **Rifts®** and *Palladium Fantasy Role-Playing Game* with new and different dragons, detailed information about dragons (complete with M.D.C. stats), the religion of Dragonwright, deific powers, and stats on scores of gods and demon lords — over 60 supernatural beings in all.

Magical and mystical material can also be found in **Ninjas & Superspies™**, **Mystic China™** (both with magical martial arts powers), **Nightbane®**, **Beyond the Supernatural™** and others. Don't forget what having a true Megaverse® with one basic game system means — endless possibilities limited only by your imagination.

Cool Reference Books

The following are just a few of the most notable books on the subject of Russia and Russian Mythology. I found them to be insightful, fun and inspirational. You might enjoy them too. All are available at most book stores (although some might have to be special ordered).

— *Kevin Siembieda, Author*

Russian Folk Belief, by Linda J. Ivanits, M.E. Sharpe Inc. is the publisher, 1992

Russia and the Golden Horde, by Charles J. Halperin, Indiana University Press is the publisher, 1987

Essential Russian Mythology, by Pyotr Simonov. Thorsons/Harper Collins is the publisher, 1997

Russian Tales & Legends, retold by Charles Downing. Oxford University Press is the publisher, 1996 (current edition).

Bury Me Standing — The Gypsies and Their Journey, by Isabel Fonseca. Vintage Books/Random House is the publisher, 1995.

Heroes, Monsters & Other Worlds from Russian Mythology, by Elizabeth Warner. Peter Bedrick Books is the publisher, 1985. Actually, this is one in a fantastic series of books on myths from around the world. I can not say enough about this series. Each and every book is exceptional with beautiful illustrations. Available in hard cover and soft. It is my impression that, while still available (at least through Amazon.com and special orders) the series has been slated to be discontinued, so get 'em while you still can, these books are worth every nickel.

Experience Tables

Night Witch & Mystic Kuznya
1. 0,000-2,080
2. 2,081-4,160
3. 4,161-8,800
4. 8,801-18,000
5. 18,001-33,000
6. 33,001-48,000
7. 48,001-65,000
8. 65,001-90,000
9. 90,001-120,000
10. 120,001-150,000
11. 150,001-200,000
12. 200,001-250,000
13. 250,001-300,000
14. 300,001-400,000
15. 400,001-500,000

Russia Sorcerer a.k.a. Ley Line Walker
1. 0,000-2,240
2. 2,241-4,480
3. 4,481-8,960
4. 8,961-17,920
5. 17,921-25,920
6. 25,921-35,920
7. 35,921-50,920
8. 50,921-70,920
9. 70,921-95,920
10. 95,921-135,920
11. 135,921-185,920
12. 185,921-225,920
13. 225,921-275,920
14. 275,921-335,920
15. 335,921-395,920

Gypsy/Hidden Witch
1. 0,000-1,975
2. 1,976-3,950
3. 3,951-7,900
4. 7,901-15,800
5. 15,801-31,600
6. 31,601-46,400
7. 46,401-61,800
8. 61,801-87,000
9. 87,001-112,200
10. 112,201-152,400
11. 152,401-212,600
12. 212,601-267,800
13. 267,801-330,200
14. 330,201-400,400
15. 400,401-470,600

Necromancer
1. 0,000-2,200
2. 2,201-4,400
3. 4,401-8,800
4. 8,801-17,600
5. 17,601-27,700
6. 27,701-37,800
7. 37,801-53,900
8. 53,901-75,100
9. 75,101-100,200
10. 100,201-140,300
11. 140,301-200,400
12. 200,401-250,500
13. 250,501-300,600
14. 300,601-350,700
15. 350,701-425,800

Old Believer
1. 0,000-2,050
2. 2,051-4,100
3. 4,101-8,250
4. 8,251-16,500
5. 16,501-24,600
6. 24,601-34,700
7. 34,701-49,800
8. 49,801-69,900
9. 69,901-95,000
10. 95,001-130,100
11. 130,101-180,200
12. 180,201-230,300
13. 230,301-280,400
14. 280,401-340,500
15. 340,501-400,600

The Slayer & Gypsy Layer of Laws
1. 0,000-2,100
2. 2,101-4,200
3. 4,201-8,400
4. 8,401-16,800
5. 16,801-25,000
6. 25,001-35,000
7. 35,001-50,000
8. 50,001-70,000
9. 70,001-95,000
10. 95,001-130,000
11. 130,001-180,000
12. 180,001-234,000
13. 234,001-285,000
14. 285,001-345,000
15. 345,001-410,000

Gypsy Thief & Gypsy Enforcer
1. 0,000-1,900
2. 1,901-3,800
3. 3,801-7,300
4. 7,301-14,300
5. 14,301-21,000
6. 21,001-30,000
7. 30,001-40,000
8. 40,001-53,000
9. 53,001-73,000
10. 73,001-103,000
11. 103,001-138,000
12. 138,001-188,000
13. 188,001-238,000
14. 238,001-288,000
15. 288,001-330,000

Born Mystic, The Gifted Ones & Gypsy Fortune Teller
1. 0,000-2,050
2. 2,051-4,100
3. 4,101-8,250
4. 8,251-16,500
5. 16,501-24,600
6. 24,601-34,700
7. 34,701-49,800
8. 49,801-69,900
9. 69,901-95,000
10. 95,001-130,000
11. 130,001-180,200
12. 180,201-230,000
13. 230,001-280,400
14. 280,401-340,500
15. 340,501-400,600

Fire Sorcerer & Gypsy Seer
1. 0,000-2,200
2. 2,201-4,400
3. 4,401-9,000
4. 9,001-19,000
5. 19,001-28,000
6. 28,001-40,000
7. 40,001-60,000
8. 60,001-80,000
9. 80,001-100,000
10. 100,001-150,000
11. 150,001-200,000
12. 200,001-275,000
13. 275,001-350,000
14. 350,001-425,000
15. 425,001-525,000

Gypsy Beguiler & Gypsy Wizard-Thief
1. 0,000-2,700
2. 2,701-5,400
3. 5,401-10,800
4. 10,801-21,600
5. 21,601-31,600
6. 31,601-42,800
7. 42,801-62,000
8. 62,001-90,000
9. 90,001-120,000
10. 120,001-170,000
11. 170,001-220,000
12. 220,001-290,000
13. 290,001-400,000
14. 400,001-500,000
15. 500,001-700,000

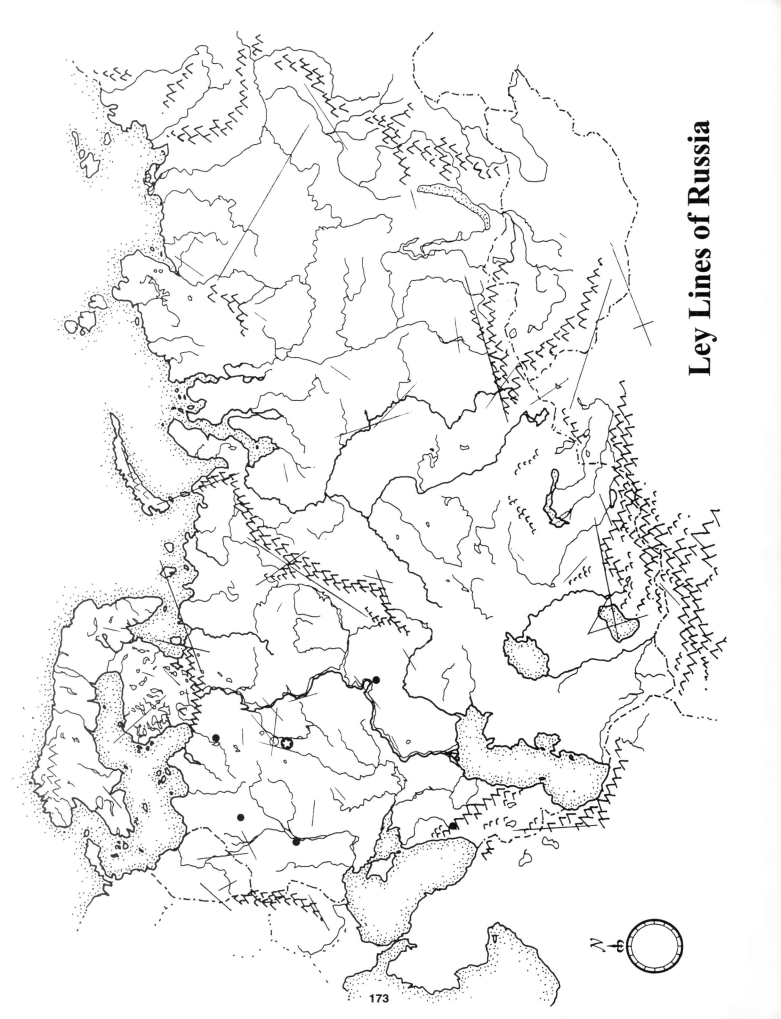

Ley Lines of Russia

173

Heroes Unlimited, 2nd Edition — 8,000 copies sold in under six months

Heroes Unlimited™ 2nd Edition is without a doubt, one of the hottest role-playing games currently on the market!

Why?

There are five *BIG* reasons ...

1. HU-2 enables gamers to create every type of comic book hero and super being imaginable!

Superhuman mutants, aliens, cyborgs, robots, psychics, gadgeteers, super-geniuses, martial arts masters, and more!

2 Create new and original super-powered heroes and villains, or characters from the pages of comic books and films.

3. *Fun!* HU-2 captures the power and thrills of superhero comic books, perhaps better than any other.

4. 352 pages for $25.00, great artwork throughout — more bang for the buck.

5. A complete role-playing game — everything needed to play is in one juicy, big book. Plus HU-2 is compatible with *Rifts®*, *Ninjas & Superspies™ RPG*, *Ninja Turtles® RPG* and the *entire* Palladium Megaverse® of games! No wonder it's hot.

Available now — don't miss out.

$24.95

Coming for Heroes Unlimited™, 2nd Ed.

Listed in no particular order of release ...

Hardware Unlimited sourcebook — by Brent Lein

Delphineous' Guide to the Megaverse® — by Doug Coughler

The Nursery™ — by Kevin Siembieda and others.

Adventure book — by Wayne Breaux Jr. & Kevin Siembieda

and don't forget about **Villains Unlimited™**, always in stock.

Teenage Mutant Ninja Turtles® & *More* Strangeness RPG

This expanded edition of the original Ninja Turtles® Role-Playing Game (hence the slight title change of "Other" Strangeness to "More") will ship late *January* and includes character updates, new artwork by the Paulo Parentes Studio, new cover by Simon Bisley, and over 20 pages of additional material.

The RPG is presented in a serious manner, containss over a hundred different mutant animals and is completely compatible with **Heroes Unlimited™, Second Edition**.

New text includes a look at the mutant underground and mutants as heroes, plus new villains and characters from the pages of the TMNT comic books. Fans of the original edition (which sold over 180,000 copies) have expressed serious interest in this title.

- **Over 100 different mutant animals.**
- **Rules for creating any sort of mutant animal.**
- **Animal powers and psionics.**
- **Villains and adventure ideas.**
- **Five adventure outlines.**
- **Written by Erick Wujcik, Siembieda and Oliver.**
- **Compatible as a sourcebook for *Heroes Unlimited™, 2nd Edition*.**
- **Retail Price: $12.95 — 128 pages.**

This should revitalize sales of the old sourcebooks and adventure books too.

1999 will be big for Rifts® RPG

After we blew our 1998 schedule, we decided to focus on getting 1999 product done *in advance* to insure product is released on schedule. Yeah, we always say we hope release product on schedule, but rarely do. You *will* see a difference in 1999 starting with the first quarter.

The Rifter #5: 112 pages — $7.95 retail. Includes material for *Rifts® Mystic Russia*, plus *Heroes Unlimited™*, *Nightbane®*, and others.

Rifts® Canada: 160-224 pages — 16.95 to $20.95 (price will defend on the final page size). By Eric Thompson.

Rifts® Splynn Dimensional Market™ (Atlantis): 160-224 pages— 16.95 to $20.95 (price will defend on the final page size). By Mark Sumimoto.

Plus other books are under development.

Palladium Fantasy RPG

The Palladium Fantasy RPG series also continues to be hot! And to keep product flying, you'll see the following new books in the first two quarters of 1999.

- **The Baal-gor Wastelands:** 224 pages — $20.95 retail. Written by Bill (Western Empire) Coffin; art by Perez; cover by Zeleznik. In final production and ships *February 5th, 1999*.
- **Mount Nimro:** 112-160 pages — $12.95-16.95 retail (depending on the final size). Written by Bill Coffin.
- **Eastern Territory:** 160-224 pages — probably $20.95 retail. Written by Steve Edwards.

If you missed **The Western Empire™** (fall 1998 release) check it out. Not only is it selling well, but the artwork is breathtaking!

Palladium Books® Inc.
12455 Universal Drive
Taylor, MI 48180

www.palladiumbooks.com

One game system.
A Megaverse® of adventure!

The Rifter™

A Megaverse® Sourcebook from the Web & beyond

What is The Rifter™?

Really, there has never been anything like it.

The Rifter is a synthesis of a sourcebook, Game Master's guide, a magazine and talent show/a fan forum.

The Rifter® is like a sourcebook because it will include a ton of role-playing source material (optional and official). This will include New O.C.C.s, NPC heroes, NPC villains, new powers and abilities, weapons, adventure settings, adventures and adventure ideas, and Hook, Line and Sinkers™.

The Rifter™ is like a G.M.'s guide because it will include special articles and tips on role-playing, how to handle common problems, how to build an adventure and so on.

The Rifter™ is like a magazine because it will come out four or five times a year (we're shooting for a regular quarterly release schedule), and because it will feature Palladium news, advertisements, serial articles and continuing features.

Most importantly, The Rifter™ is a forum for Palladium's Fans. At least half of each issue will be text and material taken (with permission) from the Web, as well as fan contributions made especially for **The Rifter™**. We get tons of fan submissions that are pretty good, but not good enough for publication as an entire sourcebook. In other cases, the submission is something clever and cool, but only a few pages long. There's lots of cool stuff on the Internet, but you must have a computer and Internet access, something a lot of fans just don't have.

The Rifter™ will reprint some of those "Web-Works™" allowing fans (and the world at large) to get a glimpse of their genius. It is one more avenue in which fans and professionals alike can share their visions of role-playing and the Palladium Megaverse with other fans. It's a chance to get published, get a little cash, get your name in lights (well, in print) and have fun.

This also means, more than any RPG publication ever produced, **The Rifter®** is yours. Yours to present and share ideas. Yours to help shape and mold. Yours to share.

Why call it The Rifter™? Because each issue will span the Palladium Megaverse of games, adventures and ideas. Each issue will publish features from people across the Web and beyond! But mainly because each and every one of us, from game designer and publisher, to Joe Gamer, traverses the Megaverse™ every time they read an RPG or play in a role-playing game. We travel the infinite realm of the imagination, hopping from one world to the next — building one world to the next. Time and space are meaningless in our imaginations as we *Rift* from one place and time to another.

In stores everywhere: 96-120 pages per issue, for only $7.95 in the stores (distributed around the world), $7.95 plus $1.00 for postage and handling for a single issue ordered through the mail.

You can't touch a sourcebook that size for only 8 bucks! Heck, these days it seems like most 96 page sourcebooks sell for $15-20 dollars! We're trying to keep the price as low as we possibly can (please recognize that the vast majority will be sold wholesale to distributors for under $3.00)!

Subscription Rate: Four issues $25.00 postage included, plus subscribers will automatically get new Palladium catalogs and maybe the occasional other odd and end, like posters and such.

First issue should ship January 1998!

Highlights

- The focus will be on the vast Palladium Megaverse, so each issue should provide new and *optional* source material for **Rifts®** and 2-5 other Palladium RPG lines — **Palladium Fantasy RPG®, Heroes Unlimited™, Nightbane™, Beyond the Supernatural™, Ninjas & Superspies™, Robotech®, RECON®** and all the rest, as well as special game ideas, previews and experimental RPG ideas.

- Most issues will present articles, commentaries, hints and tips for Game Mastering, playing, and building role-playing campaigns.
- Contributors will be from around the world. And **The Rifter**™ will be sold around the world!
- Fan stuff. This is a chance for our many talented fans and blossoming writers to see their names in print and contribute to the Palladium Megaverse. See the Palladium Website for information, updates, and all kinds of stuff going on at Palladium (*www.palladiumbooks.com*).
- As an unabashed house organ, **The Rifter**® will be dedicated exclusively to Palladium RPG products and include sections on the latest Palladium news, upcoming releases, coming attractions (art and text), scheduling changes, convention appearances, advertisements for the latest **Rifts**® and other Palladium role-playing games and products, and who knows what else.
- Cartoons, comic strips and artwork by fans and the usual gang of maniacs like Perez, Breaux, Johnson, McKenna, Siembieda, plus a bunch of new guys and promising fans.

Contributing Writers

The following professionals and freelancers will be contributing to **The Rifter**™ on a regular basis.

Kevin Siembieda	Patrick Nowak
Erick Wujcik	Chris Jones
Wayne Breaux	Kevin Kruger
Jolly Blackburn	Chris Kornmann
Julius Rosenstein	and others.

Plus outstanding, promising and fun fan works from the Web and submissions done specially for **The Rifter**™

You can be an active participant in the Rifter

If you write halfway decent and have some ideas for characters, equipment, magic, monsters and adventures, especially adventures between 2-25 pages long, let us know, 'cause maybe you'll get 'em printed in **The Rifter**™.

We're looking for funny cartoons and quarter to half page illustrations too.

The Rifter™ is a small press publication designed to inform and entertain the reader, just like any RPG sourcebook.

Source material and adventures can be based on virtually *any* Palladium RPG. However, we are most interested in material for the following (listed in no particular order):

Rifts®
Palladium Fantasy RPG®, 2nd Ed.
Heroes Unlimited™, 2nd Ed.
Ninjas & Superspies™
Nightbane™
Robotech®

"Source material" means O.C.C.s./R.C.C.s, fully fleshed out adventures, adventure ideas and settings, *Hook, Line & Sinker*™ adventures, Non-Player Characters (NPCs), villains, heroes, monsters, mutants, aliens, new magic spells, new superpowers, new psionic abilities, new robots and bionics, new weapons and vehicles, clarifications on existing spells and powers, clarifications on rules, optional variant rules, and indepth looks at particular O.C.C.s. **Note:** We will consider anything that's good and makes sense.

If you already have "good stuff" on-line, send us an Internet/Web address with a note pointing out what we should look at for consideration in **The Rifter**™. Large works may be serialized in sections over two or more issues.

You must include a signed copy of Palladium's *Unsolicited Manuscript Form* with *each* submission. It can be mailed to you upon request or pulled off our Website (www.palladiumbooks.com).

A formal agreement will be sent to you if we like what we see and plan to use your work in an upcoming issue. Nothing will be published without a signed agreement.

Payment

Palladium Books is doing **The Rifter**™ as a fan forum and to spread the word about our games. In an attempt to give our fans an opportunity to share ideas, see their work in print, hone their writing skills, and to have fun, we are trying to keep the cost and labor as low as possible. Low cost means we can keep the cover price as low as possible. It also means we are paying dirt cheap prices to contributors. **Note:** Payments may change from time to time. All payments are made in US dollars.

Writer "Flat Fee" Payment: Roughly ten dollars ($10.00) per "printed" typeset page of text (that's roughly 2 to 2 1/2 single spaced computer pages at 10-11 point size; see, we're even too cheap and lazy to figure out a per word rate). A small bonus *may* be paid to truly outstanding works if our budget allows it, and at Palladium Books Inc.'s sole discretion.

Articles and features written by two or more people will have to divide the flat payment between themselves. Palladium will send only one check to one person who represents the team or group.

Plus, each contributor will get three (3) copies of **The Rifter**™ his work appears in and he/she/they will get credit as the author of said work. Additional copies of the book in which an artist or author's work appears may be purchased at a 50% discount, as long as supplies last (may go out of print).

Writer Payment for "Reprinting" the work elsewhere will be included in the formal agreement, but is likely to be modest. Payment will be made roughly 30 days after publication.

****

Artist "Flat Fee" Payments: High quality fan and near-professional quality artists will be used to help illustrate **The Rifter**™ along with some new art from the usual Palladium artists and reprinted art.

Payment is abysmal, compared to our usual rates: Roughly $10.00 for a quarter page illoe.

$25.00 for a half page illoe.

$50.00 for a full page illustration.

Artist Payment for "Reprinting" the work elsewhere will be included in the formal agreement. Payment will be made roughly 30 days after publication.

Palladium Books Inc.

Rifter Dept.　　　　　　　　**Taylor, MI 48180**

12455 Universal Drive　　　**www.palladiumbooks.com**